CHAMELEON

by

MICHAEL K FOSTER

For Margaret

By
Michael K Foster
DCI Jack Mason Crime Thriller Series:

THE WHARF BUTCHER
SATAN'S BECKONING
THE SUITCASE MAN
CHAMELEON

ACKNOWLEDGMENTS

All my DCI Mason and David Carlisle novels are works of fiction based in the North East of England. There are so many people without whose help and support it would have been difficult, if not impossible, to write with any sense of authenticity. Suffering from dyslexia as I do, my grateful thanks go out to the late Rita Day and my dear wife Pauline, whose belief and inspiration has never waned.

I am indebted to Detective Constable Maurice Waugh, a former member of the Yorkshire Ripper Squad, and Ken Stewart, a former member of South Shields CID. Their technical assistance of how the police tackle crime has allowed me a better understanding of what takes place. Their efforts have helped me enormously.

To single out a few other names who helped make a difference to the book, I would like to thank Robert Barnes and Lynn Oakes for their encouragement and unqualified support in developing the initial cover graphics. Finally, I would express my heartfelt appreciation to the Beta reader team: Jan Duffy, Maria Jones, Mark Duffy, Daniel Inman, and Brenda Forster, without whose help this book would never have made the bookshelf.

Michael K Foster
Co Durham England
www.michaelkfoster.com

CHAPTER ONE

Chopwell Wood Monday 13 June 2016

The boy stood on his tiptoes and peered in through the car's passenger window. Nobody inside – all the doors were locked but the engine was still running. Curious, he inched his way forward through the thick undergrowth and thought he could hear a man's voice, not too far away, and close to the footpath. Oblivious to the dangers now surrounding him – the dim and vaulted green woods always had a magical appeal.

Earlier, having built a secret bird hide close to the river and just off the beaten track, he was hoping to spot kingfishers. Fledglings had been seen on the banks. Wild, spectacular, kingfishers in flight always filled him with joy. Not that he was expecting to see any, but he might if he kept quiet.

Eyes peeled through a gap in the treeline, he could just make out a dark silhouette beyond the ridge. He knew it was risky, knew he shouldn't, but he crept forward anyway. There was a man. Not tall, but portly, with a rounded face and balding hairline that reminded him of his late Uncle Arthur. What was he doing here? Who was he talking to? He was eager to find out.

Crawling forward on all fours, twigs snapped beneath his fingertips and the long knobbly ferns dug deep into his scrawny knees and caused him to wince. He didn't want to get too close as he might be seen, but curiosity had unquestionably got the better of him.

Then, through the thick undergrowth he spotted a woman's face. Motionless, eyes wide open in a look of terror, she was staring out into space as if searching for something. He could see her lips were tinged blue and her mouth wide open in a cry of revulsion, but still it didn't register. Next, he noticed the yellow cord attached to a branch and tied taut around her neck. She was bent forward slightly, knees buckled, with her feet touching the ground. She wasn't a tall woman, slim with long shoulder-length blonde hair that clung to her cheeks like ripe summer corn. Wearing an ankle-length skirt, blue cotton blouse and flat leather shoes, he noticed her fingernails were painted a bright orange colour reminding him of pyracantha berries in autumn.

Who was she?

Shifting his weight, he watched as the man extended his arms towards the heavens as a priest offering prayers. The boy had never seen a person this close to death before, and never wanted to see one again.

Without warning, the man's eyes shot sideways suddenly. His voice was threatening, cold. 'Who's there?' he demanded.

Scared out of his wits, the boy pressed his face hard against the damp woodland soil and tried to make himself small. He should never have skipped off school lessons; it was a stupid thing to do. Now caught in something he no longer wished to be part of, he didn't feel safe anymore.

Warily, he opened one eye and caught the resolute expression on the man's face.

'I'm not going to hurt you,' the man said unconvincingly. 'Why don't you come out?'

The boy wanted to say something, anything, but the words got stuck in his throat. Too scared to move, he was looking for a way out. To his right was a woodland path. Beyond that, a tangled mass of branches swayed leisurely in the sweltering summer breeze making a whispering sound. What if he ran towards the mass of woodland ferns? He was brave enough, and he might even lose him there.

What if he fell?

With every sinew in the boy's body now straining, he lifted his head a tiny fraction; enough to peer out of one eye. Closer, closer than ever before, the thought of what the man might do had put the living fear of God in him.

'I know you're in there,' the man shouted out.

Coiled like a spring, blood drained from the boy's face as the woods began to spin. His heart was pounding so fast, he thought it was about to explode. Tears rolled down his cheeks, and he felt wet fluid running down his legs.

Motionless, the man shot him another sideways glance. There was evil in his eyes, the likes of which he'd never seen before. After a few deep breaths, the boy pulled back into the thick undergrowth and hid behind a tree. He was desperate to get away from him, but nowhere felt safe anymore.

Terrified, the boy rose to his feet and ran towards the woodland footpath. Head down, shoulders slightly hunched, he sprinted as fast as his legs could carry him. He was heading for the river and the safety of the bird hide he'd built. Twenty metres, fifty metres; he thought he was going to be sick. If only he could run faster the man might give up on him. Then, reaching a bend in the footpath, it ended abruptly, and for one split second he'd lost all sense of direction. As his eyes searched for a gap in the undergrowth, he shuddered at the hopelessness of escape. He'd taken a wrong turning and there was nowhere else to run.

Then he heard footsteps approaching.

Panic came in waves as he felt the man's strong hand grab the back of his neck. He remembered the woman's face and imagined himself in her place. Somehow, he wriggled free, dropped to one knee and scrambled through a gap in the undergrowth. Thorns tore into him, like a werewolf's talons gouging through flesh. He tried to scream out, but the pain was excruciating and his voice pitiful.

Then daylight appeared, and he was standing at the top of a steep ravine searching for his next route of escape. There was none, only the sound of running water deep in the valley below. Caught in two minds, he plucked up enough courage to slide down a steep slippery slope. Everything was a blur, and his head was pounding so hard that he thought he was about to die. Tumbling headlong to the bottom, he turned. But all he could hear was the man's ragged breathing and the sound of falling rocks.

What to do next? His mouth felt dry, and the hairs on the back of neck were standing on end. Gripped by uncertainty, he decided to make a dash for it. It wasn't far, but on nearing a bend in the river he doubled back on himself and ducked inside his secret bird hide. It was dark inside – eerie – only the afternoon sunlight streaming through the tiniest of gaps in twisted branches. Then he heard the man's ragged breathing again, like the wind along a knife.

Crouching low, the boy held his breath and listened. Less than a metre away sunlight danced on the man's mud-spattered shoes. They were brown, with sharp pointed toes and his shoelaces had been tied in a criss-cross pattern. How much longer he could hold out he had no idea. What if he made another dash for it – ran towards the river and swam to the other side?

Then the man's ragged voice again.

This time he was goading him, wielding a heavy stick above his head and shouting out profanities. Half expecting it to come crashing down on top of him, the boy closed his eyes and wished himself invisible.

Only the man's irregular breathing now, and the sound of running water.

CHAPTER
TWO

It was six o'clock when ten-year-old Martin Kennedy finally arrived back at his father's house. Carrying his mud-spattered shoes in his hand, the young boy didn't know what to think. Scared out of his wits, he crept up the hallway stairs and quietly pulled the bedroom door shut behind him. The room was small and cluttered, tucked away towards the back of the house. Posters filled every wall, some of wildlife but mainly birds of prey. A central window looked out onto small factory units; it wasn't a particularly pleasant view. At least it was home and Martin felt safe here.

Quietly, not wanting to disturb his father, he stood in front of the mirror and wriggled free of his mud-spattered school uniform. There were so many unanswered questions on his mind, questions he didn't want to talk about. If he had known then what he knew now, he would never have skipped off school in the first place.

Exhausted, he flopped down on his bed and buried his head in his pillow. He'd been in some terrifying scrapes in his life, but nothing compared to this. As he let his mind drift, all around him the wind began to howl in his daydream. Fear gripped him, and he was thrown into utter turmoil again. He was running through a forest, and a wicked beast was chasing after him. It was huge, bigger than anything he'd ever witnessed before. As the illusion intensified, so did his sense of judgement. He knew it was evil, knew it was out to kill him, but there was little he could do to stop it. Then, just when he thought it was going to devour him, his dream took a different form. He was standing in a tunnel, and the ghostlike image of his mother was walking towards him. Arms outstretched, head bent low, she was pleading with him to follow her to safety and away from the wicked beast. All the while he could hear heavy footsteps approaching, and knew the beast was getting closer.

Then, in the darkest corners of his mind, he heard his father's voice. Not daring to breathe, fear ripped through him as never before. This wasn't a dream, this was reality and his father's voice was angry.

'Is that you up there, Martin?'

'Yes, Dad,' Martin called out.

'What the hell have you been up to this time?'

'Nothing, Dad. I swear it!'

'What do you mean nothing?' his father yelled back at the top of his voice. 'There's mud all over the hallway carpets and all the way up the stairs.'

Martin peered down at his bed sheets and cringed. Muck everywhere, footprints all over the floor, and his bedside cabinet was in a right old mess. His father would kill him if ever he saw his bedroom in this state – but what was he to do? He didn't have a clue how to operate the washing machine, and the bed sheets were far too big to wash in the sink. He knew his mother would have helped him, but she no longer lived at home.

His mind running amok, Martin picked up his mud-spattered shoes and slid them under his bed.

'Did you hear me, son?'

'Yes, Dad, and I took my shoes off the minute I stepped into the house.'

'Really!'

'I swear on my grandmother's life!'

The moment he caught his father's ominous shadow through the gap under the door, his heart sank. It wasn't his fault he'd messed up badly; it was Miss Crawshaw, his lousy English teacher who was to blame. Why couldn't she be nice to him like all the other teachers in school, instead of constantly picking on him all the time? He should never have peered in through the car's windows, he should have gone straight to the bird hide just like he'd planned. He hadn't, and now he was up to his neck in serious trouble.

The moment his bedroom door flew back on its hinges, Martin winced. The next thing he saw, after his father had stormed into the room, was the furious look on his face. He wanted to cry out, say he was sorry for the terrible mess he'd got himself into. But how could he possibly explain what had happened to him that afternoon, where would he even begin?

He watched as his father puffed his cheeks out and expelled a long blast of air.

'What in hell's name have you been up to this time, young man?'

'Nothing, Dad—'

'Nothing,' his father shrieked, 'just look at the state of your room.'

'I'm sorry, Dad.'

'Sorry!'

Tears rolled down Martin's cheeks, and he couldn't stop shaking. Then, in a moment of inspiration he started to count to one thousand and ten – just as he always did in times of trouble. It diverted his attention from unwanted thoughts, helped him cope in a grownup world. But nothing could save him from the beast in his nightmare, no matter how hard he tried.

'There was this stranger, Dad,' Martin began.

'What stranger. . . who?

'The man who chased me through Chopwell Wood.'

His father stared at him oddly, as he moved towards the bottom of his bed. There was nothing more frightening than an angry dad. Then, when he was least expecting it, his father lifted one eyebrow and shot him a piercing glance. 'What were you doing in Chopwell Wood. . . I thought you were supposed to be at school all day?'

'I was—'

After his father had asked him a zillion questions, he finally broke down and cried. He should never have gone there in the first place. He'd been spooked, and he didn't want to talk about it anymore.

Then silence – only the nightmare still playing on his mind.

'What did he look like?' his father asked, softy now.

'Who, Dad?'

'The man who chased after you through Chopwell Wood?'

'Just like my Uncle Arthur!'

He watched as his father's eyes darted back to the bedsheets for an instant; then returned to him, silently, resolutely for some moments. 'You'd better be telling me the truth, young man. If not, I'll stop your pocket money for the rest of your life.'

What was he to do?

He was trapped, and his mind had splintered into a thousand pieces. Nothing made sense anymore. As he pulled the bed sheets over his head, he wished he was invisible. Too scared to even close his eyes; sleep didn't come easily that night.

CHAPTER
THREE

David Carlisle pocketed his iPhone and pondered his options. It was that time of year again, and trade in the unfaithful husband and wife department was booming. Sometimes he wondered where time went. Being a private investigator could be very demanding at times, and this summer was no exception. Not since his days with the Metropolitan Police had he been so busy. The trouble was, as government cutbacks cut deep into police numbers, petty crime was on the increase. It was a never-ending cycle, and one that the politicians were struggling to cope with.

Drinks arrived, brought in on a tray by his business partner Jane Collins. He cleared a few files away and watched as Jane placed a mug of steaming hot black coffee down on the corner of his desk. She was an attractive woman. Tall, witty, with a warm, bubbly personality that seemed to resonate with everyone she met. There was a darker side, though, and one that a lot of people knew nothing about. Hers was a well-kept secret, and one that Jane never talked about. Not even to him.

Outwardly assertive and self-assured, inwardly Jane was haunted by a troubled past. A broken relationship with a married man who had presented himself as single at the time, had totally shattered her confidence in men. The scars ran deep, as if indelibly etched on her soul. Carlisle despised the man who had cheated on her and swore quietly that one day he would get even with him on her behalf.

'There's a Mr Kennedy wishing to speak with you,' said Jane with an element of urgency in her voice. 'His son's in a spot of bother, it would appear.'

Carlisle put his pen down and pushed back in his seat. 'A stocky guy with a large black moustache and unruly mop of hair?'

'I believe so,' she replied.

'Does he happen to look a bit like Boycie off Only Fools and Horses?'

'Yes, he does now that you mention it.' Jane flashed her ice blue eyes at him as she peered out of the office window. 'Shall I tell him to make an appointment?'

'No, that won't be necessary.'

Carlisle stepped out of his office and returned seconds later. Pleasantries exchanged, there was no laughter in Phillip Kennedy's eyes, only emptiness. The man looked ragged, as well he might have been. His son's harrowing account of what took place in Chopwell Wood the previous day was enough to send shivers down any father's spine.

'So,' Carlisle began. 'Why haven't you gone to the police with your son's story before now?'

'You know I can't do that. Not with my criminal record, David. Besides, I'd rather you dealt with it. . . at least I know where I stand.'

Having served a two-year prison sentence for armed robbery, Kennedy had recently been released on licence and was subject to a string of conditions. Aware that Social Services were involved with the man's son, Carlisle thought a moment.

'What if Martin isn't telling you the truth? What if he's making this up after ruining his school uniform? Kids do that sort of thing, you know. It's part of growing up.'

Kennedy shook his head dismissively. 'No. He's telling me the truth all right, I can assure you of that. He's not slept a wink all night and hasn't eaten since breakfast time yesterday morning. I know he can fantasise at times, but something serious has happened and it's scared the living daylights out of him.'

Carlisle checked his appointments book.

'Whereabouts in Chopwell Wood did you say this incident took place?'

'Close to a footpath, down by the river! He's built a bird hide there apparently. That's where he was heading after he'd bunked off school lessons.'

Carlisle raised his eyebrows a fraction. 'It sounds like Martin has grown into a bit of a Jack-the-lad since I last met him. Apart from witnessing a possible suspicious suicide, is there anything else I should know?'

Kennedy smiled bleakly. 'I'll admit he's no angel, but Martin has been going through difficult times lately. But that's the least of my worries, it seems.'

'And where is Martin now?'

'He's stopping at my sister's house. It's over in Benwell.'

Carlisle opened his laptop and studied the Google map for a moment. Concerned about reporting the incident to the police, his friend was desperately trying to keep a lid on things.

'From what I can gather, Martin's bird hide must be sited in the south of the woods. Somewhere around here. . . Lintzford.' Carlisle ran an index finger along the River Derwent tracing its route before hovering over a small built-up area. 'If he was chased for a good half mile, that would make it a lot more difficult, of course.'

'Difficult?'

'It's a vast catchment area and knowing where to start's the problem.' Carlisle blew into his coffee as he stared down at the map. Tracks led to streams, streams led to the river, but nothing was cast in stone. There were dozens of footpaths fitting the boy's description and choosing the right one seemed an impossible task. He turned to his friend, and said, 'You can see the size of the problem we're faced with. . . it's like looking for a needle in a haystack.'

'What about this black car that Martin spotted, could that have something to do with it?'

'I'm more concerned about this woman than anything. If Martin is telling you the truth, then the police will want to get involved.' Carlisle thought about it. 'Unless she's already been discovered, of course.'

His friends head dropped. 'So, it *will* involve the police?'

'I'm afraid so.'

'What will happen to Martin now? Will they want to question him over it?'

'At some point they will, especially if this woman has died under suspicious circumstances.'

'I knew it,' Kennedy said, waving a hand in annoyance.

'It's never that simple, Phil.'

'I know, but my supervising officer will obviously want to question me over it.'

Carlisle ran the flat of his hand over the top of his head in thought.

'We need to move quickly.'

'I know, I know,' Kennedy said angrily. 'Ever since me and the missus split up, Martin's been getting into all kinds of trouble. He can be a real handful at times, but he's a good kid at heart and I know when he's telling the truth.'

Carlisle stared at his friend sympathetically. 'The quicker we contact the police the better. After all, he's only a ten-year-old child and they know how to handle these situations better than we do.'

'You better get on with it then,' Kennedy sighed resignedly.

'The other issue we may need to consider is: what if this stranger decides to catch up with your son at some later stage?'

'And do what exactly?'

Carlisle stopped himself short, the expression on his friend's face warning him against continuing. He stared at the map again and did a quick mental calculation. With fifty good men, the police could cover an awful lot of ground in an hour – especially with trained dog teams. No, he thought. Time to act now rather than the police go knocking on Kennedy's door in the middle of the night.

He picked up the phone as he turned to his friend. 'I still have a few good contacts who will handle the case with utmost discretion.'

'Case?' Kennedy replied bleakly.

'This isn't an everyday occurrence, Phil, and your son's account of what took place suggests this woman may have been strangled. Besides, the man who chased after your son needs to be brought in for questioning.'

'What are you trying to say?'

Carlisle looked hard at his friend. 'The minute I contact the police they'll be all over it like a rash.'

Kennedy's face dropped as if resigned to the fact.

'I thought as much.'

'Let me make a few phone calls first,' Carlisle said, pressing the conference call button and waiting for the dialling tone to click in.

'*DCI Jack Mason, Northumbria Police.*' The speaker suddenly boomed out.

'Good morning, Jack. It's David Carlisle. How are things over at Gateshead nowadays?'

'Cut out the crap. What's on your mind, my friend?'

CHAPTER FOUR

The small knot of forensic officers gathered close to the clearing told Jack Mason where the woman's body was. Dressed in a white forensic suit, overshoes and blue gloves, the Detective Chief Inspector signed the crime scene entry log sheet and ducked under the police cordon tape. One hundred metres east of the woodland cycle trail and four hundred metres north of the River Derwent the chances of being spotted here were slim. This was dense woodland, and well off the beaten track.

He was met by Tom Hedley, the senior forensic scientist, and his colleague seemed surprised to see him. 'I thought you were still on light duties.' Hedley grinned. 'The first sniff of a bloody body bag, and you can't resist the temptation.'

Mason brushed his friend's comments aside as he moved to take a closer look.

'What have we got, Tom?'

'Slimly built woman, mid-forties, around five-foot-six. It initially looks like suicide, but I'm not convinced.'

'Who found her?'

'One of the search teams.'

What Hedley didn't know, or perhaps he did, is that it was the DCI who had initiated the search operation in the first place. The rest was a simple matter of legwork and elimination.

'No other reports of someone spotting her?' Mason asked.

'None that I'm aware of.'

Not a tall man, Jack Mason had recently been described by local news reporters as 'short and stocky'. He would have preferred compact and muscular, if the truth were known. But beggars couldn't be choosers especially where the media was concerned. He opened his notebook and studied his surroundings.

'It's well-hidden,' Mason shrugged, 'which means less contamination.'

'It's another way of looking on it,' Hedley replied.

In what was otherwise an isolated spot on the southern edge of Chopwell Wood, there was no easy access to the body. From what he could see the skin around the woman's lips and ears had turned blue with cyanosis. On further inspection, what looked like a yellow clothes line wrapped taught around the woman's neck had cut deep into the flesh. There were no visual signs of bruising, no signs that a struggle had taken place – nothing.

As the two forensic officers stood next to him moved towards the base of the tree, he recognised one of them. Neither spoke, but he knew what they were thinking. Whether she'd been assisted to shuffle this mortal coil, or some other dark forces were at work, it made no difference. This woman had died under suspicious circumstances as far as he was concerned, and all were agreed on that.

The police doctor, an unhappy creature, ran a spatula under the woman's bright orange fingernails before placing his findings into a small plastic forensic dish. How the woman had arrived on the scene had yet to be established, but the black vehicle the young boy had spotted not forty metres away, was nowhere to be seen.

'How long has she been dead?' Mason asked casually.

'Best part of twenty-four hours, I'd say.'

'Ligature asphyxiation?'

15

'It would appear so. No doubt a post-mortem vitreous chemical analysis will tell us if any abnormalities are present in her body.'

The sound of his voice had all the gaiety of an afternoon tea on the Somme, Mason thought. 'What, you think she was drugged?'

'We can't rule it out.' The doctor pointed to the woman's legs. 'Her feet never left the ground, and the position of her body suggests she leaned forward on the noose and her body weight did the rest. That aside, she died under suspicious circumstances in my opinion.'

'What, made to look like suicide?'

The police doctor gave him a cynical smile as he closed the lid of his medical bag. 'The pathologists will give us a better indication of that. After years spent dealing with dozens of similar cases, I've learnt never to pre-judge a crime scene.'

Mason stood for a moment in thought. He would have preferred to enter the investigation on more certain ground. Officially, nobody had been assigned to the case and he was hoping the Area Commander would look favourably towards him. And yes, he was the senior officer present, but that didn't mean a thing. Not whilst he was stuck on light duties it didn't. Best not get carried away, he thought. His first course of action would be to check the surrounding area, look for any CCTV footage and take it from there. Whoever had parked their vehicle close to the crime scene had obviously done so for a good reason. If nothing else, he would need to find it, and fast.

He scanned the ground close to the dead woman's feet. A woollen hat, an empty beer can, and a few discarded food wrappers haphazardly scattered about the place. It would all be bagged, tagged, and taken away for further examination in due course, once they'd established the cause of the woman's death. The doctor was right, there was nothing to suggest her body had swung from the tree branch as the cord attached to her neck was too long.

Mason crouched low as he turned to Hedley. 'We need to carry out a thorough examination of the surrounding area, Tom. My gut-feeling tells me we could be looking at a murder enquiry here.' He thought about what the doctor had said and corrected himself. 'Let me rephrase that. Let's see what the Home Office pathologist throws up before we go making any assumptions.'

Hedley had caught the suffering in Mason's voice and tried to mask it. 'Once we establish who she is, it should answer a lot of our questions.'

Mason nodded in agreement but said nothing.

'Has the boy said anything to you?' asked Hedley.

'Young Martin Kennedy?' Mason kicked the ground with the toe of his muddy shoe, annoyed with himself. 'Not yet, he hasn't. He's obviously a vulnerable witness, so we'll need to apply to the courts for "Special Measures". The fewer people who know of his existence the better, in my opinion.'

Hedley lowered his voice. 'You need to take it easy yourself, Jack. There's plenty of other good officers who can handle the case.'

'Nah! Not now I'm on the mend.'

Hedley was right, standing was his biggest problem nowadays. The Suitcase Man's horrific knife attack had caused all kinds of additional complications and infections, and it wasn't getting any easier. Had it not been for the life jacket he was wearing at the time, the serial killer's knife would have penetrated his heart. He realised that and was eternally grateful to the surgeons who had saved his life. Even so, a few more weeks of intensive physiotherapy and he'd be back in the swing of things again – or that was the plan at least.

His iPhone pinged.

He checked the display. It was Superintendent Gregory asking for an update on the monthly overtime sheets. Now back from his six-month secondment with the Nottinghamshire Police Force, the Area Commander was obviously making his presence felt.

'Yes, sir,' Mason replied. 'They're just about complete.'

'Good man!' There was a pause on the other end of the phone. 'Where are you now?'

'I'm over in Chopwell Wood. There's been what looks a suspicious suicide.'

'Who's in charge?'

'I'm the senior officer present if that's what you mean.'

'Umm.' There was a short pause, a gathering of thoughts. 'When you've finished your investigations, call by my office as there's a few matters we need to discuss.'

'Will do, sir.'

The line went dead.

The Chief Inspector slipped his iPhone back into his jacket pocket and stared at the activity close to the dead woman's feet. After jotting down notes, he noticed one of the forensic officers had started to make plaster of Paris casts of freshly made footprints. A quiet, shy, unassuming man, Williams seemed too engrossed in his work to speak. Maybe he should check out young Martin Kennedy's bird hide, Mason thought. Not that he was expecting to find much, but it was still worth a look.

Following the long winding footpath towards the river, he tried to imagine what the young boy had encountered that Monday afternoon. Scared out of his wits at having witnessed a woman's horrific strangulation, if that wasn't bad enough, he'd been chased by a man intent on beating his brains out. No, Mason thought. This case was right up his street and he was keen to take charge of it. Perhaps that's what the Area Commander was wanting to talk to him about – heading up the investigation team.

Eager to get stuck back into real crime again, he still had the police medical board to face. But that was a forgone conclusion: how could he possibly fail?

CHAPTER FIVE

Feeling on top of the world, Jack Mason slid onto the physiotherapist's treatment table in a consulting room in Forest Hall and grinned. These past few weeks he'd felt a ton better. Getting in and out of a car was still a major issue, though, and he couldn't walk fast without getting a sharp pain in his side. Other than that, he was more than pleased with the progress he was making and was ready for anything the Area Commander was about to throw at him. His consultant at the General Hospital wasn't so encouraging, though, but he was a bit of a dour sod anyway. According to him, he still had concerns about post-trauma complications and thought it would be months before he was back to full fitness again.

'Still keeping up with the exercises, Inspector?' his physiotherapist Barbara Lockwood said tersely.

'Twice a day,' Mason replied.

'Good. A couple more visits and that should be the end of it.'

'Sounds good to me.'

As Mason slid from the treatment table, another searing pain shot through his side. Desperately trying to hide it from her, Lockwood shot him an inquisitive glance. 'You're obviously suffering some discomfort. We need to keep an eye on it, as you might need a few extra sessions.'

'It's probably something I ate.'

Lockwood gave his side a gentle prod with the tip of her finger, and he nearly hit the roof. God, he thought. She knew where to hurt, and the pain had taken his breath away.

'It seems you may have some scar tissue problems from the knife wounds.'

Mason recovered his breath and slipped on his shirt feeling somewhat disappointed. He should have curbed his enthusiasm instead of running around like a headless chicken these past few weeks. There again, it wasn't in his nature and the Chief Inspector knew it. He wasn't out of the woods yet and Lockwood had been his saving grace these past few months. Without her physio and encouragement, he'd be sitting in a wheelchair, God forbid. Life in the fast lane wasn't all it was cracked up to be, and he had little choice but to trust her judgement.

'Everything, okay?' Mason asked warily.

She gave him a puzzled look. 'You can't expect your body to recover in a couple of months, these things take time.'

'Yeah, but I'm tired of staring at the four walls of my office. It's enough to drive any man crazy.'

'You'll be missed when I do finally sign you off,' Lockwood laughed.

'Oh?'

She blushed. 'I actually look forward to seeing you here every week.'

'Really!'

'What you see is what you get with you.' She smiled. 'You're not pretentious like some who come here on a regular basis.'

Mason thought about it, but not for long.

'How about you and I meeting up one night. . . go out for a meal together?'

Lockwood looked at him confused. 'What makes you think I'd want to do that?'

'Just a thought.'

'Really?'

Realising he'd overstepped the mark, he slipped on his jacket. 'It wasn't a proposal. It was meant as a thank you for getting me back on my feet again.'

'That's my job, it's what I'm paid to do.'

'Whatever,' Mason shrugged.

She handed him a new appointment card and gave him an almost guilty smile. 'Do you know what, I might just take you up on your offer one day?'

'You have my number,' Mason said approvingly.

Stepping into the waiting room rejuvenated, he checked his iPhone for missed calls, but there weren't any. It was time to give the Area Commander a call and update him with his progress. To be fair to his boss, a large consignment of drugs had recently hit the streets of Gateshead and he was under a lot of pressure. Crime figures were soaring, and the number of house break-ins had gone through the roof lately.

Still, Mason thought, a bit of good news might cheer the grumpy sod up – or give him another problem to think about!

★★★

Twenty minutes later, Jack Mason was sitting at his desk and checking a fresh batch of emails he'd just opened. It was official: the middle-aged woman found hanged in Chopwell Wood had died under suspicious circumstances. Running through the toxicity report, an elevated level of benzodiazepines had been found in the victim's body – a drug commonly prescribed as a sleeping aid and mainly used as a tranquilising anti-anxiety medication. Things were shaping up, and the fact the woman had been discovered in the kneeling position with another person known to be present, had enabled the coroner to return a narrative verdict of suspicious suicide rather than suicide.

Strange, Mason thought. According to the coroner's report, the noose around the woman's neck had been pulled tight by her own body weight, thereby cutting off the supply of oxygen to her lungs. There were no signs of vagal inhibition – a reflex that leads to cardiac arrest – allowing Dr Gillian King, the Senior Anatomical Pathology Technician, to finally reach her conclusions. All that remained now, as far as Jack Mason was concerned, was to be put in charge of the case.

He closed his computer down, grabbed a notebook and pen, and made a beeline towards his boss's office. Deep down he had a bad feeling about this and wasn't looking forward to their meeting one little bit. Mason was already running late and the Area Commander was a stickler for punctuality.

'Take a seat, Chief Inspector. You're five minutes late!'

'Apologies, sir. I got side-tracked by the coroner's report.'

Dressed in full police uniform, white collar and black tie, Superintendent Gregory's facial expression gave very little away. When Mason was a young copper working with the Metropolitan Police, he'd always had an aversion towards well educated, high ranking officers. Many were knobheads, desk-bound idiots and far removed from the real crime that was taking place on the streets of our cities, whilst others were so entrenched in their self-opinionated beliefs that he could never get to grips with the legal jargon they spouted off at meetings. He guessed it was pure waffle, as many had an answer for everything and a solution for nothing when it came to the real crime.

Gregory barely lifted his head as he took up a seat opposite. A dapper man, with grey swept back hair and high forehead, he had the eyes of a hawk, ears of a bat, and never missed a trick when it came to police procedure. Not the easiest senior officer to get along with, he rarely ventured out of his office nowadays. If he did, it was to present himself in front of media cameras at the end of every successful investigation. Mason hated press conferences at the best of times, and always regarded them as duplicitous affairs.

Fake news ran rife, and whatever you said in front of the cameras was edited and taken out of context.

'According to the coroner's report, it would appear we have another suspicious death on our hands,' Gregory began. 'Do we know who this woman is?'

'Not yet, we're still in the initial throes of our investigations, sir.'

'Given the time of death, most people would have been at work that time of day?'

Mason nodded. 'I would have thought so.'

'And the black vehicle this young boy spotted, where are we with that?'

'We're pulling together local CCTV footage, but I'm not pinning any hopes on it. The problem is, we don't have a positive description of the model or make other than the vehicle was black.'

There was a long pause.

'How are you coping with your light duties nowadays? I hear you're still seeing a hospital consultant?'

'Everything's fine, and my physiotherapist thinks I'll soon be back to full-fitness again.'

Gregory lifted his eyebrows a fraction. 'What about these new inquiries you're involved in, do you think you're up to it?'

'It's not a murder enquiry at this stage, so I would have—'

'These things can go either way, even you should know that,' Gregory interrupted.

'That doesn't mean I'm not up to it.'

The Area Commander hesitated. 'I've been giving it some thought lately, and I'd like you to take a backseat role on this one.'

Mason's face dropped. 'Back seat role, what does that mean exactly?'

'I'm concerned about your mental well-being, especially after all the physical trauma your body has gone through these past few months. This type of case can spiral out of control and before you know it, you're put under enormous strain. Long hours and pressures of work are the last thing you need right now, Chief Inspector.' Gregory lifted his head as if to make a point. 'I've decided to bring another senior officer in on the case. Only as a temporary measure, might I add. Once the police medical board have passed you fit for work again, we'll look at it again.'

'So, it's back to the desk job?'

'Not in as many words,' Gregory replied awkwardly. 'This isn't a major case as such and will only involve four or five officers at the most.'

Mason nodded, then shrugged. 'So, who do you have in mind?'

'After careful consideration I've decided to bring in DI Gamble on this one. She's a competent officer, suitably experienced, and I'm sure you'll appreciate her keenness to get involved.'

'And once I'm fully fit for work again does that mean I will take charge of the case?'

Gregory shook his head dismissively. 'Let's wait and see what the medical examiners have to say first. This recovery of yours could take weeks, and I'd hate you to have a major setback – especially after all the effort you've put into getting back to your current fitness levels.'

'So, it's down to the police medical board?'

Gregory smiled. 'I'm afraid so.'

'I see. . .'

'I'm banking on your full cooperation on this one, Chief Inspector. Detective Inspector Gamble doesn't have any axes to grind with anyone in the building, and I know the two of you will get on like a house on fire.'

Like hell, Mason thought. Offloaded from Middlesbrough Special Crime Unit to take over control of his team, that was the last thing he wanted to hear. He took a deep breath and steadied himself. It wasn't looking good suddenly, and he could think of a dozen better officers to do his job.

'Who will I report to, now that DI Gamble will be running the show?' Mason asked.

'Directly to me. Why?'

'I was—'

'Rule number one,' Gregory said, tapping the end of his pen on his desk, 'you're to observe case management protocol at all times. As far as I'm concerned, DI Gamble will handle the-day-to-day running of operations, whilst you will actively take on an advisory role. This is by no means a slant on your good character, far from it. And, I might add, it could lead to other things in the future.' Gregory shuffled awkwardly knowing his arrangements had gone down like a lead balloon. He was floundering, and Mason had picked up on it. 'You're a good officer, Chief Inspector, and no one doubts your ability. The trouble is you're not one-hundred percent fit and until you are, I'm not prepared to put my neck on the line.'

'No, I suppose not.'

Gregory took a few moments to gather his composure. 'I can sense your disappointment, but you know it makes sense. These things take time, and the last thing you need is another setback.'

Infuriated, Mason stood to leave.

'Will that be all, sir?'

'Yes, for now.'

Just when he thought he was about to take control of a murder investigation, he'd been asked to play second fiddle. Not one for shying from the action, the thought of a junior officer heading up his team infuriated him. He would need to calm down, show a little respect.

'Better get on with it then.'

Gregory's look was stern. 'I want you to think very carefully about your new role. Try keeping it simple. In a few months' time you'll be a completely different man again. Mark my word.'

Too damn right, Mason thought. It was all utter bollocks. He'd been stitched up big time and there wasn't a damn thing he could do about it. Emotionally drained, he slammed the Area Commander's office door behind him and stormed off along the corridor. It was time to put up the shutters – think about his future.

Chapter Six

Throughout his professional career, Chameleon had never failed to complete a mission. Ever. He'd come close on several occasions, but failure wasn't an option. Despite a shady past, his word was sacrosanct – as was an impeccable success rate. Everything he did was to eradicate randomness; nothing was left to chance.

Known to employees only as "Chameleon", his part in operations was always considered a done deal – a guaranteed banker many would agree. Having amassed a vast fortune providing covert services in the shadier side of society, he'd built his reputation with two golden rules.

Never renege on a client.

Never make promises you can't keep.

A few days ago, at a place called Chopwell Wood, he'd made a grave misjudgement. There was no way he could have known at the time, but the boy who slipped through his fingers now threatened to unravel everything he'd built. It wasn't looking good suddenly, and the thought had played over and over in his mind. These past few weeks had been a desperate scramble to recover the situation and take back control. Although a dozen other missions were in operation around the world, he had finally devised a plan to deal with the boy once and for all.

Today, outside the school gates, he only had one thing on his mind. To find the boy and eliminate the source of his problems. He'd learnt over the years that you never gave in to the sympathy vote. Once you did, you were finished. There was a lot at stake with his part of the operation, and if the boy talked, he could open a can of worms.

Wearing a pair of blue denim jeans, and a plain T-shirt, he merged in well with the regular parents. Not that anyone would question him over his presence here today, but it was the interfering do-gooders he feared most. That's why he wanted to get it over with. Quickly, without fuss, and made to look like an accident. There were many ways to kill the boy, and it was never going to be easy. It was how he went about it that made the difference.

He heard the school bell ring and watched as the kids spilled out onto the playground. Hundreds of them, screaming at the top of their voices and scattering in all directions like rats in a sewer. He thought he might recognise the young boy if he saw him again, but still he wasn't one hundred percent convinced. It was only a fleeting glance, a snapshot in time. Without a name, he was forced to work blind.

Adrenaline coursing through his veins, Chameleon reached into his pocket and pulled out a sketch he'd made from memory of the boy's school uniform. It was almost a perfect match – black V-necked jumper, red and yellow stripe tie, even the school logo was identical. As he peered at the sketch again, the more baffled he became. How would he pick the boy out from the rest of the children when they all looked the same in their school uniforms?

What if he killed the wrong boy?

Back at the hire car, he took out his mobile phone and frantically started to video everything that was going on around him. Nothing was obvious anymore, and everything was thrown into confusion. It wasn't his fault the boy had witnessed what had taken place that day, but two wrongs didn't make a right.

He sat for a moment, thinking.

Across the busy playground he noticed a second gate; and hundreds of kids spilling into the nearby streets. Seething with anger and frustration, Chameleon needed only a moment to make a snap decision. Slamming the gear lever into reverse, he hastily backed the hire car into one of the side streets, keeping an eye on his surroundings. Annoyed with himself, he made a slight detour around the back of the estate before pulling up twenty metres short of the gate. Next, he switched off the engine and peered out of the passenger window.

Perfect, he thought, as he discreetly fired up his camera again. He would download the images later – once he was back at the hotel.

CHAPTER SEVEN

Detective Inspector Gamble's appointment hadn't gone down at all well in Jack Mason's books. Not that he could do anything about it, but he was still reeling over the Area Commander's choice of case leader. Convinced he should be heading up the investigation, his feelings were running high. Having spent the whole weekend deliberating over his future position on the force, he'd decided to do things his way. The last time he'd felt this way about his job, he was close to chucking it in. Not this time, though. Now that he'd got his head around it all, he was determined to put up a fight.

'Morning, boss,' DS Rob Savage said, breezing into his office. 'No doubt you'll have heard about the new appointment.'

'What appointment is this?'

'Detective Inspector Gamble from Middlesbrough.'

'What about her?'

'Everyone thought that you were heading up the Chopwell case.'

'Oh! What gave you that impression?'

The sergeant stared at him, confused. 'After you turned up at the Chopwell crime scene we naturally took it for granted that you were in charge of the investigation.'

Much as Mason hated parting with hard-earned information, he wasn't giving in that easily. Matters had got off to a bad start, and a few extra nuggets of misinformation wouldn't go amiss at this stage. He took a sip of his coffee and paused in thought as he opened a sandwich carton he'd placed on his desk.

'As far as I'm aware, DI Gamble is only here on temporary assignment.'

'That's not what she told us at this morning's briefing.'

Mason looked at the sergeant inquisitively. 'Oh! What did she tell you?'

'She'll be running the day-to-day operations from now on, and anyone not pulling their weight will immediately be slung off the team.'

Mason smiled with some satisfaction. 'That's a bit harsh, don't you think?'

'It didn't go down at all well with the team.'

'No, I suppose not.'

'Bugger,' the sergeant swore. 'Sounds like I've gone and put my foot in it again.'

Mason took a huge bite of his sandwich, knowing that Savage had wanted to get it off his chest. Strange, he thought, the sergeant usually kept his thoughts to himself.

'You don't seem exactly enamoured by her appointment?'

'I was talking to—'

There was a knock on the door, and the sergeant stopped mid-sentence.

'Enter!'

The door opened.

'Ah! DI Gamble,' Mason said, wiping the crumbs from his mouth. 'Speak of the devil. I hear you are joining us?'

Mason indicated to a chair opposite him, as Savage slid from the room. Five-foot-eleven, with short blonde hair and brown eyes, Gamble was a good three inches taller than Mason. Wearing a white open neck blouse, slacks, and black brogue shoes, she seemed pleasant enough. He knew her slightly from a case he'd worked on in Middlesbrough involving a child sex offender. She wasn't part of his investigation team, but he'd heard rumours that she was ambitious and determined to climb the promotion ladder at any costs. How true the rumours were, he had no idea, but in this game, you had to cover your back.

Itching to say something, Mason waited for the Inspector to break the silence between them, knowing full well what she was up to.

'I thought we might spend a few moments together,' Gamble began.

'Always pleased to assist,' Mason smiled. 'What can I do for you?'

There was another long pause.

'I was rather hoping we might throw a few markers down . . . team strengths, budgets, that sort of thing.'

'Of course,' Mason said, feigning enthusiasm. 'I've heard you'll be running the day-to-day operations on the Chopwell case. Is that true?'

'Yes, I am.'

'In which case you'll find most of the information is already on file.'

Gamble paused for a moment then continued. 'I thought it would be much nicer coming from you, Jack.'

Mason picked up the other half of his sandwich and stopped short of his mouth. Not taking too kindly to her ease of the word "Jack", he put it down again. 'How do you see my role in all of this, Detective Inspector?'

'It's my understanding you're still stuck on light duties.'

'Yes, I am. But that doesn't mean that I'm desk bound.'

'We can both be flexible around that, Jack.'

There it was again . . . *"Jack"*. He thought about it and pushed it to the back of his mind for a moment. 'I have no objections to you throwing a few markers down, just as long as it doesn't constrain people.'

Gamble's stare hardened. 'Much as I hate taking over control of your team, we still have to work together on this one. Let's be clear about one thing, though, we're both striving to reach the same outcome.'

'Indeed.' Mason nodded. 'And I'd hate to think we got off on the wrong foot.'

'Those are exactly my sentiments.'

Bullshit, Mason thought.

Reaching over, he picked up one of the case files lying on his desk and casually tossed it towards her. 'This woman we found in Chopwell Wood, her name is Margaret Cooper.'

'Another desperate tale of woe?'

'Quite the contrary, she was a barrister in real life, married with two teenage daughters and lived in a four-bedroomed detached house in Darras Hall. Three days prior to her body being found in Chopwell Wood, she'd gone to work as normal and that was the last her family saw of her. Up until now that is.'

Gamble cocked her head to one side. 'That's unusual . . . a barrister you say?'

'Ah huh. Mind, there's a long history of depression according to Margaret Cooper's medical records.' Mason brushed the crumbs from his trousers and stood. 'Four years ago, she was off work for six months having suffered a mental breakdown. Naturally concerned about his wife's sudden disappearance, that's when her husband reported her missing to the police.'

'When did you discover this?'

'It's just what I've picked up,' Mason said, a touch of envy creeping in. 'I naturally assumed you knew about it.'

Gamble's face contorted into something unrecognisable.

'What about formal identification?'

'Yes, her husband has already carried that out.'

Gamble swallowed hard and stared at her notes. Still trying to get her feet under the table, there seemed very little logic in her approach. Mason shuffled a few papers around an untidy desk and continued to study her reactions.

'Why wasn't I informed about this?' Gamble said, lifting her head.

'You were holding your team briefing at the time the report came through.'

'A breakdown in communications perhaps?'

'Could be. I naturally assumed you'd already read the coroner's report, and that's why I contacted Dr Gillian King, the senior anatomical pathology technician at Gateshead Coroner's Office.'

'What about a written statement from her husband?'

'Laurence, as far as I'm aware, he's too busy consoling his two teenage daughters – very distressing.'

'If he hasn't made a formal statement yet, he still needs to be eliminated from our enquiries.' She opened the case folder in front of her and thought for a moment. 'What about this young boy's account of the man he saw in Chopwell Wood?'

'Young Martin Kennedy?'

'Yes,' she replied.

'From what we can gather, the boy's description of the suspect is that he looks like his Uncle Arthur.'

'Sounds like a typical ten-year-old child's account.' Gamble shook her head. 'Has anyone tried contacting this. . . Uncle Arthur?'

'Hardly, he's been dead three years.'

Gamble was quick to recover. 'Do we have any other information on him?'

'It's all on file,' Mason replied, tapping the case folder with his pen.

'What about this barrister's husband?'

Mason brushed the crumbs from his mouth. 'What about him?'

'What are your thoughts?'

'Judging from family photographs, Laurence Cooper looks nothing like the boy's Uncle Arthur. This isn't as straightforward as it appears, but I'm sure there's plenty for you to go at.'

Mason dropped the empty sandwich carton into the waste bin and made a point of tidying his desk. Taking a backseat role wasn't so bad after all – even if she was trying to pick his brains. No, he thought. The average chess player is usually three or four moves ahead of the game and he was happy to stick to his plan.

'Leave this with me,' Gamble insisted, standing to leave.

'Will that be all?'

'Yes, for now,' she replied.

He was about to say something but chose to let it drop.

'There is one other thing, actually,' Gamble said, turning before reaching the door. 'I'd like you to attend my daily briefings. If we are going to work together on the case, you need to be kept in the loop on all the latest developments.'

'Do you think that's wise?' Mason said, cocking his head to one side.

'In what way?'

'After all I am the senior officer.'

Gamble's stare hardened. 'What difference does that make?'

'Well.' He smiled, a hint of smugness creeping into his voice. 'I'd hate to think I was influencing your decision making!'

'I doubt you'll do that!'

'No. Perhaps not.'

CHAPTER EIGHT

The moment David Carlisle pulled his Rover P4 100 into the layby, he spotted the media satellite vans. Dozens of them, one behind the other like ducks in a row. He was met by Jack Mason, and they bobbed under the police cordon tape and followed the long meandering trail leading to the River Derwent. The woods were a mixture of conifers and broadleaf woodland, almost a thousand acres covering an area on the northern slopes of the Derwent Valley. To the east were the villages of High Spen and Rowlands Gill, to the west Blackhall Mill and Chopwell. It was a beautiful location, but one that Carlisle had paid little attention to over the years. Dotted with ancient and new woodlands, a sculpture trail blazed a novel adventure path through the heart of the woods. Teaming with wildlife, it was easy to see why young Martin Kennedy had chosen this particular area to build a bird hide. In places, the undergrowth was quite tall, and an adventurous ten-year-old schoolboy might easily conceal himself from view.

At the bottom of a steep incline they picked up a well-trodden riverside track which ran for a quarter of a mile before pulling up in front of a steep knoll. Mason was obviously in pain, and his hand kept gripping his side.

'I'm concerned about the safety of your friend's son,' Mason announced. 'We've received reports of a stranger hanging around the school gates.'

'What are you doing about it?'

'Not a lot actually.' The Chief Inspector looked at him, crestfallen. 'I'm still stuck on light duties, and the Area Commander has drafted someone in from another division to deal with the case.'

'You're still confined to your desk in other words?'

'In a nutshell, yes.'

'Is that problematic?' Carlisle replied.

'I'm not in a bloody wheelchair for God's sake!'

Carlisle smelt a rat. Something got under the Chief Inspector's skin, and whatever it was, it irritated him. He would need to tread carefully – find out what was really going on back at the station. He still had a few reliable contacts he could talk to, officers he could trust. He made a mental note of it and tried to delve deeper.

'You're not usually one to shy away from a problem, Jack. It's not your style.'

'It's out of my hands, I'm afraid.'

Carlisle stared out across the river, the sunlight dancing over water ripples. In days gone by, he might have challenged him over it, but not anymore. In a way, he felt sorry for his old work colleague. There were far less proficient officers around who could scale the promotion ladder, and the team had suffered badly as a result. Sometimes it was all about who you knew, favouritism gone mad.

'Anyone I know?' Carlisle asked.

'Her name's DI Gamble, and rumour has it she's ambitious.'

'Nothing wrong with that.'

'As long as she doesn't have eyes for my position.'

Carlisle smiled, knowing he was nearer the truth. 'What about your health? You're not walking very well at the moment.'

Mason kicked the soil under his foot. 'Once I'm declared fit by the police medical board, everything will be back to normal again.'

'What are the chances of that happening?'

Mason shrugged but chose not to reply.

Behind the thin-lipped smile Carlisle detected a hint of jealousy. There were an awful lot of rumours kicking about, and events had obviously got off to a bad start. Not that he had any influence over the matter but he could sense bad vibes when he saw them. The last time they'd worked together on a murder case, the Chief Inspector's powers of investigation had been tested to the limit. Mason led from the front, no matter what dangers he faced. His friend was old school, a down to earth, hands-on detective. Taking a backseat role was akin to locking a tiger up in a cage.

He watched as the Chief Inspector swung on his heels and pointed back at the tack. 'Was the barrister dead or alive when the suspect chased young Martin down here? That's what we should be asking ourselves.'

'The suspect obviously panicked knowing the boy was his only witness.'

'It's as good as any motive.' Mason shrugged.

On reaching the police cordon tape, Mason showed his warrant card to the young Constable and they stood chatting for a while. Even after Martin's bird hide had been pointed out to him, Carlisle could not see it. It was well hidden.

Mason returned his gaze. 'What was a barrister doing in the woods in the first place, you may ask?'

'Whatever happened here was clearly planned.'

'You think so?'

Carlisle nodded. 'The black vehicle that Martin spotted, the clothes line around her neck, and the suspect's attempts to beat the boy's brains out.'

'What about the elevated benzodiazepine levels we found in her body?'

'What. You think she took an overdose?'

'If she did,' Mason said thoughtfully, 'it means her suicide was definitely planned. Something's not right, and according to the coroner's report she didn't put up a fight.'

'She could have been unconscious and driven here?'

'With that number of pills in her body she would have died from an overdose, let alone putting a rope around her neck.' Mason looked at him and shrugged. 'This was made to look like suicide, in more ways than one I'd wager.'

'So, we could be looking at murder here?'

'If not, then how come her handbag and iPhone are still missing, and forensics still haven't found any empty pill containers at the crime scene?'

'What about her iPhone transmitting a signal?'

'No. Nothing.'

The private investigator screwed his face up. 'That's odd!'

'Perhaps he intended to throw us off his scent.' Mason raised a finger to his forehead. 'Think about it. If your friend's son hadn't witnessed what went on that Monday afternoon, we'd still be looking at suicide.'

'The only problem I have with that is why would a barrister walk out on her family without making contact?'

'I'm still not convinced she walked out on them.' Mason stood for a moment, thinking. 'All she had with her was the clothes she stood up in, so where did she go that weekend?'

'Perhaps it was a spur of the moment thing.'

'I doubt it,' Mason replied bluntly.

'What about close family and friends?'

'Nothing there either.'

Carlisle was taken aback somewhat. 'If she had a history of suicide attempts that puts another slant on it – surely.'

'I'm no psychiatrist,' Mason said, shaking his head, 'but according to the medical experts, they were only half-hearted attempts at taking her own life – more a cry for help than anything.' Mason's eyes toured the crime scene. 'There's more to this case than first meets the eye. Cooper was a professional, a barrister at the top of her game, so I doubt it was a spur of the moment thing.'

Carlisle scratched his brow in serious mode. 'She could have known the suspect, of course?'

'Possible, but most suicides I've attended there was either an expression of intent, or some form of written apology to the family in the form of a suicide note. Even in their darkest hour, people who commit suicide always think about their loved ones before they leave this mortal coil.' Mason hesitated, the tiniest flicker of doubt showing in his eyes. 'This looks like murder to me. I'm convinced of it.'

The seeds of doubt having been sown, they stood in silence for a moment.

'These sightings of a stranger seen hanging around the school gates,' Carlisle said. 'They need to be taken seriously. Mothers tittle-tattle tends to carry a lot of weight, especially where their kids are concerned.'

'We're dealing with it.' Mason shrugged. 'But it's more than likely to be gossip.'

'How do you propose to keep tabs on it?'

'That's DI Gamble's problem, not mine,' Mason replied brashly.

Carlisle stood for a moment, knowing how crucial the next few days would be. Get it wrong and the wolves would come knocking at the door. The boy's safety was paramount and if he could help in any way he would.

'I'm not liking it,' Carlisle said, shaking his head.

'Tell me about it.' Mason swung to face Carlisle. 'I know you've worked for me on several occasions in the past, but I'm no longer in a position to offer you a contract.'

'Thanks for keeping me in mind, but I'm extremely busy at the moment.'

'But that could all change, of course.'

Carlisle nodded. 'Always grateful to be of assistance.'

Whichever way they looked at it, there was no simple explanation for all of this. The fact that a hard-working barrister had gone about her daily business and had been found dead three days later, had cast grave doubts in a lot of people's minds. Something wasn't right, and whoever had given chase to Martin Kennedy meant the young boy's life was now in grave danger.

That much they were agreed on.

CHAPTER NINE

Three hundred metres from the airport's main terminal building and a fifteen-minute drive from Newcastle city centre, the Britannia Hotel couldn't have been more centrally located. There was free Wi-Fi, free parking, and a restaurant and cocktail bar should he require it. The last time Chameleon had flown into Newcastle on operations he'd stayed at the Premier Inn. Not that he disliked the place, it was just that he never stayed at the same hotel twice. Too risky, he considered. Especially if someone recognised you from a previous visit.

Chameleon's word was sacrosanct. Once a deal had been struck, his clients could rest assured their dreams and aspirations could continue untarnished – without consequence. Planning was his biggest forte, as everything he did was orchestrated. Today, however, as he gazed out of his hotel room window, he still had some unattended business to deal with before flying back to Heathrow.

He poured himself another coffee and gazed at the Google map he'd opened on his laptop. Having made a list of the things to do, he carefully considered his options. First, he would talk to his contact about the Sanderson Law Chambers down on Newcastle's Quayside. It shouldn't take long, and he already had a plan. His next port of call would be the boy's school. Still without a name, he'd figured it would only take twenty seconds of pressure on the carotid arteries to render the boy unconscious. Two minutes longer, and death was inevitable. Having searched through hundreds of photographs on the internet looking for the boy, he'd finally whittled it down to three possibilities. Which one he had yet to decide, but he knew he was closing in.

Surprisingly, there had been no more mention of the barrister's suspicious suicide. Not in any of the local newspapers there hadn't. He'd watched all the latest TV news bulletins and checked his phone for messages. Nothing. Perhaps the boy hadn't gone to the police after all, or maybe they didn't believe him. There again, he thought. What if they were keeping an open mind and were out there looking for him?

He'd been over this scenario a thousand times these past few days, and there was no way he was giving in to the sympathy vote. Just because a child had seen something they shouldn't have, didn't mean they were exempt. No way, Jose. The last thing he would need is for the boy to blow his cover and the whole operation go into meltdown. Not that it would, but he'd already made a note of the people he still had to deal with – and the boy wasn't at the top of his list. He was close, but these situations were fluid and sometimes you had to shuffle the pack around in order to reach a successful conclusion.

Dressed in a casual sweatshirt and jogging bottoms, Chameleon made his way through the busy hotel reception lobby and sauntered towards the Airport Tyne and Wear Metro station. It was a beautiful afternoon, and the air felt a lot warmer today. Having already sussed out where all the CCTV cameras were positioned, he was feeling upbeat. Airports were notorious for security checks, and that's why he never carried weapons. Besides, there were far more proficient ways to kill a person if you wanted to – without attracting attention.

The Metro station concourse was empty as Chameleon boarded the waiting train and stared up at the station map. He would alight at the Haymarket, then make his way to St Nicholas

Cathedral where he had important business to attend to. Churches were ideal places to contact associates – only God knew what you were up to there!

The moment the train pulled out of the station, his mobile pinged.

He checked the display.

Where are you now?

On my way, he texted back.

See you there!

He fired off his answer and pocketed his phone.

Knowing that Metro trains always carried CCTV cameras onboard, he would change the SIM card later. He wasn't that daft! The pace of events had accelerated, and in six hours from now he would back in the capital again. This was purely a reconnaissance mission – the easy-peasy lemon squeezy part of the job.

CHAPTER TEN

After weeks spent cooped up inside Gateshead Police Station, enough was enough, Jack Mason reasoned. Now that DI Gamble had clearly got her feet under the table, it was time to jump back into action again. It was part of Mason's inquisitive nature to go back over old case files. Digging up the past uncovered all kinds of new leads, and time watered down a person's memory – notably their lies.

He was thinking about this when he stepped up to Laurence Cooper's front door in Darras Hall. Located in one of the most sought-after streets in Ponteland, this remarkable six bedroomed property occupied a deceptively spacious plot of land. As his hand gripped the door knocker, Mason gave it an authoritative rap. Seconds later, movement reflected through the stained-glass panelling and a dapper man with a suntanned complexion and a look of professional arrogance appeared. He was wearing a blue denim top, black trousers and carrying a large Persian cat tucked under his arm – Mason guessed he was early fifties.

'Hello. I'm DCI Mason, and this is my colleague Detective Carrington,' the Chief Inspector explained. 'May we have a word?'

Cooper stood motionless as he peered down at their warrant cards. 'I've already made a statement to Northumbria Police when I was advised of my wife's death. Can I ask what this is about?'

'Certainly.' Mason slipped his warrant card into an inside pocket and stood for a moment. 'There's a few things we need to clarify, Mr Cooper. May we come in?'

'Yes, of course.'

Ushered into a spacious entrance hall with tiled floors and lofty ceilings, they were led into a large spacious study overlooking rear gardens. Not bad, Mason thought. Whatever line of business Laurence Cooper was in, he'd obviously done well for himself. As the suspect dropped the reluctant Persian cat onto an empty wicker chair, he turned to face them.

'Can I offer you people a drink?'

'No, thank you.'

'Please take a seat,' Cooper insisted.

'It's a very nice place you have here,' Mason said, unable to disguise the admiration in his voice. 'What line of business are you in?'

'I'm a global management consultant – why do you ask?'

'It must pay extremely well.' Mason smiled.

'It can be very demanding at times, but it does have its benefits.'

Pleasantries exchanged, Mason slipped quickly back into police mode. 'Perhaps we can talk about the statement you made to Northumbria Police.'

'About what?' Cooper replied, caught completely off guard.

'According to our records, you've been married before, have you not?'

'Yes, but that's no secret.'

'Then why didn't you mention it at your recent interview?'

'Because the question was never asked.'

'Mind telling us what happened to your first wife?' asked Carrington.

Cooper's face clouded over. 'I'm not sure where this is heading. What has this got to do with Margaret's recent death?'

Carrington rallied quickly. 'Tell me, Mr Cooper. How did your first wife die?'

'If you must know, she committed suicide. But that was almost ten years ago.'

'If I'm not mistaken, she threw herself off the High-Level Bridge in Newcastle after taking an overdose of anti-depressants.' Carrington's tone was forceful and it had the desired effect. 'According to your statement back in 2007, you'd only been married three years.'

'You don't think I had anything to do with my first wife's unfortunate death, surely? That's preposterous.'

Mason smiled wryly. 'Who mentioned anything about you being involved in anything? There again, we do deal with an awful lot of life insurance claims where the determining factor is a suspicious suicide. It's strange what some people think they can get away with.'

'Wait a minute! You're not suggesting I'm involved in some sort of fraudulent insurance claim, are you?'

'No. Merely stating a fact.'

'I'm not liking the tone in your voice, Chief Inspector,' Cooper said finally. 'It's time I called my lawyers.'

Cooper's face had drained of colour, and he was breathing heavily. As a man of standing, Mason had anticipated him to be more articulate and self-assured instead of coming across as hesitant.

'That won't be necessary,' Carrington said. 'You're not under any suspicion here.'

'Then why are you taking down notes?'

'Standard procedure,' she replied. 'It's what I'm instructed to do.'

'Really?'

Cooper's facial expression never altered, but the look in his eyes told Mason he was floundering. 'Your second wife was a barrister, was she not?'

'Yes, she was.'

Mason stared down at Cooper's shoes. He had small feet, size nine, and nothing like the plaster-of-Paris casts lifted from the crime scene. What's more, the Mercedes-Benz S500 parked on Cooper's drive was silver and not black like the vehicle spotted in Chopwell Wood. And, if he wasn't mistaken, Cooper looked nothing like the boy's Uncle Arthur. No, Mason thought. It was time to take on a new line of approach.

'Your second wife, Margaret.'

'What about her?'

'Am I right in saying she operated out of the Sanderson Law Chambers on Newcastle Quayside?'

'Yes, she did.'

'Which clients did she mainly represent?' asked Carrington.

Cooper huffed. 'Margaret was mostly instructed by the Crown Prosecution Service as well as prosecution agencies such as HMRC.'

'But she would occasionally have worked for the defence, would she not?'

'She did, but not that often.'

Carrington sat thoughtfully for a moment. 'So, she was predominantly a criminal prosecution barrister?'

'Yes, she was.'

Mason raised an eyebrow. Now that Carrington had mentioned it, his next question seemed a pretty obvious one to ask under the circumstances. 'Was your wife ever threatened at any stage in her career? Nasty phone calls, threatening text messages, hate mail, that type of behaviour.'

'None that I'm aware of.'

'Can you be sure of that?' Mason said.

'What makes you think she was ever threatened?'

'Well, being a police officer, I often come up against some very nasty people during my duties.' Mason's eyes drifted to the Persian cat and then settled back on Cooper. 'It had crossed my mind whether barristers suffered the same abusive threats as we do.'

'No. I can't say that she ever did.'

'Here's my problem,' Mason said. 'Your second wife died under suspicious circumstances, which means a Coroner has instructed the police to continue in their current line of enquiries. Hence our meeting here today.'

'I thought you people said this was an unofficial visit?'

Mason closed his notebook and glanced at his watch. 'When you first reported your wife missing to the police, did it ever occur to you that she might not come home again?'

'No, and I strongly resent such a suggestion.'

Mason hesitated, having overstepped the mark. 'Let me put it another way. On the day your wife went missing, what state of mind was she in when she left for work that morning? Did the two of you have an argument perhaps?'

'No, we did not. That's absurd.'

Carrington gave him a genuinely warm smile. 'But she did suffer from depression, did she not?'

'Yes, but that was a heck of a long time ago.'

'Two-thousand and ten to be exact!'

Cooper squirmed in his seat but remained silent.

'Was Margaret ever involved with other men?' Mason asked outright.

'Wait a minute!'

Mason knew he was treading on dangerous ground but pressed on regardless. 'The reason I ask is, three days seems an awful long time for someone to go missing without contacting close family or friends. Where did she go? Who was she with?'

'Isn't that what you people are supposed to do . . . find these things out?'

Mason's face remained expressionless. 'After you reported her missing to the police, did Margaret ever contact you via a text message at all?'

'No. Had she done so, I would have told you people.'

Carrington's brow furrowed. 'What about your daughters?'

'What about them?'

'Did they ever make contact at all?'

'My daughters would have told me had they done so.'

Mason forced a smile. 'Yes, of course.'

Cracks were appearing in Cooper's storyline and he had displayed none of the confident attributes of a global management consultant. There again, Mason thought. How would *he* react had he just lost his wife in a suspicious suicide? Pretty much the same, he guessed. Even so, this was Cooper's second wife to die under dubious circumstances and he may well be hiding something. He would need to sleep on it, check out his alibi at a later stage.

Mason stood to leave.

'You've been extremely helpful, Mr Cooper. We'll not keep you a minute longer.'

Relieved it was over, Cooper picked up the Persian cat, stuffed it under his arm and showed them to the door.

★★★

DC Carrington sucked on a fruit sweet as she stared out of the unmarked pool car's grubby windscreen. 'What do you think, boss?'

'Not a lot,' Mason replied.

The detective folded her arms across her chest in thought. 'If Margaret Cooper was last seen leaving the law chambers on Friday morning where did she go over the weekend?'

'That's the million-dollar question.'

'It's an awful long time to go missing without contacting family and friends.'

'Sounds like we're barking up the wrong tree,' Mason agreed. 'Either Cooper knows something and isn't letting on about it, or his wife was caught up in something sinister. Whichever way you look at it, the only person who is able to tell us that is the man from Chopwell Wood.'

'That worries me, boss. Whoever this stranger is, his biggest threat is Martin Kennedy blowing his cover. If not, then why give chase and threaten to beat the boy's brains in?' Carrington swung to face Mason. 'What if he recognised Martin's school uniform and decides to go after him?'

'And do what exactly?'

'Let's face it, unless we can come up with a vital piece of forensic evidence on the Chopwell suspect, then Martin is the only credible witness who can identify him.'

'Let's not jump to conclusions—'

'I'm not, but what about this man who was seen hanging around the school gates?'

Mason pondered her statement for a moment. 'I thought DI Gamble was looking into that?'

'She was.'

'What do you mean. . . was?'

Carrington gave Mason a withering look. 'Perhaps you should attend her daily briefings instead of trying to go it alone.'

'What are you getting at?'

'Don't get me wrong. I know you're desperate to pass your police medical exam and take back control of the case, but what if you fail?'

Mason screwed his face up. 'Give me a break, I couldn't stand another ten weeks of this shit.'

'It's time you faced up to reality, boss.'

'I'm not a fucking magician, I can't just pull rabbits out of a hat. Besides, the minute I go poking my nose into DI Gamble's affairs she'll go running to Superintendent Gregory.'

Carrington blew through her cheeks. 'Tread carefully, boss. You can't keep ignoring her.'

'What do mean?'

'It's obvious you are not happy about her appointment – everyone can see that. She could lodge an official complaint against you for sexist behaviour, and that could get you into an awful lot of trouble.'

Mason thought about it.

'I've heard rumours, Sue,' he said defensively. 'Gamble wouldn't think twice about taking over my position if she thought she could get away with it. That's how she got to be a DI in the first place.'

'Really?'

'I know so.'

Carrington drew back in her seat. 'That's the first I've heard of it.'

Mason fiddled with the ignition keys, then turned to Carrington and said, 'Rumour has it that Middlesbrough were glad to see the back of her.'

'I don't know about that,' Carrington replied. 'But I did overhear that Gregory doubts you'll ever pass the Police Medical Board's fitness test. If he believes that, then we could be looking at a permanent assignment here.'

Mason gritted his teeth. Convinced that a conspiracy takeover was going on behind his back, he would need to get to the bottom of it, and fast. This wasn't the first time he'd felt threatened like this before, and it wouldn't be the last. He would keep a low profile, bide his time, and choose his moment when the opportunity arose.

'Thanks for the heads, Sue,' Mason said, feeling somewhat relieved of some sound advice.

'No problems, boss.'

'You did the right thing, and I appreciate your honesty.'

Carrington shrugged. 'I just thought I'd mention it, that's all.'

More than pleased with his findings, Mason was already thinking about his next line of attack when he drove off the estate. The solution to some problems, he had come to believe over the years, lay in good team selection. Carrington knew how to handle awkward situations and was business–like in her approach. He knew he could trust her when the chips were down, and that's all that really mattered to him.

CHAPTER ELEVEN

The traffic around Chester-le-Street was heavy as they drove north past the Drum Industrial Estate heading for Beamish open-air museum. It was a bright, sunny day, and Chopwell Wood seemed a million miles from Martin Kennedy's mind. Ever since his father had spoken to the school's headmaster, life had quietened down a tad. He'd been moved to another class, and away from Miss Crawshaw whom he never liked anyway. Martin couldn't have asked for more, and just because he'd managed to stay out of trouble lately, his father had promised him a special treat.

Set in three hundred acres of beautiful rolling countryside, Beamish Museum was a working example of everyday life in urban and rural North-East England in the early 20th century. After passing through the admissions hall, Martin stood in awe as he was suddenly swept back in time. He'd never seen a working tram before – only on a postcard – and now he was clambering onboard one with his father. As they faced one another across a central wooden aisle, the conductor rang a bell and shouted for them to "hold on tight". It was a strange sensation. Although it ran on rails, it was much slower and more cumbersome than he'd ever imagined. The noise it made was incredible and reminded him of a giant beast as it rumbled and screeched along every twist and turn in the track. Suddenly the clanking noises stopped, and they'd arrived at the bustling town.

Opposite Redman Park stood a long row of terraced houses, originally from Gateshead. Among the attractions were a teacher's house, an Edwardian style solicitor's office, and the Sun Inn pub. The dentist's house was his favourite, and Martin's mind was blown away by brave and terrifying tales of young Edwardian children visiting the dentist's surgery more than a hundred years before.

Moving between exhibits was fun; browsing through each of the shops an even bigger adventure. He loved the old sweet shop where mouth-watering treats were being made in a backroom factory on large stainless-steel trays. Bonbons, cinder toffee, and his favourite black bullets were all being formed into shape by a lady dressed in traditional custom. It was brilliant watching her turn hot toffee as it cooled. The aroma was wonderful, and she explained everything she was doing.

'Lunchtime, young man,' his father called out.

Armed with a rucksack full of sandwiches, they soon found a spot overlooking the bandstand in Redman Park. It was jam-packed with visitors, and they sat on the grass verge listening to a brass band playing old marching tunes. Dressed in their bright red tunics, black trousers and shoes, the musicians looked more like Victorian soldiers than a colliery band.

The bandleader, a stout man with long sideburns and a walrus moustache, reminded Martin of his old school music teacher. Then again, everyone looked like Mr Hardaker on a hot summer's day.

'Where should we visit next?' his father asked.

'Can I take another peek at the repair works, Dad?'

'Yes, of course you can. Five minutes, and no wandering off.'

Inside the Beamish Motor & Cycle Works, Martin stood in awe at the wonderfully assembled array of amazing old cars and motorcycles on show. Strange looking contraptions with polished brass lamps and huge mud guards over each of the wheels. At the rear of the building, tucked back in a corner stood the weirdest car of them all. Called a SHEW, it had solid black tyres, open top bucket leather seats, and a large steering wheel the like of which he'd never seen before. It was a magnificent beast and he wondered what it would be like to ride in one. He imagined it would be cold, especially in winter, as it didn't have a roof and would be open to the elements.

'Fantastic looking car,' the stranger said.

Martin turned but could not see him. The crowd was so tightly packed that he could not move. Then, out of the corner of his eye he caught a glimpse of the stranger's face. He was glaring at him, evil-eyed, as if to reach out and grab tight hold of his collar. His world falling apart, Martin felt trapped. He tried to move away, but he was hemmed in so tightly that he could barely move his arms. Panic gripped him, and his heart was pounding so fast that he could barely breathe.

Then a gap opened up, and he managed to wriggle free. It was then he saw the man's shoes. They were brown, with sharp pointed toes and the shoelaces had been distinctly tied in a criss-cross pattern.

Daring to breathe, he ran as fast he could to where his father was sitting.

'That didn't take long. I thought I would need to come and fetch you.'

'It was him,' Martin said, still gasping for breath.

'Steady on, son,' his father said. 'Who are you talking about?'

'It was him, Dad. The man I saw in Chopwell Wood. He was standing right behind me inside the repair works.'

'Can you be sure?'

'Of course, I am.'

Gathering up their belongings, his father ran towards the repair works in search of the mystery man. It was busy inside, and with his father's guiding hand they soon pushed their way through the throng.

'Where is he, son?' his father called out.

'I can't see him, Dad. He's not here anymore.'

They scoured the cobbled streets outside together, but the man was nowhere to be seen.

'Are you sure it was him?' his father asked staring suspiciously across at him. 'Or somebody who just looked like your Uncle Arthur?'

'It was him, Dad. I swear it.'

His father's thick bushy eyebrows raised a fraction. 'What did he look like, this man who spoke to you? Was he bald with a round chubby face?'

'Yes.'

'You could be mistaken, son. There must be thousands of men who look like your old Uncle Arthur.' His father placed a reassuring arm around his shoulder and gave him a gentle hug. 'If you do happen to spot this mysterious man again, you're to point him out to me. Is that a promise?'

His father was right. He was constantly worrying over nothing these days, and it was slowly driving him mad. Even so, the man did bear a remarkable resemblance to his late Uncle Arthur and his shoelaces were tied in a peculiar criss-cross pattern. But it was those cold staring eyes he feared most.

It had to be him!

Twenty minutes later, after arriving at the old colliery school, Martin had already put the works repair incident to the back of his mind. Now sitting behind an old school desk, he was experiencing what it would have been like to be a ten-year-old boy in Victorian times. Back in those days, teachers were very strict, and young boys and girls were not allowed to talk unless spoken to. There were no pencils or papers, only a small piece of white chalk and a slate board to scribble your classwork on.

Rucksack in hand, it was time to head home. It had been a wonderful experience, and a day full of surprises – in more ways than one. Standing in the queue for the bus, a woman driver in a straw boater sped past in a beautiful horse and trap. Dressed in Edwardian costumes, the passengers sitting in the back of the open trap all waved across at them.

Then over the crest of the hill, two buses appeared. One was red with an open top roof, the other blue and closed in. All of his life Martin had dreamt about riding on an old bus, and now his dreams were about to come true. As the red bus screeched to a halt in front of them, the queue surged forward. Not everyone was going to climb on board, of course, that much was obvious. When the conductor finally stuck his arm out to signal it was full, all eyes now turned towards the blue bus.

Just as the red bus reached the crest of a hill, the boy froze. Panic gripped him, and the hairs on the back of his neck stood on end. It was the man from the repair works and he was sitting on the upper deck.

'It's him, Dad,' Martin called out tugging on his father's sleeve.

'Who, son?'

'The man from the repair works.'

Eyes straining through sunlight, his father peered into the distance towards the fast disappearing red bus. But that wasn't all, there was surely something more sinister in all of this – the man was waving back at them and smiling.

59

CHAPTER
TWELVE

It felt good talking to DS Savage over lunch and following yesterday's incident at Beamish Museum they both had plenty to talk about. They'd been searching for connections and finding too many – each seemed to cancel the other out. The team was clutching at straws, and the longer this went on, the further they were distancing themselves from the facts. There were too many lose ends, and not enough hard evidence to go on. Having carefully considered his options, the most crucial piece of information they had to work on was the car that Martin Kennedy had spotted in Chopwell Wood. If all the doors were locked and the engine kept running, it meant the vehicle had probably been hot-wired. If not, the suspect had a spare set of keys.

Had he missed something? He wondered.

Mason swirled the remains of his coffee and mulled over the facts. All things being equal, he had taken an instant shine to young Martin Kennedy. The fact they'd both come from similar backgrounds meant they could level with one another. He knew how tough it was to live on a rough council estate, especially when money was tight. School kids were highly competitive at Martin's age, and if you didn't wear the latest designer shoes and carry a cool backpack to school, you were ostracized. Adolescents could be cruel, and research had shown that bullying ran rife in schools. Maybe society had itself to blame for creating its own social outcasts, as few people gave a damn about those living below the poverty line.

'What's the Area Commander's view?' Mason asked thoughtfully.

'The canteen gossip is that Gregory is siding with DI Gamble, or that's the impression she gives. The boy's an unreliable witness in her eyes, and she's sticking to it.'

'And what about the rest of the team? What do they think?'

'We all agree the boy should be moved to a safe house,' Savage replied.

Mason's plan, such as it was, was to focus on the barrister's last known movements. It had been a hard slog, and the more he delved into Margaret Coopers past, the more concerned he was that something wasn't right. Everything was legally tied up in her husband's name. Their three-million-pound house, their holiday home in Cornwall, even their expensive cars. But why would a well-educated barrister allow her husband to take such control of her life? Things didn't stack up, and according to the Coopers' family solicitors, her husband had taken out a one million-pound life insurance plan on his wife's life.

With alarm bells ringing in his head, Mason sat back thinking.

'I'm still convinced this was planned.'

'What is your biggest concern?' asked Savage.

'This life insurance plan that Laurence Cooper took out on his wife.'

'Do you think this could have a bearing on the case?'

'Either he's a cunning sod, or his wife was a damn fool.'

'I doubt she was a fool. She was a top-class barrister from what I can gather.'

Mason stared at Savage. 'As a general rule of thumb, if a life insurance policy is purchased within two years before a suicide takes place, death benefits will not be paid out.'

'So, he won't receive a penny in other words.'

'That's my understanding of it.'

'What about his first wife?' Savage quizzed. 'Did he take out a policy on her?'

'Not according to his solicitors, although he did manage to retain most of the family assets but only after a long protracted legal battle through the courtrooms.'

Savage paused in thought. 'Having lost his first wife under tragic circumstances, he could have genuinely been thinking about his daughters future.'

'Who knows?' Mason shrugged. 'But why put everything in your husband's name?'

'That's how some people roll, I'm afraid. They trust their partners implicitly.'

'Even so, it still doesn't account for her walking out on her family as she did.'

'Maybe she didn't.'

The Chief Inspector pushed back in his seat and sipped his coffee. How a barrister could slip under the radar for three whole days had left him completely baffled. As he flipped through the casefiles in search of clues, he puffed up his cheeks and blew out a long steady breath.

'According to the law register,' Mason explained, 'Margaret Cooper had spent the past five years working at the Sanderson Law Chambers. I've been there on several occasions in the past and can vouch they're a reputable organisation. They don't come cheap.' Mason gave a shrug. 'Cooper's specialisms were prosecuting on all aspects of crime and she was no mug. Educated at Bristol University, she worked as a level 4 prosecutor and mostly for the CPS. Appointed Recorder in 2010, she sat in the County Courts throughout the North-East circuit and in London. A highly respected barrister in her field, she dealt mainly with criminal and regulatory cases including murder, manslaughter, death by dangerous driving and fraud. According to work colleagues, she never avoided awkward issues. What is of interest, though, is that she'd dealt with civil actions against the police on several occasions.'

'What exactly is a level 4 barrister?' Savage asked.

'Level 4 advocates will have established a reputation for excellence among court users, including the bench. They also deal with rape and serious sexual abuse casework – that type of offending.'

Savage raised his eyebrows a fraction. There was no mistaking the sergeant's interest levels had heightened. 'An experienced advocate and woman of standing by the sounds.'

Mason closed the case files in front of him. 'Has anyone else on the team spoken to the Sanderson Law Chambers lately?'

'I've heard rumours that DI Gamble paid them a cursory visit, but nothing untoward came of it. She was delving into Cooper's personal background, I'm told. Who she mixed with, who she socialised with after work. . .'

'Looking for a seedier side no doubt.'

'If she was, she didn't find one.'

Mason leaned over the table and lowered his voice. 'What about past and current cases that Cooper was working on? Did Gamble mention anything about those to you?'

'Not to me she didn't. If she did raise the question with the law clerks, then she never mentioned it at any of her team briefings.'

Mason drew back. 'That's odd. What if Margaret Cooper had been threatened in her line of work?'

'Even if she had, Gamble would never have mentioned the likes of that to us.' Savage screwed his face up. 'Why don't you ask her yourself?'

'No. Not at this stage of my investigations.'

'Oh! Is there something I don't know?'

Mason brushed the sergeant's comments aside. 'Perhaps I should pay Sanderson Law Chambers a visit.'

'On what grounds?'

'If Cooper worked mainly for the CPS, she's bound to have locked more people up than she ever set free.'

'True.'

'And there's some nasty people out there.'

'It's highly unlikely that someone would threaten a barrister, don't you think?'

Mason shrugged. 'Those bastards give *us* plenty of grief, Rob.'

'You're right,' Savage said, pointing down at the case files. 'She was a highly successful barrister in her field, so there must be plenty of angry prisoners behind bars.'

Savage was a good honest copper. He wasn't a specialist at anything, more a jack of all trades. A dapper man, late thirties and former boxing champion who knew how to handle himself. Mason liked him, and they always got on well together. Some words were best left unsaid, though, especially where DI Gamble was concerned. He would need to tread carefully, work around the fringes and see what he could uncover.

'Okay, it's agreed. I'll talk to Sanderson's.'

'It's a strange one, boss.'

Mason cocked his head to one side as he spoke. 'My money would be on some other dark secret the barrister was holding. Someone close to her.'

'A legal colleague perhaps?'

'Could be—'

Savage thought a moment. 'What about this black vehicle the boy spotted?

'There's nothing on the Police National Computer's stolen vehicles register.'

'That's odd.'

Mason made a little sweeping hand gesture. 'I've heard that Sanderson Law Chambers were broken into recently.'

'Really. DI Gamble never mentioned anything about that at her briefings.'

'They targeted a watch repair workshop next door, apparently, but nothing of any value was taken – which seems rather odd when it's in the same building.'

Savage chewed on a biscuit in thought. 'Has the boy said anything more to you?'

'I'm still not convinced the man he saw at Beamish Museum is the person from Chopwell Wood.'

'Having read his father's statement, he was ninety percent convinced.'

Mason laughed. 'Do you know what a jury would call that. . . reasonable doubt. Martin's a bright kid, and I really like him, but he does tend to live in his own little fantasy world at times.'

'Tell me a ten-year-old boy who doesn't.'

'You're right, and that worries me.'

'Gamble believes he's an unreliable witness.'

'Really?'

Savage looked at him oddly. 'Mind, she does seem to be spending an awful lot of her time in Gregory's office these days.'

Mason thought about it, but not for long. Maybe there was a plot to oust him from his current position as head of serious crime after all. Carrington had a point, and a good one at that. What if he failed his fitness test? What then? He was leaving himself wide open for failure instead of tackling the real issues. He would need to get himself back to full fitness again, clear his head of negative thoughts. If ever he was going to make a comeback, he would need to give Gregory good reason to think differently.

Mason looked at his watch. 'Anything back from forensics?'

'Nothing to write home about.'

Mason stood to leave.

'There is one other thing,' said Savage. 'When are you in front of the Police Medical Board?'

'Twelve days' time – Friday the fifteenth.'

'Fingers crossed they pass you fit for duty and you take back control of the case.'

'Let's see what the medical board say first.'

Savage looked at him oddly. 'Why, is there a problem?'

CHAPTER THIRTEEN

Sanderson Law Chambers was housed in a grade 2 listed building close to the River Tyne, and the medieval All Saints Church. For those lucky enough to live and work in this part of the city, it was easy to take for granted the sheer architectural scope and historical range of the buildings that graced the area. Newcastle has a proud architectural heritage, including the 12th century Norman castle which gave the city its name, through to the Jacobean buildings and modern development of the twenty-first century that graced the Quayside.

The barrister's clerk room was rectangular, with a low ceiling, customised furnishings, and a large Georgian central window overlooking the River Tyne. From where he was standing, Mason could see the Tyne Bridge foundations but not the upper structure. Expensive glass fronted bookcases ran the full length of one wall, and a meeting table occupied a central position. On closer inspection, tasteful period framed portraits of bewigged judges and legal advocates filled the walls, giving the room a distinct professional feel.

'Thank you,' the barrister's clerk said, staring down at their warrant cards with an element of theatrical panache. 'What brings you here today?'

'The late Margaret Cooper,' Mason began. 'I believe she was part of this practice?'

'Indeed,' Grainger replied. 'I presume your presence here today is in follow-up to Detective Inspector Gamble's call earlier this week?'

One of the more prominent clerks who worked in the building, John Grainger was a medium built man, with a high forehead and sharp swarthy features. Mason detected a soft American accent, but finally settled for Canadian. Pleasantries exchanged, the two detectives took up seats opposite and made themselves comfortable. He would have preferred to attend alone, but DC Carrington had prearranged the appointment and he was more than happy to tag along with her.

'The fact is,' Mason began, 'Margaret Cooper died under suspicious circumstances, and we've been instructed by a coroner to carry out further enquiries.'

Grainger shook his head in sympathy. 'Such a tragic loss, and so young!'

'I'm surprised DI Gamble never mentioned anything to you about a possible suspicious suicide?'

'Not in as many words, Chief Inspector,' Grainger admitted. 'If anything, we talked more about Margaret's position here at the Chambers. Who she mixed with, that sort of thing.'

Mason smiled but did not push the matter further.

'I take it you have some important questions to ask me?'

'We do,' Mason replied. 'How much do you actually know about the case?'

The barrister's clerk raised his eyebrows a fraction. 'That's always a difficult one.'

Mason considered this and opened his notebook at the desired page. 'In which case let's begin with Friday 10th June.' He smiled then looked serious for a moment. 'After Margaret failed to return home from work that evening, her husband was naturally concerned. He made a few frantic telephone calls to family and friends and when she still hadn't returned home the following morning, he reported her missing to the police. Where Margaret spent the next few days we have yet to establish, but on Tuesday 14th June, we discovered her body in Chopwell Wood. Found hanging from a branch with a cord wrapped around her neck, she had lain dead there for twenty-four hours according to the Coroner's report.'

The barrister's clerk clasped his hands on the desk in front of him, as if to jog a memory. 'Such a tragic ending.'

'I understand that Margaret was a 'level 4' prosecutor and was involved in a number of high-profile cases here in the North-East,' said Carrington. 'What type of cases was she involved in?'

'That shouldn't be too difficult,' Grainger replied. 'May I ask why you would need such information as it's not normal practice to discuss forthcoming cases openly.'

'Certainly.' Carrington confided in her notes. 'The people she was dealing with, her so called clientele, could have been involved in her disappearance.'

'You're not ruling out foul play then?'

'Let's just say we're looking into every avenue at this stage.'

Grainger pushed back in his seat. 'In all the years I've worked in the courts, I've never come across anything like that before.'

'There's always a first time,' Mason interrupted.

'Indeed.' Grainer leaned forward and wrote something down on a notepad. 'Leave it with me, I'll pull a few case files together including the ones that Margaret was working on.'

'That would be helpful.' Mason nodded.

'The one thing that has always puzzled me about Margaret's death, was her mobile phone.'

Carrington shot Mason a glance. 'What about it?'

'After her disappearance we tried ringing it on several occasions, but it was always dead.'

'It's our view it went missing at the same time as her handbag did. Neither have been recovered.'

'Ah, that would explain. We thought her phone battery may have gone flat,' Grainger replied.

Mason thought a moment. 'The listed cases that Margaret was working on. What can you tell us about them?'

'Not a lot. I do know she experienced difficulties contacting one of the key witnesses in a major fraud case she was working on. A hedge fund auditor, called Stephen Rice. Other than that, I would need to check through the case files.'

'What kind of difficulties?' asked Mason.

'Nobody knew where the witness was, apparently.'

'And when is the case due before the courts?'

Grainger seemed keen to engage. 'Not until September, I believe.'

They spent the next twenty-five minutes going over the details. It was a slow, laborious process, but after searching through the barrister's Outlook calendar, a bigger picture emerged – and one with surprising consequences. On the day Margaret Cooper went missing, she'd called in at a secretary's office to pick up a bundle of case files that she'd been working on. Nothing out of the ordinary, Mason thought, but an hour later, at 10.00 am, she was last seen leaving the building and heading towards Newcastle city centre. It was this aspect that immediately caught Mason's attention, and on checking further he noticed a single entry scribbled against Friday 10th at 1:00 pm: *must ring "R".*

'Any idea what this could mean?' Mason quizzed.

Grainger took a sip of water from a glass and stared up from behind his desk. 'No, sadly, we don't. Everyone here at the Chambers has racked their brains ever since. Whatever or whoever "R" refers to, it's obviously an abbreviation of some sorts.'

'That's strange,' Carrington said, shaking her head. 'How would you describe her general demeanour that day?'

'She seemed anxious.'

'Agitated perhaps?'

'No, more apprehensive than anything.'

Mason felt his shoulders slump. 'What about the case files she'd picked up from the secretary's office that morning, could they have caused her concern?'

'Margaret was a top barrister, Chief Inspector, so I doubt anything of that nature would have worried her.'

The Chief Inspector took his time before continuing.

'This witness who has gone missing, Stephen Rice. Could he be the "R" that Margaret Cooper was referring to in her Outlook calendar?'

'Definitely not. Rice is a hedge fund auditor who seemingly used his position to make substantial loans to holding companies in the British Virgin Islands that were never repaid. What we do know is, the loans were illegally controlled by a Russian bank according to the Crown Prosecution Service, but the defence continues to deny it.'

'Sounds complicated,' Mason said, pen posed.

'It is, very!' Grainger frowned. 'The case was originally scheduled for the High Court in London but was transferred north with a three-month delay owing to some technical hitches. I don't have all the details readily at hand, but I do recollect there being some major British household names involved, including a brewing giant, a well-known hotel chain, and several reputable property companies.'

'Quite a range?'

'Indeed. The last I heard the National Fraud Intelligence Bureau was involved, but that's as much as I can tell you at this point.'

'The NFIB.' Mason shrugged. 'It must be serious.'

'I would have thought so.'

'These technical delays, what were they about?' asked Carrington.

'When the case first came to our attention, it was claimed the extent of these illegal money transactions totalled somewhere in the region of fifty million pounds. The Crown Prosecution Service wasn't happy about it, and after further investigations were carried out by the NFIB, they uncovered several basic mathematical miscalculations.' Grainger smiled. 'The CPS were right, of course. It was closer to half a billion pounds.'

Mason sucked air through clenched teeth. 'That's a sizeable chunk of money.'

'It is.'

'And this missing witness, Stephen Rice. I take it he was assisting the CPS?'

'He'd turned Queen's Evidence apparently, which further complicates matters.'

'What do we know about his background?'

'I'm sorry, Detective Chief Inspector. I'm not privy to that kind of information. Although I do recollect that Margaret was heavily involved in trying to establish Rice's whereabouts.'

'It sounds as if this hedge fund auditor has some vital information to present before the courts,' Carrington added.

'No doubt he has,' Grainger replied. 'But only time will tell.'

A memory tugged Mason. 'This recent break-in at the watch repair workshop, what can you tell me about that?'

'The building was broken into over the same weekend that Margaret went missing.'

'Would this be Monday 13th June?'

'Yes, and that's when the police were notified after the security system had been activated.'

'I presume the watch repair workshop is part of the building?'

'It's an old storeroom at the back of the premises, but it does have its own access.'

Mason made a few notes and tapped his pen against the side of his notebook in thought. 'And when did the police first arrive on the scene?'

'Around nine o'clock that morning – a Detective Inspector Swan from Police Headquarters in Ponteland was heading up the case.'

'Do you know if anything was stolen?'

'Not as far as we know.'

'The alarm system is linked, I presume?'

'Not to the watch repair workshops it isn't.'

'So how was the alarm system activated in the first place?' asked Carrington.

'The person responsible had obviously opened an adjoining door according to DI Swan, which automatically triggered the alarm.'

Mason felt they were onto something. 'Do you happen to have the crime report number handy?'

Grainger read it out to them, and Mason jotted it down.

'Anything else, Chief Inspector?' Grainger said, looking at his watch.

There was nothing more to be gained, Mason thought. Not now, at least. Pleased with their findings, the two detectives stood to leave.

'You've been most helpful,' Mason said, holding out a hand.

Grainger shook it, and then said, 'I'm only too pleased to be of assistance.'

'Thank you,' Carrington replied with a smile.

They left into bright sunshine, much the wiser.

Chapter

Fourteen

Northumbria Police Headquarters July 2016

DI Archie Swan was a former Military Police officer who had served two years in Afghanistan with the NATO-led International Security Force (ISAF). A tall man, standing six feet two, he still carried that untrusting look in his glances as though a bad guy was lurking around every street corner. Swan was old school and had worked with Jack Mason on several occasions in the past. Not one for mincing his words, he was typical ex-military and never flinched away from the action.

'How are the old war wounds doing nowadays?' asked Swan.

'I'm in front of the medical board next Friday,' Mason replied. 'Fingers crossed, I'll pass with flying colours.'

'You're not walking very straight.' Swan grinned. 'You look all lopsided from where I'm standing.'

'By the time I fill myself full of painkillers, I'll be jumping through hoops on the day of the examination.'

'Tread carefully, Jack. Those bastards know what to look out for. After I broke my leg in a motorbike accident, they put me through my paces before declaring me fully fit for duty again. It was a right old carry on, and they had me crawling around on all fours in the end.'

'If they try doing that to me, I'll probably end up barking at the bastards.'

Swan roared with laughter.

'Sounds about right coming from you.'

'Better than being stuck in an office twenty-four-seven.'

Swan remained silent for a minute, but Mason sensed another useful nugget of information was about to come his way. 'This robbery at the law chambers you asked me about, it wasn't highly organised in my view. Whoever broke into the building was obviously an opportunist.'

'What about fingerprints?' Mason asked.

'No, nothing. We did manage to lift a set of footprints close to the watch repair workshops though.'

'Anything else?'

'He didn't wear forensic overshoes that's for sure.'

'Did he steal anything?'

'That's a strange one,' Swan replied, shaking his head. 'If it was jewellery he was after, then he left all the expensive stuff behind. It's my guess he was specifically targeting something and didn't find what he was looking for. There again, once he'd triggered the security alarm he probably left in a hurry.'

'Could it have been made to look like a robbery, do you think?'

'In what respect?'

'Staged.'

'Why would a bungler want to do that?'

'What if he was using the watch repair workshops as a diversionary tactic, whilst targeting the law chambers next door?'

'I very much doubt it. According to the barristers' clerks nothing was stolen.'

'What about CCTV footage?'

'It was disarmed.'

Mason thought about it, still not convinced that this was an opportunist thief. Okay, so nothing was taken in the way of material goods, but what if vital information had been stolen? He knew it was a long shot, but during his ten years working with the Metropolitan Police he'd come up against that sort of scenario before. Some perpetrators would attempt to confuse forensic investigators by staging a crime scene and disguising what really took place.

He took out his notebook and flipped through the pages. 'Those footprints you recovered,' Mason said. 'Can you e-mail the details?'

'Yes, of course. What are you hoping to find exactly?'

'It may not be much, but something tells me this break-in could be linked to the barrister's suspicious suicide.'

'Tampering with the evidence—' Swan pondered his statement.

'It's highly unlikely, I know, but you need to cover every avenue in this game.'

'Hmmm. What gave you that idea?'

'One of the cases listed for September has come up against difficulties. A key Crown Prosecution Service witness has gone missing, apparently.'

'Cold feet, do you think?'

'Probably.' Mason nodded. 'But it's strange that two people involved in the same trial and representing the CPS are either dead or have gone missing!'

Swan thought a moment. 'What other arrangements had the barrister made?'

'The day she went missing, scribbled against her Outlook calendar for 1:00 pm, were the words: *must ring R.*'

'Who the hell is *R?*'

'That's the million-dollar question, and nobody at the Chambers has the foggiest idea. Whatever and whoever "*R*" stands for, it's the last known point of contact we have to go on.'

Swan frowned. 'What about her court listings that day?'

'No. Nothing.'

Mason gave DI Swan a brief overview of what he knew so far – the money laundering scam, the people involved, and the details about the missing hedge fund auditor, Stephen Rice.

Sadly, little else was known about the man. If there was a connection to be had, and Mason believed there was, he would need to find Rice. . . and fast.

Sweeteners, Mason thought. What if someone had got at Rice and bribed him to steer clear of the case? He knew those kind of deals took place, and that some prosecution witnesses could be open to intimidation. No, Mason thought. The problem the CPS were faced with, was that Rice was a key witness. Without him, they were treading on thin ice.

It wasn't looking good suddenly, and there were far too many grey areas for his liking. When DI Swan had finished his story about his views on the law chambers break-in, it sort of backed his thinking up. If the perpetrator was trying to steal or even copy vital case evidence, it would clearly strengthen their hand against the CPS.

His mind clearly made up, Mason was convinced the break-in at the law chambers had been staged. It had to be. This case wasn't as easy as he first thought; no wonder they were struggling.

CHAPTER
FIFTEEN

Jack Mason stood in front of DI Gamble's crime board in Gateshead Police Station and cringed. Four weeks into the case, and not a lot to write home about. A few new post-its, several spider strings leading to a few potential suspects of interest, but nothing to send his adrenaline racing. He wished he could be more involved, liven things up, but knew that was impossible in the current situation. Despite all his efforts, DI Gamble was deliberately turning her nose up at him and complaining about his lack of cooperation. She had a point, of course, but he was damned if he was going to give up his position without a fight. He was the senior officer, after all, but that didn't mean a thing in the grand scheme of things.

The case had taken a turn for the worse, and now the media had got its teeth into the barrister's suspicious suicide, they were making life extremely difficult for everyone.

'Morning, boss,' DC Carrington said, looking up at him from behind a cluttered desk.

'Updates on the Chopwell Wood suspected suicide?' Mason asked.

'Funny you should mention that. The desk sergeant has just received a phone call from one of Cooper's neighbours claiming to have seen a blue Ford Kuga parked outside the barrister's house on the day she went missing.'

'I thought we'd already interviewed neighbours? What time was this?'

'Around three o'clock—'

'Do we have a registration number?'

'According to DVLA it belongs to Richard Drummond, a senior lecturer at Newcastle University,' Carrington replied.

Mason held her gaze. 'Why come forward at this late stage in the proceedings?'

'The witness sounds a bit doolally if you ask me. What she perceived she saw and what actually took place could be two different things, of course.'

'Mmm! She must have her suspicions about something. If not, why write down the car's registration number, colour, make, and model.'

'Fancy a ride out to Darras Hall to revisit the Coopers?'

'Thanks all the same, but I'm meeting the Area Commander in ten minutes' time.' Mason was quick to signal his thoughts. 'There's an awful lot of expensive properties over in Darras Hall, and most of them are covered by private security companies. It might be worth running it past the tech boys first. You never know, you might save yourself an awful lot of legwork.'

'Thanks, boss.'

Mason nodded. 'Let me know how you get on?'

Plans were shaping up, and Mason was really looking forward to Friday's appointment with the police medical board. His strategy, so much as it was, was to ease back on the drink for a couple of weeks and spend more time in the gym. His physio had warned against rushing back into the thick of the action, which was easier said than done. Stuck in an office pushing paperwork around all day wasn't good for his morale.

Despite all the recent setbacks, there was a new spring in his step as he strolled towards the Area Commander's office that morning. God, he felt good. The moment he poked his head around the office door, he winced. Like a gallery of achievements, Gregory's walls were graced with certificate awards, photographs of major events, and pictures of him meeting the Queen. Mason hated celebrity status, believing it a self-indulgent act of pomposity.

'How are you these days, Detective Chief Inspector?' Gregory said, barely lifting his head.

'Couldn't be better, sir. I'm before the medical board on Friday.'

'Ah, yes. I'd almost forgotten about that.'

Charming, Mason thought. It seemed the Area Commander had more important matters on his mind. It was time to make his presence felt.

'I can't wait to get my teeth back into real crime again,' Mason smiled.

'Let's see what the medical examiners have to say first.' Gregory put his pen down and stared across at him. 'Any more thoughts on taking a short holiday break?'

'Nothing planned.' Mason shrugged.

'You're missing a golden opportunity, Chief Inspector. You'll never get a better chance to take time off. A few weeks in the sun and you'll feel a different man.'

'It's not my scene. Besides, I've got far better things to do with my time.'

Gregory stared at the open case file in front of him. 'So, you think this barrister's death could be linked to the fraud case she was working on. What's the rationale behind your thinking?'

'Something's not right. First a key prosecution witness goes missing, then the law chambers are broken into on Newcastle Quayside. If that wasn't bad enough, the lead barrister involved in the Crown Prosecution's case commits suicide in suspicious circumstances.'

'I'm not sure DI Gamble would agree with you on that.'

Mason pulled his chair up.

'Oh. And why not, sir?'

'No doubt you'll have read her latest report.'

'With all due respect, I'm not at all happy with the way DI Gamble is conducting the operation.'

Gregory thought for a moment. 'Enlighten me.'

'I've asked her on several occasions to consider transferring the boy to a safe house, especially after the Beamish open-air museum incident.' Mason took stock. 'The problem is, if the Chopwell Wood suspect turns out to be connected to this hedge fund auditor's sudden disappearance, the boy could be in grave danger.'

Gregory's eyes were drawn to a stack of papers on his desk. He picked them up, thumbing them through with a flurry. 'I had considered the option of moving the boy to a safe house, but having discussed the matter with DI Gamble, I fear that Martin's not a credible witness.'

'He's a ten-year-old child for God's sake.' Mason huffed.

'That's the point.'

'Let's not forget it was Martin who initiated the case in the first place.'

Gregory looked puzzled, then affronted. 'Yes, but according to child psychology experts, Martin is prone to exaggeration and habitually overstates the truth. Even after a team of trained child support specialists spent hours working with the boy on suspect facial recognition, his account of what took place in Chopwell Wood was all over the place.'

Mason raised his hands as in surrender. 'I'm obviously missing a trick here.'

'Just because DI Gamble is junior in rank doesn't mean you can ride roughshod over her. She's a highly qualified police officer who is making great inroads on what is a very difficult case.' Gregory shook his head. 'Perhaps you should start attending her daily briefings instead of trying to solve the case on your own.'

Oh, yeah, Mason thought.

He moved to leave. 'Will that be all, sir?'

'Yes, for now. But you need to think very carefully about what I've said.'

As he stormed along the corridor, Mason mulled over the facts. How could DI Gamble not see the danger that Martin was in? Was she blind? There again, he'd suffered an awful lot of physical anguish these past few months and he was mentally worn out by it all. Frustrated by his own lack of progress, stuck behind a desk all day had finally got the better of him. This wasn't his style of policing, and he'd never been asked to take on an advisory role in his life before. Not since his days as a detective sergeant at least.

Emotionally and physically drained, Mason was thinking of chucking it all in. Perhaps a couple of weeks in the sun wasn't a bad idea after all. At least he could drink himself senseless and come back a better man.

God, what a mess.

CHAPTER SIXTEEN

Now ensconced in his own private little space, Chameleon fired up his laptop computer, confident in the knowledge he was still in control. Next, he plugged the memory stick into the USB port and typed in the sixteen-digit code. As his eyes moved instinctively down to the dropdown box at the bottom of his screen, he entered the password he'd been sent in a text message and waited for the program to load.

It didn't take long.

Strange, Chameleon thought. Why would the Organisation agree to setting up a business meeting between him and a client in Stuttgart? Not that he was questioning their judgement, but the establishment never made direct contact with its clients – only through intermediaries. It was the first golden rule, the founding principle on which the Organisation had been built.

Happy in the knowledge the information would have come from a trusted source, he decided to check on the client's credentials. Considering the vast sums of money involved, two possibilities immediately sprang to mind. Either the client had a new business proposition to put to the Organisation, or they wanted him dead.

Either way he would oblige.

He changed the SIM in his pay-as-you-go and fired off a new e-mail. The moment his phone pinged, he copied the new

Personal Identification Number (PIN) into the dropdown box on his laptop and watched as the program opened.

"RECEIVED," he acknowledged in a text message.

His phone went dead.

After minutes of poring over the new computer files, a bigger picture emerged. Soon his professional relationship with the client in Stuttgart would take on a different kind of business partnership – and one he hadn't bargained for. He Googled *Hotels in Stuttgart*. Moments later he had a full listing of what was available. The Steigenberger Graf Zeppelin Hotel looked favourable on Amulf-Klett-Platz – reserve now, pay when you stay. Perfect, he thought. Tracing an IP address back to an individual was an impossible task, especially when the Organisation were involved. He made a reservation, closed the lid of his laptop, and pondered about the future.

Two days would be enough – more would be too risky. Some things were best dealt with privately, especially if they interfered with existing plans. He would deal with the boy later, on his return from Stuttgart. The Organisation came first, and what went on in Chopwell Wood was his problem. His business alone.

He checked his watch.

The longer the police continued to believe the barrister's death was a suspicious suicide the longer he could move around freely. Without hindrance, without hesitation.

Alone!

CHAPTER
SEVENTEEN

Jack Mason could see most of the cars in the street boasted many of the latest Beemer's, Mercs, and Jags, but he was looking for a specific model. Then, set back on the driveway at the "The Willows" – a large detached property in Wylam, a small village 10 miles west of Newcastle upon Tyne he noticed a blue Ford Kuga. And, if he wasn't mistaken, it carried identical number plates to the vehicle spotted outside the barrister's house the day she went missing. Not bad, he thought. This was a part of his job he loved most – the hands-on bit.

Mason rapped on the front door knocker.

Seconds later, a man appeared in a bright green T-shirt and wearing a mask of uncertainty. 'Richard Drummond?' Mason asked authoritatively.

'Not today,' the man brashly replied. 'We don't deal with door-to-door salesmen in Wylam!'

'Really?' Mason replied, pulling out his warrant card and pushing his foot over the door threshold. 'Would that include police officers?'

'It's still not convenient right now.'

'No time is ever convenient when it involves the police.' Mason pointed to the blue Ford Kuga. 'The purpose of my call is to find the owner of this vehicle.'

'Why? Is there a problem?'

'For the owner perhaps, but not for me thankfully.'

'If you must know, it's mine.'

'Mind telling me what you were doing in the Darras Hall area on the afternoon of Friday 10th June?'

'What time would that be?'

'Three o'clock,' Mason replied stoically.

'I'm a senior lecturer at Newcastle University, and that's where I would have been.'

'You may well have been, Mr Drummond, but at 3:00 pm on Friday 10th June this vehicle was spotted outside Margaret Cooper's property in Darras Hall. What's more, she was seen getting into this vehicle before being driven away.'

'What is this, some kind of witch hunt?'

'Do you know a Margaret Cooper?'

'I may do.' Drummond went white suddenly. 'Are you quite sure it was this vehicle?'

'I'm one hundred per cent sure, and we have it all on camera. Either you're not telling me everything, or someone else was driving this vehicle that afternoon.'

'That's preposterous—'

'We need to talk. May I come in?'

Drummond looked at him in mocked horror. 'I'm afraid that's not possible, Chief Inspector.'

'Oh. And why not?'

Drummond mouthed the words: *Not in front of my wife!*

Mason knew then he was onto something and did not hang about. 'In which case you'd better accompany me to Gateshead Police Station, Mr Drummond.'

★★★

Gateshead Police Station was a twenty-minute drive from Wylam, and Drummond had barely spoken a word throughout the entire journey. After they'd checked in at the front desk, the suspect was taken straight to Interview Room One (IR-1) where his solicitor was sat waiting for him. A police station could be a daunting place at times, especially sitting face to face across an interview table staring at two determined police officers.

The moment DCI Mason activated the recording tape and announced the date, time and those present, the suspect's face darkened. It was another tense moment, and Drummond's demeanour looked strained. Cocky at first, it didn't take long before the senior lecturer had turned into a nervous wreck. What was of interest, though, was that the 'R' in Margaret Cooper's Outlook calendar against 1:00 pm on Friday 10th June, turned out to be the 'R' as in 'Richard' Drummond. They'd been having an affair, and all behind closed doors.

As Drummond's incredulous story began to unfold, Mason couldn't help pinching himself. Having driven to Darras Hall that Friday afternoon to pick up the barrister's clothes, they'd spent the rest of the weekend in a hotel room in the village of Belford, Northumberland. Two wrongs didn't make a right in Mason's books. But according to Drummond, the barrister's marriage was in freefall and she simply wanted to take a break from it all. Not so in the senior lecturer's case, he hadn't the slightest intention of leaving his wife and was probably in it for the sex.

There was more to Richard Drummond than Mason first thought. Not only was he a charlatan, he was an obnoxious self-opinionated prat who saw himself as a cut above the rest. In what had been a long drawn out first session, it was time to apply some pressure. With any luck, Drummond was about to uncover Margaret Cooper's last known movements – along with the last people to see her.

Was Drummond the killer? Mason wondered.

'Let's talk about the Blue Bell Hotel in Belford,' Mason began. 'What were you both doing there?'

Drummond struggled with his words. 'Margaret and her husband had serious issues, they argued constantly. Laurence was making life extremely difficult for her.'

'So, she decided to confide in you?'

Drummond lowered his head. 'She asked me to spend a few days away with her to bounce a few ideas off each other in an attempt to sort her marriage out.'

'Really?' Mason gloated. 'If you're such an expert at marriage guidance counselling, how come you shied away from talking to me in front of your wife?'

Drummond said nothing.

'Tell me,' DS Savage said, pulling up his seat. 'Had you noticed any decline in Margaret's demeanour over your weekend away together – her mental state?'

'No, I can't say that I did. She seemed pretty level-headed about everything.'

'Yet she was found dead in Chopwell Wood with a rope around her neck!' Drummond's head dropped as the sergeant's words cut deep, but the detective was in no mood for sympathy. 'It doesn't look good suddenly, does it, Mr Drummond?'

'No. It would appear not.'

Drummond was falling apart, and Mason could sense the home straight was in sight. The moment DS Holt entered the room and slid a slip of paper towards him, Mason read it. Having contacted the Blue Bell Hotel to verify Drummond's story, shortly after 2:15 pm Sunday 12th June, the university lecturer had checked out of the hotel having settled his account. He'd been telling the truth. The barrister had held onto her room until the following morning and checked out at 7:00 am. Even so, it still didn't mean he was out of the woods yet, far from it. They would need to recover the hotel lobby CCTV footage and check on the university's lecturer roster list.

The pieces of the puzzle slowly coming together, Savage dug deeper. 'Who else did you meet in the hotel that weekend?'

'What do you mean – meet?'

'The other guests, did you talk to any of them at all?'

'Only to say hello at mealtimes.'

'Friendly enough, were they?' Mason cut in.

'Yes, now that you mention it.'

Annoyed, Mason slid a photofit of the Chopwell Wood suspect towards the university lecturer and took up an unfriendly posture. 'For the purposes of the tape, I'm showing Mr Drummond exhibit ED 413.' Mason tapped the photofit with his finger. 'What about this man, did you bump into him at all?'

'No. Who is he?'

'Someone of interest,' Mason replied bluntly.

'Oh!'

'Let's talk about Margaret's husband for a moment,' said DS Savage. 'What can you tell us about Laurence Cooper?'

At last Drummond began to open up and according to him, the barrister's husband was a cruel manipulator who had allegedly used mental cruelty as a means of controlling his wife. By the time Savage had finished talking, Laurence Cooper wasn't the same person that Mason had previously interviewed. But Drummond was a schemer, someone who would lie his way out of a tight corner to save his own skin. That said, the notion of Cooper threatening his wife in front of their teenage daughters didn't bode well in Mason's books. No, Mason thought. This was the second wife to commit suicide under Laurence Cooper's watch, and there was still the life insurance policy to consider.

'Tell me, did you ever meet Laurence Cooper at all?'

'Good God, no—'

'Perhaps not,' Mason smiled. 'It wouldn't have been convenient, would it?'

'He's a cruel manipulator, Chief Inspector.'

'So, all of this is what Margaret told you?' said Savage.

'Yes, but I had no reason to disbelieve her. After all, she was a highly respected barrister.'

'I can't say as I can agree with you on that either, not when she was having an affair behind her husband's back.'

Drummond slumped in his seat.

'One last question, and you don't have to say yes,' Mason said. 'How do you feel about giving us a DNA swab?'

'That's not a problem.'

Mason scribbled something down in his notebook. 'Is there anything else you wish to tell us?'

'Yes. What about my wife? I don't want her to hear any of this.'

Drummond may not have had anything to do with the barrister's death, but he certainly wasn't getting off lightly. Not in Savage's books he wasn't.

'It doesn't work like that unfortunately.' The sergeant smiled gloatingly.

'Surely, there's no need for my wife to know about this.'

'It's not the police you should be concerned about, Mr Drummond. It's the media you need to worry about. Once those vultures get hold of your weekend exploits, it will be all over the national tabloids. Especially as you are a senior lecturer at Newcastle University.'

'Surely not. I—'

'Think about it: who doesn't like to read a juicy bit of scandal now and then?'

Drummond put his face in his hands and broke down.

What a wuss, Mason chuckled.

CHAPTER EIGHTEEN

It was Friday and having stuck rigidly to his fitness regime for the past two weeks, Jack Mason felt much better for it. Given the all-clear from his physiotherapist, Barbara Lockwood, he was hoping the police medical board would follow suit. His scar tissues had healed nicely but he was still having grave doubts as to what was going on inside his body. He'd heard some horrific tales from fellow officers about the medical board's rigorous tests and wasn't at all confident about passing with flying colours. Just how he would react should they declare him unfit for work, he was dreading to think.

The rain had eased when he checked in at the reception desk and made himself known. Dressed in tracksuit bottoms, sports top and trainers, he signed the pre-test medical forms and felt the knot in his stomach tighten. He'd not eaten since yesterday teatime and could have murdered a full English breakfast. Little chance of that happening now.

Directed into a side room, he was weighed, and his blood pressure taken by a male nurse who stank of garlic. Six months of worrying and it had all come down to this. Might as well get it over with, he groaned. Next, his lungs and chest were checked, and he was asked to produce a urine sample.

'Are you taking any beta blocker drugs?' the nurse asked, handing him an empty plastic container.

'No. Why?'

'If you are, it could depress your heart rate scores during the tests.' The nurse stared at him and frowned. 'I presume you've not eaten, exercised, or drunk coffee or tea in the last two hours?'

'No,' Mason said, shaking his head, 'and I'm bloody famished.'

He gave him a brief, slightly embarrassed nod of acknowledgement as if he'd heard it all before. 'I take it you've read the questionnaire?'

'Yes.' Mason nodded.

'And there are no contraindications to you performing the tests here today?'

'None that I'm aware of.'

'What about your physical health?'

'I was recently discharged from hospital and signed off by my physiotherapist.'

'No more medical appointments then?'

'None, apart from this one.'

The moment the nurse closed the medical file, Mason thought it was over. He should have known better, of course. Just because he wore a smart uniform and carried an air of authority didn't mean he was a key player in the grand scheme of things. Far from it.

His ego deflated, after handing his urine sample in at reception, he was herded into an open-plan waiting room. Two men opposite him were staring up at a muted TV screen. One was short with a wizened face, the other looked close to death.

He smiled, and then said, 'Are you two here for the tests?'

'Yeah, and you?' the wizened-faced man replied.

'Afraid so.'

Mason saw a door open and felt the rush of cool air. He tried to stay calm but knew the man fast approaching was about to put him through hell. He looked like a fitness fanatic he once knew, early twenties, exploding with energy and not an ounce of body fat. God, he thought. What was he letting himself in for?

'DCI Mason?' The young man smiled.

'That's me.'

'I'm Kevin Whitaker, and I'll be conducting your CTPWT tests today. Do you smoke, Detective Chief Inspector?'

'No, I gave that shit up almost fifteen years ago,' Mason replied proudly.

'You're a wise man.'

Mason pointed to the clipboard that Whitaker was carrying. 'I've briefly read up on it, but what do these tests entail exactly?'

'The Chester Treadmill Police Walk Test or CTPWT as it is better known, is a performance test specifically developed for the police services of England and Wales. It's a modern-day replacement to the old fifteen-metre shuttle run you may be familiar with.'

'What running backwards and forwards between two set points.'

'Yes, it's all done on a treadmill nowadays.'

'And how does that work exactly?'

'It's nothing to worry about, it's just a series of rigorous physical tests we put you through which closely replicates the real life demands of a police officer during their daily duties. It's based on several operational scenarios . . . a bit like a fitness assessment of your ability to cope with varying situations.'

Bugger, Mason cursed. Had he known that he would have spent more time in the gym instead of thinking about it. He watched as the wizened man opposite screwed his face up at the mere mention of a physical fitness assessment. If anyone was to fail it was him.

'How long does it actually last?' Mason enquired, still hedging his bets.

'In your case around an hour.'

'*An hour!*'

'After a suitable warm-up you'll be required to walk on a treadmill at a brisk pace, then every two minutes the gradient is raised by three per cent. It's pretty straightforward actually.'

'And who will be monitoring me?'

'To give it a fancy name, I'm your so-called test administrator.'

For some moments he fought it off, but the thought of pitting his wits against a computer driven treadmill was doing his head in. At least he knew what he was up against, and he wasn't out to impress. He would need to conserve his energy for the latter stages of the test if anything, and somehow muddle his way through the rest.

They moved down a never-ending corridor at speed. It was hot inside, and on reaching a pair of double swing doors, Whitaker pushed them open. The room was L shaped and reminded him of an open plan hospital ward he'd once visited. It was well-ventilated, with solid wood floors, low ceilings and large frameless windows running along a south facing wall. Then he saw the treadmill, and it suddenly took his breath away. Nothing ever panicked him, usually. But this was enormous, and full of gadgets and monitoring devices the likes of which he'd never seen before. He knew it was premature, knew it was untimely, but knew what the outcome would be.

'You must know my father,' Whitaker announced.

'Do I?'

'Sergeant Whitaker, he's worked at Gateshead Police Station for the past seventeen years.'

'Dennis Whitaker, the front desk Sergeant?'

'Yes, that's him.'

'Well I'll be damned. So, you must be the young lad who recently graduated from Manchester University?' Mason smiled to himself. 'Congratulations, you've really done well for yourself.'

Whitaker began to prepare him for the test.

'My dad often talks about you,' said Whitaker, switching on the treadmill belt.

'I hope it's not all bad.'

'As a matter of fact, he speaks very highly of you.'

'Your father's a good man, Kevin,' Mason said, tying his laces before stepping onto the impending torture machine. 'He's one of the old school police officers, and there are very few of them still around.'

The young man smiled, and Mason felt uncomfortable. Informed that if he showed any signs of over-tiredness, dizziness or discomfort, the test would be stopped, and he would be allowed to recover and cool down. He had no intentions of doing that. Stopping would be classed as failure, if not questionable in front of a medical panel.

'So, what do you want me to do here?'

Whitaker grinned and gave a pretend salute. 'It shouldn't take long, Chief Inspector, especially for someone of your calibre.'

Shit, Mason cursed. He hated false myths.

There were three things he'd learnt about treadmills over the years. How to adjust your gait, how to conserve your energy, and how to deal with incline changes if you thought you couldn't cope. This time felt different, though, as he wasn't in charge of the controls.

Cursing his luck, he nervously clipped the safety stop to his waist and prepared himself for the inevitable. Nothing was ever a doddle these days.

Slowly at first, he walked at a steady pace concentrating on feeling his back foot getting a good push off with each step. Arms bent at 90 degrees, shoulders relaxed, he felt like a steam train in motion. Doddle, he thought, as he stared out of the window at the grasslands opposite. This wasn't as bad as everyone had made it out to be, and he was slowly beginning to get the hang of it. Then, after the five-minute warm up session ended abruptly, he was suddenly thrown into confusion. Holy shit, he cursed, grabbing tight hold of the handrail as the treadmill gathered speed.

How much faster can this bloody thing go?

His feet barely touching the ground, if he stopped now, he would be flung through the window faster than a clay pigeon. Anxiety gripped him, and he was fighting to stay upright.

'Is everything okay, Chief Inspector?'

Mason blew through his cheeks as if it were his last breath on Earth. 'Yeah, sort of.'

'You're doing just fine,' Whitaker called out. 'Heart rate looking good, rhythm perfect, just two more incline levels and you're through.'

'Two!' Mason gasped.

'Just raise your hand if you require me to stop.'

This wasn't fun anymore, and as the treadmill began to tilt ever further towards the heavens, he thought he was going to slide off the back of it.

Sod this for a game of soldiers, he thought.

CHAPTER NINETEEN

It had stopped raining when DCI Mason entered Gateshead Police Station, but the ground underfoot was awash with puddles. Now that Richard Drummond had been cleared from his investigations, the finger of suspicion pointed firmly at Laurence Cooper. But these matters were never straightforward, and according to Cooper's gardener, the family had taken off to their holiday cottage in Cornwall. This wasn't in the script, so what was Cooper running away from, Mason wondered?

Thinking about this, he decided to swing by the station's front desk. Convinced he'd failed the police medical board tests miserably, he wasn't looking forward to his meeting with the Area Commander one little bit. There were still a few things to iron out, but he was now resigned to losing his position on the Serious Crime Squad.

'Morning, Jack,' the desk sergeant breezily announced.

'What's new at the zoo?'

'Two overnighters due before the magistrates court, and one stray dog if you want it?'

'No thanks.' Mason shrugged. 'Any more news on the Chopwell Wood suspect?'

'There's nothing in the report book of interest. . . were you expecting something?'

'Not really. I'm due in Gregory's office in ten minutes.'

'DI Gamble is in with him at the moment, so he could be running late.'

Strange, Mason thought, looking at his watch.

The sergeant's eyes narrowed as he looked over the top of his glasses. 'A little birdie tells me you passed your police medical with flying colours.'

'Is this a wind-up?'

'No. You've been passed fully fit for duty.'

Mason looked at him, suspiciously. 'Really?'

'Keep it to yourself, as it's not general knowledge at the moment.'

How could that possibly be, Mason thought. The last thing he remembered, after staggering off the treadmill and collapsing in a heap on the floor, was being handed a glass of water. So, unless Whitaker's son had fiddled the results and wasn't letting on about it, the sergeant could only be in on the act. Sometimes it wasn't what you did in life, it was who you knew that made the difference.

'Take my advice,' the sergeant said, leaning casually over the counter, 'don't go rushing into it, as your type of injuries can take a long while to heal.'

'Thanks, pal. I owe you.'

With a few minutes to spare, Mason called in at his office and delved into Laurence Cooper's case files. Still curious as to why Richard Drummond had told him about Cooper's use of mental cruelty, he was looking for patterns. Had Cooper's first wife jumped off the High-Level Bridge by her own accord or had she been encouraged to do it? There was nothing in the interview transcripts to suggest the latter, and nothing to cause him alarm. Even so, it seemed odd that both wives should die under similar circumstances and yet there was nothing to connect them.

Satisfied, he closed the filing cabinet drawer and grabbed his notebook and pen. There was a new spring of confidence in his step as he strode along the corridor that morning, but that was about to change.

The moment he entered the Area Commander's office, Mason's heart sank – *what the hell was DI Gamble still doing here?* Something was afoot, and whatever it was she looked incredibly relaxed. He thought he was here to talk about his future position, but the news from the Police Medicals Board still hadn't filtered through.

'Ah, Detective Chief Inspector Mason,' Gregory said, lifting his head towards him, 'we were just talking about you.'

'Something positive, I hope?'

Gamble flashed her whitened teeth at him. 'What's the latest on Laurence Cooper, Jack?'

There it was again . . . JACK! What gave her the right to call him by his Christian name? He was never on familiar terms with any of his team in front of senior police officers, so why be on familiar terms with him? Not the best of starts, it was time to put his foot down.

'Laurence Cooper is in Cornwall,' Mason replied firmly.

Gregory was quick to react.

'Yes. We were aware of that.'

Gamble turned her back on Mason and spoke to Gregory direct. 'It's strange that Cooper should take off so soon after his wife's death, sir. What is he running away from?'

'He's gone there with his daughters apparently.'

'Perhaps we should pay him a visit. . . establish if there's any truth in these mental abuse allegations that Drummond was talking about.'

'Yes. I agree,' said Gregory. 'We need to get to the bottom of it.'

Mason felt at odds suddenly and tried to intervene. 'I could arrange for the local constabulary to have a word—'

'No. That won't be necessary,' Gregory replied stoically.

'And why not?'

'I was thinking of sending you down there.'

'What, *me*. Cornwall?'

'Why not? You've asked me on enough occasions to be involved.'

'Yes, but I was—'

'There's a direct train from Newcastle to Penzance,' said Gregory pointing at his computer screen as if it had already been decided. 'You should go first class, of course. Take a couple of days out – the break will do you the world of good.'

'Wouldn't it be more fitting if DI Gamble went to Cornwall, sir? Besides, I still have a few loose ends to tie up on the Richard Drummond interview.'

Gregory stared at him hard. 'I thought we'd already eliminated Richard Drummond from our enquiries?'

'We have. It's—'

'Well then?'

Masking his fury, Mason flopped back in his seat flabbergasted. He'd been stitched up, big style, and there wasn't a damn thing he could do. He took a few moments to gather his wits before answering.

'There's also the break-in at the Sanderson Law Chambers to deal with.'

'I'm sure DI Gamble can handle that little matter for you. After all, she is in charge of the day-to-day running of operations.'

'I agree, but——'

'Good. It's settled then.'

Mason's instincts as a working detective had developed enough over the years to know when to keep his mouth shut. These bastards were joined inseparably at the hip, that much was obvious. He would need a subtle plan, something discernible, and one involving DI Gamble's grip on his position as head of serious crime. Whatever it was she was scheming behind his back, she now had the upper hand. He would need to tread carefully, think it through. Now he'd been given the heads-up the police medical board had given him the all-clear, he was in a much stronger position.

Or at least he thought he was.

CHAPTER TWENTY

After a pleasant nine-hour train journey to Penzance, Jack Mason was in pensive mood. Having caught a local taxi to the neighbouring fishing port of Newlyn, he booked into his hotel room and slung his overnight bag onto the bed. Under the circumstances, he would normally have been keen to get away from the hassle for a few days, but Newlyn was full of bad memories. The last time he'd visited the place was with his ex-wife, Brenda. Their marriage had been going through a bad patch at the time, and they were trying to straighten things out. If anything, their long weekend in Newlyn had turned into a series of disastrous bitter arguments. They stormed off to London under a cloud of mistrust, that was the last time they'd slept in the same bed together.

What the hell, he cursed.

Still deep in thought, he unpacked, showered and changed into something more casual before heading down to the bar. Still light, from the hotel lounge window he had clear unobstructed views of the busy harbour. Poised where the English Channel meets the Atlantic, Newlyn had long been a fishing port and boasted one of the largest in the UK. The place was extremely popular with tourists, and this was the busiest period of the year.

Finding a corner seat, he checked his emails, fired off a couple of text messages, and quietly admired the view. In many ways the white stone-faced granite cottages and steep narrow alleys only added to the town's quaint charm. It was a beautiful place, especially in the depths of winter where the medieval harbour walls of the North and South piers were a most welcoming sight for hundreds of returning fishermen. With over seven-hundred fishing vessels and numerous fresh fish landing stations, its busy fish market was the focal hub of the town. Newlyn had a bustling local community, and in a few weeks from now the annual Fish Festival would take place and the town would come alive under a different guise.

The lounge was heaving when Mason ordered another pint; mostly locals who seemed to prefer standing elbow to elbow at the bar. Pushing his way through the throng, he managed to squeeze back into his window seat, but only just. Now deep in thought, he was actually looking forward to his meeting with Laurence Cooper at Newlyn Police Station, but that was twelve hours away.

'Just arrived?' A rather stout blonde lady asked, now sitting opposite.

'Yes, and you?'

'I live here, have done for the past twenty-three years.'

She gave him a second glance and smiled. 'Are you down from London?'

'I grew up there, but I live in the North East nowadays.'

He pretended to be texting on his iPhone, but she wasn't giving in that easily.

'What line of business are you in?'

'I work in a sewage plant,' Mason lied, 'shovelling shit all day. What about you?'

She sipped her wine and thought about it.

'Drowning my sorrows mainly. I'm a gutter in the local fish factory.'

'Sounds interesting.'

'Not really,' she sighed, as if quickly losing interest in their conversation.

He took another mouthful of his beer and wiped the froth from his lips thinking. In all his years on the force he'd never felt as low as this before. Gregory had finally got him where he wanted him – wallowing in fish guts and a million miles from the action.

'How long are you here?' the stout blonde lady asked.

'A couple of days,' Mason replied.

'Meetings?'

'All day tomorrow by the sound of things.'

She lifted her heavy eyes towards him. 'Where's that, over at the Cornwall Drains?'

'How did you guess?'

'If it ain't fish, it's sewage,' she said, finishing the last of her drink and standing to leave. 'Other than tourism, there's not much else going on around here.'

Mason nodded. 'No, I suppose not.'

'Have fun,' she smiled.

'I will—'

Her eyes sparkled with mischievous humour as she leaned over towards him. 'If you're here tomorrow night, maybe we can have a few drinks together?'

'Can't promise anything,' Mason replied. 'But it was nice meeting you.'

Mason smiled to himself as she pushed her way through the throng and vanished beyond the lounge double doors. She was friendly enough, but definitely not his type.

With thoughts now elsewhere, he let his mind drift.

How much of Laurence Cooper's story rang true, he had no idea. There were plenty of motives for murder, including a million-pound life insurance plan he'd taken out on his wife. There was still the Cooper family assets to consider – all of them legally tied up in Laurence's name. A few hours' grilling should do the trick, by which time Cooper might buckle under the strain.

The more he thought about it, the more Mason warmed to the idea. With no reasonable explanation as to why his first wife had committed suicide, he would need to question him over their relationship prior to her death. No doubt Cooper had dozens of witnesses who could vouch he was innocent but was he responsible for his second wife's death? What if Cooper had discovered Margaret's affair with the university lecturer, Richard Drummond? He could have done – simply put two and two together and hired someone to carry out his dirty work. There were so many unanswered questions, so many motives for murder, and every one of them seemed plausible at this late hour.

No, Mason thought. He would need to sleep on it – work through the possibilities – tomorrow was another day.

CHAPTER TWENTY-ONE

Still reeling over his visit to Cornwall, Jack Mason was still no closer to the truth. His interview with Laurence Cooper at Newlyn Police Station had gone badly, and he was left with more questions than answers. As things now stood, nothing seemed to make sense anymore. He still had his suspicions, of course, but with insufficient evidence to press charges, Cooper was allowed to walk free – for now at least.

Mason would have liked to think that Cooper was involved in a million-pound life insurance scam, but he very much doubted it. The way he now saw it, either the global management consultant had hired someone else to take care of his dirty work, or the Chopwell Wood suspect was involved in something more sinister.

Now sitting at his desk, he quietly mulled over his options. In what had been a bizarre chain of events, his impulsive actions had probably cost him dearly. He'd cocked up big time, and on arrival back to Newcastle, he'd taken it upon himself to enter the Coopers house without a search warrant. He'd found nothing, of course, and the Area Commander was rightfully demanding answers. Not that Mason had any to give. He didn't, but the whole affair was unfortunate and regrettable.

Much to DS Savage's surprise, Mason threw his warrant card down on the desk and contemplated his future. The whole business churned his guts and changed everything, and all because of a stupid hunch that Cooper was holding back on something.

Worse still, DI Gamble was cock-a-hoop over his distinct lack of self-control and was laying it on thick with the Area Commander. Sadly, the rest of the senior staff couldn't agree with his actions either, and the Chief Inspector was now staring down the barrel of yet another disciplinary investigation.

Mason gave Savage an almost guilty smile. 'I'm faced with the same old problems, Rob. Only this time it's much more serious.'

'It was a bad move, boss.'

'Tell me about it.'

Savage caught Mason's eye. 'Do you still think Laurence Cooper has something to do with his second wife's death?'

'A part of me says he has, and he's the only person who stands to gain from it.'

'You mean this million-quid life insurance policy he took out?'

'That amongst other things.' Mason nodded.

'Hang on a minute, I thought the insurance brokers were questioning its validity?'

Mason thought for a moment. 'If both Laurence Cooper and Richard Drummond are innocent, then who else do we have in the frame?'

'Apart from the Chopwell suspect, nobody.'

'Exactly,' Mason replied. 'What if Cooper had hired someone to get rid of his wife?'

'The only problem I have with that,' Savage said, shaking his head, 'is why haven't we picked up on it during our interviews?'

Mason was adamant. 'The break-in at the law chambers has to be connected to this barrister's death. I'm convinced of it.'

Savage looked at him oddly. 'DI Gamble still isn't persuaded this break-in was staged. She thinks it's another red herring you've dreamt up.'

Mason's face suddenly darkened. 'What else has she been saying?

'Not a lot. She spends most of her time in Gregory's office nowadays.'

'What about this auditor, Stephen Rice? Has she said any more about that?'

'Not to me, she hasn't.' Savage frowned. 'There again, I'm deliberately kept out of the loop these days.'

'Watch your back, Rob.'

'Tell me about it. I'm not sure I can trust her anymore.'

'What makes you say that?'

'She seems to have a hidden agenda if I'm honest.'

'Oh!'

'It could be nothing, of course.'

Mason's fingers tightened round the armrest as he tried to steady himself. All things being equal the boy was his biggest concern, and without proper police protection he was extremely vulnerable.

'We could be heading for trouble,' Mason said.

'In what way?'

'Young Martin Kennedy. Without close protection the boy could be in serious trouble.'

'You're not the only one who thinks that. I've heard rumblings.' Savage shrugged.

'About what?'

'DI Gamble.'

'What about her?'

'She has Gregory's ear.'

Mason thought a moment. 'This case is going nowhere, Rob.'

'I know, but it's out of our hands unfortunately.'

Mason sat back thinking. The decision he'd struggled so hard to make had just been made for him. In a way it was inevitable. 'This isn't a suspicious suicide we're dealing with here, this is a full-on murder enquiry.'

'What, you think everything's connected?'

Mason looked up sharply. 'Whoever broke into the Sanderson Law Chambers, knew what they were after. Find the answer to that, and we're well on the way to solving the case.'

'Yeah, but nothing was stolen.'

'It could have been photographed.'

'What, case files?'

'Tell me why not?'

Savage shook his head dejectedly. 'What about Cooper's house, did you find anything of interest?'

'No, nothing.'

'So, it wasn't such a clever idea after all. What the hell were you thinking of?'

'Trying to get ahead of the game. Besides, I trust Laurence Cooper as much as I trust politicians delivering on their promises. He's a creepy bastard, and he's definitely holding back on something.'

'Had you asked me beforehand, I would have arranged a search warrant for you.'

'I know, I know. . . it's too late for that now—'

'As always.'

Mason swung to face Savage. 'If you're not prepared to ruffle a few feathers in this game your leads go cold on you. It's the first rule of being a good detective.'

'Yes, but neither is breaking and entering into someone's property without a search warrant.'

Mason stared at him as he pulled out a bundle of documents he'd been working on. No matter how hard he tried to get his head round the case, obstacles were being thrown in his path. A copper's luck was hard earned, without which you got nowhere.

'So, where do we go from here?' Mason asked.

'That's DI Gamble's call—'

Mason slapped the desk with the palm of his hand in moment of temper.

'You need to calm down, boss. Think this through logically.'

'And do what exactly?'

Savage drew breath. 'I've been looking into the regs, and it's my belief a police officer can enter someone's property to look for evidence without a search warrant if they have reasonable grounds to believe there is evidence.'

'Thanks, Rob. I'll give it some consideration.'

Savage winked as he turned. 'No show without punch, eh!'

'Don't push it.'

CHAPTER
TWENTY-TWO

As the main landing struts extended to their full travel with a clunk, the cabin stewards of the Airbus A320 made their final preparations for landing. The flight into Heathrow Airport was now running forty-minutes late, and they were in a holding pattern circling London. Another hour should do the trick, Chameleon thought. Once he'd cleared customs.

Folding the seat tray away, he saw the outside temperature on his in-flight entertainment monitor was showing twenty-two degrees and humidity forty percent. Slightly cooler than when he left his temporary accommodation in Filderstadt in southern Germany that morning. It was still a pleasant day, nevertheless.

Minutes later as the plane juddered and broke through a heavy cloud formation, from his window seat the long black ribbon of the River Thames extended to the horizon and beyond. Below, he could see Canary Wharf and the skyscrapers now a dramatic, established part of London's skyline. They were a landmark he never failed to admire, as he'd done a lot of business there and he was itching to do more.

Feeling his ears pop from the sudden change in cabin pressure, Chameleon sucked hard on a boiled sweet. Travelling business class from Stuttgart was always a bit of a ball-ache, but that was the least of his worries. Wearing a dark grey business suit, white shirt and red tie, the Russian businessman was desperate to get back into the swing of things again. Not a tall man, stocky with a rounded lived-in face. Behind the deep-set brown eyes lurked a tough, uncompromising personality.

Something had seriously gone wrong, but where? He was desperate to find out. Questions were being asked at a higher level and his services were urgently required elsewhere. He'd only been out of the country a couple of days, and contracts were coming thick and fast. But you could only be in one place at a time, no matter how much pressure the Organisation put on you.

The moment the plane banked steeply, Chameleon's nostrils twitched. He could see the woman sitting next to him was terrified of flying and he could almost smell the fear. As the plane shuddered and descended towards its final approach, her face contorted beyond all recognition. She looked mid-forties, blonde, with beautifully manicured nails and a mouth full of whitened teeth that reminded him of a toothpaste ad in a glitzy magazine. He knew she was Turkish the passport poking out of her handbag told him that. It was a country he despised, a place full of bad memories.

He glanced at his watch.

It would be happy hour back at his favourite bar in Regent Street, but he wasn't going to make it. Not now he wasn't. Already running late, he hated airports at the best of times and they always pissed him off. With nothing to declare, and only a weekend bag to worry about, he was hoping to fast-track through security. He preferred travelling light, especially business class, as the stewards always gave him preferential treatment and it made him feel at ease. Not like the people stuck in cattle class – grappling for leg room and packed like sardines in a tin. Those plebs drove him crazy on short haul flights, especially the amount of luggage they carried with them. God knows what Customs made of it. Get a life, he cursed.

Once the plane was taxiing, he switched his mobile on and waited for an internet connection. It pinged, and he checked the display.

Where are you? The text message read.

Just landed.

Same place?

He fired off a change of plan and pocketed his phone.

Twenty minutes later after clearing Border Control and Customs, he was heading north on the London underground – standing room only. Excited to be back in the capital again, he was looking forward to seeing how the new house renovations were progressing. It was a large Regency Georgian terraced property just on the outskirts of Belgravia. A Middle East Arab sheik had owned it and he'd fought tooth and nail to secure a good deal. Twenty-million pounds, a snip at half the price. Money was no object, luckily. He'd done his sums, and if he did need more cash he knew where to find it. This was the second most expensive property Chameleon had acquired in the past six months; the other was in New York. Long Island, Upper Brookville, a spectacular forty-acre property facing the Atlantic Ocean.

Nothing came cheap nowadays, and there was no such thing as a free lunch ticket. Everything had a price, and those that thought otherwise were deluded. Smiling inwardly to himself, Chameleon was beginning to enjoy his new business ventures into the exclusive offshore property market. He'd done well for himself considering. Most of his hard-earned cash had been salted away into legitimate assets, which was more than he could say for a lot of fellow business associates he knew.

As the train screeched to a halt inside Leicester Square tube station, a new sense of excitement washed over him. He was close, and ten minutes from now he would be sitting in his favourite bar and drinking a much-loved pint of British beer. He watched as the man opposite craned his head as people started to get off. Having spent the best part of his journey hiding behind his newspaper, did he really think he was invisible?

His mobile pinged, and he checked the display.

Where are you now?
Five minutes away, he texted back.
I'm on my way.
He could hardly wait!

CHAPTER TWENTY-THREE

The moment Jack Mason pulled into Gateshead Police Station car park, heavy rain struck the windscreen. For once the weather presenters had got it right, and ominous black storm clouds gathering over the North Sea that morning, were now unleashing their fury. As he sat quietly and waited for the worst to blow over, he thought about his future. Policing wasn't the same anymore, and detectives like DI Gamble were working their way into good positions at the expense of talented young officers. It wasn't right, and something had to give.

With bloodshot eyes, he ran up the entrance ramp and took the stairs two at a time. Dressed in his favourite leather bomber jacket, jeans and black trainers, Mason looked anything but a senior police officer involved with the Serious Crime Squad. Well, he thought, as he knocked on the Area Commander's door, might as well get it over with. The last few weeks of bickering had finally come to a head, and morale had reached an all-time low.

'Good morning, Jack,' the Superintendent said sounding ominously upbeat. 'Two important visitors are joining us today.'

Mason detested the term – *important visitors*. It had a condescending ring, as if a class above the rest. Something was afoot, and whatever it was, he didn't like the sound of it. Yes, he'd overstepped the mark, but what the hell were two Special Branch officers doing here?

Formalities over with, he took up a seat opposite.

The senior officer seemed capable enough, despite his youthful appearance. At a glance Mason thought he looked ex-military. Dressed in an immaculate grey suit, white buttoned-down shirt and tie, his highly polished shoes were the giveaway.

'I'll come straight to the point,' the senior Special Branch officer suddenly announced. 'The man you've all been looking for is a former officer of the Russian FSB.'

Mason stared at him in stunned silence for a moment. This was the last thing he'd expected to hear, and it had knocked him for six. 'I presume we're talking about the Chopwell Wood suspect here?'

'Yes, I am.'

'Who is he?'

'Known as Chameleon, his real name is Grigori Yavlinsky and he operates out of Stuttgart with known connections in London and New York. Born in the Soviet Union, he served as an army special service officer and is known to have worked for the Russian foreign intelligence division. In 2010 he was sent to spy on expatriates who had moved to the West after the dissolution of the Soviet Union, and soon made a name for himself as a ruthless operator. One of his missions was to identify and deal with former Russian Oligarchs who were known to be passing on intelligence and technology to the Americans.'

'What is he, a Russian secret agent?'

'We believe so.' The officer paused. 'After returning to St Petersburg, two years ago he took up a position in the banking industry. We now know it was a cover for clandestine work he was doing for the FSB's foreign intelligence division, which may account for his current position.'

Mason cocked his head to one side. 'Which is?'

'Dealing with the seedier side of off-shore banking.'

Mason listened intently, pleased at the fact this was no longer a disciplinary hearing. There was determination in the officer's voice. Forceful. As though keen to get his point across. He'd met his like before, but still couldn't decide whether he was working for Counter Terrorism Command or directly for Security Services (MI5).

'Who is Yavlinsky currently working for?' Mason asked outright.

'That's a difficult one.'

'So, what's his connection with Newcastle?'

The senior officer's brow corrugated. 'Six months ago, the Metropolitan Police were given secret documents highlighting several money laundering red flags involving a series of wire transfers through shell corporations with accounts in Russia. It's a complex operation, involving dozens of countries. So far, we've managed to obtain documentary evidence that shows the money is being wired to banks in South America, then wired back to accounts in Switzerland and London. We're talking billions of dollars here, dirty money which is being laundered into luxury apartments and high-end capital investment around the globe.'

'And you suspect Yavlinsky is using his banking connections as a cover?'

'Either that, or he's involved with the Russian Mafia.'

Mason thought about it. 'So, what's the connection between Yavlinsky and this Newcastle barrister, Margaret Cooper?'

'Good question,' the nameless second officer replied. 'We now have compelling evidence that proves Yavlinsky is linked to a massive money laundering scam with wider links across Europe and the USA. It's a sophisticated set-up, and one involving lawyers, bankers, and politicians with connections to several East European investment banking firms. And, might I add, all with offices based in London.'

Mason suddenly noticed a large green folder stuck on the corner of Gregory's desk. It belonged to the second officer who kept drumming it with the end of his pen. It was marked: CLASSIFIED. He made a mental note of it and turned to address them.

'So why are you telling me all of this?'

'We believe that Yavlinsky came to England with the sole intention of disrupting the Crown Prosecution Service's case listed against one of the Russian investment banks.'

'I presume this was the case that Margaret Cooper was involved in?'

'That's correct. Naturally the main accused. . . the so-called people at the top . . . are keen that their identities are not disclosed. Of course, the Russian government deny any involvement in the matter, but we know of at least two top embassy officials who are implicated in the scam.' The senior officer raised his eyebrows a fraction before continuing. 'The solution to ending this problem lies firmly with Moscow – but that's never going to happen, of course. Which means it's left to the British Government to resolve.'

Here we go, Mason thought.

'This is beginning to sound like Spooks,' Mason remarked.

'Indeed, and we're merely scratching the tip of the iceberg here.'

'That's all very well and good but how does this involve me?'

The senior officer nodded as he opened the large green folder, he'd brought with him.

'Looking at your service records, I see you were brought up in the East End of London, and close to the docklands.' Mason shot him a glance but quickly thought the better of it. 'Known as a bit of a risk taker, after several years working with the Docklands Division as a Detective Sergeant you were selected for the Metropolitan's Murder Investigation Team (MIT).'

'What is this?' Mason asked finally. 'A retirement selection committee, or am I—'

Superintendent Gregory who had sat quietly throughout suddenly raised his hand. 'Hold on a minute, Chief Inspector. Let's hear the officer out.'

'I'm impressed.' The second officer smiled. 'It's little wonder the Northumbria Police were keen to recruit you as they did. I admire a man who speaks his mind.'

Mason held his composure, but only just.

'Here's my problem,' the second nameless officer continued. 'We're convinced Margaret Cooper was murdered for what she knew. In representing the CPS against one of the Russian investment banks, it meant she had direct access to all of the case files.'

'So that's what all this about?'

The officer nodded. 'Looking at the evidence, forensic foot casts recovered from Chopwell Wood are a direct match to those taken from the Sanderson Law Chambers, and a property of interest in London. In other words, we now have three positive links to Yavlinsky.'

'Sometimes you get lucky.' Mason shrugged.

'Not in this case. You'd obviously figured out the break-in at the Sanderson Law Chambers was connected to this barrister and followed it up at your meetings with DI Swan at Ponteland Police Headquarters.'

When he'd finished, Mason stared at him in stunned silence. Holy shit, he gasped. These bastards were five moves ahead of himcatch-up. This meeting wasn't about local criminals anymore, this was way over his head.

'So, you now believe Yavlinsky was responsible for killing the barrister?'

'No, I didn't say that. Neither did I say he killed her. What is fact, though, is that when Yavlinsky broke into the Sanderson Law Chambers we believe he may have photographed vital evidence that would incriminate the Russian investment bank at the forthcoming Newcastle trial. Not only that, we're still unable to trace one of the key witness's whereabouts.'

'You mean the hedge fund auditor, Stephen Rice?'

The senior officer nodded. 'Yes, and he was auditing one of the city banks at the time of his disappearance.'

'I had an inkling that Rice was implicated. If not, then why did he go missing?'

'You were certainly on the right track, Chief Inspector.'

'So, what's Rice's connection in all of this?'

'Shortly before his disappearance, we know he was working for one of the Russian leading banks and was backed by some very prominent people.'

'Like who?'

'Off-shore financiers, lawyers, corrupt politicians—'

'So, Rice is obviously a key player in this money laundering operation?'

'Very much so.' There was a hint of impatience in the senior agent's voice, suddenly. 'When Rice realised what he was letting himself in for, he wanted out. But it's never that easy, not where the Russians are concerned. Having decided to come clean, he went to the Metropolitan Police with his story.' The senior officer smiled cynically. 'Once the Joint Intelligence Committee were involved, they quickly realised the threat that Rice posed to our national security – and that's when he took flight.'

'So, where is Rice now?'

'Nobody knows – not on our side of the fence at least.'

'Is he still alive?' Mason asked.

'We know that British Intelligence has contacted him on several occasions, and that Rice seemed willing to turn Queen's evidence. But there lies another problem. . . how much information did Rice give to other people involved in the trial?'

'It sounds like Yavlinsky's sole mission is to hoover up anyone with insider knowledge of this Russian banking scam?'

The officer shook his head mutely. 'That's our understanding of it.'

Nerves jangling, Mason gripped the tubular metal armrests to steady himself. 'What I can tell you, is that a few weeks prior to

Margaret Cooper going missing she'd arranged to meet someone regarding Rice's whereabouts.'

'Which suggests she was probably set up, then silenced,' the second officer added.

'By whom? Yavlinsky?'

Gregory leaned in closer without holding eye contact. 'He certainly fits the bill.'

'So, why was the trial moved to Newcastle and away from the capital in the first place?' Mason asked.

'That was the Joint Intelligence Committee's decision, along with the Home Office,' the second officer confirmed. 'They were testing the water out – tugging at the shirt sleeves of the Russian investment bankers in the hope that one of them might break.'

'If Yavlinsky broke into the law chambers and copied Cooper's Outlook calendar, he would have known all of her contacts and movements,' Mason replied.

'Besides important information regarding the trial.'

'Shit!' Mason gasped.

'These people are ruthless professionals, make no mistake about that.' The two Special Branch officers exchanged glances as if to emphasise the point. 'Had this young boy not spotted Yavlinsky at work, I fear this case would have gone unnoticed.'

Mason folded his arms across his chest, a defensive stance. 'I always thought that Cooper was caught up in something sinister. If these people are prepared to eliminate anyone with incriminating evidence against them, then young Martin Kennedy is now in serious trouble.'

'We've already taken care of that aspect,' Gregory replied authoritatively. 'He's been moved to a safe house.'

The senior officer shifted his weight and smiled. 'How would you describe your current fitness levels, Chief Inspector? Let's say on a scale from one to ten?'

'If you're trying to pension me off, I feel fucking terrible,' Mason replied.

'And what if we're not?'

'Then I've never felt better.'

The two officers stared at one another and burst out laughing.

It was Gregory who spoke next. 'This case has obviously taken on a whole new meaning. Knowing your previous background working with MIT, how would you feel about taking on a special assignment?'

'What are you proposing, sir? Another shit advisory role?'

'No, no! This would be a front-line policing position.'

The senior officer stared across at Mason and smiled. 'Your number one priority would be to protect the boy, and anyone remotely connected in this forthcoming trial. We know what Yavlinsky is capable of, but that's a matter for you people to consider.'

'I presume we're looking at a close protection role?' Mason said pointing at the files.

Gregory shrugged. 'I'm confident you're the right man for the job.'

'Yeah, and I'm no James Bond,' Mason smugly replied.

'Why not sleep on it and give me your answer in the morning?'

The second officer spoke next. 'I don't have to tell you that this case is covered by the Official Secrets Act. Signing it has no effect on which actions are legal, as the act is law, not a contract. In other words, you are both bound to it, whether or not you have signed up to it.'

Alarm bells ringing in Mason's ears, the senior officer's words suddenly hit home hard. This was a dangerous assignment he would be undertaking, so it had to be on his terms.

As the two Special Branch officers stood to leave, the senior officer turned to them, and said, 'Thank you, gentlemen. As soon as you've given us the green light to proceed, we'll set the wheels in motion.'

Mason let out a long sigh of exasperation, still unsure what to make of it all. One thing for certain, though, he was back in the driving seat again.

CHAPTER
TWENTY-FOUR

With every movement sending shooting pains throughout his body, Jack Mason gingerly made his way towards Superintendent Gregory's office. It had been quiz-night at the Ship Inn in Benwell the previous evening, and his team had come in last as usual. After crawling their way to some seedy backstreet Indian restaurant in Forest Hall, the last thing he remembered was falling out of a taxi. The rest was awash in a haze of alcohol confusion, and the mother of all hangovers.

It was part of Mason's nature to worry when caught in two minds. Ever since childhood he detested making life changing decisions. Now that Special Branch was involved, it didn't take a rocket scientist to work out that this would be a dangerous assignment he would be undertaking. It was never easy. The last time he'd worked with the Security Service was back in 2003, and that concerned a consignment of arms that were being supplied to splinter terrorist groups in Africa. He'd been stuck in a private room in the Travellers Club on Pall Mall at the time, whilst two floors down a group of MI6, CIA and Libyan intelligence officials were having a very long lunch over a major arms deal. He was much younger back then, and more agile.

Reluctant to get involved, Mason knew the enormous risks he would be undertaking. But he loved the buzz he got from it – the unbelievable adrenaline rush from catching the bad guys and bringing about their downfall. But there lay a bigger problem, as you never knew who the real enemy was. Once government intelligence officers were involved, you always knew you were working alongside double-agents – people whose allegiance lay on both sides of the fence – risk takers who knew the consequences of being found out. Those days were behind him now, although yesterday's meeting had certainly given him a lot to think about.

The moment the Area Commander looked up from behind his desk, he could see his mood was upbeat. 'Ah, Detective Chief Inspector. Coffee?'

'I'd love a cup, sir.'

'It's on its way over.'

Eyes glazed over, Mason took up a seat opposite and flipped open his notebook. The last thing he wanted to hear was another round of questioning. Pen poised, brain stuck in first gear, he sat back and waited for the punchline.

'Have you come to your decision yet?' Gregory began.

'No, sir,' Mason relied flatly. 'I'm still wrestling over the problem of team selection.'

'Let's not get too hung up over that, we have far more important issues to discuss.'

'It's a simple matter of principle, sir. Now that I'm fully fit for duties, I resent having to take my instructions from a junior ranking officer.'

Gregory let out a long slow breath, his expression grave. 'I've just had the Chief Constable on the blower, and he's already been in contact with Special Branch. It seems the latest intelligence reports coming out of Millbank confirm the Russian Mafia could be involved in this money laundering scam – and in a big way, apparently. Some of the information is highly sensitive, of course, and we're not getting the full picture. That said, the CC is naturally keen we get moving on our part of the operation.'

Coffee arrived, brought in on a tray by a young secretary with the Times newspaper tucked neatly under her arm. Mason waited for the door to close behind her before continuing. 'Does this mean the Chief Constable will be overseeing our part in the protection operations?'

'No. That still remains with me.' Gregory stared out of his window and stroked his chin in thought. The man looked at odds with himself, as though his retirement plans had suddenly been put on hold. 'He still has an active interest in the proceedings, of course, especially now that Joint Intelligence Committee are involved.'

Curbing his emotions, Mason mulled this over. Change unsettled him, and the landscape had altered considerably these past few years. Political correctness had gone mad, and far too many officers were too scared to speak openly, not to mention cultural appropriation. Not so in Mason's case, he was determined to get his point across no matter whose toes he trod on.

'What will my new role entail exactly?'

'I take it you're still interested in heading up the operation?'

'As long as I have a say in team selection.'

Gregory nodded in reluctant agreement and exhaled through clenched teeth. 'What came over rather strongly at yesterday's meeting with Special Branch was our role in keeping the local community safe. Who else at the Sanderson Law Chambers knew about these illegal money transfers with the Russian investment banks – that's what we should be asking ourselves.'

'Apart from a few clerks, no one, I suspect.'

Gregory looked strangely unnerved as he put his pen down in thought. 'We need to be absolutely certain. If not, the consequences could be catastrophic.'

'What about the other Russian banks involved?'

'That's a matter for the Home Office and Special Branch to sort out, as much of it involves shell companies who are registered in overseas tax havens. Who is responsible for the wire transactions is none of our concern.'

'I take it our task is to hunt down Grigori Yavlinsky and bring him to justice?'

'Far from it,' Gregory replied, looking troubled. 'Our role is purely one of close protection – looking after the likes of young Martin Kennedy and anyone else who is caught up in this.'

'Are you saying that this is purely a holding role?'

'If the Russians are refusing to cooperate with the British government it means we'll be working closely with the Joint Intelligence Committee. Once your team's in place, the Chief Constable will give us a broader indication as to what is expected of us.' Gregory shook his head as if resigned to the fact. 'I take it you *do* have a few people in mind?'

'Yes and no. I was—'

Gregory raised a hand to interrupt. 'Good. You'll need to keep your team small. No more than a dozen officers. Any more and it won't be manageable. We also need to consider giving young Martin Kennedy adequate protection during the daily school runs.'

'It sounds like you already have a plan in mind?'

'Social Services are looking at a foster mother in Seaton Sluice, and he may need to be given a new identity at some point. That said, the Chief Constable isn't at all keen on the idea, as it could throw up all kinds of problems.'

'I tend to agree with him on that.' Mason nodded. 'I presume the boy's father's house isn't suitable?'

'Phillip Kennedy is still out on licence; it's not a viable proposition.' Gregory glanced at him sternly. 'Once you've made your final team selection, I'll be holding a briefing in my office. In the meantime, we've set up a firearms refresher course for everyone involved in the case.'

'What about Special Branch will they be involved?'

127

'Not at this point. They will be acting as an intelligence gathering service, of course. Any additional support will come via the Chief Constable.'

Mason whistled through clenched teeth. 'This is beginning to sound like the real deal.'

'Make no mistake about it, Chief Inspector. This is a dangerous assignment.'

'It's definitely not your everyday police operation, that's for sure.'

'Good, we understand each other perfectly then.'

Mason checked his notes. 'There is one further question if I may – team selection. Does that include taking on specialists?'

'Specialists?'

'I was particularly thinking about David Carlisle and his criminal profiling skills.'

The Area Commander thought a moment. 'Allow me to run it past the Chief Constable Constable, as I'd hate us to get off on the wrong footing especially at this early stage in the proceedings.'

Mason nodded and scribbled down some notes.

'Will that be all, sir?'

'Yes, for now. In the meantime, I'll make the necessary arrangements with Special Branch and let them know of your decision.'

'Thank you, sir.'

As Mason stood to leave, he felt another searing pain in his side. Recovery was painstakingly slow and a constant reminder as to just how close to death he'd actually come. Loath to admit, there had been some on the force, only a few, who questioned whether he would ever make a full recovery at all.

CHAPTER
TWENTY-FIVE

Chameleon was up at the crack of dawn, and after a jog through the quiet suburban streets of Belgravia he arrived back at his luxury apartment just in time for the seven o'clock news bulletin. He showered, changed into a T-shirt and tracksuit bottoms and poured some cereal into a bowl. Breakfast wasn't his thing usually, he preferred eating in the evening. It was a habit he'd adopted from his military days, as troops fought better on empty stomachs. It had served him well over the years, and if it meant you could run faster and dodge bullets, he was happy to stick to the plan.

At the kitchen table thinking, he fired up his laptop. Always suspicious of the British postal system, he stared down at the bubble padded envelope and wondered how people could be so trusting. The Organisation had been quick to respond after his whistle-stop visit to Stuttgart, and he was quite looking forward to his new venture. Never one for shying away from a hazardous assignment, he knew what the envelope contained. Sometimes they carried an official rubber stamp under the postmark: FRAGILE DO NOT BEND.

The most crucial element, as far as Chameleon was concerned, had it been tampered with? He held the envelope up to the light and checked to see if the minute strand of hair was intact on the seal. Not that it made one iota of difference, as the data on the USB memory stick inside would be encrypted. Curious, he slid the kitchen knife under the sealed flap and removed the contents from within. After loading the memory stick into the laptop USB port, a password box appeared. Next, he typed in the eleven-digit code and waited for the file to upload. Seconds later a dozen high density images burst across his laptop screen, and he read the large caption:

STEPHEN RICE – HEDGE FUND AUDITOR.

Next, he checked his subject's physical features, including height, physique, and most importantly his outward appearance. He had handsome, fair-skinned looks, and a good head of ginger hair. Not that he took much notice, but Rice wasn't wearing a wedding ring.

'Hello, and welcome to the real world,' Chameleon whispered softly.

As his cursor hovered over a central tab box, he clicked on it and a street map of Bristol popped up. His first impressions were how much investigatory effort had gone into the operation. Six locations, all highlighted and supported by a wealth of information including contacts, summary sheets, building diagrams and possible escape routes. Not that it was a problem to him, but of all the places Chameleon had visited over the years he'd never been to Bristol before. He'd read about it in his military training days, but that was as far as it got. There again, he thought. It could work to his advantage as nobody in Bristol knew him from Adam, let alone what he would be doing there.

Flicking through the files, his next item of interest was a large spreadsheet containing known areas that his target regularly frequented. It was all there. Weeks of intelligence work and all at the press of a button. How could he possibly fail?

He closed the lid of his laptop and took another sip of his coffee. Plans in place, he would meet Rice in one of his favourite haunts, after they'd completed the deal. He knew the hedge fund auditor was desperate to leave the country, and he had the perfect place in mind. What nobody knew, not even Rice, was what would be waiting for him on his arrival there.

Some plans were easy to execute; not this one. He would need to keep his wits about him, blend into the background and cover his tracks. He knew how the British intelligence services worked – who he could trust and who he should stay clear of. Only a few people knew how to contact him in the event of an emergency, and that was via his pay-as-you-go phone. He only used a SIM card once, changing it for a new one after every text message or call. Too many people cloned mobile phones in Britain nowadays, and he was always conscious of government hackers. Big Brother wasn't a mere word in a book, it was lurking on every street corner.

Distracted by noises outside, he peered through a gap in the window blinds. Two men dressed in bright orange jackets were dragging heavy wheelie bins around in the yard. They were loading them into the back of a refuse lorry without checking to see what was inside. Not that he cared, but it had crossed his mind that it would be an effortless way to dispose of a body should he require one. He made a mental note of it and moved back to his laptop again.

Next, Chameleon checked the flight times to Bristol Airport and quickly decided against it. Far too risky, he thought. Too many security checks, too much traceability. After he'd fired off e-mails from three different accounts, he checked the train times out of Paddington Station. He would take an overnight bag and check into a cheap hotel. Nothing flash. Privacy.

He didn't do abortive missions, it wasn't part of his itinerary. Neither was failure; that was for idiots and fools.

CHAPTER
TWENTY-SIX

Jack Mason leaned against the unmarked pool vehicle and weighed up his options. Less than a mile from the village of Old Hartley, the new safe house had been well chosen. Close to Seaton Sluice harbour and overlooking the southernmost point of the rugged Northumbria coastline, the village had approximately 4000 inhabitants. It had a post office, chemist, beauty salon, and a local convenience store. Apart from its pubs, the only other tourist attraction was a local fish and chip shop and tea room. Mason had eaten there on several occasions, and knew the place served generous portions and played great sixties music.

The North Sea air filling his lungs, he unzipped his leather bomber jacket and strolled purposefully towards the harbour whilst checking the lay of the land as he went. It was a beautiful day, clear blue skies and not a single cloud to be seen. Moored up in shallow waters, a dozen small fishing boats were waiting for the tide to turn. Further north, across long stretches of golden sands, lay Blyth. Not the prettiest coastal town in the brochure, but the people who lived there were the salt of the earth and always made you welcome.

His head full of kidnapping scenarios, Mason was looking for holes in his plan. He'd been over this ground several times that afternoon but still wasn't satisfied. Now 3:15 pm, he watched as a blue Vauxhall Insignia pulled onto the kerb opposite and flashed its headlights. Seconds later, Detective Susan Carrington slid from the driver's seat and stood for a moment. Wearing a bulletproof vest under her jacket, it gave the impression she'd put on weight.

Now a well-established member of his team, Carrington was destined for higher things. Not pushy like the others, she was intelligent, incredibly quick witted, and had a wry sense of humour that Mason found difficult to comprehend. He genuinely liked her, she was a reliable team player – a person he could trust. And yet, beneath the angelic smile lay a ruthless streak, and one of the key requisites of close protection selection.

'What do you think?' Mason asked.

'I've spoken with the school's head teacher, and young Martin Kennedy can start his new placement on Monday.'

'What about Social Services?'

'They're more than happy to go ahead with the new arrangements and are pleased we'll be accompanying the boy to school every day. It's only a five-minute drive away, and once the main gates are locked it's a safe environment to be in.'

Mason shielded his eyes from the direct sunlight. 'Good. What about his new foster mother? Is she happy with your plans?'

'She seems to be. Although she's still apprehensive as to why there's a heavy police presence in the cottage next door.'

'What else did she say?'

'She asked how long his father would be working away.'

'And was she happy with your explanation?'

'She didn't object, but she's bound to quiz young Martin over it.'

'No doubt she'll put two and two together at some later stage.'

'I'll talk to her again about it, boss.' Carrington confirmed.

Mason stared at the Kings Arms pub opposite, his mind full of possibilities. 'I presume DC Richie is happy in his new role?'

'Everything's fine,' Carrington nodded. 'The two of us work well together.'

'Good.'

'I've also asked Social Services to keep in regular contact with me. I know his teachers will be keeping a close eye on the boy whilst he's in school, so we don't have any worries there.'

'Do they know you are undercover police officers?'

'They know we work at Gateshead Police Station, that's about all.'

'What about young Martin, has he said anything to you yet?'

'He knows his father is working away and seems quite excited about his new move.'

Mason smiled. 'Let's hope it's just a couple of weeks and not another one of those long drawn out protection operations.'

Carrington held his glances. 'What will happen to DI Gamble's team now? Will they disband it, or will it run as a parallel operation?'

'Do you have a problem with that?'

'No. It just seems strange that we're not allowed to discuss our new roles with anyone else on the team.'

'All will be revealed in good time.'

Carrington cocked her head to one side. 'If I'm completely honest with you, I'm only too glad to get away from DI Gamble's way of running things.'

Mason smiled. 'Those are strong words coming from you.'

'You know my thoughts on that, boss.'

Mason remembered, ten years ago, as a keen young detective sergeant being in a similar position as DC Carrington now found herself in. Changing allegiances could be testing, as team trust carried an awful lot of weight amongst your colleagues. But some officers were a natural choice for special assignments, others not. Carrington was a level-headed police officer who was about to advance up the promotion ladder. Besides, her selection had taken him all of six seconds to think through. His was a formidable team. He knew every one of them would give him one hundred percent. No, he thought. It was time to ease off the throttle – keep the young detective's interest levels heightened.

'Let's see what tomorrow's team briefing brings.' Mason grinned. 'It's probably the worst or the best decision you'll have ever made in your career.'

Carrington raised her eyebrows a fraction. 'If it's not of national importance, then I can't see what all the secrecy is about?'

Mason smiled inwardly to himself. Never a truer word spoken in jest, he mused.

His iPhone pinged, and he checked the display.

It was his physiotherapist from Forest Hall, Barbara Lockwood.

'DCI Mason. How can I help?'

'You sound very official this morning, Jack.' Lockwood giggled. 'Have I caught you at an inconvenient time?'

'Not at all, Barbara. What can I do for you?'

'That depends,' she coyly replied.

'Oh! Is there a problem?'

The connection went quiet for a moment. 'The last time you were in my treatment room, you asked about going out for a meal together one night—' her voice tailed off.

'Yes, and it was meant as a thank you gesture,' he defensively replied.

'How does Thursday night sound?'

Speechless, Mason stepped back a couple of paces as if not believing his ears. 'Yes, Thursday's fine,' he whispered. 'What time and where?'

'I'll leave that entirely to you.'

A vision intruded, and something began to stir inside of him, something, very, very, dangerous. He pocketed his iPhone and tried to think positively.

Chapter
Twenty-Seven

Mason felt refreshed after he'd showered and changed into his work clothes. It was Thursday, and he was looking forward to his night out with his physio Barbra Lockwood. He still hadn't decided where to take her, but he was working on it. He had a couple of places in mind and was definitely out to impress. *Stay clear of the usual dives,* he told himself.

By the time he'd reached the third-floor landing at Gateshead Police Station, he'd run out of steam. He stood for a moment as two uniformed police officers approached along the corridor. It wasn't looking good suddenly and he pulled out his iPhone and pretended to text.

'Ah, Detective Chief Inspector Mason,' the familiar high-pitched voice screeched out from the floor level below. 'Have you got a minute?'

As DI Gamble faced him from the bottom of the stairwell, Mason felt a sudden rush of adrenaline. 'I'm in a hurry,' he replied, 'can it wait?'

'It will only take a minute, so we might as well get it over with.'

'How can I help?'

'It's about this recent meeting you've set up involving some of my team.'

Mason looked at her oddly. 'What about it?'

'It would have been courteous to ask me first.'

'Tell me, DI Gamble. Do you always decide who is guilty then look for the evidence to support it? Is that how things are done back in Middlesbrough?'

'What are you inferring?'

'If I want to hold a meeting, I will do.'

'Who is charge of the operation here?'

Mason rounded on her. 'I once knew a police officer in London who used to operate like you do. Two good detectives lost out on promotion because of him.'

'Is this another one of your sarcastic remarks?'

'No, but I'm—'

'If it is, then this isn't the right time and place.'

'Tell me. Why didn't you give young Martin Kennedy police protection when I asked you to?'

'I didn't think it necessary.'

'You didn't think!'

Gamble pointed a finger at him – bad mistake.

'How can you trust a boy who is constantly up to his neck in trouble. If I'm not mistaken, he was lying his way out of trouble after bunking off school.' She sucked in the air. 'Young Kennedy's nothing but a troublemaker, anyone who meets him will tell you that.'

'I'm one of your old school police officers,' Mason calmly replied. 'I like to assemble the evidence and see which way it points before I make a decision.'

'Tell me,' she said. 'Who's responsible for the daily running of operations?'

Not any longer, Mason thought.

'Have you talked to Martin's father lately. . . listened to what he has to say?'

'No, and I have no intention of doing so either.' Gamble hunched her shoulders. 'Like father, like son, the man has a criminal record as long as your arm and cannot be trusted.'

'So, you do judge a person by their appearance then look for the evidence to incriminate them?'

She lowered her eyes a fraction. 'And what are you suggesting?'

'You're treading on thin ice, DI Gamble.'

'Really?

'Yes, you—'

'You know I'm right,' Gamble seethed. 'You were too pig headed to even ask me for a search warrant when you broke into Laurence Cooper's property.'

Hold your nerve, Jack.

'You're forgetting who the senior officer is here.'

Gamble's face contorted into something almost unrecognisable. 'Don't try and pull rank on me,' she snarled. 'You've criticised my every move the minute I first set foot in the place and took charge of your team.'

'What the—'

'You can't live with it, can you? You feel threatened by it.'

'It's not about rank, it's about the respect.'

'You've not heard the last of this.'

'No, I suppose not.'

She glared at him, all colour drained from her face. 'Just because you're the senior officer on the case doesn't mean you can trample all over me.'

'It's not what you do that annoys me,' Mason continued unruffled. 'It's what you don't do when I advise you to do something. That really gets under my skin.'

It had finally come to head, and Mason was surprised at the calmness of his voice. Yes, she had a valid point. He had felt threatened, but she was conniving behind his back with an eye on his position. Not any longer. Not now he was back in the driving seat. No doubt she would go running to Gregory's office with her tales of woe, but that didn't bother him either.

Proud at having kept his temper under control, there was a new spring in his step as he moved back along the corridor.

***

It was red hot inside Meeting Room One, even with all the windows open. Mason felt a new excitement inside as he stood in front of the assembled team. As the crown prosecution's case crumbled all around them, the Home Secretary was keen to put a stop to it. Whoever was tangled up in this international money laundering scam had certainly done their homework. Events were piling up too fast, and Mason was having to work flat out just to keep his head above the waterline. If the worst happened, and Yavlinsky did manage to penetrate his security ring, he would be ready and waiting for him. This wasn't about law and order anymore, this was a matter of survival. Knowing that MI5 were involved, only added to the seriousness of the situation.

Mason had kept his team small and compact. Everyone present that morning was a trained firearms expert and knew how to handle a range of weapons. He'd been down this avenue before, but the world had moved on since then. This time felt different, though. More hazardous, especially knowing the Russian mafia could be involved.

There was a knock at the door and DS Savage entered.

'You said your office, boss.'

'Sorry, George. Last minute changes,' Mason apologised.

Superintendent Gregory was next to appear in the doorway and everyone sat to attention.

'Good morning everyone,' he announced. 'I'll not keep you longer than necessary.'

MR-1 was subdued, and after grabbing a coffee from a side table, Gregory gave a brief overview of the Chief Constable's plans. The mere mention of the Home Secretary had certainly gained their attention, and by the time he'd finished you could have heard a pin drop.

'So, this is purely a close protection operation?' asked DS Holt.

'Yes. Operation Drawbridge as it is now known, will be controlled from here in Gateshead – although our key source of intelligence will come via Special Branch. Our main remit is one of containment, protecting those involved in the Crown Prosecution's forthcoming trial against the Russian investment bank. Although only a small part of a much bigger operation, it is an important one nevertheless.'

'Could there be an overlap in the operational structure, sir?' asked DC Carrington.

'No doubt there will be. That said, I have the Chief Constable's assurances that whatever we need to bring this operation to a successful conclusion will be made available to us.'

DS Savage raised a hand to speak. 'What do we know about this Russian agent's movements, sir?'

'As far as we know, Grigori Yavlinsky is still in the capital and locked in a pattern of high escalation. No doubt the Joint Intelligence Committee will fill us in with any new developments, but I'm informed the chatter lines coming out of the Russian Embassy have recently intensified, which means that something is about to take place.'

'Do we know what?'

'Rest assured, the minute I'm informed you'll be kept in the loop. Which reminds me,' Gregory said, opening his hands expansively. 'This operation is covered by the Official Secrets Act, so anyone who is unfamiliar with what that entails, I suggest you read up on it before you put pen to paper.'

With that the Area Commander replaced his peaked cap and briskly stepped out of the meeting room, leaving Jack Mason to get on with it.

CHAPTER

TWENTY-EIGHT

As soon as he ended the call, Jack Mason stood thinking about young Martin Kennedy's security arrangements – or lack of them. Now that DCs Carrington and Richie had established a regular school run, he decided to shuffle things around. Still paranoid of Martin possibly blowing his own cover at his new school, Mason wasn't sleeping at all well at night. If there were flaws in his plans, a trained agent would uncover them.

Mason, faced with a difficult decision, looked out from the surveillance house in Seaton Sluice and across at the North Sea. Martin's first week at his new school had gone well considering, and the team's defensive shield was beginning to run like clockwork. His biggest concern was what to do during the school summer holidays. That worried him. If the Russian was to make a kidnap attempt, that would be the best time to do it. However vulnerable the target of a professional assassin might be, it wasn't going to happen on his watch.

Sliding his hand around the butt of his trusty Smith & Wesson 36, Mason checked the safety catch was on. Next, he fiddled with the holster and tightened the strap. Apart from regular visits to the practice range, it seemed a lifetime since he last carried a firearm on operations. It felt good working on close protection again, but the risks were enormous. One momentary lapse in concentration, a careless slip of the tongue, and it could all end in disaster.

Nothing was ever straightforward in this game. Even if you'd prepared for every eventuality the enemy would always find your weakest spot. No, Mason thought, his best line of defence would be to vary the boy's daily routine. Mix things up – no two days the same. This was an anxious waiting game they were playing, a simple matter of holding their nerve.

Like most senior detectives he knew, Mason always felt uncomfortable when entering a strange environment. As he ran a beady eye over Martin's foster mother's property next door, he was looking for cracks in their armoury. Barely twenty metres away from the surveillance house, with clear unobstructed views overlooking the street, it was a formidable fortress to penetrate. The tech team had done a fantastic job installing CCTV cameras, and every room in the property had been fitted with movement detectors. Even the foster mother's phonelines were monitored, and there was little chance of anyone entering the property without the surveillance team knowing.

Mason could hear music coming from the back of the building. Penny Lane, a Beatles track and one of his favourite songs. It had been years since he'd last heard it played, and the memories all came flooding back.

Then he heard footsteps approaching.

Wearing a Ralph Lauren black sweater shirt, casual trousers and trainers, DS Holt cut a dash as he entered from the hallway. 'What's the latest on Stephen Rice?'

'Still nothing from the UK Border Force,' Mason replied.

'He's obviously skipped the country.'

'It would appear so.'

The surveillance house had an empty feel, sparsely furnished and devoid of character. Set back from a large bay window a large camouflage net stood. Although restricting the light, any internal movements would not be spotted from outside the building. Taking centre stage was a high definition professional camcorder, and behind that a large folding table crammed full of sophisticated surveillance equipment. It included monitor screens, listening devices, and a communication system linked directly to police Central Control.

Mason was about to say something when his iPhone pinged.

He answered it.

'What's the weather like up there?'

He immediately recognized the cockney accent. It was the Special Branch officer he'd met in Gregory's office a few days earlier. Strange he should make direct contact on his iPhone, Mason thought.

'It's ninety-five degrees, and everyone up here is sweating their bollocks off.'

'Pull the other leg, it's not what I'm seeing on my webcam.'

Mason grinned. 'What can I do for you?'

'I've been asked to keep in regular contact with you and hope it's not inconvenient.'

'Of course not.'

'Good. Now that's over with I thought I'd bring you up to speed with the latest developments. There's a lot of mixed chatter coming out of Europe lately. Two days ago, Grigori Yavlinsky flew into London on a European flight out of Stuttgart and checked into the Russian Embassy in Kensington Palace Garden. This is his third flight in as many weeks, and we believe it's in connection with this money laundering scam he's tied up in.'

'What makes you think that?'

'We know he's been in regular contact with the bank's defence lawyers, a company in Oxford Street. But that's none of your concern.' The officer sighed. 'What is, though, is that around the time your barrister went missing he was known to have been in the country.'

'Do we know where?' Mason quizzed.

'At first we thought he was stopping at a local address in the capital, but it later transpired he wasn't.'

'So, he could have travelled to Newcastle in other words.'

'He most likely did.'

'Where's Yavlinsky now?' Mason asked.

'He's recently purchased an upmarket Regency Georgian terraced property in Belgravia and is having extensive renovations carried out. We know he's using it as a meeting place, and it's been on our radar for several months.'

Mason jotted down some notes. 'He's obviously using it as a base.'

'We believe so and have some great footage to back it up.'

'Any chance of sending me a copy?'

'No problem. I was intending to do that anyway.'

'That would be very useful,' Mason added.

'There's something else you should know. Twelve months ago, Yavlinsky purchased several exclusive apartments in New York and we know the FBI are looking into it. From what we can gather, he's building up a portfolio of fashionable properties in several other major capitals around the globe.'

Mason shook his head. 'It sounds like he's offloading his dirty money into non-traceable tangible assets.'

'He is. On the surface everything looks legit, which makes this impending Newcastle trial much more important to these people.'

'Which is probably why they're keen to disrupt it?'

'Right again.' The senior officer chuckled. 'Once we've established which other banks are involved in the scam, we'll know the true extent of their operations.'

'I though you already had a list of those involved?'

'It's not that simple.'

Mason looked at the monitor screen, then checked the street outside. 'Do you know who else Yavlinsky has been in contact with lately?'

'According to our man at the embassy, he's very much involved with the renovations at the Belgravia property he's having done. Builders, plasterers, painters and decorators, you name it, they're all in there. It could be a front, of course. We know he has a network of intelligence agents working behind the scenes, along with a bunch of people at the Russian embassy.'

'He's a busy man by the sounds.'

'It's my guess he's waiting for further instructions from Moscow before he makes his next moves.'

'And how will you know when that happens?'

'We've tapped into their phone calls, and that's when the chatter lines go crazy.'

Mason thought a moment. 'This property in Belgravia he owns, is it bugged?'

'No, these people are experts at uncovering intelligence devices, and we don't want to spook them at this point. Whoever's behind this money laundering scam is determined to see this through. Having taken out a prosecution barrister and tampered with vital evidence at the Sanderson Law Chambers, there's no limit to what these people are capable of.'

'They seem determined to eliminate the source of the problem?' Mason added.

'The way things are going, the Crown Prosecution won't have a case to present before the courts before long.'

'What about this hedge fund auditor, Stephen Rice?'

'There's still no feedback as to his whereabouts, so he could have already slipped out of the country by now. The last we heard he'd left the capital having moved south somewhere.'

'Do we think the Russians could have got to him?'

'It's possible, who knows. We've had dozens of potential sightings of Rice and every one of them has drawn a blank. If we do hear anything, I'll let you know.'

'Thanks, that would be useful,' Mason acknowledged.

'Stay vigilant and whatever you do, don't drop your guard.'

There was a click on the line.

Then silence.

Mason sipped his coffee as he glanced out of the surveillance house window. It wasn't the best news he could have wished for, but at least it was candid. If the Russians were intending to eliminate anyone who was a risk to them, it didn't bode well for young Martin Kennedy.

He stared at his watch, then out at the rugged coastline. It was time to go with instincts – run back over the school's security arrangements again. Not that there were any flaws in his plans, but contentment was a breeding ground for complacency, he mused.

CHAPTER TWENTY-NINE

A warm wind had whipped up through the streets of Gateshead as Jack Mason entered the police station that morning. Still, he thought. His night out with Barbara, his physiotherapist, had gone better than planned. He definitely felt passionately drawn to her, and they'd got on like a house on fire. He mustn't rush into, though. Take things easy, see what develops. . .

The front desk was busy, and the sergeant in charge seemed his usual jovial self as he whistled an unrecognisable tune that was driving everybody mad.

'It's official,' Sergeant Whitaker excitedly announced, waving a fist in the air.

Mason screwed his face up. 'What the hell are you on about now?'

'DI Gamble, she's gone back to Middlesbrough.'

'When was this?'

'Last night, according to Rob Savage. Now you're back in charge of the case, it seems her temporary assignment has finally come to an end.'

Throughout his career, Mason had come to expect the unexpected and that some matters were never quite what they seemed. If you needed to know what was going on in the world, you either asked the cleaning ladies or stopped by the sergeant's front desk. Tittle-tattle ran rife throughout the building, and some people had a knack of sniffing out information.

Two days away from his desk, and the DCI's in-tray had given birth. It didn't take much, and paperwork was the bane of every police officer's life. Nothing got swept under the carpet these days. If you wanted a new notebook and pencil you had to sign for one. Government cutbacks ran deep, and everyone was accountable.

First, he fired up his computer, then checked the overnight serials. Two break-ins in the Felling, a pub brawl in Bensham, and a sixty-four-year-old man badly beaten up on Gateshead High Street by drunken revellers. In all a busy night, Mason thought. The local scumbags had certainly been active. Everything ran in a cycle, which meant the cells would be busy these next few weeks. As he leaned across his desk in search of a file, it was then he spotted the sealed brown envelope, marked confidential in thick bold red letters. He opened it and removed a CD sent from his MI5 contact, half expecting to see a note inside – there wasn't one.

Next, he loaded the CD onto the computer tray, pressed the start button and adjusted the sound. The first shots, he guessed, were surveillance footage of the suspect's large Regency terraced property in London. Guarded at the front by a high wrought iron fence, a large metal skip stood close to the pavement's edge with a long white plastic chute attached to it. As the camera lens panned in, he noticed it ran all the way up to the second floor and was attached to the support scaffolding. He could see a workman dropping building rubble into it, and it was throwing up a lot of dust.

Then, through the ground floor main entrance, two men appeared. One looked professional and carried a briefcase in his hand, the other was short and thickset. He looked mid-forties with a round face and clean-shaven head. As the two men went their separate ways, he made a mental note of their features.

The next video footage was of the Executive VIP Lounge at Heathrow Airport. He'd been there on several occasions in the past, whilst working on an undercover sting operation involving people smuggling. Very little had changed, and as he familiarised himself with the layout, he adjusted the focus. Two people were sitting on high stools chatting at a bar. The man on the right was obviously Grigori Yavlinsky, and the woman on his left was blonde, slim, elegant looking, with long shapely legs. Their conversation appeared relaxed, as if they knew one another intimately.

Seconds later he was staring at the departure gate for an 11.30 am Aeroflot flight to Moscow. As the VIP passengers were being called forward to the flight check-in desk, he watched as the suspects moved towards it together.

Mason ran the video through several times, freeze framing at intervals. He knew that Russian passports were red in colour and carried a double headed eagle on the front cover, but these were burgundy with REPUBLICA MOLDOVA and the word PASAPORT inscribed below the coat of arms. As they entered the departure hall together, it was then he noticed that the man was carrying a diplomatic bag tucked under his arm – which seemed kind of odd when he thought about it.

Pleased with his findings, he grabbed a couple more screenshots and ran off several prints. If this was the same man that young Martin Kennedy had spotted in Chopwell Wood, he now had a good set of images to present to him. Even so, Yavlinsky looked nothing like the family photographs of the boy's Uncle Arthur, but that didn't mean a thing. Hopefully the shock of seeing his assailant again might spark the boy into making a positive identification – or run the risk of sending him into his shell again!

There was a knock at the door and DC Manley breezed in.

'What can I do for you?'

'It might not be much, but we're getting reports of a couple of burnt-out vehicle wrecks over in the Stanley area. They think one of them could be the vehicle the boy spotted in Chopwell Wood.'

'Good work, Harry. Contact Road Traffic and get them to run a check on the vehicle's VIN.'

'Will do, boss.'

Mason was having a good day, but that could change in the drop of a hat. If this was the stolen black Volvo that Yavlinsky had driven to Chopwell Wood, it could be the breakthrough he was looking for. Just to make sure, he rang the local constabulary with the instruction to carry out a door-to-door enquiry, reminding him to keep an eye out for CCTV footage.

After the call, Mason stood there, pondering over the case. Who was this man who could attract so much attention and keep cabinet ministers up late into the night? Anxious to find out, it suddenly felt good being back in control of his own destination again. Things were looking up, in more ways than one, he thought.

His iPhone rang – but it wasn't the news he'd been expecting to hear.

CHAPTER THIRTY

Earlier that morning, having searched through a large selection of mugshot images of Grigori Yavlinsky taken at Heathrow airport, young Martin Kennedy was unable to make a positive connection. It was the setback the team had been dreading, but not all was lost, thought DC Carrington. These things took time, and there were other ways of gleaning information out of the boy without having to force the issue.

The minute the school bell rang, hundreds of children spilled onto the playground and walked towards the main entrance gates. It was Friday, and Carrington was eagerly looking forward to a few days off from her close protection duties. It had been a difficult week, and Martin was severely testing her patience, as he was always the last to appear out of class.

After the two CP Officers had waited a full five minutes, and Martin still didn't show, Detective Carrington walked towards one of the side gates. As the last of the stragglers sauntered aimlessly into the nearby estate with their minders, she began to fear the worst. Something was wrong, and the moment the school caretaker appeared from one of the side doors she felt her stomach lurch.

'We're here to pick up young Martin Kennedy,' she said authoritatively. 'Has he been held back after class for some reason?'

The caretaker looked at her quizzically. 'Martin Kennedy you say. Give me a minute and I'll find out for you.'

As her mind lapsed into troubled thoughts, Carrington slipped back into protection mode. Where the hell was he? Martin had never done anything like this before – so *why now?* She could see the lollipop man was preparing to leave, and no other children were in sight.

The tension inside now building, she wanted to scream out.

Then, through the main school entrance the headteacher appeared.

'We've checked with the history teacher and Martin left along with the other children in his class.'

'Well he's not here!'

'Have you tried the other school gates?'

'No. Martin has strict instructions to meet us here after school every night.'

The headteacher's phone rang.

'I'm sorry, but we've searched the building thoroughly and he's definitely not here.'

'Where is he, then? I thought you people were responsible for his safety during school hours?'

The headteacher looked at her bemused. 'I'm sorry. He must have slipped through the net and made his own way home?'

'Hardly,' Carrington replied, 'you know he's not allowed to do that.'

'In which case I think we'd better send a search party out for him.'

Carrington felt the hairs on the back of her neck prickle as she made a few frantic calls. The moment she rang Jack Mason, a full-scale operation was thrown into place. Her heart sank. Please God, she thought. If Martin was last seen hanging around the school grounds with classmates, could the Russian have got to him?

***

Blue lights flashing, DS Savage at the wheel, the unmarked police car sped south along the A193 towards Whitley Bay. It was 6:15 pm, and two boys wearing black school uniforms had been spotted close to St Mary's lighthouse. It wasn't a lot to go on, Mason thought, but at least it was the first real sighting since the alarm was raised. Missing children were every policeman's nightmare as you never knew what to expect. If Martin had been snatched from under their noses, then how had Yavlinsky penetrated his security ring?

At the north end of the Links mini golf course and opposite the crematorium, Savage swung left along a narrow lane hugging the coastline. It was a tense few minutes, and as the unmarked police vehicle sped towards St Mary's lighthouse the car radio kept spewing out undecipherable updates. Two long hours had passed since Mason's full-scale search had been put into operation, and he was now fearing the worst.

'There, boss,' Savage suddenly announced. 'Over by the point.'

Pulling up short of the concrete causeway, Mason clambered out of the passenger seat and stood for a moment. He could see the tide was on the turn, and an hour from now the small rocky tidal island would be cut off from the mainland. Further north and hugging the North East coastline, he noticed two dark silhouettes scrambling amongst the rocks. Whoever they were, they were searching for something and oblivious of the dangers now surrounding them.

Fighting back his fears, Mason set off along the rugged shoreline to the sound of crashing waves. The North Sea seemed angry today, madder than ever. Half a mile from the causeway, he noticed the tide was creeping in. Then, two hundred metres to his left, he could just make out the boys' black school uniforms.

His handset crackled.

'I'm getting reports of two boys out searching for fossils,' DS Savage said. 'They were spotted by a local fisherman about an hour ago.'

'Roger that,' Mason replied. 'I'm fast closing in on them.'

It wasn't often he lost his bravado, but the moment he spotted young Martin's mischievous face, Mason let out a sigh of relief. Having lost all track of time, the two young boys seemed oblivious of his presence.

'What the hell are you two up to?' the Chief Inspector yelled out.

'Nowt much.'

'I thought we'd agreed you were to report to the main gates after school?' The young boy shrugged as though he couldn't have cared less, and Mason remonstrated in his sterner authoritarian voice. 'Are you listening to me, son, or are your ears stuffed full of cotton wool?'

'Nah, but look what we've found, Jack.'

Mason flinched. 'What the hell—'

Martin handed him a small rock. 'It's a brachiopod.'

'A what?' Mason shrieked.

'A brachiopod, it's a marine animal and it's millions of years old.'

'Never mind how old it is, who said you two could come here after school?'

'Me and my mate Dez decided to take a look.'

'Why didn't you ask me before deciding to come by yourselves? The last time you did that you—' Mason cut himself off mid-sentence. Still straining at the bit, he glared at the boy, and said, 'Well?'

'Cos.'

'Cos what?' Mason insisted.

'If you must know, we were planning on coming here during the school holidays.'

'Who else knows you are here?'

'I talked to my foster Ma, and she said it would be okay.'

Deep down Mason saw the funny side but wasn't letting on about it.

'Did she now?'

'Yes, and she said she would talk to you about it.'

Mason stared at Martin's partner in crime and almost burst out laughing. What his mother would think of him when she saw the state of his school uniform was anyone's guess. 'And what about you, son,' Mason said sternly. 'Does your mother know where you are?'

'Nah, but she knows I'm with Marty.'

Mason stood for a moment and wondered what he'd let himself in for. Armed police officers everywhere, a Russian assassin on the loose, and two ten-year-old boys sending his blood-pressure soaring sky-high. This sort of thing hadn't happened to him in a long time, and he'd almost forgotten how to deal with it. Not since his own daughter had gone missing in one of the local shopping malls, had he worried as much as this before. Even then she'd only been missing a few minutes. Not two bloody hours like these two reprobates, he cursed. At least they were both safe and it hadn't turned into the disaster he thought it would.

His handset crackled into life again.

'Need any assistance, boss?' DS Savage asked over the airwaves.

'No, they're both fine.' Mason looked at the small rock that Martin had handed him and then said. 'Tell me, Rob. What do you know about brachiopods?'

'Not a lot. Isn't that a Russian football team?'

'I don't think so.' Mason chuckled.

'Never heard of it before, boss. What is it?'

'I'll talk to you later about it.' Mason stood for a moment and tried to clear his head. 'Best call the rest of the search team off, Rob. Stand everyone down.'

'Roger that.'

Never a dull moment, Mason thought.

The tide was well in when they scrambled over the rocks and finally made it back to the unmarked pool car. As water lapped the causeway, twenty minutes from now and St Mary's lighthouse would be completely cut off from the rest of the mainland. It had been a hair-raising experience, and Mason was glad it was over with. But how to occupy a ten-year-old boy's mind over the school holidays was an even bigger nightmare. They could hardly rely on his foster mother to keep him entertained; not in a million years. No, Mason thought. He would need to come up with a better plan, and one that would keep the boy out of mischief. Maybe he should have gone with his instincts, played on his injuries instead of pig-headedly volunteering for a child protection role.

Then he saw the funnier side.

'Okay, you two, it's time to head home,' Mason said, opening the rear door of the Ford Focus.

'Just five more minutes, Jack.'

'Five minutes, my arse,' Mason said firmly. 'You two have caused enough havoc for one day.'

His phone rang. It was DC Carrington and she sounded in a right old state.

'Anymore news on Martin, boss?'

'We found him ten minutes ago.'

'Is he okay?'

'He's as bright as a button.' Mason laughed.

'Thank God for that. The little bugger sneaked out through the back gates according to one of his classmates and never bothered to tell anyone.'

'Tell me about it. We need to come up with a plan 'B', Sue.'

'Why don't we just strap a ball and chain to his foot,' Carrington sighed.

'You wish!'

'I doubt my nerves could stand any more of this, boss. This close protection malarkey is all but doing my head in.'

'Tell me,' Mason said thoughtfully. 'What do you know about brachiopods?'

'Never heard of them. Isn't that something to do with Star Wars?'

'I don't think so.'

'Why don't you try Googling it, boss?'

'Just thinking about my next quiz night at the Ship Inn, that's all.'

'Brachiopods – what are they?'

Mason frowned. 'They've got nothing to do with Star Wars, nor a Russian football team. I'd never heard of them myself until a ten-year boy told me about them.'

'So, what are they?'

'I'm keeping it for a future quiz night.'

His phone went dead.

CHAPTER
THIRTY-ONE

Chameleon sat on his bed at the Premier Inn in Bristol and stared at his watch. It was 9:30 am, and most businessmen had already checked out of the hotel that morning. Through his room window overlooking the roundabout, he could see the A38 was busy. Six hours from now he would be boarding the train back to St Pancras and another mission tucked under his belt. His was a watertight plan, and all that remained now was to execute it.

The aroma of fried bacon hit his nostrils, but he wasn't hungry. It was wafting in through the open hotel window, so he shut it. After logging out of the hotel Wi-Fi, he closed his laptop down and got ready for the task ahead. Down at the reception lobby, he handed in his key card, and slid into the back of a waiting taxi. Everything was paid for by cash. If anyone did ask for his card details, he always walked away from them – nothing was ever traceable that way.

He glanced at his pay-as-you-go phone for messages.

Just one. An important one, nevertheless.

Following the long trail of red stop lights, they inched forward at a snail's pace towards Bristol city centre. He knew they were close, as he could see the university buildings through the cab's tinted windows. After navigating several busy road junctions, he reached forward and tapped the driver on the shoulder.

'How much do I owe you?' Chameleon asked.

'That will be ten pounds, sir.'

'I need a favour.'

'Sure,' the cab driver replied, 'what can I do for you?'

'Fifteen minutes from now, you're to ring this number and ask for me by name.'

He handed the cab driver a slip of paper with Stephen Rice's name written on it, along with a roll of bank notes. As the taxi pulled up outside a Barclays Bank branch, he caught the driver's eye in the rear-view mirror. He was eyeballing the wodge of fivers he'd given him, and his brain was all over the place.

'Sure, Mr Rice. Leave that with me,' the cab driver said turning to face him.

Chameleon looked down at his watch, then into the driver's rear-view mirror again. The street outside looked exposed, dangerous, and full of CCTV cameras.

'Your fifteen minutes starts from now!'

'No problem, sir.'

'Have a good day!'

***

The coffee shop wasn't overly busy, and Chameleon soon spotted Stephen Rice. He was sitting in a corner seat overlooking the high street and watching the world go by. The hedge fund auditor looked gaunt under the strip lighting, as well he might have been. The man had given the Organisation a lot of unnecessary grief lately, but that was about to change.

He pulled up the seat opposite.

'How are you?'

'Fine,' Rice replied.

'Looking forward to some sun time?'

Rice steadied himself. 'I take it you have everything ready for me?'

Chameleon opened his weekend bag and pulled out a portfolio of exclusive properties he'd brought with him along with a bunch of keys. Placing them on the table in front of him, he caught the trace of a smile on Rice's lips. He knew what the man was thinking and let him do the talking. That's where most of his information came from, and he knew which side of the fence Rice was sitting on. Running away from the authorities was one thing, but you never knew who you might bump into in the middle of the night.

'I'll come straight to point with you,' Rice said, as he stroked the outline of his jaw. 'I'm setting up a new business venture in Spain and have a few irons in the fire.'

'What sort of business venture?'

'Wreck diving.'

'Sounds interesting, what made you come up with that idea?'

'I was looking at Malta initially, but it's overexposed.'

Rice was growing in confidence, and Chameleon had picked up on it.

'In what way?' he asked, pretending to show interest.

'Too many people, and too few wrecks,' Rice replied. 'They've recently sunk a few old naval vessels in shallow waters, but it's not the type of wreck diving I'm looking for.'

Rice fiddled with the teapot lid, and Chameleon's eyes lit up.

'So why L'Estartit?'

'The funny thing is,' said Rice, 'when you finally came up with this long-term property plan it really set me thinking. It's perfect. Spain's perfect. And the minute I saw the villa you had to offer, I knew it was for me.'

'Glad to be of assistance. A man who knows what he wants. . . there's nothing wrong with that.'

'Now that the contracts have finally been signed, I can't wait to get started.'

Chameleon tapped the keys with the flat of his hand and fiddled with the key fob. His hesitant, but flawless English, was delivered with an unmistakable Eastern European accent. 'It sounds like you've done your homework, Mr Rice. When exactly do you intend to fly out to Spain?'

'Later tonight.'

'*Tonight!*' Chameleon repeated, accentuating his surprise.

'Yes. I'm booked on the seven o'clock flight to Girona.' Rice pushed back in his seat looking hesitant. 'I was thinking. Would it be possible to take the property keys from tonight? I know it's a week earlier than we agreed, but I'm willing to pay extra.'

Chameleon nodded and then said, 'I can't see that being a problem.'

'That's great,' Rice grinned. 'When you deal with money all day, you know who you can trust.'

'Indeed.'

Chameleon had thought long and hard about a lot of things lately, and how best to finish the job. There were plenty of methods to choose from, and the list seemed endless. Hemlock was an old favourite with the ancient Greeks, and about eight leaves of the plant usually did the trick. Aconite was another preferred toxin used by some of his connections, but he hadn't given it much thought. Also known as wolfsbane, aconite left only one post-morten sign that he knew of, that of asphyxiation as it caused arrhythmic heart function which led to suffocation. But he wanted a much slower death, subtle, and dimethylmercury had crossed his mind. The only problem with that was, it usually took ages to take effect.

It had all come down to something a little more suitable in the end. A slow but silent killer with no known cure. His associates had demanded he use a chemical nerve agent and had insisted they supply him with it. What type, he had no idea, but knew it had effectively been used on former defectors and well-known critics of the State. Some had taken all of three weeks to die, others a little longer. He knew the risks he was undertaking, but all traitors had to die at some point. It was simply a matter of principle.

Chameleon peered over at Stephen Rice's teapot again and checked in his pocket for the small container he'd brought with him. No time was ever convenient in this game, and it would need to be done with the utmost discretion. This was an extremely dangerous substance he was dealing with, and he wasn't taking it lightly.

Then those magic words!

'Is there a Mr Rice in the room?' the waitress suddenly announced.

Still holding up the café telephone receiver in her hand, the moment Rice moved towards the service counter Chameleon was onto it like a flash. First, he checked the surrounding tables, then slipped on the rubber gloves. Next, he carefully screwed the lid of the container open and poured the contents into Rice's teapot. As the hedge fund auditor continued to argue his case over the telephone, he gave it a quick stir.

Perfect!

Rice looked confused as he sat down at the table again. 'Sorry about that . . . some asshole of a taxi driver must have got his wires crossed.'

Chameleon smiled as Rice poured himself another fresh cup of tea. Just one mouthful would be enough! He tapped the property portfolio with an index finger and then said, 'It's an excellent choice, might I add, and the diving around the Mediterranean is all the rage now.'

Rice thought for a moment. 'What about staff . . . cleaners, fresh linen, that sort of thing?'

'Leave that with me, Mr Rice. Everything is taken care of. We can even supply a cordon bleu chef should you require one.'

Rice's face lit up. 'I'm ever so grateful for everything you've done for me, I can't thank you enough.'

The Russian assassin cocked his head to one side and smiled. 'May I ask when you intend to start this new business venture of yours?'

'I was hoping to start in a few weeks.'

'That soon?'

Rice looked at him and frowned. 'That's if everything goes to plan, of course.'

'It's a very popular location, and I know a lot of people who go diving there. You should do really well for yourself, especially with the number of new wrecks that keep popping up.'

Rice took another huge swig of his tea and wiped the corner of his mouth with his napkin. 'If things turn out as I'm hoping they should, I may even wish to extend the lease. Do you see a problem with that?'

'Absolutely not, Mr Rice,' Chameleon said trying his utmost not to laugh. 'Who knows, twelve months from now and you could be the richest man in Spain!'

Rice's grin broadened as he finished off the dregs of his tea.

'Only time will tell, Mr Tarik.'

Indeed, Chameleon smiled inwardly – *and pigs might fly!*

CHAPTER THIRTY-TWO

Seahouses August 2016

They couldn't keep young Martin Kennedy indefinitely cooped up in a safe house over the school holidays, something had to give. Having sought advice from the National Crime Agency, Jack Mason had finally sanctioned a short break to the Farne Islands. Just a few hours, nothing elaborate. At least it made sense, and there was more than enough armed protection officers to keep the boy safe during their visit.

It was a beautiful day; rays of sun were streaking through the unmarked pool car's windscreen as Detective Carrington sped north along the rugged Northumberland coastline towards Seahouses, with Martin keeping her company. She'd taken an instant shine to the boy. They got on well together, and he was not like some of the toe-rags she'd encountered during her time on the force. A little boisterous perhaps, but he was always well-mannered.

Given the choice, she would have preferred to have taken some time off herself, but that wasn't possible now that the Chief Constable was involved. Planning anything nowadays was a nightmare come to think of it, as Operation Drawbridge had taken over her life.

'What kind of birds are those?' Carrington asked.

Martin shielded his eyes from the strong morning sunlight and pointed to a small flock of birds. A dozen or so, skimming the water at speed. 'They're black Guillemots,' the boy explained. 'They breed among the rocks at the base of the cliffs and dive into the water to catch their prey.'

'What are they searching for?'

'Fish and crustaceans mainly. The mad thing is, it's possible to tell if the bird is left or right handed by the way the fish points in their mouths when they carry them.'

'You're joking.'

'I know it sounds crazy, but it's true.'

'You're quite the little expert, aren't you?'

'Nah.' Martin shrugged, as if unaccustomed to praise. 'It's just what I've picked up on the internet.'

'It's all new to me,' she confessed. 'I know nothing about birds except those that come into my garden every day.'

'Do you feed them?'

'Not as often as I should.'

Martin screwed his face in a show of disappointment. 'Poor birds,' he sighed.

Located on the Northumberland coast between Beadnell and Bamburgh, Seahouses was a popular tourist attraction due to its beautiful sandy beaches. Known as the 'Gateway to the Farnes', this quaint little fishing village was an Aladdin's cave of giftshops, arcade amusements, cafes, and fish and chip shops, all centred around its bustling harbour. Most of the fishing vessels were out at sea today, but there were at least a dozen small trip boats hugging the harbour wall in wait of adventurous tourists.

Carrington stopped at a pedestrian crossing to let a young woman with a child in a pushchair cross and could see the iconic Bamburgh Castle in the distance. Once home to the ancient kings of Northumbria, its stunning location not only attracted thousands of tourists to its grounds every year, it was also a major attraction for the Hollywood movie industry.

Her communications earpiece sprang into life.

It was DS Holt who was travelling in convoy with DC Hedley barely a hundred metres behind them. 'How's it going?' asked Holt.

'Just fine. He's never stopped talking from the moment we left his foster mother's house.'

'What about the Chopwell Wood suspect, has he mentioned anything to you yet?'

'I'm working on it,' Carrington replied. 'I'll talk to you later.'

'Roger that.'

As the airwaves fell silent again, Carrington caught the curious look on Martin's face. She'd tried to engage with him on several occasions about the incident, but he was still refusing to talk. God, she thought, he probably felt like sliding under the car seat rather than talk to her about it. It wasn't the kind of encounter that any ten-year-old child should ever have to witness, let alone discuss with grown-ups. No psychiatrist herself, it was difficult to imagine what was going through the young boy's mind. Bad thoughts, probably.

Shortly before ten, they pulled into a small car park overlooking the little fishing harbour. Seahouses was extremely popular, and today was no exception. Not that they were anticipating trouble, but as DS Holt drew up alongside them in an unmarked blue Skoda Octavia, three armed police officers seemed more than adequate protection if any trouble broke out.

Carrington spoke directly to DS Holt through her headset.

'The boat's moored up over by the harbour wall. Once I've paid my parking ticket, I'll make towards it and you two can follow.'

'Don't rush it. Stay focused,' DS Savage advised.

'Will do.'

'Keep your eyes peeled for stragglers hanging around the fringes,' Manley added, annoyingly sucking on another hard boiled sweet.

Normally, Carrington kept a cool head in situations such as these. Not today. No sooner had she displayed her parking ticket on the dash screen, when an eerie sensation crept up on her. As her stare hardened, any one of a thousand tourists could be a potential threat, and there was no way of knowing where the danger might spring from.

At the end of the pier they arrived at the boat's check-in kiosk and paid their money to a man in a blue bib and brace. Deep down, Carrington was quietly looking forward to her venture out to the Farne Islands. The day felt full of promise, despite her headache.

'Harry and I will catch up with you later,' said DS Holt as the three-armed police made their final preparations.

She watched as Detective Constable Manley ran a check on every passenger stood in the queue and signalled his approval. As the last person scrambled aboard, the captain slipped the mooring lines and made towards the harbour entrance. Having sat quietly throughout, a man in a Beanie hat and bright green trousers stood to take a few photographs with an expensive looking camera. Swaying unsteadily on his feet, he nearly lost his balance on several occasions before he finally sat down again.

The islands are split into two groups according to the skipper's running commentary and are known simply as the Inner Group and Outer Group. The Inner Group, which they were now heading for, consisted of several islands including Knoxes Reef and the East and West Wideopens. At very low tide they were all joined together, but not today they weren't. The tide was in and they were separated by a heavy two-metre swell.

'Look,' Martin suddenly pointed out. 'Razorbills and puffins – thousands of them.'

A stout man in a white baseball cap aimed his camera at them, and shouted, 'They look like sea parrots to me, son.'

Martin screwed his face up, annoyed at the man's stupid remarks. 'They're actually a member of the auk family and breed here between April and late July.'

'Is that so,' the man smiled mischievously. 'So, what happens to them for the rest of the year?'

'They fly out to sea, overwintering on the water and return here to raise their young.'

'You certainly know your onions.'

Martin cocked his head to one side and addressed the man directly. 'Puffins don't nest on the rocks, they dig rabbit-like burrows to nest in.'

Having met his match, the man turned sheepishly away as though thoroughly humiliated.

As the boat pitched and yawed in the heavy swell, they slowly made their way around the Inner Farne. Keen not to miss the lighthouse where the Victorian heroine Grace Darling along with her father had rescued survivors from the wreck of the Forfarshire, Carrington stood to take a closer look. As for the doe-eyed grey seals that lolloped on rocky ledges and frolicked in the sea, she couldn't have cared less. It was a wonderful sight; but the rocking motion of the boat and cold salt spray wafting in her face had left her feeling queasy. Gripping the handrail with both hands, she was determined to ride it out. It was a weird sensation, but to everyone's amazement young Martin kept up with his running commentary throughout.

Within seconds of the captain warning of choppy waters ahead, the passengers were thrown into sudden turmoil. To the sounds of human voices in various stages of dismay and excitement, the boat pitched and rolled in a heavy swell as it made its way back to the harbour. Buffeted in all directions, huge clouds of sea spray were sent in all directions, as passengers held on for dear life.

★★★

Back on dry land, and now working in close protection mode, the three-armed officers approached the car park with caution. As Carrington stepped aside to let an old man in a wheelchair pass through, she kept a close eye out for any suspicious movements. Seahouses was busy, and it only took a second. A knife to the throat, a bullet to the head, that's how these people liked to operate.

'That man over there,' Martin suddenly announced. 'He looks like my Uncle Arthur.'

Everyone froze.

It was only a fleeting glance, but Carrington's reaction was instantaneous. Immediately grabbing hold of the boy, her free hand reaching towards the Glock pistol, she felt an adrenaline rush. In what seemed to her to be in slow motion. . . not fifty metres away the suspect had homed in on them and was closing down at speed.

Not a short man, thickset, with a rounded rubbery face and balding hairline, he carried the look of uncertainty in his glances.

Who is he? Carrington wondered.

'Holy shit,' Manley called out. 'It's him—'

'Not so fast,' the sergeant replied, calmly tugging on Manley's shirt sleeve. 'He's much too tall to be our suspect.'

With no time to think, time seemed to go into suspension.

Unfazed, DS Holt sucked in air through gritted teeth. 'If it is him, he could be carrying a gun.'

Manley patted his pistol holster. 'I'm on it, Sarge.'

'Don't get carried away, let's see what transpires first.'

The distance between them closing, Carrington bundled Martin into the back seat of the unmarked pool car and told him to lie down. There was little doubt what the stranger was intending to do, and everything was moving so quickly. As she slid to the rear of the vehicle, she unholstered her Glock pistol and pointed it to the ground by both hands.

She teased back the safety catch and prepared to take aim.

'Take him from both sides,' she shouted. 'I'm locked and loaded.'

Manley moved first.

Stepping to his right, his hand was hovering over his pistol holster like a gunslinger in a Western Movie, Carrington felt the hairs on the back of neck prickle. Holt moved next – darting to his left and crouching low as he went.

The man approaching faltered, then stopped.

'What is this?' he protested.

He wasn't as tall as Holt had first made him out to be, not more that five-foot six. He wore a white button-downsweat shirt and black pants and carried a cross-body bag over his shoulder. After a moment of posturing, Manley rushed forward spun him round and slammed his body against the nearest car's bonnet.

'What the hell is going on?' the man shouted.

With one hand holding the man's arm up his back, the other holding his warrant card to his face, Manley read him his rights.

It was over in seconds.

As Holt ran forward and applied his handcuffs, he spun the man around again. He was muttering something inaudible, but the sergeant never took his eyes off him as he searched the man's pockets. Recovering the suspect's iPhone, Holt punched a number into the keypad and waited for the phone to boot up.

'He's not our man,' the sergeant announced.

The stranger looked at him confused. 'Who the hell did you think I was?'

'Sorry,' said DS Holt, removing the man's handcuffs. 'You're free to go, sir.'

'What's happening?' the man insisted.

Holt returned the man's iPhone and pointed towards the harbour wall. 'Thank you for your cooperation, please be so kind as to move away from the area.'

Still protesting his innocence, the man stormed off in a huff.

Yet another false alarm, Carrington thought. Everyone was getting tetchy and it was definitely time to make tracks.

CHAPTER

THIRTY-THREE

Earlier that morning

Relaxed in the knowledge that young Martin Kennedy was now in safe hands, Jack Mason entered Newcastle law courts unaware of the events taking place further north. They were now entering the fourth day of the trial, and the media circus never ceased to amaze him. Some cases hung in the balance and getting a conviction could be extremely difficult at times. Not so in this case. The prosecution evidence stacked against Angelica Glebova, an 18-year-old Estonian illegal immigrant charged with two counts of murder, was overwhelming, and there was little doubt the jury would find her guilty.

With little room for manoeuvre, Glebova's defence lawyers were claiming their client was still suffering from traumatic brain injuries following a stolen police vehicle chase she was involved in. They were getting nowhere, of course. Mr Armstrong QC, counsel for the Crown Prosecution, had thrown their claims out of the window as utter nonsense. By the time he'd finished, everyone in Courtroom One was under no illusions where the truth lay.

The case was a complex one and centred around her dead partner, serial killer Patrick Stanley – responsible for five counts of murder. Having lured their prey back to Stanley's house, they strangled and dismembered their victims' bodies using a surgical power saw. And to muddy the water, to overcome the difficult task of getting rid of the bodies they had transported them around in suitcases and dropped them off at local refuge tips. Everyone accused had the right to a fair trial, Mason thought, but these crimes had gone 'beyond the pale'.

As he walked down the long marble corridor towards Waiting Room One, Mason kept getting flashbacks. He could vividly recollect being stabbed by the serial killer, but the rest was lost in a haze of confusion. In truth he owed his life to a lot of people, including a quick-thinking ship's medical doctor, paramedics, emergency crash teams, and the surgeons at Newcastle Royal Victoria Infirmary who had stopped massive internal haemorrhaging. He'd been extremely lucky, and every single one of them had contributed to saving his life.

'Ah, DCI Mason,' the Area Commander said as he approached from one of the side rooms carrying a bundle of case files under his arm. 'What time are you due in the witness stand?'

'Ten-thirty, sir.'

'Fingers crossed, eh?'

Dressed in police uniform, Area Commander Gregory seemed in a jovial mood, which was always a sign to tread cautiously. Mason took a step back. 'Yes, sir. Let's hope the jury agrees with us.'

'It's all going swimmingly well according to Mr Armstrong QC, and we should get the conviction we are looking for. It's a pity Patrick Stanley won't be around to face the music, but his death will save the taxpayer a lot of money.' The Area Commander stared at him quizzically. 'The strange thing is, we're getting reports that Stanley's been seen hanging around the court building. Have you heard anything to that effect?'

'No, sir. I haven't.'

'Just as a precautionary measure I've bolstered up our security arrangements. It's probably nothing, but you never know with these things.'

Mason thought a moment. 'You obviously have some reservations, sir.'

'With this amount of media coverage, we cannot be seen to be doing nothing.' The Area Commander shook his head. 'Mind, it's probably a hoaxer who wants to have their two-penneth. . . better safe than sorry, eh?'

'No show without punch.' Mason chuckled somewhat relieved.

Gregory fell silent, thinking.

God forbid that Patrick Stanley was still alive, Mason thought. Despite a huge search operation taking place after throwing himself off the Amsterdam Ferry, the Suitcase Man's body had never resurfaced again. Missing, presumed drowned wasn't the result the police had been hoping for, as it always left an element of doubt in people's minds. Even so, the River Tyne was notorious for its strong tidal undercurrents around the North Shields Ferry Terminal, so it may well have been washed out to sea.

'Any more news from Special Branch, sir?'

'No, it's all gone quiet.'

'That's odd. I would have thought they'd be in regular contact with you?'

'Not lately, they haven't. I suspect they're onto something.'

'There is that aspect to it.'

Gregory held his gaze. 'I hear you've despatched young Martin Kennedy to Seahouses for the day. Do you think that's wise?'

Mason was quick to react. 'As a matter of fact, I ran it past the National Crime Agency and they were quite happy with our security arrangements. Besides, a boat trip to the Farne Islands might do the lad the world of good.'

'What makes you say that?'

'Letting off steam, sir. The boy's bored out of his mind at being cooped up in a safe house all day, and I was hoping he might open up and tell us a few of his concerns about what took place in Chopwell Wood.'

'There is that element to it, I suppose.' Gregory stared at his watch. 'The last thing we want is for him to go wandering off on his own again.'

'Not with a trained security team around him, he won't.'

'Tell me,' said Gregory pensively. 'What arrangements have we put in place with his current school?'

'Regarding what, sir?'

'His identity. . . how secure is it?'

'Other than social services and what he's told his foster mother, I doubt anyone knows his background.'

The Area Commander hesitated and then said. 'Children talk, Jack. If Martin doesn't know the danger, he's in, then he's bound to engage with other children about his past.'

'He'll not do that, sir. Even the specialist teams couldn't get a squeak out of him about what he saw in Chopwell Wood, so I doubt he'll want to discuss it with school mates.'

'It's not my understanding of kids. They like to fantasise, show off in front of their peers. We need to keep a watchful eye on him, make sure he doesn't let the cat out of the bag!'

'Not with the amount of team effort that's gone into the operation, sir. Even if he does, what use is it to them?'

Gregory checked his watch again as if time was a premium. 'Before I forget, there's been another break-in at the Sanderson Law Chambers. Ponteland are currently dealing with it, and I've asked Tom Hedley to get involved.'

'Anything stolen?'

'It's still early days,' Gregory replied. 'One of the clerks believes it could have been an opportunist thief, as they'd masked one of the windows with heavy duty duct tape before smashing it to gain entry. It set off the burglar alarms and Forth Bank Police Station were onto it within minutes.'

'Coincidence perhaps?'

'Let's hope so, but I doubt it's connected.'

They were joined by the court usher, a stout man with a hooked nose and wearing a long black gown. 'Ah, Detective Chief Inspector Mason,' he said, staring down at his clipboard. 'I have you down for Courtroom One at ten-o'clock.'

'That's correct.'

'I'd be obliged if you could make your way to the waiting room, sir.'

'And Miss Glebova,' Mason asked. 'Will she be in attendance today?'

The usher wrinkled his nose. 'In body, but not in mind, I'm afraid.'

'Still refusing to cooperate, is she?'

The usher nodded. 'Those were your words not mine, sir. She's a strange individual, that one. Never says peep in court, just sits and stares at the judge all the time.'

'Past experience tells me she's faking it.' Mason shrugged. 'But it's up to us to prove she's guilty and she's obviously making us work for our money.'

'Only time will tell.' The usher smiled, as he took off down the corridor and disappeared into the back of the building.

'I'll leave you to get on with it,' the Area Commander acknowledged. 'It seems you have a rather busy day in front of you.'

'Never a dull moment.' Mason smiled.

★★★

That evening in the lounge of the Ship Inn, in Benton, Jack Mason was aware of the minutes ticking by. After another hard-fought day in court, he was really looking forward to another relaxing evening with his physiotherapist friend, Barbara Lockwood. It was a funny old world, Mason thought. One minute you were down on your luck, the next you were in seventh heaven.

He took a deep breath and stared at the text message again – *7:30's fine, X.*

Mason's marital life had been a total train wreck, there were no other words to describe it. Ever since the divorce he'd struggled to settle into a regular routine. His financial affairs were a mess, and the thought of being stuck in the same house on his own for the rest of his life was slowly driving him insane. He felt ready to freshen things up in his life, start up new adventures with a new partner.

He was about to order another pint, then thought better of it. Instead, he let the dregs hang in the bottom of the glass. The more he thought about it, the more he was looking forward to meeting up with Barbara again. She was an extremely good-looking woman, intelligent, and above all else, he'd shared a lot of his troubled past with her. Yes, he was attracted by her, and they did have a lot of things in common. But he didn't want to rush into it and spoil things, that was the last thing he wanted to do.

'Good evening, Jack. Still working hard, I see?'

'Hello, Barbara. You are looking beautiful tonight.'

'Thank you.' She smiled. 'It's nice to get out of my working clothes for a change.'

Mason gave her a warm agreeing smile. 'I know the feeling.'

'You need to loosen up. Those injuries of yours won't just mend overnight.'

He ordered a round of drinks, and they sat in a corner seat.

'So, what do you have planned for me tonight?' she asked inquisitively.

Shit, Mason thought. He hadn't organised anything special, let alone book a table for two.

'What kind of night were you thinking of?'

She wiggled her eyebrows. 'Anywhere that serves nice food.'

Mason groaned inwardly. He was floundering and gagging for another pint to steady his nerves. *Easy does it, Jack. Don't go and spoil it!*

'I do have a place in mind,' he whispered.

'Oh,' and where might that be?'

There was a look in her eyes that he'd not seen before. Inviting, sensual, that had instantly taken his breath away. He'd not felt like this in a long time and he'd forgotten how to handle it. Yes, he'd dealt with some hair-raising moments in his time as a senior police officer involved in serious crime, but nothing compared to this.

He steadied himself. 'If I told you that, I'd giving my secrets away.'

'Umm. . . this sounds like I'm in for a real treat.' Lockwood gave him a sensual look as she placed her hand on his shoulder. 'I like a man who has everything under control.'

Mason took another mouthful of beer, then let his head fall back. Never in a million years did he ever imagine she would fancy him, and here he was on his second date. He still hadn't the foggiest idea where he was taking her, or where they'd end up for that matter. With any luck he would come up with somewhere nice to eat – an upmarket Italian restaurant where they served good food and the finest wines.

But right now, he couldn't think of one.

CHAPTER
THIRTY-FOUR

Stephen Rice wasn't feeling at all well. Having been up most of the night suffering severe stomach cramps and vomiting, he felt he was coming down with a fever. At first, he thought it was Norovirus, but he didn't have diarrhoea. Feeling distinctly sorry for himself, he crawled out of bed, made a fresh pot of coffee, and shuffled awkwardly onto the balcony overlooking the fishing village. Nestled at the foot of the Roca Mountain and lapped by the azure Mediterranean, L'Estartit's picture-postcard beaches were unfolding before him. It was pure Catalonian charm, not that Rice cared much about picturesque charm at six o'clock that morning. His head was pounding, and the temperature had already reached eighteen degrees Celsius.

Having flown into Girona airport the previous evening, he'd picked up a Hertz hire car and driven straight to his newly rented luxury apartment before crashing out on the king size bed. Sweating profusely, Rice put it down to cabin fever or something he'd picked up at the airport.

He'd read somewhere it wasn't the recirculated cabin air you breathed that was the problem, it was those nasty little microscopic bugs that came out to bite you in the middle of the night. According to one top lab research technician, most deadly bugs were spread via surfaces found in a variety of indoor environments. Aeroplane dropdown tables were a particularly nasty place for picking them up, as were airport toilets. Avoid the aisle seats, the article had warned, they were the most likely contaminated areas. According to one report, a group of passengers – all sitting in aisle seats – experienced norovirus symptoms within hours of stepping off the plane. It was the very definition of the shit show according to one scientist, and Rice had every sympathy for them.

Earlier that week, having arranged to meet with his Spanish lawyer Cornelius Casillas, he had been looking forward to his trip to Barcelona. The two of them were old friends, and the last time they'd lunched together was at Cornelius's daughter's christening.

How could he ever forget that?

Feeling like shit, Rice opened the lid of his suitcase and changed into a clean sweatshirt and some comfortable knee-length shorts. It was eight o'clock, and after another bout of vomiting he knew he wouldn't make it to Barcelona. Not in this heat. Not sat in a car for two hours knowing he could throw up at any moment. Whatever he'd picked up on his journey over from England it had certainly got a grip of him. His joints were aching, and his head felt like it was about to explode.

Grabbing a bottle of water from the fridge, he decided to give Cornelius a call.

'*Que Paso?*'

'It's me, Cornelius—'

'Stephen! How are you? It's lovely to hear your voice again.'

'I'm not feeling at all well, Cornelius.'

'Oh, what's the matter with you? You sound terrible.'

'It's something I've picked up on my journey over from Bristol,' Rice replied.

'Planes are shit, airports are shit, and nobody gives a damn about spreading germs about anymore. Let's leave it a couple of days – you can always give me a call when you're feeling better.'

'What about these new business plans?' asked Rice.

'We still have a fortnight to sort things out; it's you I'm more worried about.'

'Are you sure?'

'Of course, I'm sure. I've already started the ball rolling with the new boat owners, so there's nothing to worry about. This is an amazing new business venture of yours, and everyone is talking about it. What's more, the ship's captain is a good friend of mine and I'm certain you'll get on like a house on fire.'

'I'm sure we will.'

'He's very excited about it and keen to show you what the Catalonian coastline has to offer. Besides, he has a few innovative ideas of his own he wants to share with you.'

'Sounds good.'

'It is, and you've certainly caused quite a stir amongst the local dignitaries. Anything that's good for the tourist industry is good for Spain.'

'Exciting times, eh?'

'Very much so. Once you're back on your feet again, I need to talk to you about a few little opportunities of my own – more about that later.'

'I'm so sorry to be such a pain, Cornelius, but there's no way I could face the long drive to Barcelona in this heat'

'You need to rest, Stephen. It's not a problem. Now you're back in the country we have all the time in the world to sort things out.'

'Thanks— You're a gem.'

'You take care of yourself, and I'll call you back in a couple of days.'

With that Cornelius hung up.

Seconds later Rice made another dash for the toilet pan, oblivious to the terrible death he was now facing.

CHAPTER THIRTY-FIVE

The day had started bright and breezy, and the North Sea sparkled like jewels in a crown as Jack Mason strolled along the clifftop close to Old Hartley village. Despite all his planning, the team were bored out of their minds. The operation had stagnated, but the minute you dropped your guard it was Murphy's law that something big would kick off. He'd not heard from Special Branch in a while, and Operation Drawbridge was going nowhere, it seemed.

A creature of habit, Mason hated complacency at any level. Now back in the driving seat, failure was no longer an option. Earlier that week, he'd run several mock kidnapping exercises at Martin's school, but still wasn't satisfied. Practice made perfect, but there was nothing like the real deal when it came to focus the mind.

His phone buzzed in his pocket – number withheld.

'*Jack Mason!*'

'Where are you now?'

Speak of the devil, he thought. It was the senior Special Branch officer whom he'd met in Gregory's office.

'I'm out walking.'

'See any penguins?'

'It's the middle of July for God's sake!"

'I didn't think you got much sunshine up in Newcastle.'

Mason chuckled inwardly having seen the funnier side. 'How can I help?' he asked.

'We've been seeing an unusual upsurge in activity around the Russian Embassy lately, and the phone lines out of Eastern Europe have never stopped. Tell me, what sort of security arrangements do you have in place?'

'Probably not enough.'

'You may wish to reconsider your options then.'

'And do what?'

'If you have any reservations about the boy's safety, I'd strongly advise you move him somewhere else. I'll keep you informed if any new developments crop up – but we're getting bad vibes.'

'Do you suspect something is afoot?'

'We believe so. Despite all the hullabaloo, the Kremlin doesn't want problems with the UK government. Not that they're squeaky clean, but Moscow is never happy to see anti-Russian headlines in Western newspapers.'

'I thought the Russians denied all knowledge of these international money wire transactions?'

'Let's just say there's a lot of individuals in high places with offshore banking interests. Not all are Russians, might I add, and I don't have to tell you that.'

'So, what's Yavlinsky's interests in these recent wire transfers?'

Mason's phone went quiet for a minute. 'We know Yavlinsky has been making £20k daily transfers into his personal bank account to pay for a recent loan he took out. We've been through his account details and found he uses a bank line of credit. It's another clever scam, as the daily payments he's making are for money he owes so it doesn't show up as a cash transaction, it shows up as a negative loan balance.'

'What does that mean in layman's terms exactly?'

'Anyone who checks Yavlinsky's bank account details sees a negative balance, which means the real money is invisible.'

'How much does he owe?'

'Ten-million-pound sterling.'

'What!'

'I thought that would excite you, and it took a team of financial experts three days to fathom that one out.'

'Why don't you just arrest him?'

'Easier said than done. Besides, it's not exactly illegal what he's doing – it's where his daily income is coming from that's the real issue. Yavlinsky's the target of a larger set-up, so were we to question him over it the whole operation would be thrown into jeopardy.'

Mason shook his head in disbelief. 'And those involved.'

'Exactly. It's not just young Martin Kennedy who is at risk here, there are hundreds of individuals caught up in the scam.' The line went quiet for a moment. 'This Newcastle trial is merely the tip of the iceberg, and there are dozens of interested parties monitoring the situation. This isn't just about money laundering anymore, it's about moving dirty money into legitimate assets—'

'So, what are your plans?'

'The Home Office are keen to come down hard on these people . . . make them think twice about using the UK financial system as their base. That's why the Home Secretary is personally involved. . . they want to put a stop to it.'

'Holy crap.' Mason sighed. 'Now I see what this is all about.'

'It's not general knowledge, of course, so I'd appreciate you keep this to yourself.'

'Yes, of course.'

'Our response must be decisive, and proportionate, and based on unmistakable evidence. That's why we're closely monitoring Yavlinsky's Belgravia apartment. There's been an awful lot of people activity taking place there lately, which has nothing to do with the ongoing renovations he's having done.'

'Where's Yavlinsky, now?'

'He's still in the capital as far as we know, but he's an elusive operator to pin down.'

'Hence the codename – *Chameleon.*'

'Exactly.'

'What about credit card transactions?' Mason asked.

'That's already been taken care of. If he hires a car, books a flight or train ticket to Timbuctoo we'll immediately know about it.'

'That could be useful.'

'Not really as he uses cash most of the time or gets someone else to pay for things.'

'What about undercover surveillance?'

'If we do get a sniff he's heading north, you'll be the first to know.'

Mason felt an adrenaline rush. 'Before you hang up, this video you sent me. The one involving the woman boarding the plane at Heathrow airport with Yavlinsky. Who is she?'

'Her name's Tatiana Meshkova and she works at the Russian Trade Delegation building in West Hill Park. We've checked with the UK Border Force and she's a regular passenger on the Moscow to Heathrow flight. From what we can gather, we believe Yavlinsky may have teamed up with her on a previous flight as we're unable to find a connection.'

'In other words, keep an eye out for Tatiana!'

'Precisely. We know she carries a Moldovan passport and lives in Moscow, so she could be operating incognito.'

'It all sounds a bit fluffy to me.'

'I'm afraid so, but we do have a reliable source at the Russian Embassy —' The officer's voice tailed off.

'And?'

'It's nothing for you to worry about – not at this stage of our investigations.'

'Thanks anyway,' Mason replied.

His line went dead.

Mason turned to DS Savage who was staring over the harbour wall. 'We need to tighten up on our security arrangements. . . got any thoughts?'

The detective stared at him and frowned. 'What are the rules of engagement, boss?'

'It's still weapons–free according to the Area Commander.'

'A shoot on sight policy or simply bring them to ground?'

'I just want these bastards kept off my patch. How we achieve that depends on what Yavlinsky intends to do to the boy. I'm praying he's forgotten about the Chopwell Wood incident, as I'm—'

'Do you honestly believe he'll do that?' Savage cut in.

'Probably not. But it's a nice thought.'

'We've been down this avenue before. It's not enough to just kill someone, you need a plan in place beforehand. Believe me, these foreign agents will do their homework before they make any moves.' Savage frowned. 'Where's Yavlinsky now?'

'Somewhere in the capital according to Special Branch.'

'It's my view he's planning to head north,' Savage said thoughtfully.

Mason scratched his head in bewilderment. 'What gives him the divine right to go after a ten-year child?'

'Most foreign agents are self–employed entrepreneurs who are paid to do a job. Once all the pieces of the puzzle fall into place, they don't give a toss who they kill.'

'You've been watching too many movies, Rob.'

'Bollocks!'

Mason nodded as he wrote something down in his notebook. 'Yavlinsky's main interest lies in money laundering, turning dirty money into legitimate assets.'

'There's more to it than that. The clients who employ people like Yavlinsky want to know what they're getting for their money.' Savage glared at him. 'And they certainly don't want their identities exposed.'

Caught in two minds, Mason felt his throat tighten. 'Is that how he's making his money, do you think – a professional hitman?'

'It wouldn't surprise me. Especially knowing the type of people he's dealing with.'

'In which case we need to make life difficult for him.'

As they climbed into the unmarked pool car and slammed the doors shut behind them, minds began to focus. They'd been over this ground at least a dozen times – each time was more intense. If the Russian was about to strike, they would need to be ready for him.

Shoot to kill and cover up later.

Chapter
Thirty-Six

The idea of slipping into a wet suit and vomiting into a face mask somehow didn't appeal to Stephen Rice. Not in a month of Sundays. One thing was for sure: obtaining a medical certificate to certify he was fit to dive in Spain was completely out of the question. He was ill and he couldn't put a finger on it. His mind all over the place, Rice shuffled awkwardly along L'Estartit port's cobbled streets feeling decidedly miserable. Everything was an effort these days, and it wasn't getting any easier. Apart from developing lower back pains, large clumps of hair were falling out of his head. If matters didn't improve drastically within the next twenty-four hours, he would need to check in at the town's medical centre – which he knew was open daily from ten o'clock onwards.

As the sun beat down on the back of his neck, Rice thought he was going to pass out. There wasn't a cloud in the sky, and it was going to get even hotter according to the forecast. His face as white as the lighthouse walls, no matter how much water he drank he still had a raging thirst. No, Rice thought. This wasn't a virus he'd picked up, this was something more serious.

On nearing the end of the pier, he spotted *"Barracuda"*. She wasn't a large vessel, but as dive boats go, she looked every inch the part. Barely a week ago, Rice would have given his right arm to be clambering onboard and venturing out to sea. Not today.

The thought of being tossed around in a heavy swell didn't sit well with him. Despite having taken a couple of sea sickness pills, he felt he was going to throw up.

Rice stood for a moment as a man in his late fifties moved several oxygen bottles towards the aft of the boat. Some were green and red, the others yellow and silver. After he'd checked out a couple of diving regulators, he watched as the man dropped them into a wooden crate full of fishing harpoons and stared up at him over the starboard side.

'Looking for someone?'

'Yes,' Rice replied. 'I've arranged to meet with Captain Fernando Perez.'

Wiping his brow with a rag pulled from his pocket, the man worked his way towards the front of Barracuda. 'You've found him,' he replied in broken English, 'and you must be Stephen Rice?'

'Yes, I am.'

'Welcome aboard, Mr Rice,' Fernando said, extending out a hand. 'I'm so glad you could make it, I wasn't expecting to see you here today.'

'I've not felt well since the day I first set foot in Spain,' Rice said pitifully. 'It's something I've picked up on my journey over here.'

'Yes, Cornelius told me all about it. Let's hope it's nothing serious and you make a quick recovery.'

'I'm sure I will.'

The moment he stepped onto the swaying walkway, Rice felt his stomach lurch. He thought he was going to be sick, but somehow managed to crawl his way to the back of Barracuda. As the first of the maritime pleasure cruisers noisily drew alongside them, it caused him to lift his head.

'I'm not up to any diving today,' Rice weakly admitted, 'but perhaps we can take a leisurely cruise around the Medes Islands and sample what's on offer.'

'The Medes is for novices, Mr Rice. There's far better diving further out to sea. We have a good sonar navigation system onboard, and I can show you where the best dive wrecks are located.'

'How far out to sea is that?'

'About an hour's sailing at the most, but it's more in line with this new business venture you are proposing.'

Rice gulped hard. 'An hour!'

'Barracuda is an amazing boat and is more than capable of handling any kind of weather you care to throw at her.'

'I'm sure she is, Fernando, but I certainly don't feel up to it today. Perhaps we could glimpse the coastline and get a feel for how she handles.'

'Anything you say, but I doubt you'll see any of the decent dive sites.'

Rice hesitated, still unsteady on his feet. 'No, I guess not.'

'Are you sure you're up to this? You don't look at all well to me.'

'I'm fine. . . just a little wobbly on my feet, that's all.'

Fernando shouted something through the boat's hatch in Spanish, and a head suddenly appeared. A short man, balding, with the muscular physique of someone who worked out regularly.

'I'd like you to meet Jose.' The captain smiled. 'He's an experienced scuba diver who has been part of my crew for the past three years. The other crew member is also called Jose, but he'll not be joining us today.'

'Two Jose's?'

'Yes, but to stop confusion we call the other one Soriente – which roughly translates as *jovial*.'

Rice nodded as he flopped down on an upturned catch box; he wasn't up to humour. Sweating profusely, his energy levels felt zapped and he could hardly concentrate let alone make business decisions.

As the captain fired up the twin engines, Jose loosened the mooring lines and jumped into the moving boat. Slowly at first, they slipped effortlessly out of the port of L'Estartit before hitting the open sea. Now moving at a leisurely speed, Barracuda glided effortlessly towards the northernmost tip of the largest island in the group. He could see the 19th century lighthouse and several steep rocky outcrops jutting out of the sea, and an armada of small fishing vessels hugging the foot of the cliffs. La Meda Gran wasn't the kind of diving spot he'd dreamt of, but at least he'd been forewarned. Besides, the way he felt right now he couldn't have cared less what the hell he was looking at, if only the head pains would go away.

Barely a mile from shore another small flotilla of diving boats came into view. This was obviously where beginners learnt their diving skills and his interest levels quickly waned. Pity, he thought. If only he'd felt up to it, he would have hit open sea to more interesting waters.

'We call this Novices' Bay,' Fernando pointed out with a smile.

'So I see.'

'In Spain we have a saying that little fish soon grow to be enormous fish. The same goes for inexperienced divers they're always on the lookout for new adventures.'

'I'd considered that when I was setting up the business.'

'It's a clever idea, Mr Rice, and I'm sure Barracuda will serve you well.'

'I'm sure she will,' Rice replied, tapping the side of the boat as if to emphasise his point. 'She's a striking vessel and everything I had in mind.'

'Once you feel up to it, I'll show you the new wreck sites we've recently discovered. Many are war ships sunk by mines or attacked by British submarines during WWII. There's blue shark out here too, which all adds to the fun. One thing for sure, the visibility in this part of the Mediterranean Sea is very good . . . sixty-five to one hundred and thirty feet is quite normal.'

'Do you get many heavy seas?'

'Sometimes, but they are quite rare. Besides, we can always find somewhere else to dive when the weather gets too rough.'

'Sounds good.'

'You have no worries with us, Mr Rice. Once we sign the contract papers, we can start advertising on the internet. And if you agree to our terms, I can also set up a small booking office in the centre of town which should generate a lot more interest.'

'Yes. That's a wonderful idea.'

'Now that Cornelius has taken over the legal side of the business, everything should slot into place.'

'I'm sure it will.'

Totally drained, Rice closed his eyes and stretched his aching limbs. Whatever he did, nothing seemed to ease the pain anymore. As the boat pitched and rolled in a one metre swell he suddenly felt his grip on the handrail slacken. The next thing he knew, after opening his eyes, he was staring up at the sky and his whole body was on fire.

'You okay, Mr Rice?' Jose said rushing to his assistance.

'No, I feel terrible. I can hardly breathe.'

'Try to lie still,' Jose insisted, 'we'll get you back to port as quickly as we can.'

The words had barely left the crew members lips when Barracuda's twin engines roared into action. Nothing had ever prepared him for this, as the deck beneath his body shuddered and vibrated, he fought to stay conscious.

The next thing Rice remembered, after they'd stretchered him into the back of a waiting ambulance, was an oxygen mask being strapped to his face. He knew he was in deep trouble and considered the agonising fate that could be awaiting him.

As the doors to the ambulance slammed shut, he overheard the driver garble some inaudible instructions into his radio handset and the warning siren wailing. Everything was a blur, and his whole body was convulsing in pain.

As the ambulance eased forward over uneven ground, every bone in his body jarred with pain. Trying to stay conscious, he knew he was fighting a losing battle. As his mind began to drift, his eyelids felt as though they had lead weights attached to them and he was tumbling into a bottomless pit. It was then that the penny finally dropped.

He'd been poisoned.

CHAPTER

THIRTY-SEVEN

Stephen Rice's demise had sent shock waves throughout the backroom senior staff at Northumbria Police Headquarters, and the Secret Intelligence Service (MI6) was now in top-secret discussions with their Spanish counterparts the Centro Nacional de Intellencia (CNI). Rushed to L'Estartit medical centre, Rice had then been transferred to a Spanish hospital in Barcelona where tests found he'd been suffering from radiation poisoning. Not only that, both the British and Spanish governments were now locked in talks as to where Rice had initially been poisoned. Some national secrets spread like deadly wildfire, and once the international press got hold of a story it was never out of the headlines.

Not the best of starts to his day. Mason was facing an even bigger challenge – *what to do with the boy?* The game plan had changed and as he walked towards the Area Commander's office, his phone rang.

He answered it without stopping.

'Call me back later, it's not convenient right now,' the Chief Inspector said.

The moment Mason stepped into Superintendent Gregory's office, he wasn't surprised to find a Special Branch delegation sat waiting for him.

'Good morning, gentlemen.'

'Take a seat,' said Gregory guardedly, 'coffee is on the way.'

He recognised the nameless senior officer from their previous meeting, but the other officer he'd never seen before. Wearing a neatly cut blue mohair suit, he had an owl face and wore a thick pair of horn-rimmed glasses across a high forehead.

The senior officer spoke first. 'Fun at the zoo, Chief Inspector?'

'Tell me about it.'

'Rice's death has certainly come as a bit of a surprise to everyone, but it was inevitable, I fear. Either Yavlinsky has been active again or one of his Russian counterparts has beaten him to it.'

'What's going on?' Mason asked outright.

"Officer Jay" as he was known, gave Mason a sullen look. 'Working with the Spanish Centro Nacional de Intelligence, we know Rice boarded an evening flight to Girona in northern Spain using a false passport. Having picked up a Hertz hire car at the Spanish airport, he then drove to the coastal resort of L'Estartit where he'd taken out a twelve-month lease on an exclusive property there.'

'Any idea what he was up to?'

'Rice was involved in a new business venture in the port — wreck diving apparently.'

'How was he poisoned?'

Officer Jay didn't fit into any particular pigeonhole in Mason's books, and names didn't mean a thing in this game. Good operational officers always had a number of different cover stories with specialist departments within the intelligence services whose job it was to maintain those covers. Times had moved on since his days in the Metropolitan's Murder Investigation Team (MIT), and a lot more preparation and research went into the intelligence role these days.

'We believe his drink may have been laced with some form of radioactive poison.' The officer's eyes narrowed a fraction.

'We've been down this avenue before, of course, and it's the preferred choice of the Russians. Alexander Litvinenko was a prime example, so we know what we're up against.'

'How come the Russians were able to trace Rice's movements when British intelligence couldn't?'

'Let's not forget that Rice initially worked for the Russians before he came over to us, so they obviously had a covert operation in place and were monitoring his activities.'

Mason thought a moment. 'So where was he poisoned?'

'Nobody knows for certain where the poison was administered, as there are still fragments of evidence out there that need to be pulled together. Who ordered it is a completely different matter, of course.'

'These people obviously mean business,' the Area Commander added.

'Never underestimate their will to succeed, Superintendent, they have very dubious pasts.' Officer Jay muttered something inaudible under his breath, then turned to face Mason. 'When the Russians got wind that Rice had defected to us, that's when they wanted rid of him.'

'So, you believe Rice was deliberately assassinated?'

'I'm convinced of it. That's what happens to you when you change your allegiances in this game. Rice was not only a liability to the Russians, he was a risk to our national security. According to government sources some nerve agents used by these people are a trillion times more toxic than hydrogen cyanide. That's why most agents prefer to use this method of elimination as it demonstrates to future defectors what will happen to them should they step out of line.'

'This is straight off the pages of a political spy thriller.' Mason shrugged. 'If you now have hard evidence to prove that Rice was poisoned by these people, then why haven't you arrested Yavlinsky?'

'Good question.'

Mason raised his eyebrows a fraction. 'And—?'

Officer Jay gave Mason a cold look. 'It's not that simple, I wish it was, but some things are best left untouched. One thing you can be rest assured of, we've never had such a high-ranking Russian agent under our radar before and we'll never get another opportunity like this one again. Rice knew how the international banking system worked, and how to lose money in it. That's what made him such a catch for the Russian oligarchs – they used him to filter their dirty money away and turn it into tangible assets. The fact he was acting as a double agent makes this a much more complicated operation. Not only did Rice know the names of the people involved in the Russian banking scam, he knew who the main benefactors were.'

'Surely by allowing Yavlinsky to walk free means you're allowing him to go after another unsuspecting victim. Isn't that the case?'

'Think about it. Yavlinsky is our best source of intelligence gathering right now. The list of bankers he meets, the lawyers he dines with, and his meetings at the Russian Embassy. These people are all potential links to the missing pieces of a bigger puzzle that we're trying to piece together. Not only that, his every movement at his Belgravia property is under our watchful eye. The British Secret Intelligence Service aren't daft. Take Yavlinsky out of the equation and we lose our biggest source of intelligence gathering.'

Officer Jay pushed back in his seat. He wasn't a tall man by appearance, slim, with a pale complexion and blue piercing eyes. Every now and then he made a funny little clicking noise with his tongue, which intrigued Mason.

The Chief Inspector turned his gaze back to Officer Jay. 'So, it's now a waiting game?'

'Rice was a traitor who sold his soul to the devil for his own financial gain. When the stakes got too high for him, that's when he wanted out. But that's not how the Russian Federation's ethical code of conduct works. Turn your back on the Kremlin and you virtually sign your own death warrant.'

'Now that Rice is no longer a threat to the Russians, where does that leave young Martin Kennedy?'

The Special Branch officer gave Mason a withering look. 'The question you should really be asking yourself is, who's pulling Yavlinsky's strings? Is it the Russian mafia, a rogue state, or do his orders come from the Kremlin direct? Yavlinsky's a hired man, make no mistake about that. It's not that simple as these people offer their services to the highest bidder and are trained to eliminate their targets as and when the situation dictates.'

Officer Jay was self-driven and spoke with an air of confidence, which Mason had picked up on. He sat silent for a moment, and then said, 'What else do we know about Yavlinsky's background?'

'In what way?'

'His past?'

Officer Jay bristled, then shot Mason a pensive glance. 'During the collapse of the Soviet Union, the Russians were looking for potential military intelligence officers to support the new Russian Federation cause. At the time, Yavlinsky was an army major with connections going back to the old-style KGB. He was an ideal candidate with impeccable credentials and that's why he was recruited into their fold.'

'So, who's pulling Yavlinsky's strings?'

'We're convinced he was recruited by the Russian Mafia, but we're still not one hundred percent.'

'This doesn't get any easier,' Mason sighed. 'What about this fraud trial that's now listed for the 19th September?'

The senior Special Branch officer interjected. 'If the Crown Prosecution still has enough hard evidence to support a conviction, then the trial will go ahead. If not, we suspect the Russians will be eager to switch to other banks.'

'Which ones exactly?'

'Who knows at this stage, that's why we haven't arrested Yavlinsky as he still remains a key figure of interest to us.'

Mason thought about it, but not for long. 'And young Martin Kennedy?'

'That's your decision. It's what you agreed to do in the first place – protect the boy and any other potential targets involved in the trial. No doubt the Russians will find other ways of getting at the Crown Prosecution's case, and their lawyers will demand disclosures at some point. This isn't a straightforward operation.' Officer Jay opened the folder in front of him and stared across at his Special Branch companion and said, 'A part of me says that Yavlinsky is a bit of a loose cannon.'

'What, you think he could be working for himself?' Mason replied.

'Whoever's behind this money laundering scam are keen that their identities are kept secret. The minute they find out that Yavlinsky's cover is blown, they'll want rid of him too – and quick.'

'Holy shit,' Mason gasped.

'That's how the system works – everyone is expendable in this game.'

'Then apart from the Russian Mafia, who else are we dealing with?' Mason questioned. 'Could some other Eastern European rogue state be involved?'

'If we knew the answer to that, we'd all be national heroes.'

The Area Commander eased forward in his seat. 'Whoever's responsible for this reckless and discriminate act needs to be brought to justice. But that's a matter for you people to sort out. Our task is to protect those caught up in the future trial. We know of at least two individuals who have been murdered, but how many more are out there?'

Officer Jay smiled. 'Now you see the full extent of the task we're faced with.'

'So, what's our next move?' asked Gregory.

'Most chemical weapons have a footprint to them, so we're able to trace where they were manufactured. Not that it is any of your concern, but we now have a possible radiation trail that leads us back to a Girona flight into northern Spain.'

'So, Rice could have been poisoned in England in other words?' Mason argued.

Superintendent Gregory sat back thinking. 'Either this was a deliberate act by the Russian Federation, or during the breakup of the old Soviet Union, they lost control of one their catastrophically damaging nerve agents and allowed it to fall into the wrong hands.'

'There is another theory, of course,' Officer Jay pointed out. 'When a country uses a chemical on another country's soil, it never uses its own chemicals. It uses the chemicals of another country to throw investigation teams off its trail.'

'Is that why you think the Russian Mafia is implicated?' the Area Commander added.

The Special Branch officer adjusted his position. 'Who knows. This could all come down to a political trade off in the end.'

'What, plea bargaining?'

'Isn't that how the police handle some affairs?'

'Yes, but on a much smaller scale and one that doesn't involve national security.'

'You'd be surprised at what goes on behind closed doors.' Officer Jay smiled. 'Especially where international diplomacy is concerned.'

'Nothing surprises me anymore,' Mason said, shaking his head.

'Think of it as two sides locked in a deadly game of Russian roulette knowing there can only be one outcome.'

The Area Commander cocked his head to one side, and then said, 'What about moving the boy to another safe house?'

'I would think it unadvisable at this late stage. . . perhaps you should talk to Central Intelligence. It's my view the further you move the boy away from his natural environment, the more stretched your lines of communications will become. It's a matter of holding your nerve. Now that Rice is out of the equation, we still don't know how these people will react.'

Mason checked himself. 'If Yavlinsky's a loose cannon, then who else is he in bed with?

'Your task is to ensure the British public remains safe. Whoever's behind this money laundering scam will no doubt be looking for a replacement for Rice – someone in the banking industry with insider knowledge who knows how the international banking system works. Let's hope we've scared these people off enough for them to move their operations to another country.'

'Chance would be a fine thing,' Mason groaned.

Officer Jay made the funny tongue clicking noise again as he pocketed his pen. 'Before we go making assumptions, let's see what the bigger picture throws up.'

Wise words indeed, Mason thought.

CHAPTER
THIRTY-EIGHT

Chameleon rose at 6:30 am, excited about the day ahead. According to the latest news bulletin, the London-based hedge fund auditor Stephen Rice was lying in a Spanish mortuary having died from toxic poisoning. Believing Rice was poisoned on Spanish soil, the British government was playing events down – hiding behind the mask of uncertainty whilst covering their own tracks. He knew that some chemicals were highly radioactive and extremely toxic materials to handle. Even so, it wasn't the kind of death that he would ever fancy. These were slow and silent killers that attacked the blood cells, followed by the liver, kidneys, bone marrow, gastrointestinal tract and central nervous system. It would be virtually impossible to trace it back to him, as he'd used a third party to lease the Spanish property using Rice's personal banking details.

It was amazing what a fresh pot of tea could do to a person, though!

Thrilled with his findings, Chameleon switched on his laptop and Googled Sky News Live for the latest news updates. Now that the case against the Russian bank was beginning to collapse, he was starting to look at life differently. With one less witness to worry about, he decided he might as well abandon his clean-up operation at the Bristol Premier Inn. It was too risky. Besides, Rice had died in a Spanish hospital and it would be weeks before the authorities got to the bottom of it – by which time he'd be long gone.

The boy was Chameleon's biggest concern, and he was high on his priority list. There was some good news on that front, and his undercover networks had been working flat out to get to the bottom of it. Having picked up on a ten-year-old boy who had moved to a school near Seaton Sluice, he'd heard the police were providing close protection. It had to be him, and he'd paid good money for someone to install surveillance cameras covering the school grounds.

Staring down at his computer screen, he changed the SIM card in his pay-as-you-go phone and fired off a few text messages. Next, he pulled up the Google map of Seaton Sluice, and began to work out a plan. Concerned about driving north, he checked the train times to Newcastle and booked a single room at the Marriott Hotel in Gateshead. With British intelligence involved, he needed to think differently.

After logging into his streaming account, Chameleon looked into the benefits of installing additional surveillance cameras inside the school. They wouldn't come cheap, but money wasn't an object in this game. Next, he scanned the school perimeter fence and made a mental note of all the exit points. He was looking for escape routes, a place where he could kidnap the boy and make a quick getaway. He preferred busy roads, with potential for weaving in and out of heavy traffic. If the police were to give chase, he would need to know where the safest escape routes were – and he'd already worked out a plan.

Thinking about this, a whole raft of school blueprints appeared on his computer screen and he began to study them. Knowing that most school authorities were mad hot on security, it would be a difficult nut to crack. One possibility was to use the tradesman's entrance at the rear of the building. It wasn't foolproof, but it had plenty of potential, nevertheless. He made a quick call to the installations engineer and gave him a load of new instructions.

After he'd finished his coffee, he showered and shaved, then threw a few things into an overnight bag. This was purely a reconnaissance trip, a means of gathering information. Nothing could be rushed in this profession – everything had to be meticulously planned. If there were flaws in the police's security arrangements, he would uncover them. Only once had he ever spontaneously killed a person on active service, and that was in self-defence.

Closing the zip on his overnight bag, it was time to make tracks. In many ways, Chameleon was looking forward to his trip north. Two days away from the capital and a chance to get his head around another mission. What could be better than that?

***

The city was bathed in sunshine as the train screeched to a halt at Newcastle's Central Station, but it hadn't been the best of journeys. Full of noisy cricket fans, who drank their way to Durham. Much quieter now – easier to think straight. Chameleon could never get to grips with the rules of cricket. One man throwing a ball at a guy with bat in his hand whilst trying to knock his stumps down. Crazy game, he reasoned. It was like watching paint dry. He preferred the contact sports, more physical, much easier to get excited about.

Easing his way through the busy station concourse in heavy disguise, he made for the taxi rank. He loved this part of the world, and Geordies were very friendly people. No one had any time for you in the capital cities these days; it was the same the world over.

As he slid into the back of a taxi, the driver pulled out of the rank. The interior smelled of fir trees and something a little stronger. Cannabis. As his thoughts began to drift, he wondered who the previous occupants were, and what they got up to during their day. It was strange how your mind worked when you entered unfamiliar territory, you always looked at things differently.

A talkative man, Raj the taxi driver told him everything he wanted to know about the city. The best places to eat, the liveliest dives to drink, and where to have the most fun. There were some bars he wouldn't be seen dead in at night, let alone frequent.

Now caught up in heavy traffic, the taxi crawled along Neville Street. The town was crowded, and at the junction with St James' Boulevard, Raj turned left and drove towards the Redheugh Bridge. Chameleon always felt at ease here, it reminded him of home. Wherever that was!

The moment the taxi pulled up outside the Marriott Hotel opposite the Metrocentre, he gave Raj a twenty-pound note and told him to keep the change. The hotel lobby was buzzing. Mainly young people settling their accounts and checking out. The receptionist was jovial enough, smartly turned out in a clean-cut blue uniform and wearing a large pink cravat, reminding him of an undercover agent he'd once met in Japan. Her fingernails were painted an unusual rust colour, which sort of matched her hair. She handed him a check-in slip and he started to fill it in. When he explained that his credit card had expired a couple of days earlier, he paid for everything by cash. Much safer that way.

Even numbers to the right, odd to the left, he placed the electronic pass key against the door lock and waited for the green light to flicker. Seconds later he was inside his room and checking for hidden wiretaps, which was standard procedure nowadays. The room was 'T' shaped, bland. It had an en suite, sliding wardrobe, and a table with coffee making facilities. The Queen-sized bed looked inviting, sending his mind spinning in other directions.

Little time for that now!

Closing the room curtains, he threw his overnight bag into the corner of the room and changed into tracksuit bottoms and sweatshirt. Feeling a prickle of unease, he fired off a couple of text messages and signed out of Outlook. Next, he logged into his streaming account and checked to see if the surveillance cameras were working. Apart from a few glitches around the school perimeter fence, everything looked fine.

The school had a relatively modern layout. High roofs, good security, and plenty of quiet corners where a person could get lost in. He took a screenshot of the perimeter exits and considered his options. The best way to move around the area would be to pose as a wannabe jogger. Nobody took much notice of joggers these days, it was as if they were invisible. The only drawback was you could never stop long enough to weigh things up. Not that the streets around Seaton Sluice would be busy this time of day, but they might be at school finishing time.

Closing the lid on his laptop he popped it into his overnight bag and peered out of the hotel window. The carpark was empty, and there were not many people about. The tourists were doing what tourists did best – looking at sights of interest. Many of them were Americans, the men in loud checked shirts and a thick wodge of money stuffed in their back pockets.

Time to get going!

Down at reception Chameleon picked up the Hertz hire car keys and made a mental note of the mileage. Next, he eyeballed the hotel security arrangements and noted the pulsating lights on the side of the main control panel. If he did have any problems during his stay here, he knew how to deal with it. Not that he was expecting trouble, but it was always best to err on the safe side.

'Will you be wanting a full English breakfast tomorrow morning, Mr Twining?' the receptionist asked.

Chameleon shuddered at the thought. *In your dreams, sweetheart.*

Never start your day on a full stomach, especially when moving in for the kill!

CHAPTER THIRTY-NINE

It was a bright, sunny day, and apart from a man out walking a golden Labrador, there wasn't a soul in sight as Jack Mason strolled along the clifftops close to Old Hartley village. His mind now in turmoil, matters had taken a turn for the worse and there wasn't a quick fix. One thing for certain though, Grigori Yavlinsky was a slippery customer to pin down. Neither he nor Special Branch knew of the Russians whereabouts, and that worried him. He'd plugged a few gaps, tightened up on security, and generally made his presence felt. If Yavlinsky was about to try anything stupid, he would be ready and waiting for him.

Well that was the plan, and Mason was sticking to it.

It was still early morning, and a calm warm breeze was generating small ripples of shimmering light over the North Sea. It was a beautiful sight, but Mason had more important things to think about right now. This wasn't the first time he'd come up against a problem such as this before, and he'd always found a way round it. He'd taken on some dangerous assignments over the years, especially during his days with the Metropolitan Murder Investigation Team (MIT). Some operations invariably carried a high element of risk with them, and those were the ones that always left a nasty taste in your mouth.

His phone rang, and DC Carrington's number popped up on the screen.

'Morning, Sue. What can I do for you?'

'We're receiving reports of a stranger seen hanging around the school gates.'

'From who?'

'A young woman on her way to the shops.'

'Did she give you a description?'

'She thought he was a jogger – middle aged, five-six, wearing a blue T-shirt and black tracksuit bottoms.'

'What else did she tell you?'

'She didn't get a good look at him as he was wearing a baseball cap, but thought he was acting suspiciously.'

'What do you mean – acting suspiciously? I thought the school was shut for summer holidays?'

'Well, he was touring the school's perimeter fence as if checking on the building. She thought he might be a paedophile and that's why she rang the police.'

'Something's not right.' Mason admitted. 'What time was this?'

'Shortly after ten.'

It was uncanny, the Chief Inspector thought. One-minute things were relatively quiet, the next they were up in the air.

'Did he have a car?'

'No, he was on foot.'

'Ten o'clock, you say!'

'Yes.'

Mason was having to think on his feet. The children would still be on holiday, so what was the suspect up to?

'Any thoughts?' he asked.

'He could be genuine. . . but I'm not convinced.'

'Okay,' Mason replied. 'If he was seen hanging around the school perimeter for any length of time, he's probably up to no good.'

'Those were my sentiments, boss.'

'The trouble is, there must be dozens of men answering to that description in the area. Get hold of uniforms, let's run a few checks to see if anyone answering to that description has been acting suspiciously near the school gates lately. When you've done all that, have a word with the school caretaker and get him to look at his security arrangements.'

'What are we looking for?'

'We need a list of anyone who has entered the school premises during the summer shutdown. Maintenance men, contractors, cleaners, that sort of stuff.'

'Do you think it could be Yavlinsky?'

'I've absolutely no idea, but we know what he's capable of. It could be nothing, of course, but we need to respond to it – and quickly.'

'I'll set the wheels in motion, boss.'

'Good.' Mason made a little grimacing gesture. 'When you talk to the school caretaker, set up a meeting with him for me. Sometime later this afternoon.'

'What shall I say it's about?'

'Tell him I'll be looking at their security shutdown arrangements. Try keeping it simple. I don't want him to go around thinking we have a problem, that's the last thing we need.'

'Will do.'

Mason pocketed his iPhone as he made his way back towards the surveillance house. He'd started with a clear diary that morning, and now it was filling up. If a Russian hitman had arrived in the North East, he could only be here for one reason. Safe houses were easy buildings to secure but protecting a vulnerable child witness was a totally different matter. Martin's case was slightly different, though, as he'd been chased through the woods by someone who didn't want to be identified. If this was Yavlinsky seen hanging around the school gates, then how the hell did he know the boy was here?

★★★

The school caretaker was stood waiting for him, when Jack Mason pulled into the teachers' car park. A gaunt, hard-faced man, with a bright red nose, Harold Carpenter was just shy of his sixty-fifth birthday. Not the sharpest tool in the box, he walked with a limp as if he had a nail in his shoe and retirement couldn't come fast enough.

A radio was playing in the background as they entered the school rear entrance, along with a strong whiff of paint. He watched as a man dressed in white overalls and carrying a tin of paint moved freely around the corridor, and guessed he was one of the decorators. Mason had never cared much for school himself and had always considered it stressful. Classed as a slow learner by the age of ten, he was always in trouble over it. Not that he didn't put his back into studying hard he did but his classmates were much brighter than him and he was always having to play catch up due to his dyslexia.

'Busy times, I see,' Mason said, pointing to the dust sheets scattered along the corridor.

'We're all but done here, Chief Inspector.' The caretaker smiled. 'The kids are back to school on Monday, but there's still plenty of finishing off to be done.'

Mason's mind turned to other thoughts.

Ever since he was first involved in the case, kidnapping was Mason's greatest fear. Nothing was ever straightforward when it came to be protecting vulnerable children, and he could never quite get to grips with it. But he trusted his team, and not one of them would hesitate should the occasion arise.

'How long have you worked at the school?' Mason asked casually.

'Thirty-five years.'

'That's almost a lifetime. What will you do with yourself when retirement day eventually arrives?'

'God knows. I'm dreading the thought of it if I'm completely honest with you.'

'It happens to us all someday.' Mason nodded.

The office was small and compact, crammed full of old filing cabinets waiting to be thrown out. A tottering stack of books were piled in one corner, many of the them tattered and torn. From the caretaker's office window, he could clearly see the school playground, but the main gates were obscured from view. He made a mental note and took out his notebook and pen and placed them on the table in front of him.

'We had a couple of police officers here earlier,' the caretaker remarked. 'They were asking about school security.'

'Did they find anything?'

'Not a lot. They asked a few questions and we had a quick look around the school.'

'Anything of interest pop up?'

'Nah, they seemed more concerned as to whether we'd had any break-ins lately. Broken windows, forced door locks, that sort of thing.'

Mason cocked his head to one side. 'Have you?'

'None that I'm aware of, and there's nowt in the report book to that effect.'

He pointed to it.

'I take it this place is alarmed?' Mason asked.

'Yes, it is.'

'So, you would have known if anyone had tried to enter the premises without authorisation?'

'Ah-huh.' The caretaker leaned forward and flicked open the pages of a large maintenance log as if it were the be all and end all of everything important in the running of the school. 'The security system was checked only last week, and the guy who came here installed some additional cameras and gave us a twelve-month clean bill of health.'

'New cameras?' Mason said, glancing up at the ceiling.

'Seemingly, it's a new scheme the school authorities are introducing. It's due to a recent spate of arson attacks in the area – something to do with the school's insurance policy.'

'Closed circuit television cameras – were they?'

'Yes, mainly external.'

'I take it these new cameras are linked to a central control room and monitored 24/7?'

'Yes, that's right.'

'Do you happen to have the security company's contact details available?' Mason asked pen poised.

'They're based over in Blackburn somewhere. I've rung them on several occasions in the past and always found them helpful.' The caretaker screwed his face up as he ran an index finger over the maintenance log. 'There you go,' he said, reeling off the telephone contact details.

Mason tapped the number into his iPhone and waited for a connection. '*Hi. DCI Jack Mason, Northumbria police – can I speak to someone in authority please?*'

He swung to face the caretaker.

'If someone did manage to break into the premises and set off the intruder alarms, I presume the security people would contact the police first or one of your chosen key holders here at the school?'

'Ah-huh, that's how the system works.'

The moment Mason was transferred to one of the security managers, it didn't take long to establish that something was wrong.

'Is there a problem?' the caretaker asked, sounding a little uneasy.

'The engineers who run your intruder alarm system know nothing about fitting additional CCTV cameras.'

'They must be a mistaken – surely.'

'I don't think so,' Mason replied, pocketing his iPhone.

'I could have sworn the guy who installed them said they were directly linked to the existing system.'

'They may well be, but your security providers in Blackburn know nothing about these new installations.' Mason tried to arrange a neighbourly smile as he stood to face a bemused looking caretaker. 'Can you show me exactly where these new cameras are?'

'Yes, of course. There's three covering the front of the building, two at the rear, and one linked to a movement detector inside the main assembly hall.'

'What about the ones at the rear of the building?'

'One covers the loading entrance, the others are monitoring the kitchen and canteen.'

Alarms bells ringing in his head, Mason made another quick call – this time to police headquarters. Something didn't sit right, and whatever it was he was determined to get to the bottom of it.

Chapter Forty

Whilst DS Savage and the rest of the team searched the building for hidden cameras, it had taken the tech boys all of five minutes to establish that someone had tampered with the school's security system and installed a secondary monitoring device. Fitted with Wi-Fi to send video and audio signals to either a mobile phone or PC, it was the news that Mason had been fearing. The more he thought about it, the more he was resigned to the fact that Yavlinsky was determined to get to the boy. If there were any scraps of comfort to be gained from all of this, it was that he'd uncovered part of the Russian's plan.

He stared at the main control box and pondered his options. 'Okay. Let's skip the technical jargon, what exactly is going on here?'

The senior technician, a man in his late forties, stared down from the top of a set of step ladders, notably dubious. 'It's a stand-alone system and has nothing to do with the school's current security arrangements.'

'Meaning?'

'Whoever installed it, can view it from anywhere in the world.'

'Spy cameras in other words?'

'You could say that, yes.'

Mason thought about it, but not for long. 'And if we dismantle this rogue system, whoever installed it will instantly know we've cottoned on to them?'

'In a nutshell, yes.'

To do that would lose the initiative, Mason thought. He would need to focus on a new line of attack – something less drastic. Whoever was monitoring the school's activities he didn't want to spook them, but how could they get around that?

Mason gestured around the room. 'What are the chances of distorting the images to make it look like a system fault?'

'Why would you want to do that?'

'If it doesn't work, someone may decide to come back and fix it.'

The senior technician screwed his face up as he clambered down the step ladders. 'We could fit a foil blocking device to deflect the radio waves, but it may affect the entire system.'

Mason swore quietly to himself. 'Let's do it.'

'I doubt anyone will return, though.'

'What makes you say that?'

'If someone's monitoring the school twenty-four-seven, they will have spotted us by now.'

'True,' Mason nodded, 'but if it's linked to a mobile phone or PC, they could be randomly monitoring the school.'

'They could be—'

Mason turned sharply. 'That's why I'm a copper and you're a technician. I know how these bastards operate.'

DS Savage joined them.

'We've found a couple more cameras, boss.'

'Where?' Mason asked, swivelling on his heels.

'One close to a rear fire exit door, the others monitoring the tradesman's entrance.'

'Two more cameras the caretaker knew nothing about.' Mason's stare hardened. 'What are these people planning to do?'

'The rear entrance seems the most obvious place to slip in and out of the building unnoticed,' Savage confirmed, 'especially with thousands of kids running riot around the place.'

Mason caught Rob Savage's apologetic glances and made a mental note of it. A tall man, around six-foot two, the sergeant wasn't one for mincing his words. He levelled his eyes at him. 'Any more vulnerable entry points?'

'None that I can see. Once the school gates are secured, this place is virtually in lock down.'

'Good man.' Mason nodded. 'No doubt these two new cameras you've discovered are linked to the same system.'

'I would have thought so,' said Savage.

The senior technical was quick to react. 'We can soon determine that.'

'Okay.'

Mason studied the school's layout blueprints and thought about it. He knew that once the close protection officers had dropped young Martin Kennedy off at the school gates, it was down to the school to look after the boy's security arrangements. Of course, he thought. Once inside the building the police had absolutely no control over the proceedings. There again, surveillance would have been an extremely costly option and there was no way the Area Commander would sanction additional manpower to cover the premises all day. Clever, he thought. Why hadn't *they* thought of installing a CCTV monitoring system inside the building during the shutdown? It was all too obvious in hindsight, but with so many regulations protecting children's rights these days no one had the balls to go there.

Convinced he was on to something, they moved to the rear of the school. At least they were agreed on one thing – whoever had installed the additional CCTV cameras had wanted to spy on the children. But why? Was this the Russians doing, a paedophile ring, or someone else at work?

Mason frowned. 'I doubt someone is currently staring at a monitoring screen 24/7, it's too time consuming. They're probably using a laptop and randomly checking on the place.'

'You could be right, boss,' Savage agreed.

'Let's hope so.'

Savage shuffled awkwardly. 'There again, if it is the Russian, he's obviously monitoring the kid's movements.'

Mason studied the new camera installations. Savage had a point; and a good one at that. The rear service door to the school was the most likely place to slip in and out of the building unnoticed. No keypad locks to worry about, quick access to a getaway vehicle, and less teacher contact. It was perfect. He checked the surrounding area and made a few notes. He would need to heighten his security arrangements, step up patrols, and cover every eventuality. If this was Yavlinsky's doing, and he still wasn't convinced, he would need to be ready and waiting for him.

The question was – *should he move the boy to another safe house?*

CHAPTER
FORTY-ONE

The moment Chameleon logged into his streaming account he could see the surveillance system wasn't working. Annoyed, he smashed his fist into the bedside cabinet and glared at the computer screen again. It was useless. All he could see were ghost like images and sounds resembling sausages frying in a pan. Two days of nothing, and shit loads of grief to deal with just didn't bear thinking about. He should have dealt with it himself, made a proper job of it instead of letting some asshole cock things up.

Still furious, he made a quick call to the installation engineer and threatened to chop his hands off if the system wasn't operational within the next twenty-four hours. Not the best of starts to his day, Chameleon got the impression it had been done on purpose. If there was ever a man he would need to deal with, it was him.

Forty minutes later, after driving to Blyth, he parked in one of the side streets and prepared to jog to Seaton School. He was less noticeable on foot, and people never bothered you. His biggest nightmare was someone spotting the car, especially a hire vehicle. But all the time he was thinking. How to kill the boy, and where to dispose of his body?

His phone rang. It was the installation engineer, and he sounded in a right old state. Not that it bothered Chameleon, just that he fixed the system.

Now running on pure adrenalin, on nearing the school gates the Russian saw the streets were full of parked cars. It was the same every day, you could almost set your watch by them. Parents were creatures of habit but dropping your kids off as close to the school gates as possible was absolutely ridiculous. Not that he could blame them, not with individuals like him hanging around the streets.

Ignoring the double yellow lines, a short woman with blue rinse hair and bright orange trainers pulled up in a bright green Mondeo. As her two boisterous kids shot out of the back seats and ran into the playground screaming, he gave them a once over. Next to arrive was a stout man in a rusty red Nissan and carrying a yappy black poodle in the back. It annoyed him intensely. If only he had a gun, he would fill it full of lead and put an end to its miserable life.

Frustrated, he crossed the road and sauntered back along the other side, whilst keeping a watchful eye out for unmarked police cars. Which make or models he was looking for Chameleon had no idea as no two days were ever the same. This was never going to be an easy operation, he knew that, but he was convinced the police protection car would soon show up. Then, barely ten metres away, a rather tired black Ford Mondeo juddered to a halt and three young children clambered out of the back of it. If he'd have known that security was going to be this lax, he would have videoed everything.

What to do next?

Chameleon's initial reaction was to storm the building, but knew it was futile. He would need to calm down and come up with a better plan. Then, through the main entrance doors, the sudden appearance of a male in a black coat gave him concern. He was important looking, late thirties with a thin-set face and mouse like eyes that scanned the playground as if he was looking for someone. *Who was he? What was he doing there?*

Once the school gates were locked, this place would become an impregnable fortress again. He stared at his watch.

Time fast slipping away from him, he pulled his baseball cap down over his face and felt like a juggler holding a whole lot of spinning plates in the air. Everything was heavily stacked against him. His surveillance cameras didn't work, he still had the boy to identify, and he knew the police were out looking for him. But that wasn't all, there was something much bigger niggling away at him – the Organisation were beginning to ask questions.

Not wishing to hang around, Chameleon began to make tracks for Blyth. As his pace quickened, he let his mind drift. Then in a moment of inspiration another idea popped up in his head – *and this one was watertight.*

CHAPTER FORTY-TWO

Dennis Fudge, Seaton School's headteacher, peered out of his office window and onto the empty playground below. Many teachers considered summer was officially over once the children had returned to school. Not true, thought Fudge. September was usually the best month of them all. Shorter daylight hours, but still plenty of warm sunshine to look forward to. A much bigger issue, as far as Fudge was concerned, was the school had been under-performing lately and he'd come under a lot of pressure from the board of governors because of it. A bit of a dark horse, Fudge was hoping his new curriculum would improve matters for the better. But change was always difficult to introduce at Seaton School, especially among the older teachers who were too stuck in their ways and always put up resistance. Failure wasn't an option this time, and he was determined to put the record books straight.

His desk phone rang, and he picked it up.

'Seaton School, how can I help?'

'Good morning, Mr Fudge. This is Inspector Clamp, Northumbria Police. One of your pupils who is under our protection, is he in school today?'

'Yes, he is. Why do you ask?'

'Thank goodness for that. I need a favour, old boy,' Chameleon replied.

'How can I help, Inspector?'

There followed an awkward silence between them – a gathering of wits.

'We are holding an identification parade later this afternoon, and I'm instructed to pick up the boy at twelve o'clock and take him to Gateshead Police Station. Do you see a problem with that?'

Fudge thought a moment before answering.

'What's the boy's name, Inspector?'

'It's the young lad we chaperone to school every day.'

Fudge wasn't prepared to be pushed around that easily. Besides, he was in enough trouble as it was with the educational authorities and there was no way he would release a child without proper consent.

'It's not that simple,' said Fudge. 'I would need written authorisation to do that.'

Chameleon's voice suddenly sounded hollow. 'Why. . . he's already under our protection?'

'I'm sorry, Inspector. Those are the rules.'

The phoneline went dead.

Fudge thought about it, but not for long. Things didn't add up, and the fact a senior police officer couldn't remember the name of the boy he was protecting sort of backed that up. He rang reception, and seconds later he was put through to Gateshead Police Station.

★★★

Jack Mason was sorting through a pile of witness statements when his phone rang. He was having a shit day, and everything that could go wrong had gone wrong. Covert policing wasn't all it was cracked out to be, and the amount of paperwork he had to fill in was mind boggling at times. He'd often wondered what it would be like to be a prison officer and stuck in a cell block all day. At least criminals could walk free once they'd served their sentence – no such luck for prisoner officers, he thought.

'DCI Jack Mason. . . how can I help?'

'Good morning, Detective Chief Inspector. It's Dennis Fudge, headteacher at Seaton School. Do you have a minute?'

'Yes, of course. What can I do for you, Mr Fudge?' Mason replied disgruntledly.

'It concerns young Martin Kennedy.'

'What about him?'

'I've just had a telephone call from one of your fellow officers informing me that Martin is required to attend an identity parade at your police station this afternoon.'

'What time is this?'

'He's to be picked up at the school gates at twelve o'clock.'

Mason made a note of it. 'Identity parade, you say?'

'Yes, I'm not trying to be awkward, but can you confirm if that's your understanding of the situation please?'

'Hold on a minute,' Mason replied.

Seconds later, after he'd checked with the desk sergeant and DS Savage's office, he picked up the office telephone again. 'Sorry about that, Mr Fudge,' Mason began. 'It seems that nobody at the station knows anything about an identity parade taking place this afternoon. Can you give me the officer's details please?'

'Yes, of course. It's an Inspector Clamp.'

Suspicions aroused, Mason checked the duty roster. 'The name's not familiar and he's not on the station's register. Did he say which area or division he was from?'

'Northumbria Police, I believe.'

Puzzled and curious, Mason checked the area manning lists and shook his head disconcertedly. 'There's no one answerable to that name on our records.'

'Well, that's who he told me he was, Chief Inspector.'

'Is Inspector Clamp with you currently?'

'No, he contacted me over the telephone.'

Panic momentarily gripped him. Still plenty of time to make it to Seaton School, Mason thought. He pushed his office door open and signalled for DC Carrington to join him. If this was Yavlinsky's doing, then it was an audacious plan. He took several deep breaths, opened his office desk drawer, and took out his Smith & Wesson 36.

'Thank you, Mr Fudge. Under no circumstances is Martin allowed to leave the school premises. Do I make myself clear on that?'

'Yes, of course.'

'Officers are already on their way, and I'll be with you in thirty minutes.'

DC Carrington stared at him. 'Something a matter, boss?'

'You could say that.' Mason cleared his throat as he slipped on his jacket. 'Someone purporting to be a police officer has just phoned Seaton School and asked for Martin Kennedy to be made available to them.'

'For what reason?'

'An identity parade that's supposedly taking place here at two o'clock.'

'That doesn't sound right, boss.'

'Those were my sentiments.'

'Do you think there could be a mix-up somewhere?'

'I doubt it. The officer involved calls himself Inspector Clamp and claims he's serving with the Northumbria Police.'

'Never heard of him, which area is he from?'

'There's only one way to find out,' Mason said picking up his keys, 'let's ask him.'

CHAPTER
FORTY-THREE

The drive to Seaton Sluice took Jack Mason all of twenty-five minutes. It was late-morning and there wasn't much traffic along the coast road. Dressed in a casual bomber jacket, jeans, and carrying a loaded Smith & Wesson 36 housed in its holster, the Detective Chief Inspector was taking no chances. Met at the school gates by DS Savage, they moved at a pace through the large assembly hall and into the heart of the building. School kids everywhere, along with a smell of fresh paint, he felt he was stepping into bedlam.

The headteacher was staring out of his office window and deep in thought when they entered the room. 'Ah. Detective Chief Inspector Mason,' said Fudge, as he swung to address them. 'I'm so glad to see you.'

'Have you had any further contact?' Mason asked.

Fudge clearly looked nervous. 'No, nothing.'

'Good.'

Mason perched on the edge of the headteacher's desk and made himself comfortable. It was 11.24 am, and still ample time to finalise his plans. With two unmarked police cars stationed outside the school gates, and four armed officers covering the perimeter fence, it would be a difficult nut to crack – unless the suspect was already inside the building, of course.

'Where's Martin Kennedy now?' DC Carrington asked, showing her concern.

'He's down in the staff room with one of the teachers and the two detectives who brought him here today.'

At least the boy was in safe hands, which pleased Mason no end. He glanced out of the office window and tried not to be nosey, but he was a police officer and that's what he was trained to do. It was obvious now why someone had installed monitoring cameras around the building – they were snooping on people's movements including their own presence here today. Martin's cover had been blown and he was having to think differently. But what to do with him was the question. Yes, there was a highly trained response team at his disposal, but guns and school children didn't mix.

His iPhone rang. It was the Area Commander.

'Morning, Chief Inspector. What's going on?'

'Someone is attempting to snatch the boy out of the school, sir.'

'So, I'd heard. Do we have any idea who it may be?'

'No, but it doesn't take a rocket scientist to guess who's behind it.'

Gregory fell silent for some moments, and Mason knew what he was thinking.

'You need to consider getting young Martin away from there, it's becoming too dangerous.'

'I couldn't agree more, but where to is the question?'

'You need to get in touch with social services again.'

Mason hesitated. People were looking for answers and he didn't have any to give. Only uncertainty. He steadied himself before answering. 'The question I keep asking myself is how did Yavlinsky trace Martin to Seaton School?'

'That's immaterial at this stage,' Gregory replied stoically.

'But it's still a big mystery nevertheless.'

Mason sat for a moment and thought he could almost predict what the Area Commander was about to say next. He wasn't far wrong.

'You need to give it some thought, the boy's safety is paramount. If this leaks out to the press all hell will be let loose.'

As he ended his call, his mind went into overdrive.

Please God, don't let me screw up on this one.

DS Savage's police-issue radio suddenly crackled into life. One of the unmarked stationary pool cars close to the school gates had spotted a Volvo XC60 parked suspiciously. Seconds later, after checking the automatic number plate recognition system (ANPR), it was down as a Hertz hire vehicle which had been dropped off at the Gateshead Marriott Hotel the previous day.

Stay calm, Mason told himself. Don't rush into it.

'Okay,' he began. 'This place is virtually in lockdown, so let's try to contain this off the school premises and away from the children. Whoever this person is, he needs to be stopped, and fast.'

Nods of approval gathered pace.

Just as a precautionary measure Mason ordered the two unmarked police cars to move away from the scene and another two to take their place. If this was Yavlinsky's vehicle parked up outside the school gates, it could all end up in a high-speed chase. Given the choice, like all other detectives, he would have preferred it to be as far away the school as possible. But Yavlinsky didn't give a damn whose life he put in danger, just that he achieved his objectives.

His patience fast running out on him, matters had reached crisis point. He took a deep breath. If he had a pound for every time he'd been in this kind of situation, he'd be a rich man. Hold your nerve, Mason told himself. Stay calm.

★★★

The engine ticking over, Chameleon stared out through the Volvo XC60 driver's window and across at the school entrance. His foot covering the accelerator pedal, he had plenty of humph under the bonnet should he require it. It was 11.59 am, and still no sign of the boy showing. He would need to move soon – *and he knew his way around the area.*

A flash of light caught his attention, and he noticed a silver Ford Focus move off in a westerly direction. He wasn't sure, but if that was an unmarked police vehicle, he would need to keep his eye on it just in case.

Sunlight dancing through the windscreen, he hadn't felt at all well that morning. The more he thought about the poison he'd administered to Stephen Rice, the more he realised that something had gone horribly wrong. He'd followed the instructions explicitly – even down to wearing rubber gloves. Having carefully transferred the container back to the jacket pocket he was wearing, he wondered if cross contamination had taken place?

Just how much exposure he'd been subjected to, he had no idea. But it was sure scaring the living daylights out of him. Cellular degradation due to damage to your DNA wasn't the kind of death he was up for, but there wasn't a lot he could do about it right now. He should have thrown his jacket away the moment he placed his surgical gloves inside the pockets, and now he was having grave doubts about his health. Rice would have suffered in agony, and God forbid he was facing a similar fate.

Annoyed with himself, he tried to think positively. He only had one more mission to take care of in Newcastle, and he didn't want to screw up on this one. Thinking about this, there was no way the headteacher would release the boy without written consent. Definitely not. He should have done things differently, gone in heavy handed instead of pussy-footing around. He hadn't, and now he was faced with an even bigger challenge.

Chameleon glanced at his watch and checked the school entrance door again. Without access to a closed monitoring system, he was having to work blind.

Should he risk ringing the headteacher again?

He fiddled with the air conditioning control, but still couldn't get it to work. It was mad hot inside the hire car, and he'd forgotten to bring his water bottle with him. Not wishing to hang around any longer, he dropped into first gear and slid away from the pavement and joined the steady stream of traffic heading west.

What he didn't see, or perhaps he had, and it hadn't registered, was the unmarked Beamer estate now trailing in his wake.

CHAPTER
FORTY-FOUR

In the early hours of the following morning, Jack Mason stood with his hands in his pockets and stared down at the hotel layout stretched out on the bonnet of the Road Traffic Unit Vauxhall Insignia estate. It was a clear night; but a dull neon glow hung over the city with ominous uncertainty. Just off the A1(M) and close to the Gateshead Metrocentre, the Marriott Hotel stood in partial darkness. Nearby, and hidden from view, a team of armed police officers wearing anti-ballistic armour and black helmets were making last-minute preparations to storm the building. In addition to a Tactical Firearms Unit presence, a rapid response 4X4 from the Northumbria Ambulance service was waiting in an adjacent street in anticipation of a shootout.

Ten miles north, in what was now a joint coordinated operation, armed police officers were descending on other properties owned by a well-known Russian Oligarch. Elsewhere across the cities of Gateshead, Sunderland, and Newcastle, dozens of search warrants were about to be executed on smaller properties of interest. In what was a massive showdown of strength, team confidence was running high.

Having selected a small line-up of hand-picked officers including a dog unit to stay close, Mason was banking on an element of surprise. Events were moving at a pace, and as the hunt for Grigori Yavlinsky intensified nothing was left to chance.

A figure approached, and he was waving his arm in the air.

'Everything is ready to go,' DS Savage confirmed.

Mason looked at his watch. Three minutes to zero-hour.

'I'm still waiting for team *Seven* to report back.'

Savage grinned 'Let's hope our suspects are all tucked up in bed, cos they're about to receive a rude awakening.'

'Any more news from hotel reception?'

'Yeah. A *do not disturb* notice has been placed on room 27's door, and they believe it's occupied.'

Mason thought about it. According to Special Branch, Yavlinsky was moving around the area under several different names. Tetley, Grey and Twining's were among his favourites. Either the man had a warped sense of humour, or a strong liking for tea. He had yet to decide.

'What's the latest on the Hertz hire vehicle?' Mason asked, gesturing towards the hotel carpark.

'The engine's stone cold, boss. It hasn't budged in hours.'

'Good. . . which means he can't be far away.'

'I wouldn't bank on it.'

Mason gave Savage a puzzled look. 'What about fire escapes, are they all covered?'

'Everything's been taken care of, boss. If he's holed up inside the building, there's no escape for him now.'

'Okeydokey.'

Just as he was about to make his move, Mason's earpiece suddenly sprang into life. He turned the volume down. One of the ops teams north of the river was experiencing difficulties. An old man suffering a suspected heart attack was in desperate need of medical attention. Shit happened, but the thought of a three-ton ambulance entering the area somehow didn't appeal. The slightest whiff of a police presence, and the Russians would evaporate. No, Mason thought. He would need to come up with a plan, and one that wouldn't jeopardize the entire operation.

'What time do we go in?' DS Savage asked anxiously.

'Three am.'

'It's almost that now.'

I know, I know. Give it a few more minutes.'

The sergeant screwed his face up. 'Twenty-four hours into the planning and some old geezer decides to have a heart attack.'

'Some things are unavoidable—'

'Yeah, but not on our watch!'

Mason looked up at Savage briefly. 'For what it's worth, all teams will go in simultaneously.'

Savage blew into cupped hands as Mason stared at the hotel reception lobby. If they could maintain the element of surprise, the Russian had little or no chance of escape. But what if the room was booby tapped – fitted with a low-level explosive device enough to maim several officers? Just because Yavlinsky's hire vehicle hadn't moved in hours, didn't mean a thing.

Patience, Jack. *He who dares wins!*

He pressed the call button on his police-issue Airwaves Unit and whispered into the mouthpiece. 'Let's stop the ambulance well short of the suspect's property and send in the paramedics on foot to deal with the old man.'

'Roger that,' came back the reply.

'How far are we talking from the suspect's house?'

'It's directly opposite, boss.'

'Shit!' Mason cursed.

Headlights flickering along the Western Bypass, his mind all over the place, he would need to give the order regardless of the consequences.

He glanced at his watch again.

One minute to zero hour.

He loosened the clip on his holster flap in readiness. If they hung around much longer, they would lose the initiative of surprise.

Mason gave the signal.

Thirty seconds before zero hour, the assembled line of armed police officers moved quietly through the hotel's entrance lobby. Weapons at the ready, the lead officer carried an enforcer battering ram in his hand, the second an anti-ballistic shield. Following in their wake, Mason teased back the safety catch on his nine-millimetre Smith & Wesson 36 and wrapped his fingers firmly around the stock. It had been years since he'd last worked on an armed response operation but knew he wouldn't hesitate.

Silence at first, then everyone shouted at the top of their voices.

As room 27's door burst inwards with a crack, the frame gave way under the strain. Seconds later a dozen armed officers piled in through the tiny opening, their weapons loaded and locked. Then, through the mist of uncertainty, a young woman's head appeared from beneath the bed sheets. She looked frightened, confused, as if the tan had been sucked from her complexion.

'Where is he?' Mason said calmly.

She winced, her surprise unquestionable.

With a dozen Heckler & Koch assault rifles bearing down on her, Mason stepped forward and read her the riot act. 'Don't mess with me, young lady. Where's Grigori Yavlinsky?'

Still no response.

As the hotel room was taken apart, the woman was led away in handcuffs and placed into the back of a waiting police vehicle before being driven away at speed. What had taken forty hours of planning, was over in a matter of minutes. Although the operation had run like clockwork, their suspect was nowhere to be seen.

'Anything?' Mason asked.

'We've searched the building from top to bottom,' Savage confirmed, 'and there's no sign of the Russian.'

'He's here somewhere—'

'He must have got wind we were coming, boss.'

Mason looked at the sergeant bleary-eyed. 'If he left with all of his possessions, the woman is obviously a decoy.'

'It's looking that way.'

'Let's see what the dog teams throw up.'

Back at the hotel reception desk, Mason took a copy of the hotel's guest list along with CCTV coverage as forensics poured all over the Hertz hire vehicle. It didn't take long. Fingerprints lifted from the steering wheel and fed into the AFIS database system soon established a match.

An Airwave Unit sprang to life nearby, causing Mason to lift his head.

News from the other coordinated raids didn't look good suddenly. The Russian had gone to ground and had vanished without a trace. Distraught, Mason reached for his iPhone and searched through the list of numbers.

Seconds later the dialling tone kicked in.

'Sorry to drag you out of bed, my friend. But I'm in tight corner.'

'Christ, Jack. It's four in the morning, what the hell is going on?' David Carlisle yawned.

'Only the early bird catches the worm they say.'

'This had better be good.'

'It's the boy,' Mason sighed, 'young Martin Kennedy.'

'What about him?'

'I know it's short notice, but I'm looking for a safe house for a couple of days.'

Mason could hear movement in the background, and guessed the private investigator was now out of bed. At least something was working in his favour.

'How can I possible help?'

'I'm looking for a big favour.'

'Hold on a minute, I'm—'

'The last time we met you said if I needed your assistance, I just had to ring.'

'Yes, but I—'

'Good, I'll be with you in twenty minutes.'

'Wait on a minute, I didn't mention anything about—'

Mason pressed the end of call button and shouted over to where DC Carrington was standing. 'We need to move the boy,' he said in a tired but firm voice.

'Where to, boss?'

'I'll talk to you about it later. . . follow me.'

Carrington jumped into action as they took off together. His mind already made up, Mason was on a mission and nothing would stop him now.

CHAPTER FORTY-FIVE

David Carlisle was eating breakfast cereal when the front doorbell rang. Still trying to get his head around Mason's early morning wake up call, the private investigator had searched all the local TV news channels to see if anything of interest popped up. It hadn't.

He answered the door.

'Can I come in?' Mason said, his foot firmly over the threshold.

'You already are,' Carlisle replied sternly. 'What the hell is going on, Jack?'

Mason turned and signalled towards the unmarked police car now standing on Carlisle's drive. Confused at first, the private investigator stood flabbergasted as DC Carrington and young Martin Kennedy slid from the back seats and hurriedly ran towards his front door.

No words were spoken, only smiles.

'I know this is short notice,' Mason explained, 'but we need to keep Martin off the streets for a couple of nights – somewhere safe!'

'What's wrong with a local B&B, there's plenty of those in the area?'

'Nah. Bed and breakfasts are not the ideal place under the current circumstances.'

'And what circumstances are these?'

Mason looked on apprehensively. 'Yavlinsky's gone to ground and I'm concerned for the boy's safety.'

'What about the safe house in Seaton Sluice, I thought you had it covered?'

Mason nodded. 'We did.'

'And?'

'The boy's cover has been blown so we're closing that part of the operation down.'

'Great.' Carlisle shrugged. 'So now you want to get me involved?'

They were inside and sitting around his kitchen table now, drinking coffee and catching up on the latest developments.

'I know it's a big ask, but until social services can come up with an alternative plan Martin needs to be kept out of sight for a couple of days.' Mason looked at Carlisle sympathetically. 'Before you even think about going there, there's no way I'm going to lock him up in police cell twenty-four-seven. It's not going to happen!'

Carlisle gave his friend a withering look. 'I'm a Private Detective, not a bloody foster mother.'

'It's only temporary—'

'I know you of old, Jack. A couple of days becomes a couple of weeks and before you know it the boy's a permanent fixture here. Besides, you can't just dump him in a house on his own all day.'

'I've been thinking about that aspect too,' Mason said thoughtfully. 'I was planning on DCs Carrington and Richie looking after him until we can come up with something more permanent.'

'Oh, yeah! And turn my place into a full-blown operations room. It's not going to happen, Jack. And you know it. I've got a business to run; clients to meet, meetings to attend and—'

Mason held his hand up as he stared into empty space. 'Trust me, it's only a couple of nights.'

It was Carrington who spoke next. 'We're in a tight corner, David. Besides, Martin's no trouble and I know he'll fit in perfectly here.'

Carlisle looked at her pensively. 'So, you're in on this too? What about my welfare?'

'I can always cook you breakfast,' Carrington replied.

Carlisle slumped back. 'You're forgetting, young lady. I've known his father for years and know what mischief his son gets up to. Isn't that how we got into this mess in the first place?'

Martin was playing games with Benjamin the cat when he turned his head sharply towards them. This was all about trust, and the young boy had obviously overheard their conversation.

'If I do stay here, can we visit Marsden Grotto, Sue? There's thousands of sea birds around Marsden cliffs this time of year, and the beaches are full of fossils.'

Mason turned to Carlisle. 'See what I mean, the boy already feels at home here!'

Carrington's phone rang, but she let it ring out.

Carlisle cradled his mug in his hands and blew onto his black coffee. He knew it made sense, knew it was their best option, but he was struggling to come to terms with it. The problem was, once he agreed to Mason's terms his property would be turned into a mini-fortress. There again, Carlisle thought. There was no way that Martin could venture outside the house, not with a Russian assassin breathing down their necks. Security would be tight, and everyone involved in the operation would be on the highest alert. Guns everywhere, surveillance cameras on every street corner, Whitburn village would never be the same again.

The more he thought about it, the more he turned his nose up at the idea. Perhaps a police cell wasn't a bad place after all. Surrounded by doting police officers all day, five-star room service, and as much food as the boy could eat.

No, Carlisle thought, he would need to put his foot down.

Mason glared at him. 'Well?'

'Two nights. That's all.'

Mason grinned. 'Good. I knew you'd see sense.'

'And after that?'

His old colleague sat quietly thinking for a moment, but Carlisle knew what he was up to. Mason was pig-headed and that was the crux of the matter. Once the Detective Chief Inspector got his teeth into a problem, he couldn't care less whose toes he trod on – just that he got the job done.

God forbid, Carlisle thought. What had he let himself in for?

CHAPTER FORTY-SIX

Jack Mason was studying their faces: raised eyebrows, twitches, and the regular throat-clearing. Words were being muttered, but he could not make them out. He knew they were listening, but minds were elsewhere. Directly over his shoulder was a crime board full of post-its and new possibilities. Nothing was black and white anymore, and Yavlinsky had completely vanished without trace. Having broken into an adjoining hotel room and stolen a set of car keys, the Russian had made good his escape barely hours before they'd arrived on the scene. There had been dozens of raids on properties in outlying districts, but nothing of interest had shown up. He was out the somewhere, but where was the question?

Then, through a gap in the team, he observed Detective Constable Manley. He was fiddling with his mobile phone as if texting someone.

Get a grip, Mason cursed.

'Something more interesting, Harry?'

All eyes turned to the Detective Constable.

'No, boss,' Manley replied, annoyingly sucking on another humbug sweet. 'I was Googling cross contamination, particularly secondary exposure.'

'Crikey, I never realised you were into chemistry.'

Titters of laughter broke out.

A family man who doted on his kids, nothing ever fazed Harry Manley. The joker in the pack, he could talk the hind leg off a donkey, and invariably did. He did have a serious side, though, and one that habitually threw up some useful nuggets of information at times. Today was one of them, it seemed.

'It's a pretty fair bet that it was Yavlinsky who poisoned Stephen Rice, and that's what got me into thinking about cross contamination.'

'If there is any, don't you think Special Branch would have already picked up on it?'

'They might well have done, boss. What if they're keeping it under wraps?'

DS Savage looked at Mason with interest. 'Harry has a point. Anything's possible where Special Branch are concerned.'

'If we knew what we were looking for it would be, but we don't.' Mason shrugged.

Manley's face darkened. 'Well, if there's the slightest forensic trace of it around on any of Yavlinsky's past movements, it could prove or disprove his involvement.'

Mason made a note of it, as Manley's words lingered almost menacingly.

Earlier that morning, having spoken to Superintendent Gregory about the latest developments and concerns, Mason was beginning to have second thoughts. Not that he was expecting an immediate answer, but at least Gregory had given him some sound advice about the boy's temporary new arrangements. Now high on Yavlinsky's priority list, this recent incident had sort of backed that conversation up. No, Mason thought. He had every right to ask David Carlisle for his assistance in sheltering the boy.

It was DS Miller who broke the Chief Inspector's thoughts. A member of NARTs – Northumbria's Armed Response Team – Vick Miller had a keen eye and a cool head for detail when it came to tight situations.

'These additional CCTV monitoring cameras we found at the Seaton School,' Miller said.

'What about them?'

'At first, we thought the Russians had installed them, but it turns out the culprit is a well-known local criminal called Colin Glover. He was identified from fingerprints found on one of the camera lenses and brought in for questioning late last night.'

'Has he told us anything?'

'Not a lot. Glover is adamant these were legitimate installations he carried out.'

Mason shook his head in disbelief as he exchanged glances with Miller. 'What's Glover's connection with the Russian?'

'There isn't one as far as we can gather,' Miller replied. 'Glover was contacted by an anonymous third party and swears he knew nothing about any Russian connection.'

'We need to work on it,' Mason sighed.

'One thing for sure, now that Glover is locked up in a police cell there's no way these people can get to him.'

Mason stood for a moment, thinking. 'What about Glover's phone contact details, anything show up?'

'No nothing. As everyone suspected, Yavlinsky is obviously using a pay-as-you-go phone as a hotline and changing the SIM card after every call and text message he makes.'

'If we can get hold of this third party that Glover contacted, his phone could open up a Pandora's Box.'

'That's never going to happen, boss. Especially when Yavlinsky is operating over such a wide area with contacts far and wide.'

'No, I suppose not. But we still need to look into it, nevertheless.'

DS Holt entered the room and raised his hand to speak. He was wearing a Hi-Vis jacket and carrying a clipboard in his hand, and his face bore a look of resignation.

'Yes, George?' Mason nodded.

'We've just received reports of the BMW stolen from the Marriott Hotel. It's been found at the Washington Services.'

'What about Yavlinsky?'

'There's a search party out looking for him as we speak.'

'Heading south, was he?'

'Hard to say, boss.'

Mason's eyebrows rose a fraction. 'Anything else we should know?'

'Yes. The two Road Traffic Unit officers present at the scene say there's a black holdall on the back seat of the stolen vehicle.'

Time to get involved, Mason thought.

'Get hold of Tom Hedley. . . tell him to meet me there in thirty minutes.'

'Will do, boss.'

His mind full of possibilities, Mason grabbed his jacket and dished out a few hurried instructions on keeping the boy safe. He then swung to face the rest of the team.

'Okay, everyone. It's time to jump into action again.'

★★★

After taking the slip road towards Washington Services, Jack Mason could see the Road Traffic Unit Audi S3 blocking one of the lanes. He stopped in front of it and made himself known. It was then he noticed a small knot of officers gathered around a blue BMW. Its doors had been flung open, and someone had his head stuck under the bonnet.

'Any sign of the driver?' Mason asked, pulling up alongside it.

'Nothing yet, sir,' the officer replied in a broad Geordie accent.

Mason gave a shake of the head. 'Was the engine cold or warm when you found it?'

'It hadn't long been driven here.'

Curious, Mason sat for a moment and weighed things up. All they had to go on was circumstantial evidence – a telephone call to a headteacher claiming to be a police officer wasn't enough to press charges. If Yavlinsky was attempting to snatch the boy from under their noses, they would need to catch him in the act. This was no ordinary criminal they were dealing with, this was a professional at the top of his game. And another thought had crossed his mind that morning: what if they'd blown the lid on the security services surveillance operations? What then?

No Mason, thought. He just wanted Yavlinsky off his patch – but *how* was the question. The more he thought about it, the more complex his task was becoming. This wasn't a simple matter of arresting someone on suspicion of murder, there was more to it than that. In many ways it was down to the Joint Intelligence Committee to weed out the ring leaders involved in the money laundering scam – not his. The difficulty was, neither the Spanish authorities nor the Metropolitan Police could determine where and who had poisoned Stephen Rice for definite. They had their suspicions, of course, but nothing was cast in stone. Manley was right. Even if Yavlinsky had left a toxic contamination trail behind, Special Branch were dead against taking him out as the Russian was their main source of intelligence gathering. It was a vicious circle, and he would need to curb his enthusiasm and let those in higher office deal with the decision making. There again, he argued, it wasn't in his nature to sit back and do nothing.

Still deep in thought, Mason watched as Tom Hedley pulled into the empty parking bay opposite. Dressed in a dark blue suit, white button shirt and silk tie, the senior forensic scientist slid from the driver's seat and calmly ambled towards them.

'Having fun?' Hedley announced, as he slipped on a pair of rubber gloves and stuck his head in through the open BMW driver's door.

'Harassed more like.' Mason groaned.

Hedley turned to face him. 'Looks like the occupant left in rather a hurry.'

'Spooked, I'd say?'

'Probably, by the look of things.'

After a moment's consideration, Hedley unzipped the holdall, sat on the backseat of the stolen BMW and casually peered inside. Apart from a change of clothing and an old Pittsburgh Stealers baseball cap, there was little to spark his interest.

Mason pointed to it. 'Not a lot to go on by the looks?'

'You'd be surprised,' Hedley smiled, holding up a USB memory stick concealed in one of the holdalls side pockets.

Mason drew back. 'Good lord, that could be useful, Tom.'

Dropping the USB into a clear forensic bag, Hedley pointed to the vehicle's ignition. 'He must have had a set of keys by the looks.'

'He did. He stole them from an adjoining hotel guest room.'

'That would account for it as this model is fitted with an excellent anti-theft security device.' He watched as Hedley reached inside the glove compartment still looking for clues. 'Our friend is becoming complacent. Either his mind's elsewhere, or something is seriously bugging him.'

Mason looked at Hedley confused. 'What makes you say that?'

'It's strange he should take off and leave the vehicle unattended with his possessions stuck on the back seat, unless—'

'What made you open the holdall in the first place?'

'Just curious.'

'What if it had been booby trapped?'

'You've been watching far too many James Bond movies, Jack. These people have more sophisticated ways of getting rid of us if they need to. Besides, car bombs are mainly for terrorists nowadays.'

Mason stood with his hands in his pockets as a couple of onlookers were stopped at the police cordon tape. One of them was frantically waving his arms in the air and kept pointing to the northbound services. Seconds later, the young constable guarding the crime scene moved purposefully towards them.

'Can I have a word, sir?'

'Yes, of course. What is it, Constable?'

He was young, Mason thought, fresh out of police training school but he still came across as capable. The constable turned towards the group of onlookers now standing behind the police cordon tape. He pointed at them. 'A few of these people saw the driver get out of his vehicle and cross over the skywalk. He was last seen heading towards the northbound motorway filling station, but quickly disappeared from view.'

'What else did they tell you?'

'Not a lot. When I informed them that this was now a crime scene, they asked me to find out what was happening about their vehicles.'

'Did anyone mention what the driver looked like?'

'He wasn't a tall man, balding, with a round rubbery face, excusing the expression.'

'Sounds like Uncle Arthur,' Mason smiled, turning to Tom Hedley.

'Sorry, sir!'

'It's nothing, Constable.'

The officer looked at him somewhat confused. 'What shall I tell these people in the meantime, sir? They're obviously keen to get back to their vehicles.'

Mason thought about it. 'We need written statements from anyone present who saw anything. Tell them we'll deal with their vehicles in due course.'

'Will do, sir.'

'And well done,' Mason acknowledged.

As the constable turned on his heel, the anxious group of onlookers surged towards him but were quickly held back by a determined second officer. Mason felt sorry for them. Not until their investigations were finished here could anything be touched or moved.

Hedley swivelled to face Mason. 'In all honesty there's not a lot more we can do here. I've arranged for the stolen vehicle to be taken back to the compound for further forensic examination, and—'

'And the USB memory stick?' Mason asked.

'I'll get the Tech Crime Unit to fast track it through their system.'

'That could be useful, Tom.'

Hedley shrugged. 'Who knows?'

'It must be of some use I would have thought.'

Hedley pointed to a familiar figure fast homing in them. 'It would appear the vultures have already got a sniff of the dead carcass by the looks.'

'Shit.' Mason whispered under his breath. 'Christopher Sykes. I wonder where that sleazebag got his information from?'

The newspaper reporter exchanged glances as if itching to say something. Not very well liked, an edge of irritation entered Sykes' tone as he brushed the flecks of dandruff from his jacket. 'Good morning, gentlemen. Care telling me what this is all about?'

Mason almost burst out laughing. 'Run out of petrol, have we?'

Sykes eyes narrowed a fraction. 'No, my tank's completely full as it happens.'

'How can I help?' Mason asked.

'Is this the BMW that was stolen from the Marriott Hotel?'

'It could be. Why do you ask?'

'Anything to do with this Russian agent that everyone is talking about?'

Mason's heart sank. How could Sykes have possibly known all that?

CHAPTER

FORTY-SEVEN

The Cumberland Arms wasn't open for business, but the side door was unlocked. Having managed a broken night's sleep, Jack Mason had arrived there early that morning and was seated in a back room. Still with unfinished business to attend to, he was hoping his informant would show. He'd lost all track of the cases he'd worked, but this one was testing his patience. But sometimes new lines of enquiry emerged from nowhere, and the lucky breaks just happened.

The lounge door opened, and a short man appeared. He was holding out his hand, and Mason shook it.

'How are you keeping, Inspector?'

'Fine. And you?'

'Had a few nasty scares lately, but I'm still managing to stay clear of the wooden box.'

The Chief Inspector smiled. There were two potential candidates on his "want to talk to list" and Ronnie Flanigan was one of them. Mason's eyes narrowed as he checked his surroundings. For a moment he was back at David Carlisle's house in Whitburn and thinking about the boy's safety. Police work was all about contacts, people who lived on the edge who could tell you what you wanted to know.

'How's the missus nowadays?'

'She's fine,' Flanigan replied chirpily, 'she finally packed in her little part-time job at the local supermarket. It was her hands. . . full of arthritis. We're still managing to make ends meet, but only just.'

'Keeping out of trouble, are we?'

'Trying my best, Inspector.'

Formalities over with, Mason reached into his pocket and pulled out a photograph of Yavlinsky taken at Heathrow Airport. He pointed to it. 'I have a little job for you, Ronnie.'

Flanigan stared at the monochrome image and shrugged. 'Never seen him before. Who is he?'

'His name's Grigori Yavlinsky, but he may go under a few different names.'

'What's he been up to then?'

'It's a long story and I'm tired of telling it. Besides, no one bothers to listen to me anymore.'

'Try bending my ear, Inspector.'

Mason filled him in with the details. Not about the Russian banking scam, more on the barrister's suspicious death. The press had been silent these past few weeks owing to a high court action taken out on reporting restrictions, so most of what he was telling him hadn't reached the streets. Flanigan seemed keen, and Mason was encouraged by it. Besides, his informant was well connected, and valuable information could save him a lot of legwork and time. It was a fine balancing act but compared to policing overtime rates it was a quick and cost-effective method of intelligence gathering.

'So,' said Flanigan. 'What is it you're wanting me to do?'

Mason explained. 'Yavlinsky travels light and pays good money for other people's services.'

'Better rates than you're offering, no doubt?'

'Sod off.' Mason groaned. 'It's me who's kept you out of trouble all these years. . . remember?'

'Try telling that to the missus.'

Mason nodded. 'You need to be mindful that Yavlinsky's a dangerous individual to deal with and may have connections with the Russian mafia.'

'Big fish in little ponds are easier to spot.' Flanigan laughed. 'What's on your mind, Inspector?'

'I need you to find him for me.' Mason handed him an envelope stuffed with money. He took it and shoved it into a pocket – quick like. 'When you do find him, you're to ring that telephone number. Don't get involved, leave that to us.'

Flanigan hunched his shoulders – a habitual stance that told Mason he was interested.

'What's this guy's main interests?'

Mason pointed a finger at Flanigan as he played on the informant's heartstrings. 'This isn't for general knowledge, but there's a ten-year-old boy depending on you finding him for me.'

He told him more but chose not to elaborate.

'This must be the kid who saw this barrister commit suicide, I take it?'

Mason nodded. 'Yes, but that's as far is it goes.'

'I guess the kid's a key witness?'

'No more questions, Ronnie.'

In a way Flanigan was never a bad crook, just one of life's losers. In and out of prison most of his life, he'd finally grown tired of the disruptions. He'd recently been diagnosed with terminal cancer and was desperately trying to put his house in order before the big day eventually arrived. He knew he could be trusted, and a little extra cash wouldn't go amiss in the Flanigan household budget right now. It was a no brainer as far as Mason was concerned, and he was happy to oblige.

Flanigan rounded on him. 'Give me a few days, but I can't promise you anything.'

'Stay safe, Ronnie. Don't get too close to this man!'

'It's not my style, Inspector. And you know it.' Flanigan cocked his head to one side as if to make a point. 'Talking about staying safe, a little bird tells me you had a narrow escape yourself a couple of months back.'

It was Mason's turn to laugh. 'You know me, Ronnie, it'll take more than a madman to put me down in a wooden box.'

Flanigan gave him a haunting look. 'We all have to face up to it someday, Inspector. It's one of life's inevitabilities.'

Mason guessed what Flanigan was driving at and decided to level with him. 'Stay out of trouble, Ronnie. Find Yavlinsky for me, and I promise to look after you and the missus when the going gets tough.'

Time was running out for Ronnie Flanigan, and the informant knew it. Not the best of situations to find yourself in, Mason thought. At least Flanigan now had a purpose in life, and a decent wodge of money in his pocket to enjoy a few extra luxuries. Life could be cruel at times, but some people had nothing but bad luck all their lives, and Flanigan was one of them.

CHAPTER
FORTY–EIGHT

Northumbria Police Headquarters, home to the sixth largest police force in England and Wales, was just a thirty-minute drive from Seaton Sluice. Located on the outskirts of Ponteland, a district north of Newcastle, it was one of Jack Mason's old stomping grounds. He still had a strong affiliation with the place, although he was glad to see the back of it if the truth was known. But he was here for a reason. A sighting of Yavlinsky had been reported, and it could be of major interest.

Clearing security, DCI Mason and DS Holt were met at reception by Detective Inspector Swan. After brief introductions, together the three plain clothed police officers moved at pace towards the rear of the building. All kinds of emotions tugged Jack Mason as he walked along the long narrow corridor – both good and evil. He'd been in this kind of situation before, and inside this very building come to think of it.

The old operations room looked exactly as he'd left it, and that was almost three years ago. He wondered where time had gone and realised just how short life really was. Close to the back wall he caught a glimpse of his old glass fronted office, and his emotions were running high. Except for the sign on the door which read: DETECTIVE INSPECTOR ARCHIE SWAN, very little else had changed. There were no smiley face stickers attached to windows like the good old days, though. Swan was ex-military, a disciplinarian who ran his team with an iron rod. Having spent several years on active counterterrorist operations out in Afghanistan, he even had the office desks meticulously lined in a neat and orderly military fashion.

The moment he stepped into his old office, Mason's heart sank.

'Same old furniture, Archie?'

'It goes with the position, I'm afraid.' Swan smiled.

'Tight bastards, it's the same old crap that I had.'

'It may not look much, but I can assure you that the coffee has improved.'

Mason closed the door behind him and took up a seat opposite. His head full of memories, he stared at the crime board to the left of Swan's desk. Faces he didn't recognise, a case he knew nothing about. From what he could gather, another drugs gang was about to get its comeuppance, and he knew the area they were operating in. No longer in charge here, it wasn't his case, but the past all came flooding back.

'So, what's the latest on this Sanderson Law Chambers break-in?' Mason asked.

'Twice in six months, only this time we've managed to arrest someone.'

'Local, was he?' asked Holt.

'Sad case, not the sort of person we were hoping to catch.'

'You can't win them all, Archie,' Mason smiled.

'No, I suppose not.'

Mason recognised the disappointment. 'How did you manage to nab him?'

'It wasn't exactly difficult. Apart from cutting his wrist on a broken window pane and leaving his DNA all over the watch repair workshops, he was caught on CCTV cameras.'

Mason burst out laughing. 'He sounds like a real bungler?'

'He is, and he admitted to it the moment we pressed charges.'

'Well at least he wasn't trying to steal case files.'

It was Swan's turn to burst out laughing. 'Adding to his own more likely.'

Coffee arrived, brought in on a tray by a young lad in his mid-teens. Too young to be a trainee, Mason thought. He was keen, and probably here on a work experience programme.

'So,' Swan began, easing back in his seat, 'what's the latest developments regarding this Russian fraud trial?'

Mason filled him in with the details, but he was more interested in hearing what Swan had to say about Yavlinsky than anything else.

'Have you been watching the news bulletins lately?' asked Swan.

'No. Why?'

'According to the former head of British Counter Terrorism, this hedge fund auditor, Stephen Rice, may have been poisoned at Bristol Airport.'

'I've heard no mention of that. What else did they say?'

'Not a lot. A spokesman for the Metropolitan Police said they believe it was a case of mistaken identity, which tells me it's a cover up.'

Mason took a sip of his coffee. 'Sensationalism gone mad, eh?'

'The Commissioner of Police is to make a brief statement tonight about it, so that should put an end to the matter.'

'Any mention of the Russians' involvement?' asked Holt.

'No, nothing.'

Clever, Mason thought. Feed the press with false information, then stand back and light the blue touch paper. Nine times out of ten the media would interview some trumped-up self-opinionated political commentator to give their spin on events and stir up as much public opinion as was humanly possible. Fake news ran rife, it seemed. On both sides of the fence.

There was knock at the door, and a medium built man, early forties, dressed in a dark suit and carrying a pile of case files under his arm, entered the room.

Swan signalled him towards an empty seat.

'I'd like you to meet DCI Jack Mason and DS George Holt from the Serious Crime Division over at Gateshead, Cyril. Can you fill them in about this recent Yavlinsky sighting?'

Sergeant Kent said nothing for a moment, then gave a brief jerky nod. 'I'll not bore you with the details, as you guys are far more familiar with the case than I am.'

Mason opened his hands expansively. 'Just tell us what you know?'

'Three days ago, I was working on a drugs bust over in the Walker district when I bumped into one of my regular informants.' The Sergeant fidgeted uneasily. 'One thing led to another and we both got around to talking about this fraud case that's due at the Newcastle law courts.'

'Which case is this?' Holt asked, pen poised notebook at the ready.

'The one involving the Russian banking scam.'

'And what did your informant tell you?'

'I know he likes to waffle on a bit,' said Kent, 'but he's good at extracting information out of people. The thing is, he was approached by a man who bears a remarkable resemblance to this Russian guy *you* people are looking for.'

Mason felt a sudden adrenaline rush.

'You mean Grigori Yavlinsky?'

'Yes.' The sergeant nodded.

'And what was Yavlinsky wanting with your informant exactly?'

'He was looking for a guy called Colin Glover.'

Christ, Mason thought, the very man who had installed the CCTV cameras at Seaton School.

DS Holt leaned forward. 'What did Yavlinsky want with Colin Glover?'

'He said he had a job for him and was willing to pay him good money.'

Mason looked at Holt and guessed what his companion was thinking. 'So, what did your informant tell Yavlinsky?'

'Not a lot.'

Mason drew back in his seat.

'What do you think?' asked DI Swan.

'It sounds like Yavlinsky all right,' Mason replied. 'Glover's been charged in connection with breaking and entering into Seaton School and installing a shit load of CCTV monitoring cameras. He claims he was working for a third party and denies all knowledge of any Russian connection.'

Swan eyed Mason with suspicion. 'Do you think our informant could be lying?'

'I doubt it, but it seems that Glover may have had a lucky escape by the sound of things.' Mason swung sharply to face Sergeant Kent. 'This informant of yours, will he talk if he's brought in?'

'He will if he's paid,' the sergeant said, rubbing his fingers together.

'Good man.' Mason smiled, still unsure where this was heading.

Swan turned to Sergeant Kent. 'Let's start with a written statement and we'll arrange for your man to be picked up and taken across to Gateshead Police Station.'

Mason thought about it, and then said, 'Send me a copy and any CCTV footage you can get hold of, and I'll get the facial recognition experts involved. If we do have a "look- alike" on our hands, we need to eliminate him from our enquiries.'

The room fell silent.

CHAPTER FORTY-NINE

Dressed in the clothes he'd picked up from a charity shop, Chameleon moved ill at ease through the streets of Newcastle. Convinced he was suffering from radiation poisoning, stomach cramps had kept him awake for most of the night. Still left with a bitter taste in his mouth, no matter how much liquid he drank, the back of his throat felt as though it was on fire. Poking his finger into the corner of his mouth, he checked to see if his gums were bleeding. Not that they were, but it was a sure sign of radiation sickness he'd read. Nothing normally fazed him, but this worried him stiff.

It was well after eleven o'clock when Chameleon sauntered into Grainger Street. Still clinging to thoughts of Stephen Rice's painful death, he was now having reservations about his own health. Convinced his hair was dropping out, he kept rubbing his head to see if it was. Not only was he sweating profusely, the fear of what toxic poisoning might do to him had finally taken hold.

Nobody paid him much attention as he slipped into Grey Street. Having found shelter from the rain in a pharmacy store, he was trawling the aisles for something to settle the stomach cramps. The pains had got worse, and more frequent by the hour. He'd thought about returning to London but getting there was the problem – the police were watching all the stations. The irony was, he was having concerns about the property developments at his Belgravia apartment. He knew how British builders liked to operate, and if you didn't keep on top of them, they would rip you off as soon as look at you.

Worried sick the police would catch up with him before he could complete the operation, he entered the Newcastle City Library a nervous wreck. Despite all the frustration, on reaching the third floor his contact was sitting waiting for him and he heaved a sigh of relief. He was a plump man, with a large ginger beard and inquisitive goat-like eyes that danced in their sockets as though attached to elastic bands. Awash with excitement, he immediately homed in on him.

'How are you doing?' the man asked as he lifted his head.

Chameleon shot him a sideways glance whilst checking his surroundings. He needn't have bothered. Nobody had paid much attention to him, and their heads were buried in books.

'Have you got what I came for?'

'It's all there,' the man said, pointing to the cool bag at his feet.

'How much do I owe you?'

'Not until I know what you're intending to do with it.'

'Exactly what it says on the tin.' Chameleon grinned.

The man eyes sparkled with mischievous humour. 'You do realise this is lethal stuff?'

'That's why I'm paying you good money for it.'

The man forced a smile, as though he had wind. 'We agreed four hundred.'

Chameleon reached into his pocket and pulled out a wodge of used banknotes. He handed it to him. The man was standing now, checking the money as if his life depended on it. After he'd finished counting, he slid the cool bag towards him with the instep of his foot.

'Don't you trust me, you mother-fucker?'

'It's not that I don't trust you,' the man said warily, 'it's all about traceability nowadays.'

Chameleon shot him a daggers look. 'What have you heard?'

'Nothing. Why?'

'What! You think I'm some sort of undercover police officer or something?'

'You never can tell these days.'

Chameleon considered his options, picked up the cool bag and tucked it under his arm. As the doors to the lift slid open again, he stepped inside and pressed the descend button. He could see the man's reflection in the lift mirror and knew he was being watched. No surprise there, he thought.

The moment he reached ground level, and just to be sure, he decided to head for Grey's Monument. *Bugger the lot of them*, he cursed in Russian. Now he had what he came for, he was itching to finish the job.

★★★

Later that day, the weather had picked up, and Ronnie Flanigan was feeling on top of the world. He'd heard on the grapevine that the man he was looking for was holed up in one of the back streets in Walker. He was in no hurry. The silver BMW parked up in front of him hadn't moved in days. It was a 08 registration, Flanigan noticed, and it belonged to a guy two streets away. A good sign, he chuckled, as nobody gave a damn about anything around here.

After hours sat in his car watching the property opposite, there was still no sign of the Russian showing. Sometimes you got lucky, but most times you had to dig deep. There was always the back entrance, of course, but he'd covered that with an electronic breaker switch which he'd fitted to the suspect's door stanchion. Nothing elaborate, but if anyone did try to open it, it would transmit a bleeper signal to a receiver he carried in his pocket. It was a trick he'd learnt whilst in prison, and it had never failed him yet.

He stared at his watch.

In many ways Flanigan didn't mind the long hours spent shadowing suspects. He'd been paid well for his services, which was always a bonus in this game. Besides, he didn't have a lot of energy these days, not since the chemo treatment. Getting out of bed was a monumental effort, even the pain-relieving medication never completely took away the discomfort. It had been a long emotional rollercoaster ride, and he still wasn't out of the woods yet. Not by a long chalk. There again, Flanigan thought. If he could buy himself a few more extra weeks of time it would have all been worthwhile in the end.

A figure approached from the bottom of Welbeck Street. A short man, middle aged, portly, and wearing a stupid grin on his face. At a glance he looked remarkable like the man that Jack Mason had asked him to hunt out – but he wasn't one hundred percent sure.

He lowered his car window just as the man had levelled with him and tried to get a closer look. 'Excuse me for asking,' Flanigan said almost apologetically, 'do you happen to know if Caroline Cummings lives in this area?'

'Just a minute,' the man said, eying him up and down. 'I'll ask my partner. She's bound to know.'

The man had barely been gone a few minutes before he returned carrying a large brown paper bag in his hand. Half expecting trouble, Flanigan fired up the car's engine just in case his hunch was right. Then, as the man stooped down alongside the driver's door, he slid his hand inside the brown paper bag and pulled out a long hypodermic syringe and pointed it towards Flanigan's face.

The informant froze.

The next thing that Flanigan felt, was his body being trussed back and his head hitting the headrest hard. Dazed, he tried to struggle free, but his seatbelt had locked solid and prevented him from moving. Then, he caught the man's arm as it slowly rose to eye level, followed by a sharp searing jab to the side of his neck.

Flanigan yelped out loud. 'What the—'

'Take that, you bastard,' the man smiled.

Within seconds of being injected, Flanigan felt a tingling sensation running through his fingers; followed by a numbness travelling down his arms. He desperately tried to fight it, but his brain was too jumbled up to think clearly and he was slowly losing control of his movements. As his foot hit the accelerator pedal hard, the man shot sideways suddenly, and banged his head against the car's door frame. At first, he thought he had killed him, but Flanigan wasn't hanging around to find out. He cried out, but nobody came to his rescue and he was fighting it every inch of the way.

But there was something else that was fuelling Flanigan's anger, something more sinister he couldn't put a finger on. Whatever substance had been pumped into his veins, he knew it had to be lethal.

He needed to act fast, get himself to a hospital!

Slipping in and out of consciousness he somehow managed to stay in control of the wheel. Speed was vital. It was his only hope of survival.

The pain now unbearable, he tried to stay focused.

A narrow main street, a church and three pubs. Barely a mile from the hospital's A&E, he saw the stationary vehicle at the very last minute and swerved to avoid it. Then he saw people standing at the bus stop – their faces white and etched in fear as he bore down on them at speed. Dozens of them, scattering in all directions as though under attack.

Shit, shit, shit, Flanigan screamed out.

Hands gripping steering wheel, eyes firmly shut, he swung on the wheel as hard as he could. What Flanigan didn't see, not until the very last second at least, was the nose of the 20 Ton dump truck now bearing down on him.

CHAPTER
FIFTY

The news of Ronnie Flanigan's sudden demise had hit Jack Mason hard, but the report from the Coroner's Office made for even more disturbing reading. Confused at first, then mortified, Mason laid the slip of paper down on the desktop in front of him and tried to get his head around it all. It had taken emergency crews the best part of forty-five minutes to free poor Ronnie from the wreckage of his beloved Ford Escort estate, and it was in one hell of a mess. According to Road Traffic, the force from the impact was so great that it had pushed the engine block back into the driver's seat crushing Flanigan to death in the process. At least it was instant and no one else had died in the incident, but it was little consolation to Mason.

He sipped some water from a jug, checked the overnight crime serials, and made a few phone calls to set the wheels in motion on another full-scale murder investigation. It wasn't the fact that Flanigan had been blamed for the incident that upset him, it was the fact he'd been injected with a massive dose of black mamba snake venom. According to a leading zoologist at the Kruger National Park in South Africa, just two small drops of the stuff were enough to kill a person in as little as twenty minutes.

Not only did it contain fast-acting neurotoxins that shut down the victim's nervous system causing paralysis, without antivenom the fatality rate from a black mamba bite was almost 100 percent. No, Mason thought. Flanigan must have been close to death minutes before the incident occurred. This was a massive dose he'd been injected with, and a highly lethal one at that. One of the deadliest snakes on earth, these speedy reptiles could move faster than a human could run. But that was in real life, and this was a lethal neurotoxin that had been injected into Flanigan's neck using a hypodermic syringe.

As he stared in bewilderment at the spider's web of prompts now pinned to the crime board, Mason began to wonder – *where on earth could anyone have acquired such a deadly serum?*

It wasn't looking good suddenly. This wasn't an everyday poison and would have been extremely difficult to obtain. Having searched the rented property close to where his informant had been injected, he found the perpetrator had long gone. There were no eyewitness accounts, no CCTV coverage, and nothing following a door-to-door enquiry. Part of him wanted to make amends for Flanigan's death, as if it was his fault. Yes, he'd sent him to do a job for him, but he'd warned him to stay well clear of the Russian. He hadn't, and Flannigan had paid the ultimate price because of it.

Mason looked down at his notes.

'So, you found no traces of the deadly serum in the property?'

'No, nothing,' Tom Hedley the senior forensic scientist replied.

'Where in hell's name would someone obtain such a poison?'

Tom Hedley scratched the side of head confused. 'More importantly, we've picked up the slightest traces of a military toxic nerve agent in the property, which the experts are currently analysing.'

'The same chemical footprint as that used to kill Stephen Rice?'

'According to Porton Down, it's believed to have come from a batch developed by the Soviet Union in the 1970s.'

'Sounds like we're making some progress at last?'

'Not really, everyone's refusing to comment.' Hedley stared at him from across the desk. 'It may prove one thing, though. Has Yavlinsky inadvertently contaminated himself whilst handling the stuff?'

Mason drew breath. 'Courier or hit man, do you think?'

'It's hard to say.'

'What is it with these individuals, Tom? Why are Special Branch feeding us full of crap and treating us like mushrooms in the dark for God's sake! They've known for weeks that Yavlinsky was implicated in Stephen Rice's murder, as minute traces of a military type toxic nerve agent were found on the steering wheel of the Russians hire car.'

Hedley hunched his shoulders as if he didn't have an answer to give. 'The Foreign Office is obviously facing a dilemma and trying to keep a tight lid on things for reasons of national security. If the Russians *are* willing to cooperate, then there must be more to this than they are letting on about.'

'Like what?'

'Let's face it, military type toxic nerve agents are in no way exclusively used by the Russian State, or non-Russian mafias for that matter.'

'Meaning?'

'Other countries who have already developed these agents have been in the public domain for at least a decade. We know the USA and Israel have it, not to mention China, Japan and various other Eastern European nations—'

'What are you driving at?'

Hedley held Mason's gaze. 'Counterintelligence is way beyond us mortals, especially where threats to national security are involved.'

Mason thought about it.

'Maybe Rice's death was a way of deterring other Russian agents from defecting?'

'Undoubtedly,' said Hedley, 'and you need to bear in mind that some nerve agents can kill without delay. As far as we know, there are some radiation compositions that do not set off standard radiation detectors because they emit only alpha particles. What makes them ideal for a would-be assassin is that they are easy to conceal and transport across borders and can be diluted in a bottle of liquid or carried in crystallised form. Detecting them is not only time consuming. . . it requires an experienced analyst to identify them.'

Mason considered the facts. His conversations with MI5, his meetings with the Chief Constable, and his discussions with Superintendent Gregory. Hedley was right. This was way over his head and had nothing to do with everyday policing in the slightest. It was his job to protect the public, nothing more, nothing less. One thing for sure, though, now that Yavlinsky had gone to ground having injected Flanigan with a lethal dosage of deadly snake venom meant he was capable of almost anything.

This was the wakeup call that Mason had been dreading, which meant that anyone remotely involved in the forthcoming trial against the Russian bank was now a potential target. The question was, who else was pulling Yavlinsky's strings?

Mason felt the burden of responsibility just as strongly every time. It wasn't that simple, though, and Flanigan's tragic demise had certainly put the cat among the pigeons – in more ways than one.

CHAPTER
FIFTY—ONE

The boy had long gone when Chameleon returned to Seaton School that morning. Waiting at the school gates, it was amazing how much gossip you could pick up. Rumours ran rife, and the woman standing next to him couldn't keep her mouth shut. He'd only been there a few minutes, but in that short space of time she'd told him everything he wanted to know. Who the boy's foster mother was, the special protection needs he'd received at the school – everything. In many ways, Chameleon knew how to extract information out of people and how to pull at their heart strings. Street gossip was priceless, but this woman's nattering was doing his head in.

It was a beautiful day, unseasonably hot for September. Dressed in a white open neck shirt, black trousers and brown shoes, the Russian assassin felt ill at ease as he strode towards the Kings Arms opposite Seaton Sluice harbour. The view across the shoreline was superb, reminding him of Kerch in Autumn – not that he was wistful. He wasn't.

Nearing the long row of cottages, he took a deep breath and paused in reflection, thinking about the task ahead. All those weeks spent trying to find the boy's whereabouts, and here he was closing in on the kid's foster mother's house. His plan was simple enough, but it was strange how some events developed. One minute you were riding the crest of a wave, the next you were scraping the bottom of the barrel and trying to stay afloat. If he'd have only known then what he knew now, he wouldn't be in the mess he now found himself in.

He opened the gate, walked up to the large brass knocker, and gave it a sharp rap. His knock was answered by a short slender woman in her early-fifties wearing a rust-coloured dress and a pair of bright green slippers.

'I'm sorry to trouble you,' Chameleon said, 'you must be Mrs Broadbent.'

'Yes, I am. How can I help you?' she warily asked.

'I was wondering if I might have a word?'

She looked him up and down, and then said. 'And you are?'

'Let me introduce myself,' Chameleon said, holding out a hand. 'I'm Peter Tetley and it's about the cottage next-door. I work for one of the local estate agents, and before we can put the property back on the market again, we're having some alterations done to the place.'

'Can I ask what you're doing?'

'Certainly. We're extending the back bedroom and the whole place is having a major makeover before the new owner moves in.'

'New owner?' she said, with a look of surprise. 'It's not going to be turned into one of those second homes, is it?'

'Why do you ask?'

'Because most of them are usually let as holiday rentals.'

'It's nothing of the sort.' Chameleon replied, intrigued by the warmth of her tone, and the notion that he may have finally won her over. 'It's actually a well-known crime writer who has bought the cottage, and she intends to make it her permanent home.'

'An author,' she gasped. 'What, here in the village?'

'Yes. Isn't that wonderful?'

'Do I know her?'

'Unfortunately, I'm not allowed to divulge the client's name but I can tell you her books are extremely popular.'

'Goodness – and she'll be living next door to me?'

'Indeed, she will.'

'When is she moving in?'

'If the work goes to plan, we're hoping to have everything done and dusted within the next few weeks.'

'An author. I've never met one of those before.'

Chameleon was quick to signal his thoughts. 'I hear you're a bit of a celebrity yourself, Mrs Broadbent.'

She looked at him oddly but refrained from answering.

'You're a foster mother, I believe.'

'Who told you that?' she countered warily.

'One of the police officers who handed me the keys to the property. He said you were recently looking after a young boy?'

'Yes, I was.' Her head dropped momentarily. 'But he's no longer living with us anymore.'

Bullshit! Chameleon groaned. *Just give me his name!*

He gestured with his hand as if to take in the whole of Seaton Sluice. 'Taken to school in a police car every day, he must have been the talk of the village.'

She smiled. 'I'm not sure about that, but we were all sorry to see young Martin go.'

There was a hint of sadness in her voice, but the mere mention of the boy's Christian name sent shivers down Chameleon's spine. All he needed now was a surname. But these things took time, and time was a luxury commodity and he was desperate to get going.

'Where did Martin go?'

'I've absolutely no idea, Social Services were dealing with it as far as I know. It all happened so quickly,' she confessed. 'One minute he was here, the next he was whisked off to another place.'

'What about the boy's parents. . . are they still alive?'

'His father is. He has something to do with the building trade, I believe.'

Chameleon's eyes narrowed a fraction. 'Really? What's his father's name?'

'Why would you want to know that?'

'Builders are in high demand, Mrs Broadbent. Me being an estate agent, I may have some serious work to offer him.'

'It's Kennedy,' she replied.

'*Kennedy!*'

'Yes, and now that you mention it his father is working down in Nottingham, I believe.'

Still unsure of what he was up to – or what his intentions were – she'd fallen into Chameleon's trap. He swung to face her. 'You mentioned social services, do you happen to have a contact name?'

She shot him a glance as if the realisation had suddenly hit home. 'Why would you want to know that?' she asked brashly.

'Just curious, that's all.'

'It's a rather an odd question for an estate agent to be asking?' she glowered.

He could see she was agitated and noted her stubby fingers were trembling slightly. He'd considered strangling her, but quickly thought the better of it the minute a white van pulled into the street. Besides, he wasn't in the game of killing old women, and certainly didn't want to rouse unnecessary panic in the village. Not now, he didn't. Not until he'd finished his mission.

Pleased with his findings, he decided to call it a day.

'It's been a pleasure talking to you, Mrs Broadbent. If the builders do cause you any problems over the next couple of weeks, you're to give me a call.'

'And your number is?'

He pointed to the cottage next door. 'As soon as I'm done here, I'll pop one of my business cards through your letter box.'

Eyes full of suspicion, head full of uncertainty, she hurriedly closed the door behind her.

Chapter

Fifty-Two

The news back from Social Services wasn't good, and David Carlisle had all but given up on Martin moving out of his property. Furious at having given in too hastily to Jack Mason's appeal for help, he was trying to come to terms with it all. In many ways the house wasn't his own any longer – even Benjamin the cat wasn't happy with the arrangements. Apart from feeding time, his feline partner spent most of the day sleeping on top of the wardrobe nowadays.

'I'm bored,' Martin suddenly announced. 'When can we visit Marsden Grotto?'

'Not today,' Carlisle replied.

'But it's only a couple of miles away.'

Carrington looked at the boy quizzically and smiled. 'It's not up to David. It's up to DCI Mason to decide if you can go. Besides, he's trying his best to find you a more permanent place to stay.'

'What's wrong with my Auntie Glenis's house, why can't I stay with her?'

Carrington spoke sympathetically. 'You can't keep moving around willy-nilly or you're never going to make any new friends.'

'But this place is boring, and there's nothing to do here.'

'Try reading a book, there's plenty upstairs.'

'I've looked at them, and they're boring.'

Carlisle took a deep breath and thought about Martin's predicament. There had to be something that could be done to improve the situation, surely the police could come up with a better solution. Cooped up inside his house all day wasn't good for morale – no wonder the boy was turning rebellious. There again, he thought. Now that a would-be Russian assassin was on the loose, nowhere was safe it appeared.

Mason clearly had a plan up his sleeve and he wished he knew what it was. Something was going on behind the scenes, and he guessed it was coming from higher levels. Although not directly involved, Carlisle knew what government agents could get up to, as he'd worked with them often enough in the past. What if they were trying to lure Yavlinsky into a trap – using his house and the boy as bait? It was a frightening prospect, but it was a strong possibility, nevertheless. On the other hand, in the carnivorously competitive world of Russian politics, an assassin wouldn't think twice about killing a ten-year-old child if it got in the way of their plans. The FSB's cavalier attitude towards the niceties of political etiquette was non-existent when it came to the art of elimination. No, Carlisle thought. Something was afoot, and whatever it was he didn't like the sound of it.

Thinking about this, he remembered his time spent serving as a criminal profiler with the Metropolitan Police. He was younger then, more passionate about his job. But life had moved on, and nowadays trained assassins at the very least were more articulate and smarter with their movements. Many would live in the UK, searching through local cemeteries to find a deceased child that had passed away young. Taking that identity, if the checks worked out, they would create a false myth – take up a foreign passport and blend into Western society with ease. There had to be a darker side to this, and one involving huge sums of dirty money.

This wasn't the kind of operation that Carlisle would have felt comfortable working on – far from it. What with armed police officers lurking on every street corner, his life wasn't the same anymore. Not only was Yavlinsky a threat to national security he was a threat to anyone he came in contact with – and that worried him.

The more he thought about it, the more the private investigator realised the urgency of the situation. Yavlinsky didn't carry guns; his method of killing was silent and deadly. Finding him wouldn't be easy either. Besides, what had the Russian to lose? An ex KGB officer, he would have been trained to defend his corner at any cost. That was the nature of the beast – that's what made would-be assassins a cut above the rest.

Carrington's brow corrugated. 'I know Jack Mason has the boy at heart, so maybe we should have a word with him about a visit to Marsden Grotto?'

'Don't involve me,' Carlisle replied, lifting his arms as in surrender. 'I'm up to here with Jack Mason and his harebrained schemes.'

Carlisle's phone rang, and he answered it.

'David Carlisle—'

'Good morning, Mr Carlisle. A colleague of mine tells me that you are a private investigator?'

'Yes, I am. And you are?'

'James Horniman.'

'How can I help, Mr Horniman?'

'My workmate has asked me to contact you on his behalf, it's about his son.'

'And what is your colleague's name, may I ask?'

'Phillip Kennedy.'

Carlisle trod cautiously. 'And how do you know Phil?'

'We are working on a construction site together here in Nottingham.'

'I see. What can I do for you?'

The line went quiet for a moment.

'Listen, Mr Carlisle. I'm travelling north this weekend and Phil has asked me to drop a birthday present off at your office. It's for. . . Martin.'

'Sure. Do you have my office address?'

'Yes, I do.' There was another long pause. 'How is Martin keeping incidentally? I hear he's moved away from his foster mother's house in Seaton Sluice?'

'He's doing fine.'

'Where is he now?'

Carlisle paused to consider the question. Strange, he thought.

'I've absolutely no idea,' he lied, 'but I would have thought his father would have been able to tell you that.'

'No. He's never mentioned it to me. I'm just curious that's all.'

'Will that be all, Mr Horniman?'

'Yes, for now.'

His phone went dead, and he noticed the caller's number had been withheld and made a mental note of it.

Carlisle looked at the calendar pinned to the kitchen wall and checked his future arrangements. It was Friday, and he'd promised a weekend fishing trip away with his father. The way things were going there was little chance of that happening now. Besides, Jack Mason was stuck in his ways and rarely listened to other people's point of view. No, Carlisle thought. There was no way his old workmate was going to relax his security arrangements – not in a million years. The boy was in grave danger, even he knew that. But how to get around the current stalemate was the problem.

Benjamin arrived on the scene to see what all the fuss was about. Licking his paws, he stared at the female detective and then warily across at the boy. The cat was hungry, but after making a bee-line for his food bowl he was working out his options. His life wasn't his own anymore, and he was tired of all the attention he was getting.

Still thinking about Mr Horniman's call, something didn't sit right in Carlisle's mind. Although the caller had most of his facts right, his story didn't add up. Phil Kennedy had spent an awful lot of time in prison these past few years, and the emotional strain on the family had taken its toll. Separated from his wife, Martin had suffered unimaginable disruption because of it. No, he thought. If Phil had anything to give to his son, he would have delivered it personally. That's how his friend rolled these days – nothing got swept under the carpet.

'When is your next birthday, Martin?' Carlisle asked casually.

The boy looked at him dumbfounded. 'Not until December. Why?'

Shit, the private investigator cursed. *Had Yavlinsky finally caught up with them?*

CHAPTER
FIFTY-THREE

In the early morning light, DS Holt peered down on the street below and raised his eyebrows a fraction. It was five-thirty, and some idiot jogger had stopped to tie his shoelaces. What was it with these people, why couldn't they get a life?

After filling in the log sheet, Holt checked his watch and took another sip of his coffee. Next, he stared at the tiny monitoring screen covering the rear lane of the private investigator's house. Adjusting to the light, apart from a big fat ginger cat staring up at a flock of squawking seagulls in the hope that one of them might land, the street was relatively quiet. Time spent in the surveillance house wasn't all it was cracked up to be, and long hours spent staring at the house opposite was slowly driving him mad.

Holt shook his head and sighed. It was all getting out of hand. Sometimes he wondered what all the fuss was about, as there seemed little chance of a Russian assassin turning up in Whitburn village. The man was probably in London or smuggled out of the country in the back of a private jet.

As the door to the bedroom swung open, the sergeant's understudy appeared. Lean in stature with short cropped blond hair, Albert Blanch was one of the new up and coming stars on the force. Mid-twenties, with barely two years' service under his belt, Blanch was as keen as mustard. In a few years from now he would probably think differently, Holt thought. Promotion was thin on the ground, government cutbacks having put paid to that. Not like the good old days when it was much easier to advance up the promotion ladder through natural retirement.

'Anything to report?' asked Blanch.

Holt shook his head. 'Nah, same old, Albert.'

The sergeant folded his jacket over his arm as he prepared to leave. The room had a foist smell and stank of Chinese takeaway – the evidence left poking out of the waste bin. Holt paused at the door and pointed towards a small wooden table positioned at the back of the room. 'A new list of stolen vehicle registration numbers has been sent over from Road Traffic, so you'll need to keep an eye out. If you do happen to spot one, you're to contact Central Control.'

'Will do.' Blanch sighed as he shifted his weight. 'Any more news on the suspect's whereabouts?'

'Nothing yet. He's probably back in Russia if the truth was known.'

'Sounds about right,' Blanch agreed with a nod.

Pleased it was over, Holt smiled as he moved towards the top of the landing stairs. He could still hear the constable's mutterings, but the words were lost in the sound of his size twelve shoes hitting the bare foot treads at the end of another long shift.

***

Meanwhile across the street, Chameleon stretched his legs, thinking. It was pure genius how he'd conned the boy's previous foster mother into making her mouth go. And, unless he was mistaken, the boy was holed up inside the private investigator's house. Now that he had a name to work on, his plans were falling into place. Finding the school's photographer was genius – obtaining the boy's photograph priceless. This would never have happened back in Russia, not in a zillion years. The moment you tried to obtain another person's details, the FSB would be onto you like a flash.

Still feeling drained, the opportunity had come sooner than Chameleon had expected. It was Sunday, early morning, and most of the occupants in Whitburn village were fast asleep in bed. Having parked his stolen Fiat just a few streets from the private investigator's house, he didn't want to arouse suspicion. Stay calm, keep your eyes peeled and everything will fall into place, he told himself.

Chameleon knew how the British police system worked, and how they liked to cover each other's backs on operations such as this. Besides, the private investigator's house was probably bugged, so breaking into it would be risky. Now that he'd fitted electronic tracking devices to several unmarked police cars, it was much easier to keep tabs on their movements. And, if he ever did get into any kind of trouble with the law, he still had a few vials of snake venom at his disposal.

Eyes scanning the house opposite: the street was long and narrow. A few properties had driveways, but not all of them. Cars parked on either side of the road were a problem, as they made life difficult for manoeuvring around in. That's why he preferred to jog here on foot. Much easier, and less complicated. The more he thought about it, the more he knew he'd made the right decision. This was the second time in as many hours he'd checked the property out, and he'd finally found the chink in the police's armour.

Still undecided how to finish the job, he was hoping to finalise his plans. He would need a subtle distraction, something to flush the boy out of hiding without causing too much alarm. He could always set fire to the building in the middle of the night, of course, but would it guarantee success? Probably not. There again, he thought, if the kid played on his computer all day, then maybe he could deliver a pizza laced with deadly sea snake venom.

There was a thought!

As he made his way past the house with the large upstairs bay windows, he sensed preying eyes. It didn't take much, but to a trained eye the slightest movement caused him to flinch. Mad as it was, the private investigator was a bit of a geek as far as Chameleon was concerned. Who in their rightful mind would want to drive a beaten-up old Rover around all day? Not that it worried him, but it did make him smile.

Then from an upstairs bedroom he caught movement. It wasn't much – *the slightest chink in the curtains.* As he bent down to tie up his shoelaces, he noticed the man upstairs had moved to his left a few feet. Dressed in tracksuit bottoms, black T-shirt and carrying a newspaper tucked under his arm, he didn't look out of the ordinary. Maybe he was overreacting, worrying about nothing. There again, this wasn't the friendliest of places to hang around in either.

If he was being watched, it would be from an upstairs bedroom. Chameleon had his suspicions and knew how police covert operations worked. Stay clear of the windows, remove any mirrors in the room, as any sudden change in the light might draw people's attention towards you. It wasn't rocket science, and he knew that most British police offers were trained in the art of camouflage techniques.

He stared hard at the house again.

Tucked back on the driveway, he noticed a stationary silver Ford Focus and remained perfectly still for a moment. There were fumes coming from the exhaust, and he could hear the engine running. Adrenalin pumping, and knowing the police were out looking for him, Chameleon continued on down the street. Either these people were careless, or they were about to spring a trap.

He looked all around and behind him, but the street was silent and empty. He should have approached this differently, made alternative plans instead of waiting to see what unravelled.

Concentrating now, he doubled back on himself and approached the private investigator's house with caution.

Why hadn't the boy shown his face?

His mind running amok, Chameleon suddenly felt an urge to finish it. His was a simple plan. Slip in through the back door, climb the stairs, and inject the boy full of snake venom. Excellent idea! Executing it a different matter, of course.

Peering up at the bedroom window opposite, he distinctly caught movement this time. Unsettled, he jogged to the end of the street, turned right, and made his way back to the stolen Fiat. Nothing was ever easy – everything disorderly and confused. Narked at having to abort his plans a second time, he was keen to leave the area. Sooner or later he would need to finish the job, regardless of the dangers that surrounded him.

Next time, he thought.

CHAPTER

FIFTY-FOUR

Jack Mason wasn't in the best of spirits after he'd taken the call from DS Savage. Not that he was expecting good news, but the moment the sergeant confirmed the cause of Ronnie Flanigan's tragic death was due to snake poisoning, he breathed a sigh of relief. The sad thing was, even a powerful antidote wouldn't have saved his informant according to the Home Office Pathologist's report. Flanigan's immune system was so low after chemotherapy treatment that he would probably have died of heart failure anyway.

The team had worked tirelessly in tracking down the source of supply, which pleased him immensely. After a string of coordinated police raids in and around the city of Newcastle, five people were now under investigation. They did have a main suspect in mind, and Mason was keen to find out his connection with the Russian. But something was muddying the water, and as the Chief Inspector eased back in his seat, IR1 fell uncannily silent.

'*Dendroaspis polylepis*,' Mason began. 'One of the deadliest snakes in the world. I've never cared much for snakes myself. They're sly bastards and have a nasty habit of jumping out at you when least expected. Tell me, apart from owning a pet shop, what's your particular interest with Black Mamba snakes?'

Larry Hollins, a forty-six-year old local weirdo, swallowed hard. Interview Room 1 wasn't the friendliest place to be in when the chips were down, especially when the room temperature had been turned up to thirty-six degrees. Known locally as *Monty Python*, Hollins owned a small pet shop close to the city centre of Newcastle and was well known for his dodgy dealings in exotic reptiles and amphibians – especially amongst teenagers and a bunch of individuals who just happened to like snakes.

The problem was, international law decreed these creatures be bred in captivity, and not plucked from forests and rivers in some far-off foreign land. Even so, the European Union had allowed the import of over 20 million of these creatures in a ten-year period between 2004-2014, and in the US alone, millions of households owned at least one reptile. Popularity, it seemed, had spawned an enormous illegal trade, and Hollins was at the top of his game. In and out of the court rooms at least once a month, his criminal record was beginning to read like a zoologist's journal in Mason's judgement. Most of it involving the illegal trade of exotic species, and the abuse of CITES – a treaty which prohibit species threatened with extinction from being commercially traded across borders unless bred in captivity.

Hollins laughed as he rubbed a heavily tattooed arm. 'Snakes are fun, Inspector. You should try keeping one yourself.'

Mason shuddered at the thought. 'What happens to you if you get bitten by one?'

'It depends on what type of snake it is.'

'What about Black Mambas?'

'Now you're talking.'

'Just two drops of the potent black mamba venom can kill a person, I'm told.'

Hollins chuckled through blackened teeth. 'That's what makes them such an exciting species to breed.'

'So, you do deal in the deadly species?' Mason frowned.

Hollins turned sharply. 'Who said I did?'

'You just did,' Mason replied, staring down at his notes.

'They have been known to come into my pet shop from time to time.' Hollins shook his head despondently. 'Sub-Saharan African black mambas are incredibly fast and can outrun most men. They're aggressive, territorial, and their poison is neurotoxic.'

Hollins was extremely knowledgeable with regards to deadly snakes, and Mason had picked up on it. The Chief Inspector lifted his head from his notebook, and then said, 'What do you mean by neurotoxic exactly?'

'Unlike most poisonous snakes, black mamba venom attacks the central nervous system, shutting down the major organs. Twenty minutes after a bite, you lose the ability to talk. After an hour you're probably comatose, and after six, without an antidote you're dead.'

'You seem to know an awful lot about snake bites,' Mason glowered. He slid a photograph of Grigori Yavlinsky towards Hollins and watched for a reaction. 'What do you know about this man?'

'What about him?'

'Have you ever sold him a black mamba snake?'

'Can't say that I have. Who is he?'

Mason muttered under his breath. Not a good start, he thought. Hollins stank of pet shop food and something a little stronger – stale sweat. The more he levelled with the man, the more he despised him. But he was fighting a losing battle and didn't know which way to turn. One thing for sure, if Hollings was in bed with Yavlinsky he was about to throw the book at him.

'Now here's my problem,' Mason said, producing a photograph of the vial that Yavlinsky had dropped during his escape from a rented property in Walker. 'Your fingerprints are all over this container. What's more, the contents have been forensically analysed and identified as black mamba venom. Now I'm not a gambling man, but I'd say you're currently facing up to two years imprisonment for dealing with endangered exotic species, even more once we've taken your pet shop apart.' Mason paused for effect. 'Do you see where I'm coming from?'

Hollins turned to his legal advisor and muttered something inaudible as he held his hand in front of his mouth.

'Where did you find this vial?' asked Hollins' solicitor.

'Let's just say the man who last handled it is now of major interest to us.'

'The venom was stolen,' Hollins suddenly announced.

'In which case how come this man's and your fingerprints were all over the container?' Mason tapped the picture of Yavlinsky with an index finger, and the pet shop owner drew back in his seat.

'It was stolen.'

'Really?'

'No shit,' Hollins replied.

'When?'

Hollins was angry, and the words couldn't come out of his mouth fast enough. 'Ten days ago, my pet shop was broken into. The only thing that was stolen was my stockpile of snake venom from the freezer.'

'And you reported it to the police, no doubt?'

'No. Why would I?'

Mason looked at him hard. 'Tell me, what were you intending to do with this so called – stockpile?'

'It was to be used as an antidote.'

'By whom?'

'I regularly donate it to a local laboratory.'

Mason was suddenly on the backfoot again. 'Which one?'

Hollins gave him the details and told him more.

Bollocks, Mason cursed. Just when he thought he had the answers in the palm of his hand, the truth was slipping away from him. But failure to report the theft of a deadly poison was still a serious crime, nevertheless.

'Okay,' Mason said, letting out a long drawn out exasperated sigh. 'How many vials of snake venom were actually stolen?'

'A dozen, maybe more.'

'And what types of venom were they exactly?'

Hollins stared at him annoyed as he reeled off a list of deadly snakes.

'This Inland Taipan,' the Chief Inspector questioned. 'I've never heard of it before. Where do they come from?'

'Australia.'

'Another deadly species, is it?'

'A single bite from one can kill a man in less than an hour.'

'What is it with you people, are you on some sort of a death wish or something? Is that why you collect dangerous reptiles?'

'It's the buzz you get from handling them, it's like being on a rollercoaster ride.'

'What else can you tell me about Inland Tiger snakes?'

'They're generally shy reptiles and prefer to avoid conflict. If cornered they will hiss loudly and inflate their bodies.' Hollins collected his thoughts, then turned to Mason and laughed. 'They hate being disturbed. If provoked further, they will lash out at you and bite with their deadly fangs.'

Charming, Mason thought. If what Hollins was telling him was true, then Yavlinsky had obviously turned his attentions towards another deadly method of poisoning. What lengths some individuals would go to kill another human being beggared belief. And, if the Russian was intending to kill the boy using deadly snake venom, then he now had a lot of thinking to do.

Mason pushed back his seat as he began to recognise the scale of the problem he was faced with. Carlisle was right, Yavlinsky was a lone wolf who preferred to kill his victims by stealth rather than force. Guns were a no-no, knives too physical, as neither could guarantee certain death. Not all poisons were lethal, though, but deadly snake venom had to be far easier to handle than radioactive toxins. The only issue now, was what to do with *Monty Python.*

Hollins' knowledge of reptiles was invaluable, and Mason was already working on a dozen ways to approach the problem. If the Russian was intending to inject the boy with reptile venom, he would need to make a list of all the stolen vials. It wasn't that simple, though, as there were deadlines to consider, known antidotes to trace, and where to keep a stockpile in the event of an attack. He closed his notebook, leaned over and switched off the interview tape.

'What will happen to my client's pet shop now?' Hollins' legal advisor asked.

'He needs to fit better door locks to his premises and install a decent CCTV system. If not, he could find himself in a whole load of serious trouble.'

Hollins looked at Mason gobsmacked, whilst his legal advisor sighed with relief.

'And who pays for this shit?' Hollins asked.

Mason smiled. 'That's not my problem, I don't keep dangerous snakes.'

Still unable to come up with a plausible explanation as to why the Russian had targeted this particular pet shop, Mason still required the owners help. And if he refused, he swore he would tear his shop apart and close it down indefinitely.

Not all was unwelcome news, though. He now had a future plan of action and a string of new leads. As for Hollins' possible connection with the Russian, he would need to sleep on it and force the issue at a later date.

Pleased with his findings, it was time to contact Special Branch – find out what else was going on in the world of money laundering. No doubt he would be put under the spotlight again and he wasn't looking forward to it one little iota.

God loves a trier, Mason groaned.

CHAPTER

FIFTY-FIVE

Just after 2.00 pm, DC Carrington slipped the key into the unmarked pool car's ignition and heaved a sigh of relief. Recognition at last. At least Jack Mason had finally agreed to young Martin visiting Marsden Grotto, which in itself was a monumental breakthrough. The plan, in as much as she had been able to understand it, was to keep a watchful eye on the boy whilst allowing him to let off steam.

Still no news from Social Services. Carlisle's frustrations were evident. It was never meant to happen, and Mason's thin promises of finding Martin a permanent residence had fallen on deaf ears. Although everyone in the house got on well together, it wasn't the ideal environment to be caught up in. They worked in teams, around the clock, and were cooped up like chickens in a pen. Changes were needed, and fast, before their frustrations spilled over.

Carrington waited for Martin to fasten his seat belt before moving off.

'Okay, young man, we have two hours. No more.'

'Is it okay if I bring David's binoculars with me?' Martin asked excitedly.

'It seems you already have.' The detective smiled. 'As long as you look after them, everything should be fine.'

No sooner had she turned into Poplar Drive when she spotted DS Holt's unmarked pool car following in her wake. Relieved that two-armed detectives were close at hand was always a welcome sight on close protection operations. It was a bright, sunny day, and after passing Souter Lighthouse the coastline began to open up in front of them. She knew the area well, and always enjoyed long walks along the sea front.

Ten minutes later, Carrington pulled into an empty parking bay. Known locally as "the Grotto", Marsden Grotto was a public house located at the base of the cliffs and close to the shoreline. One of a very few remaining cave bars in Europe, it could be accessed by a lift at the top of the cliffs, or via a steep staircase attached to the rock face. The irony was, the Grotto was said to be haunted by a smuggler nicknamed John the jibber who was supposedly lowered down the lift shaft in a bucket and left to starve to death. His crime, according to the fable, was for ratting on his smuggler friends to HM Customs.

The beach was full of holidaymakers as DS Holt led the way down the steep cliff stairs. With DC Manley guarding the car park, there seemed little chance of anyone snatching the boy from under their noses. Following the somewhat precarious decent, the moment they reached the little beach, Martin excitedly ran towards Marsden Rock.

'Stay close,' Carrington insisted.

'Will do, Sue.'

Now half its size – after the famous archway collapsed back in the 90s – Marsden Rock was home to thousands of sea birds. On Carrington nearing the rock face, hundreds of kittiwakes swooped low overhead. It was a wonderful sight, and with the sea lapping the shoreline it made for a welcome break after days spent cooped up inside the private investigator's house.

Carrington's headset crackled into life.

Manley had spotted someone acting suspiciously close to the clifftop stair head. His face hidden from view, he was described as wearing grey tracksuit bottoms, white T-shirt, and a bright orange baseball cap. To make matters worse, having run an automatic number plate recognition check on the suspect's vehicle, it was coming up as stolen.

Alarms bells ringing, it was DS Holt who reacted first.

'Stay close,' he commanded.

Not fifty yards away, in a mixture of horror and curiosity, Holt pointed to a man matching the suspect's description. Something wasn't right, and whatever it was the detective's face had suddenly hardened.

'There!' Holt shouted out aloud. 'Thirty feet from the bottom of the cliff staircase.'

Carrington froze.

'I see him,' she replied.

Grabbing hold of Martin's arm, she instinctively pulled the boy close to her side. Not normally one for panicking, she called out to the sergeant to watch his front. There was concern in her voice, unnerving, and the boy still hadn't fully responded to it.

Reaching the shoreline, the suspect now ran at speed towards them. There was determination in his posture, threatening, as if he meant business. Then slowing in his stride, from a brown paper bag he pulled out a long hypodermic syringe and he pointed it at them.

Carrington's heart sank.

'Stay back,' DS Holt demanded, reaching for his Glock service pistol.

Stooping down low, the suspect grabbed a handful of sand and threw it into the sergeant's face. It happened so quickly, and all Carrington could do was watch in horror as the sergeant fell to his knees as though temporarily blinded. As a man in his late sixties rushed to the sergeant's aid, he too was knocked to the ground.

Now panting from his sprint, the suspect scooped up another huge fistful of sand and threw himself towards her at speed. He was quick, but not fast enough. Arm fully extended, body perfectly still, she aimed her Glock 26 pistol directly at the centre of Yavlinsky's chest. As she drew back the safety catch, she shouted out to him at the top of her voice.

'Armed police! Get down on the ground, or I'll shoot!'

In what seemed to take an eternity, the Russian hesitated, dropped the hypodermic syringe from his grasp and slumped to the sand on one knee. At first, she thought he'd given up on her, but the look of determination on his face told her otherwise.

'Keep your hands where I can see them,' she commanded.

Anxious, she would need to hold her nerve – and distance.

Arms extended like a priest in prayer, she could see the Russian assassin wasn't armed. Then in the blink of an eye, he scooped up another huge fistful of sand and threw it towards her direction. Eyes firmly shut, still protecting the boy, she ducked and prayed he hadn't picked up the hypodermic syringe.

She opened her eyes again and adjusted to the light.

In those few vital seconds Yavlinsky had sprang to his feet and taken off at speed towards the rocks. He was making his getaway and she knew what he was intending to do.

Extending her pistol arm, Carrington took careful aim.

Then, just as she was about to pull the trigger, an innocent bystander came into her sights. *Shit*, she cursed, as she quickly applied the safety catch and altered her position to take a better shot. Still running in a zig-zag pattern across wet golden sands, the Russian was getting away from them.

Moments later she heard sirens wailing and knew that backup was close at hand. Her mind all over place, she knew that Martin was safe and that's all that mattered to her. Fifty metres away she could see where the Russian was heading, but it was impossible to give chase.

Then she felt her shirtsleeve being tugged.

'Over there,' Martin said, pointing to the glistening hypodermic syringe.

'Don't touch it whatever you do.'

Now joined by DC Manley, she could see that Holt was badly in need of help.

'You okay?' the Detective Constable asked.

'We're both fine, but I think George could do with some assistance.'

Now operating in close protection mode, Manley pointed towards the general direction of the cliff face. 'Which way is he heading?'

'Towards the cove, but I doubt he'll get far.'

It was Martin who spoke next. 'He didn't look at all well to me, Harry. His face was as white as a ghost's, and his shirt was soaked in sweat.'

Carrington's immediate thoughts turned to radioactive poisoning. And yes, their suspect looked decidedly ill. It wasn't over yet, not by a long chalk and the Russian was still capable of inflicting terrible damage. Seconds later, as dozens of uniformed armed police officers appeared at intervals along the clifftops the realisation suddenly hit home. Yavlinsky had been barely inches away from killing the boy.

Then Jack Mason's voice boomed out over headsets demanding an immediate update. Within minutes of Manley confirming their position and findings, the beach was swarming with police officers.

'*There!*' young Martin pointed out.

As the constable bent down to pick up the hypodermic syringe with his handkerchief, his hand hovered warily over the top of it. From what Carrington could see, it was huge. It had a long silver shaft and plunger, and whatever substance the opaque barrel contained inside, she knew it would be deadly.

'What if it's full of radioactive chemicals?' Manley said, sounding uncharacteristically nervous after Martin's thought-provoking comments.

Carrington looked at Manley in panic. 'Don't touch it. Best leave it to the experts.'

'Are there no limits to this bastard's armoury?'

Carrington held her nerve.

'We need to get the boy off the beach, but I doubt we can take him back to Carlisle's house.'

'I wouldn't have thought so,' Manley said, pointing towards the cliff staircase. 'Talking of the devil, Jack Mason is already on his way down here.'

'Bugger!' Carrington cursed.

'I know. Let's hope they capture the Russian before the Chief Inspector goes into one of his rants.'

Martin tugged on Carrington's sleeve again, as if to draw her attention to something else. '*There!*' the boy suddenly announced.

'What is it?' she gulped, sounding clearly on edge.

'Over there!'

'Where?' Manley demanded.

'It's a cormorant and it's just caught a massive fish in its mouth.'

Her brain in bits, Carrington stared at Manley in disbelief. As the boy lifted the binoculars to his face and began scanning the rockface, she almost let out a scream.

'Unbelievable!' Manley said, despairingly shaking his head.

Chapter

Fifty-Six

Batabatabata.

The minute the helicopter came into sight, all eyes strained skywards. It was a wonderful sight, and a welcome addition to the team's search ability. Now on the front foot, Jack Mason was pleased with the way his operation was going. Nothing could move in and out of Marsden according to him. As hundreds of highly trained police officers set about their task, the whole village was in lockdown. Even the surrounding area at the base of Marsden cliffs was now being clawed over by river police, and it was only a matter of time before the Russian's position was finally uncovered.

As the focus of attention now shifted towards Sunderland and South Shields, Mason was having to rethink. If someone wanted to assist the Russian in his escape, they would find it difficult to penetrate his security ring. Now the country's most wanted man, a plan began to hatch in the Chief Inspector's head. Even the Kremlin was keen to put a stop to Yavlinsky's mafia type exploits – or so they claimed.

No sooner had the Rover P4 100's engine shut down, then the familiar figure of David Carlisle emerged on the scene. Wearing white paper coveralls, latex gloves and overshoes, the private investigator approached the major incident support vehicle with trepidation.

'Off to a fancy-dress party, are we?'

'I wasn't sure what the dress code was, and there wasn't a Scenes of Crime Officer in sight,' Carlisle replied.

Mason shook his head. 'It didn't take you long. I appreciate you coming.'

'Any more news on Yavlinsky's whereabouts?'

'No, nothing. He's gone into hiding somewhere and it's a matter of flushing him out.'

'He'll be a difficult nut to crack.'

'Tell me about it.' Mason turned to Carlisle. 'He's ex-military and trained in the art of survival, so he'll know when to make his next move.'

'In which case he'll probably move when you least expect it.'

Behind the narrow-lipped smile, Mason detected concern. He studied the map briefly and turned to face his companion again. The problem was, with hundreds of curious onlookers now gathered along the clifftop, any one of them could be the Russian. If Yavlinsky was to make good his escape, he'd melt back into the crowd unnoticed. There again, every street corner North, South, East and West of the area was now under the team's watchful eye. Even Border Patrol had tightened up its security arrangements, and Newcastle Airport and the Tyne Ferry Terminals were all on heightened alert.

Pleased that David Carlisle had now joined in the fray his criminal profiling skills would be priceless. Mason was already indebted to his colleague for getting him out of a tight corner, and it felt like old times again. What a lot of people didn't know, or perhaps they did, was now that Yavlinsky had declared his intentions to kill the boy, a shoot on sight policy had been sanctioned by higher command. It was a high-risk operation, and no one could rest easy until the Russian had been brought to justice.

Mason pointed to the kettle. 'Coffee?'

'I'd love a cup.'

Mason waited for the private investigator to wriggle out of his forensic suit before continuing. Knowing that young Martin Kennedy was now in safe hands, he heaved a sigh of relief. Having witnessed the boy slipping into the back of an unmarked police car and being driven away under heavy armed escort, at least that part of his operation had reached a satisfactory conclusion.

'What's your initial thoughts?'

The private investigator scratched his head in thought and took a sip of his coffee.

'Whoever's pulling Yavlinsky's strings will want him out of here.'

'Or, want him dead!' Mason quickly added.

'There is that possibility, of course.'

Still looking for inspiration, Mason stared into space.

'What about his property in Belgravia?'

'Anything's possible, but I doubt he'll return to the capital. Not with Special Branch breathing down his neck. It's my view he'll try and head back to Russia.'

'Talking of which, I can't thank you enough for looking after young Martin at such short notice.' Mason stared at his colleague sheepishly. 'In truth, I had no other alternative left open to me.'

'Where's Martin now?'

'Social Services are looking after him, so you'll finally get your house back.' Mason rolled his eyes. 'Send me the bill, but don't go over the top this time, especially if you still want to work for me again.'

Carlisle smiled with satisfaction but remained tight lipped.

'Fucking birds,' Mason said, thinking out aloud. 'The boy's obsessed with them and that's all he thinks about all day.'

'He's only a ten-year-old child, Jack. . . and it keeps him out of trouble.'

'*Out of trouble!*' Mason shrieked. 'Let's not forget that this all kicked off because of a sodding bird hide he'd built in Chopwell

Wood. What with trips to the Farne Islands, and now Marsden Grotto, I'm sick to the back teeth of having to wash bird shite off my car.'

'Think yourself lucky he's not into elephants—'

Mason saw the funnier side and burst out laughing.

'What with having to deal with birds, and now poisonous snakes, what the top-brass make of it all I'm dreading to think. They probably think I'm turning into a zoologist.'

'You've certainly got your hands full,' Carlisle smirked.

'Hands full—'

'He'll grow out of it. Most boys his age usually do.'

Mason shook his head in thought. 'The strange thing is, I actually like the lad. He reminds me of me when I was his age.'

'What. A twitcher?'

'Sod-off!'

The major incident support vehicle was now a hive of activity, and after a series of interruptions they spent the next twenty minutes going back over the missing snake vials.

'So,' Carlisle began, 'what's the latest on this money laundering scam with the Russian bank? Is the Newcastle trial still set to go ahead?'

Mason's grin broadened. 'Remember the USB memory stick that Yavlinsky kindly left in the back of the stolen BMW at Washington Services? Well, the Crown Prosecution Service is having a field day apparently.'

'So, the Tech Crime Unit finally managed to crack the cypher code?'

'Yes, and we now have dozens of names of those involved in the scam.' Mason's eyes widened. 'According to the Chief Constable, the National Fraud Intelligence Bureau are claiming it's nothing short of gold dust.'

'What have they uncovered exactly?' asked Carlisle.

'It's a sophisticated set-up involving lawyers, bankers, and politicians with connections to several East European investment

banking firms – all with offices based in London. The trouble the
Home Office are faced with is, will these people simply disappear
off the face of the planet or attempt to clear their names?'

'I bet you're pleased it's not your problem?'

Mason shrugged. 'The sooner Yavlinsky is off my patch, the
better I'll sleep at night. Talking of which—'

Mason stopped mid-sentence as DS Holt tipped his forehead
in salute and entered the major incident support vehicle. Now
recovered from the suspect's sand attack, his eyes still looked
bloodshot and sore.

'The tide is on the turn, boss.'

'What are the chances that Yavlinsky is still hanging around
the cliffs?'

'We still have a few more hours of light, but it's not looking
good.'

'In which case we need to switch to thermal cameras.'

'It's already covered.'

'Good.'

The sergeant screwed his face up. 'The media's our biggest
concern. Those bastards are everywhere.'

Mason groaned. 'Give me a few minutes and I'll provide them
with a brief statement. If nothing else, it might buy us some
breathing time.'

'I'm not sure that's a clever idea, boss.' The sergeant shrugged.

'Probably not, but another million pair of eyes won't go amiss
at this stage.'

Holt studied the map and screwed his face up again. 'Let's
hope your hunch pays off, boss. If not, you'll have an awful lot of
explaining to do in the morning.'

'Shit sticks,' Mason replied, as he pocketed his notebook and
pen. 'Besides, we can't just sit around and do nothing.'

Mason habitually stuck his hands into his pockets as he moved
towards the vehicle's back door. The public was his best source of

information gathering. It was a no brainer, and he was happy to oblige.

No matter what bullshit they printed in their newspapers!

Chapter
Fifty-Seven

Two-thirty in the morning and the streets around Hebburn were quiet. Apart from a few security lights covering each of the loading bays, the rest of the supermarket delivery yard was bathed in total darkness. One of the lights had a fault and kept flickering on and off every few seconds. It was driving Chameleon mad, but there was nothing he could do about it.

He took a deep breath and tried to steady himself. His hands were shaking, and his whole body felt like it was on fire. With thoughts of cross contamination never far from his mind, he was seriously contemplating injecting himself full of snake venom. It would be quick, and he knew which vial to use if push came to shove.

He removed an old woollen hat from his pocket, put it on, and crept forward to investigate the side of the building. He could hear people talking and thought it might be security guards. These individuals never stuck to a regular routine and constantly hung around in the shadows at night. There was a lot of money tucked up inside the building and they weren't in the habit of giving it away.

Close to a security fence, he spotted a line of cars. Not willing to chance his luck, it was a scooter that had grabbed his attention. Propped up against the warehouse wall, it probably belonged to one of the nightshift workers.

He moved in to take a closer look.

Through a side door, a figure emerged. He wasn't a tall man, sturdy, with a huge pot belly bulging beneath a bright orange shirt. Then a second man appeared, and then another. This had to be an official smoke break, he thought. If not, these people were skiving. As headlights flickered in the distance, all kinds of emotions tugged at him.

The moment Chameleon broke cover, one of the workers eyeballed him.

Hold your nerve. Don't move another muscle!

Seething with anger and frustration, he slipped back into the shadows again. Nerves on edge, he searched for a better option. The walls to the building were irregular and tall, with hidden CCTV cameras stationed at intervals high on the eaves. If he could only reach the scooter, he would be home and dry. There again, there was still the ignition to sort out, but he knew how to fix it.

Bubbling inside with excitement, Chameleon sneaked forward a few paces. It was a gamble. A massive gamble. But he was confident it could work. Moments later a grey-haired man appeared from a side door and stood perfectly still in the shadows. As he lit up a cigarette and blew out a long smoke trail, he turned towards his companions and pointed. Words were being uttered, and it was putting him on edge. But there was something too coincidental about the men's timing, as if none of them should be there.

When everyone had disappeared back inside the building again, Chameleon decided to make his move. Creeping forward he checked the scooter's steering lock and found it wasn't working. At the rear of the ignition he removed the cover and cut the wires leading from the back of it. Next, he hit the kick start and fired up the scooter's 50cc engine.

Mission accomplished.

Well not quite!

Seconds later, one of the unit side doors flew open and a well-built guy in his mid-twenties and a face like an angry wasp ran determinedly towards him. He was shouting abuse, and waving his arms in the air and threatening to punch his head in. What is it with the English race, Chameleon cursed? Everyone screams obscenities at you at the slightest provocation.

Now stuck on full throttle, the moment the scooter shot forward he almost ran the guy over. It was pitch black, and he still hadn't figured out the lights. Knowing his presence wasn't wanted here, he aimed the scooter towards the security gates and threaded his way through the tiny gap. It had been ten years since he'd last ridden on two wheels, and he was fighting it all the way.

The cool air brushing his face, at the junction with Leam Lane he hung a sharp right towards Low Fell. Not the fastest getaway bike in the country, at least he was making steady progress. Easing back on the throttle, he caught the blue flashing spinner lights in his mirror – two hundred metres over his shoulder and travelling towards him at speed. Not impressed, he gathered his composure, wound up the accelerator throttle as far as it would go and watched as the distance between them increased.

Take that, you bastards!

. Moments later, he turned his head sharply and his heart sank.

Less than twenty metres away, sirens blaring, a BMW's bonnet was up close and intimate. Maybe they'd been called to a house break-in somewhere; there again, maybe not! As he wound the accelerator throttle up again, he felt a sudden adrenaline rush.

A gap was opening up!

CHAPTER
FIFTY-EIGHT

Moments earlier Officer Smith thought he was having a quiet shift, up until now, that is. As the TaoTao Thunder 50cc motor scooter flashed past in front of his stationary marked patrol vehicle, he could see the driver wasn't wearing a helmet. Not the best of moves, thought Officer Smith. Not this time of night. Either the driver was over the drink driving limit, or the scooter had been nicked.

Determined to find out, he slipped into first gear whilst his shift colleague ran the scooter's registration details through the DVLA licensing system. Not that it made one iota of difference, as the idiot up ahead had already stepped up a gear. Racking up driving offences as if there was no tomorrow. The Officer put his foot down.

At the roundabout with the A184, his colleague switched the blue spinner lights on as Officer Smith hit the accelerator hard. He'd seen it all over the years, and his success rate was second to none. At least the perpetrator knew what he was letting himself in for, and that's all that really mattered to him. Speed bumps were his biggest nightmare, the damn things were everywhere. If you didn't keep your wits about you, they could cause a lot of damage.

In your dreams, Officer Smith thought, as he spun hard on the steering wheel and felt his seat belt tighten. Then, in his rear mirror, after entering the Leam Lane Estate, he caught the blue flashing lights of another fast approaching response vehicle. What had started as a routine road traffic incident, was now a full-blown police pursuit.

Officer Smith loved the thrill of the chase, and always got a buzz from it. High speed pursuits and attending traffic accidents was what he'd been trained to do. Usually the suspects would decamp thinking they were getting away from him, but his partner was fast on his feet. It wasn't the smartest pursuit that Officer Smith had ever been involved in, and after he'd been led a merry dance through the Leam Lane Estate, they re-joined the main road again. Now hitting speeds approaching 45 mph, they were hot on the suspect's tail.

'*Stinger in place*,' a voice boomed out over the radio waves.

Officer Smith remembered two years ago being caught up in a similar incident to this. He'd been hot on the tail of a stolen Harley-Davidson motorbike after the driver had been involved in a pub brawl. Twenty minutes later, after a high-speed chase involving a stinger had taken place, the driver had hit a brick wall. Not the best of endings, Officer Smith thought, as he was left to pick up the pieces.

As more and more units joined in the chase, escape now seemed futile. Keeping his eye on the road ahead, the officer guessed what Central Control were up to and took his foot off the accelerator pedal. Manoeuvring through Wrekenton, blues spinner lights bouncing off buildings, he suddenly screeched to a halt. Fifty metres up in front of them, on the B1296, the road resembled a war zone. As he pulled in behind one of the stationary patrol cars, he stared at the fireball confronting him. A parked Nissan Note was well ablaze, and the remains of the TaoTao Thunder 50cc motor scooter was trapped under it. Having slid across the road at speed, the scooter had exploded on impact.

His head full of questions, Officer Smith tried to piece together the last few minutes' events. People were starting to gather from all directions, some stood frozen, others pointing their phone cameras at the unfolding events.

Was the driver alive?

'Which way did he go?' the approaching sergeant shouted.

'We never saw him decamp, Sarge,' Officer Smith replied almost apologetically.

Joined by a team of fellow officers, they began a search of the surrounding streets around Ravensworth golf course. Seconds later the sergeant returned carrying a flashlamp in his hand.

'Best leave it to the dog team's lads,' the sergeant announced.

'He'll not get far,' a young constable acknowledged, 'not if he's badly injured.'

The sergeant aimed his flashlight towards a clump of bushes.

'Keep your eyes peeled.'

As Officer Smith bent down to check out the scooter parts strewn across a wide stretch of the road, he blew out a sigh of relief. Best not touch anything – not till Road Traffic had completed their findings at least. And if he was completely honest with himself, this had to be more than just a police pursuit.

The sergeant reappeared this time carrying a clip board.

'Did you get a good look at the driver?'

'Around five-seven, balding, with a round ugly face,' Officer Smith replied.

'Sounds a bit like the Russian the Serious Crime Squad are out searching for.'

'Could be,' Officer Smith replied.

As the Tyne and Wear Fire and Rescue Service Volvo FL appliance arrived on the scene, the firefighters raced into action. Flames spreading from under the bonnet of the Nissan Note, had quickly engulfed the rest of the vehicle.

The sergeant stood for moment, uncertain of what to do next.

'Whoever the driver was, Central Control have certainly pulled out all the stops to catch him. I've never seen so many armed response units as this before.'

'Me neither,' Officer Smith acknowledged with a nod.

The officer watched as the sergeant redirected the arrival of the dog handler van closer towards the golf course area, then returned to confront him.

'We could be staring at tomorrow's headlines by the looks.'

'Yeah, but I can't see any reporters around, Sarge?'

'Give them time. Those bastards can sniff out a storyline as flies find a camel's arse.'

With thoughts elsewhere, if this was the Russian hitman they'd been chasing, then it was a close-run thing. If only he'd hit the kerb at the A184 roundabout, then matters would have turned out differently. He hadn't, cursed Officer Smith, and the suspect was probably miles away by now.

CHAPTER FIFTY-NINE

The moment Jack Mason walked into Meeting Room One, the team was sat waiting for him. News travelled fast, and the latest intelligence rumours coming out of Gateshead Police Station were that Yavlinsky had been whisked to the Channel Islands in a private jet. If true – and Mason had his doubts – then Special Branch would have arrested him the moment he stepped onto the plane.

Yavlinsky's exploits had certainly gone beyond the pale, and whichever side of the fence you sat on, he'd overstepped the mark. Now in hiding, it was only a matter of time before they caught up with him and finally brought him to justice. Not all was plain sailing, though, as there were some daring members of the public who would take it upon themselves to hunt him down. With no mention of a Russian mafia connection to the press, Mason was hoping to get to him first. If not, then Yavlinsky wouldn't think twice of breaking someone's neck if it meant evading capture.

The Chief Inspector ran his eye down a whole load of stats and considered his options. Another weekend down the pan, and everyone looked exhausted. At least the boy was in safe hands, and that was one less problem to worry about. With all kinds of emotions tugging him, Mason figured there was no unearthly reason why the Russian would want to hang around in Newcastle anymore. There was still the fraud trial, of course, but that was a foregone conclusion.

He turned to face the assembled team.

'Right,' Mason began. 'Analysis back from the lab confirms the contents of the hypodermic syringe picked up from Marsden beach was Tiger snake venom. Discussions with the reptile keepers at Edinburgh Zoo suggest it belonged to the same batch stolen from Monty Python's pet shop in Newcastle.' He waited for the noise levels to die down. 'What it does tell us, though, is that Yavlinsky has stepped up his killing game so you'll need to be vigilant.'

Faces dropped.

'Anymore feedback from uniforms?' asked DC Manley.

'No. None.'

It was DS Holt's turn to speak next. 'What about Yavlinsky's contacts?'

'With the amount of media coverage, we're getting, I doubt anyone would want to give him assistance, let alone contact him. It's far too risky.'

Mason moved towards the crime board, thinking. He would need to work out a plan, and one exposing the Russian's weaker side. His biggest concern was Yavlinsky reverting back to his pre-trial disruption tactics but stopping him was the problem.

'Okay,' Mason said. 'Our last sighting of Yavlinsky was at three am.' He pointed to the B1296 at Wrekenton on the wall map. 'We know he slipped into Ravensworth golf course as the dog teams picked up his scent there. Where did he go?'

DS Savage held his hand up to speak. 'It's my view he's back in Newcastle, boss.'

Holt shot Savage a glance. 'I doubt it.'

'And why not?'

'His main interests lie in London, and that's where he'll be heading.'

Mason thought for a moment and took a tentative sip of his hot coffee. He needed a moment of inspiration, something he could get his teeth into.

'Anyone got any ideas as to how he knew the boy was staying at Carlisle's house?'

Savage was quick to react. 'It appears that several tracker devices were fitted to our fleet of unmarked police vehicles, boss.' The sergeant shook his head. 'He's obviously been monitoring our movements, which is how he ended up in Whitburn village.'

'Holy shit. When did you discover this?' Mason asked.

'Just before the meeting, boss. They've since been removed.'

'Good work, Rob. If he can penetrate our security ring that easily, what else is he capable of?'

'What about young Martin Kennedy?' asked DC Carrington, showing her concerns for the boy's safety. 'Have we heard any more from Social Services?'

'He's been moved to Scotland, Sue.'

'Do we know where?'

'No. It's still a well-kept secret.'

'What about Special Branch?' asked Harry Manley. 'What have they been up to lately?'

Mason let his mind drift for some moments. Questions were being asked, and he was having to think on his feet. Not good, he thought.

'If Special Branch do anything to report, they're not letting on about it.'

Tom Hedley, the senior forensics scientist, pointed to the map. 'If this Russian banking trial is still set to go ahead, he's bound to continue with his disruption tactics.'

'And do what exactly?'

'Protect the names of those who paid him to do a job,' Hedley replied firmly.

The room fell silent.

Insider knowledge could be very useful, Mason thought. Even so, now wasn't the time to reveal what Special Branch had told him about the upsurge in the chatter lines coming out of the Russian Embassy. Yavlinsky had overstepped the mark, and the Kremlin were keen to put an end to his exploits. There again, nothing was ever straightforward involving the Russians. That much he'd learned over the years.

Still struggling to come to terms with it all, the Chief Inspector turned to the wall map again. Something didn't fit, and whatever it was he couldn't quite put a finger on it. If the Kremlin had other plans in mind for Yavlinsky, what were they intending to do? More to the point, what if the supposed private jet to the Channel Islands was purely a diversionary tactic? Experience had taught him the Russians often blew hot and cold in situations such as these – but did they really want to get rid of one of their top agents? If not, then what were they up to? The last thing he wanted was a bunch of Russian mafia thugs roaming the streets of Newcastle – gangsters taking the law into their own hands.

Mason took a deep breath and turned to face the team again.

'Anyone got any thoughts?' he said, tapping the map with the back of his hand.

'Tom's right,' said David Carlisle. 'Yavlinsky's a paid man, and if the trial goes ahead, it could implicate an awful lot of high-ranking Russian officials including some eminent British businessmen with dodgy offshore banking accounts.'

'Interesting.' Mason nodded. 'So, you think he'll strike again?'

'What has he to lose?'

Caught in two minds, Mason's look was stern. He still hadn't been completely honest with his team, but some intelligence reports were too hot to handle and he'd given his word to keep schtum. He thought about it. Apart from uniforms searching the area around Wrekenton, there had been dozens of sightings matching Yavlinsky's description.

'Imagine it was you knowing everyone in the North East was out looking for you,' Mason went on. 'What would *you* do?'

'I'd lie low for a couple of days,' Manley replied. 'Bide my time and wait for the dust to settle down.'

'Exactly,' Mason agreed.

'Shoot on sight?' said DC Rogers.

Mason's grin broadened. 'With your eyesight, Dick. I doubt you'd hit a barn door if it was put in front of you.'

Laughter broke out, but nerves were jangling, and Mason had sensed unease. If it did come down to a shootout, he would be ready and waiting for him. His problem was, that Russian agents were renowned for springing surprise attacks when you least expected them, and conventional wasn't Yavlinsky style. Whatever line of attack the Russian hitman would adopt, it wouldn't be a pleasant one.

It was agreed. Yavlinsky was hiding in Gateshead somewhere and they would need to flush him out. As the team broke into smaller groups, Mason gave out another set of instructions. It was a large catchment area and nobody was under any illusions as to the size of task that lay ahead. The Russian would need to break cover at some point – he had no other option left open to him.

Mason's phone rang, and he answered it.

A man resembling Yavlinsky's description had been spotted close to Birtley and it was time to set the wheels in motion again.

CHAPTER SIXTY

Mid-morning, and Chameleon wasn't feeling at all well. He knew his motivation levels were at an all-time low and he was fast running out of steam. Not only were his gums starting to bleed, his tongue was threatening to choke him and he could hardly breathe. Desperate, he would need to get himself to a hospital before his body completely shut down on him.

Having spotted another high-speed Intercity train thundering south along the tracks, he decided to head north. He knew that Lamesley wasn't too far away, and he was making steady progress towards it. Intent on hitching a ride on one of the many freight trains leaving Tyne Yard, he was keen to get there. Anywhere was better than Birtley, and he couldn't get away from the place quick enough. What at first seemed a crazy idea, was now his only salvation. He'd initially planned to travel to Hull, where a skipper of a fishing trawler had arranged him safe passage to Murmansk. But now that UK Border Force had stepped up their surveillance operations, that was no longer possible.

Seething with anger, and still limping badly from his disastrous motor scooter mishap, Chameleon pushed on. He'd screwed up big style, failed miserably in his mission to halt the Newcastle trail, and all because of the boy. He should have taken care of it the moment he first clapped eyes on him. He hadn't, and now he was up to his neck in serious trouble. Just how the Organisation would deal with it, he had no idea. Not only had he put a lot of prominent people at risk, he'd jeopardised the entire money laundering operation.

If he did have a plausible explanation to give, he could always blame the hedge fund auditor, Stephen Rice. The man was an out and out traitor who had not only betrayed Russia, he'd duped the British Intelligence Service into believing he was working for them. He wasn't, of course. Having got into bed with the CIA on the promise of a foreign passport and a three-million-dollar money transfer into a personal account, the bastard had sold his soul to the devil.

If there was ever a man who deserved to die, it was Rice!

In truth, Chameleon wasn't one of those daft idiots who kept all of his information stored on a hard drive. He was much smarter than that. Assured in the knowledge that if anyone did try to break into the cryptic files without the correct passwords, the files would go into self-destruct. Okay, he'd mislaid an important USB memory stick in a moment of haste, but that was down to the radiation poisoning. If not, what else could he blame? He was a highly respected professional at the top of his game – *the agent known as Chameleon.*

With every movement sending searing pains throughout his body, he let his mind drift. He knew the police were out looking for him as he could hear the helicopter clattering overhead. If ever he was going to make good his escape, he would need to get a move on, and quick. It was the police dogs he feared most, as he knew how efficient they could be in tracking people down. If only he could get to Byker, he had the perfect remedy to stop them dead in their tracks – meat laced with Black Mamba venom!

See how you cope with that, you miserable mutts!

At the far end of the street Chameleon spotted a strip of wasteland, and beyond that, a row of disused lock up garages. Never stay in the same place twice, he told himself, it was the number one rule of engagement. Maybe he should hunker down for a couple of hours – build up his energy levels and make another push in the dark.

With different scenarios playing out inside Chameleon's head, he kept thinking about the new property developments back in London. His builders would have robbed him blind had he let them – and all because he was a foreigner. Not that he was squeaky clean, but at least he wasn't a down and out cheat like these individuals were. He would need to deal with them. His way – disrupt their assets once and for all. He had a few contacts he could rely on, and they were good at what they did. Bankruptcy was their favourite line of business, and it never failed to amaze. Closing companies down wasn't a problem these days. If you didn't have a roof over your head and the cost of a loaf of bread in your pocket, you simply starved on the streets.

Chameleon's instincts as a hired assassin had taught him many things over the years, but he'd never failed to complete an assignment. Never ever. This time felt different, though, and he was struggling to keep his wits about him let alone think straight. The moment he broke cover, the police would be onto him in a flash. He would need to stick to the plan – it was the only option left open to him.

Chameleon heard a helicopter hovering low overhead but could not see it. It was flying in circles, as if it had spotted something. Panic gripped him as never before as he slipped into the nearest garage lockup. It wasn't much of a hiding place, but at least he felt safe here. Then he heard dogs barking and his body locked solid.

Tomorrow would be his lucky day – surely!

Chapter

Sixty-One

Within minutes of Jack Mason calling for backup, two helicopters came into view, fifty metres apart. He watched as two teams of Counter Terrorist Special Firearms Officers (CTSFO) dropped down scaling ropes and onto an embankment close to an old carriage shed nearby. Dressed in familiar black body armour and armed to the teeth, they were here to finish the job. It was a massive show of strength, and Tyne Marshalling Yard would soon be the talking point in every pub in the land.

After relaying his team whereabouts and the suspect's last known position, Mason waited for further instructions. He didn't wait long. As the lead helicopter hovered low over the distant treeline above the Ravensworth Arms Hotel, the second flew off in a southerly direction and over the rooftops of Birtley.

'Command One to Peter Rabbit,' came the reply. 'Unless your men are in imminent danger, you're to hold your current position.'

'Roger that,' Mason replied, straining to listen above the din of the clattering helicopter's rotor blades. 'Do you want me to take up a defensive stance?'

'You can do, but you're to stay put until I give you further instructions.'

Moving at a pace, he watched as two teams of specialist firearms officers fanned out in a V formation and advanced along the railway embankment. Then through a break in the clouds, the second helicopter reappeared. Equipped with a Nita Sun 30 million candlepower searchlight and thermal imaging camera, it was hovering freely between the long lines of stationary freight wagons as if looking for signs of life. With hundreds of places to hide, the downdraft from the helicopter's rotor blades was throwing up huge clouds of dust and making life difficult. He knew Yavlinsky was ex-military and trained in the art of combat survival, but how would he cope against a team of highly trained specialists?

Then some sixty paces to his left, the Russian broke cover. Stooping low, he was limping heavily as he made towards the road bridge connecting Lamesley and Eighton Banks. He'd lost one of his shoes and his shirt tail was flapping in the breeze as he ran. Mason pointed towards him and a small coppice close to the railway embankment opposite. Having guessed the Russian's intentions, the risks he was taking were enormous. Events were moving at a pace, and no matter how well you planned your operations, the unexpected happened.

Out of his peripheral vision, Mason checked the marshalling yard layout on his iPhone and tried to get a fix on his bearings. One hundred paces to his right, he could see a team of armed officers were making steady progress towards a line of stationary freight wagons. Caught in a pincer movement and with little or no room for manoeuvre, there seemed no way back for the Russian now.

Dressed in a black bulletproof jacket and carrying what looked like an HK G36 modern assault rifle in his hand, the senior officer signalled his intentions. Seconds later and with split precision timing, the two teams began to close down on the Russian's last known position. It was surreal, like watching a ballet performance in slow motion. If Yavlinsky didn't react soon, he would be caught in their crossfire and die under a hail of bullets.

★★★

Seething with anger, the pain in his foot was excruciating. Hobbling on one leg, Chameleon could see the extended lines of armed officers advancing towards him, but there was nothing he could do about it. His plan, insomuch as he had one, was to reach the sanctuary of the small coppice opposite. He would need something more secure in the long term, but for now he would make do and mend.

After a few minutes of lying still, he heard the crunching sound of loose ballast being walked on and felt a sudden prick of apprehension. Barely thirty metres away, back arched and weapon cocked ready to fire, the senior officer was almost on top of his position. He wasn't a ferocious looking man, lean, with mouse-like eyes peering out through a slit in his black balaclava. What Chameleon didn't know, or perhaps he did, was that if he didn't act soon all routes of escape would be cut off to him.

He felt in his pocket for the hypodermic syringe.

Still there!

Nothing would stop him now. No matter what dangers he faced.

His index finger covering the hypodermic plunger, he pulled off the needle cover and prepared for the inevitable. Just a few more paces and he would take the senior officer by surprise. It would be quick – just as the others – and with this amount of lethal snake poison flowing through his veins he would die in a matter of minutes.

Crawling forward on all fours, beads of sweat rolled down Chameleon's face. Less than a quarter of a mile to his front – beyond the high-speed tracks – the small coppice looked even more inviting to him now. The problem was, reaching it would be almost impossible as he would be cut to pieces the moment, he broke cover.

Hoping the senior officer hadn't spotted him, Chameleon prepared to grab his loaded weapon. He knew he was capable, knew he wouldn't hesitate, and his determination was unwavering.

Then he heard a rumbling sound – faint and growing louder. As the ground beneath his feet began to shake, he caught the flickering halogen lights of a slow approaching freight train and craned his neck to take a better look. It was trundling towards him with ease and making light work of the uphill gradient. He knew it was a long shot, knew he had to run the gauntlet, but he might even catch these bastards napping.

It was perfect!

His foot cut to ribbons from the sharp track ballast crushed stone, he crawled beneath the long line of stationary freight wagons and waited. His mind running amok, what he wouldn't give for a size nine shoe and an AK-47 Russian assault rifle right now. Crouching low beneath the skyline, he tried to get a better fix. There was a strong stench of diesel fumes, and it almost caused him to sneeze.

It was all about timing and making the right decisions. One false move and he would die under a hail of bullets and his body taken to a crematorium for overnight disposal. That's how these bastards operated. Out of sight and out of mind.

The rumbling noise grew louder.

It was close!

He pocketed the syringe and crawled forward a fraction. Nerves jangling on edge, at the very last second, he scampered in front of the slow-moving freight train and caught the sheer look of horror on the engine driver's face.

Textbook, he smiled, as a warning horn almost caused him to scream.

Then over his right shoulder, Chameleon caught the unbelievable look of astonishment on the senior armed officer's face – he was almost home and dry.

CHAPTER
SIXTY-TWO

Jack Mason nearly jumped out of his skin the moment the helicopter swooped low overhead. Hovering some forty feet above his position, he watched as two smoke grenades were thrown from an open doorway. He could see the slow-moving freight train passing in front of them, and Yavlinsky breaking from cover. He was slipping away from them, looking over his shoulder and hobbling into the swirling white mist.

Outfoxed, there seemed little chance of catching the Russian now. Having made good his escape, he was making towards the small coppice opposite just as Mason had predicted he would. In what seemed to take an eternity, the freight train finally cleared their path. The next thing he heard, as Mason crossed over several lanes of high-speed track, was the warning horn of a fast-approaching Intercity train.

He stiffened.

Then, all hell was suddenly let loose.

First, a short burst of automatic gunfire, followed by sporadic single round gunshots. He could hear shouting to his left, but his visibility was impaired by swirling smoke. Mason's first reaction was to take on a defensive stance, confront the Russian if he tried to retreat.

As gaps opened up in the smoke, his grip on the Smith & Wesson tightened.

'What the fuck's going on?' Mason demanded.

'Yavlinsky's surrounded, boss,' DS Savage replied, closing down on his position and pointing. 'There, just below the road bridge.'

Eyes straining through white mist, not sixty metres away Mason could see a group of specialist firearms officers huddled in a circle. One of them, the senior officer, kept pointing in a southerly direction as if giving out instructions.

Mason pushed forward.

Still no sign of the Russian showing, these people seemed far too relaxed and he was itching to take back control. Then someone shouted out to him, and it caused him to jerk his head.

'What's going on?' Mason demanded. 'Where the hell is Yavlinsky?'

'Somewhere between Lamesley and Birtley,' came back the reply.

'What?'

'Relax, Chief Inspector. All railway lines between Newcastle and Durham have been shut down for safety reasons.'

Not until reaching the road bridge did Mason see the full extent of the damage – and it wasn't a pretty sight. Normally in charge of operations such as these, he now was forced to play second fiddle to Special Branch. This was his patch, his territory, and he didn't like it at all. He'd been here before, of course, but this time felt different.

Then out of the corner of his eye, he spotted a severed arm. It was lying trackside along with other chunks of human flesh. Moving forward to take a closer look, the area suddenly resembled a slaughterhouse.

'Who's in charge?' Mason demanded.

A sturdy built man in his late thirties stepped forward and was quick to signal his position. 'We're all but done here, Chief Inspector. It's down to you now.'

Mason glared at him. 'What happened here exactly?'

'It seems your man ran into the path of an oncoming high-speed Intercity-Express and never saw it coming.'

'Blimey,' Mason gasped.

'I doubt there's much left of him, especially the speed the train was travelling at. He would have burst open like a balloon full of water.'

'He ran in front of it, you say?'

'Well that's what my report will say,' the officer nodded.

As it slowly began to sink in, Mason had calmed down a tad. 'Is this all that remains of him?'

'Sadly, yes. But he'll not give you any more trouble.'

'Anyone else hurt?'

'None of my team, that's why we insisted you people stay put.'

Feeling a right prat, Mason stood for a moment, thinking.

'I saw him break cover but the moment he ran into the smoke screen I lost all track of him.'

'He was obviously disorientated.' The officer smiled. 'Smoke and stun grenades only adds to their confusion.'

Mason stared at him. 'I thought I heard gunshots. What was that all about?'

The officer was quick to react. 'Once my men have returned to base, they'll all be debriefed. That's how it works, I'm afraid. No more questions.'

'Yes, of course,' Mason acknowledged, knowing he'd overstepped the mark.

This wasn't the kind of ending he'd hoped for, but at least it meant less paperwork. Soon the transport police would arrive, and a major clean-up operation would begin. It wouldn't take long, and in a few hours from now everything would be back to normal again – whatever normal meant. God, what a mess.

Mason turned his head instinctively as the two police helicopters came into view again. Hovering low above a small piece of waste ground some twenty metres to his left, the specialist armed officers swiftly clambered onboard. Minutes later, they were airborne and skimming the rooftops over Birtley and heading in a southerly direction.

Mason shifted his position as his radio crackled into life. It was his counterpart from Special Branch.

'Sorry about the mess, old boy. You deserve better.'

'No problem,' Mason replied.

Relieved it was over, the Chief Inspector began to take it all in. Seldom did the ground troops ever receive accolades for their achievements as it was considered part of their job. Once the dust had settled and the diplomatic channels had been smoothed over, no doubt the senior officers would be looking favourably at the annual honours list. It was strange how some officers crawled out of the woodwork on occasions such as these. It was an all too familiar occurrence – people you'd never met before, faces you didn't recognise, the cockroaches from under the floorboards.

More than pleased with the way his team had handled the operation, Mason began to think about his future. At least young Martin Kennedy was safe, and that was a major plus.

His iPhone rang, and he checked the display.

It was Barbara Lockwood, his physiotherapist. 'How can I help?'

'I hope I'm not interrupting anything important.'

'I'm rather tied up at the moment, Barbara,' he replied, staring down at what remained of Yavlinsky. 'Can I call you back later?'

'Is everything on for tonight?'

'Yes, of course. I wouldn't miss it for the world. Why do you ask?'

'Its just that I have a little surprise in store for you.'

His mind all over the place, Mason could barely contain himself. God, he thought. He'd never felt like this in a long time.

His friend hung up.

'I take it you'll not be joining us for tonight's pub quiz final?' DS Savage said desperately trying to avoid eye contact.

'Not tonight, Rob. Something rather urgent has cropped up.'

'Pity,' Savage sighed, 'because tonight's the big one.'

Indeed, Mason thought. In more ways than one.

CHAPTER SIXTY-THREE

Jack Mason felt upbeat when he entered the Chief Constable's office the following morning. Now that Yavlinsky was no longer a threat, he could turn his attentions towards the other exposed people involved in the trail. He still had a few loose ends to tie up, but that was mainly paperwork and the odd interview he'd arranged. It had been one hell of a ride, not to mention his spat with DI Gamble. He'd lost control as usual, and it had almost cost him his job because of it. But that was behind him now, and he was really looking forward to some quality time off.

He stared at his notes and smiled. Never in a million years did he dream that his physiotherapist, Barbara Lockwood, would agree to them taking a long weekend break away together. Italy, Florence, where they could take in a few tourist attractions and get to know one another better. Nothing serious, of course, and it was all new territory. There was so much to talk about, and they'd reached a point in the relationship were past secrets were about to unravel.

'It's not general knowledge,' the Chief Constable began, 'but I've just been informed by the Home Office that Special Branch had been shadowing Grigori Yavlinsky's for a considerable length of time.'

'You're joking, sir.'

'That's Secret Services for you, but I thought you should know.' The Chief Constable's frown lines tightened. 'Which reminds me, Counter Terrorist Command will want to interview you over the Yavlinsky incident. It's purely a clean-up exercise, but they'll probably ask a few awkward questions nevertheless. . . national security and all that.'

Mason thanked him, and then said. 'What about the trial itself, sir?'

'I've spoken to Special Branch about that, and according to sources in Whitehall they've now uncovered at least another dozen new fake companies connected with this money laundering scam. Apart from the usual suspects, they've revealed an important link to a bank in China.'

'Really?'

The Chief Constable cocked his head to one side. 'No thanks to you, the CPS now have enough hard evidence to prove that much of the dirty money coming out of Russia is being routed through South American banks including several branches in Mexico. From there it can go anywhere, and I'm told a trail involving 48 countries and over 15,000 offshore banking transactions has since been uncovered.'

'Blimey, that's unbelievable, sir.'

'And all because of a tiny USB memory stick no bigger than your little finger.'

Mason drew back in his seat. 'No doubt the National Fraud Intelligence Bureau are cock-a-hoop over this.'

'They are, as most of the money that vanishes into the twilight world of offshore banking is difficult to track down. It's a well thought out operation, and one that cleverly mingles fake transactions with real ones. Once the money lands in offshore accounts it simply vanishes into the London property market. Having said that, the problem that Special Branch are now faced with is that at least one in ten of the properties in the London borough of Kensington & Chelsea are owned through a "secrecy jurisdiction" such as the British Virgin Islands, Jersey, and the Isle of Man.'

'Do we know who is masterminding it?'

'That's one for the Home Secretary to sort out.' The Chief Constable put his pen down and gave Mason a guarded look. 'If nothing else it shows the true extent to which these people are willing to go.'

Mason thought a moment. 'Stephen Rice had certainly done his homework, and there was little wonder why the Russians were keen to get rid of him as they did.'

'Money laundering is rife, Chief Inspector, and the British government is keen to put a stop to it.'

'Do we know who Yavlinsky was working for?'

'We do,' the Chief Constable said, matter of fact. 'He was employed by a Russian organised crime group which mainly operates in Europe with connections to the political underworld. Corrupt Russian Oligarchs mainly, and several well-known dishonest British businessmen who between them have set up a network of dummy offshore accounts. Now that Yavlinsky's undercover operation has been blown, things should quieten down a tad.'

'Is this how the Russians are able to buy into the London property market, using corrupt British property agents?'

'Indeed, and it just goes to show what we're up against.' The Chief Constable looked at his watch as if time was a premium. 'When are you due to meet the press?'

'Eleven-thirty, sir.'

The Chief Constable folded his arms and gave him a serious look. 'I'm instructed by Special Branch to divert the media's attention away from any mention of a Russian connection. As for Yavlinsky's death, we need to convince the public that he took his own life by jumping in front of a high-speed train rather than face the reality of a hefty prison sentence.'

'He probably did.' Mason smiled. 'But what if they question me over the barrister's death?'

'Let's stick with our original story on that. As far as the press are concerned, we're still in the throes of investigating a suspicious suicide and are keeping an open mind about it. Six months from now, and everyone will have forgotten that the case ever existed.'

'And Stephen Rice? How do you wish me to handle that?'

'Rice had nothing to do with the Northumbria Police as far as I'm concerned – that's strictly a matter for the Metropolitan Police to sort out.'

Mason checked his watch as he stood to leave. 'I better get going, sir.'

'There is one other thing—'

He turned sharply back from the door. 'Yes, sir.'

'There are a few aspects of your conduct that appear to have fallen well short of that expected of a senior police officer. No doubt the Area Commander will fill you in with the details.'

'Regarding what exactly?'

'I'm led to believe there's been an official complaint lodged against you.'

Mason smiled. 'That wouldn't be Detective Inspector Gamble, would it?'

The Chief Constable lifted his head as if the matter had already been decided. 'If you do have plans for future promotion, may I suggest you curb your hostility towards junior ranking officers. Anger is a normal, healthy emotion. But it's unhealthy when it flares up and spirals out of control.'

'Will that be all, sir?'

'Only to say that I'm more than pleased with the way you and your team have handled the operation, you've done the Northumbria force proud. This has been an extremely demanding case and you have tackled it with the utmost professionalism under very difficult circumstances.'

Mason closed the door behind him knowing full well he wasn't in line for any future commendations, let alone a mention in any New Year Honours list. No, Mason thought. Best leave that to the top brass to sort out, and let the grassroots officers get on with what they do best. . . fighting the real villains.

CHAPTER

SIXTY-FOUR

Twenty minutes later, Jack Mason was sitting in his office answering emails. At least the CPS now had enough hard evidence to make corrupt Eastern-European bankers think twice about moving their ill-gotten gains into British shores again. More importantly, the barrister Margaret Cooper hadn't died in vain. It wasn't the greatest ending he could have wished for, but after months spent trying to bring about Grigori Yavlinsky's downfall, he'd finally stepped into the path of an oncoming high-speed train rather than face the cruel death of toxic poisoning. It wasn't general knowledge, of course, but he knew that cross-contamination had played a major part in all of this.

Thinking he was having a good day, his desk phone rang.

'Jack Mason, how can I help?'

It was his old boss back at the London Metropolitan, and his voice was in sombre mood. 'I hope it's not inconvenient, Jack.'

'Everything's fine. What can I do for you, sir?'

'I'm sorry to be the bearer of bad news. It's about your ex-wife—'

'What about her?'

'Brenda was involved in a tragic road traffic accident at 7:32 am this morning and was pronounced dead at the scene.'

Mason sat stunned. His head was spinning, and he could not stop shaking. Even though they were never on good speaking terms towards the end, he still had a lot of fond memories.

'Dead?' he whispered. 'What, Brenda?'

'I'm sorry Jack, but that's as much as I know at this stage.'

'Was she driving. . . alone. . . what happened?'

'All I can tell you is that it occurred on the northbound carriageway of the M25, and a male passenger who was with her at the time was also pronounced dead at the scene.'

'This is awful—'

His phone went quiet for some seconds.

'There is a helpline number you can ring, and I'm sure they will tell you more than I can.'

Mason picked up a pen and couldn't stop his hand from shaking. Nothing made sense anymore, as if his entire world had suddenly been turned on its head and he was spiralling out of control. He wrote the number down and repeated it back over the phone.

'If there's anything I can do to help, you know where to find me.'

'Thank you, sir.'

The phone went quiet, then dead.

Still deep in shock, Mason stared out of his office window and tried to think straight. Never in a million years had he imagined it would all end like this. He'd experienced death in the family before, many times, but nothing compared to this.

Somewhere in the distance a phone was ringing, and he let it ring out.

It was his fault their marriage had broken up, and he wasn't trying to make excuses. Not now, he wasn't. They'd had so many happy times together during those early years, but the good times were never meant to last. It took two to tango, but he still couldn't stop blaming himself for everything that had happened between them.

He loved his job, it was like a drug to him, and that's where the real problem had lain. Being totally committed to your work clearly wasn't a crime. Surely not. The more he thought about it, the deeper he sank. He'd been living in a bubble all these years, married to his job, and now it was catching up on him. But you can't turn back the clock, and time and tide wait for no man, he thought. Brenda was dead – snuffed out on the M25 carriageway and no one there to comfort her.

It wasn't guilt that was dragging him down, it was the long hours he'd spent away from home all those years. The pressures of work, the late-night drinking sessions, and not being there to see his daughter growing up. He'd thought a lot about his job lately, and what it would be like to give it all up. No, he thought. It had never been easy for him either, and this wasn't a time for self-pity. They should have handled matters differently, separated on amicable grounds instead of tearing each other apart as they had.

His iPhone rang, and he checked the display.

'Hi, Dad?'

The moment he heard his daughter's voice, Mason's heart sank even further. How would he break the news to her? How would she react?

'Where are you now?' Mason asked softly.

'I'm at home with the baby, where did you think I was?'

He needed to say something, anything, but he was struggling to find the words. The phone went quiet for a second, and he took another deep breath.

'There's something important I need to tell you.'

'What's up, Dad?'

'It's about your mother, she's——'

Chapter

Sixty-Five

Newcastle September 2016

The first satellite vans arrived at breakfast time. Dozens of them. Parked up along Newcastle Quayside in front of the Law Courts. News travelled fast, and the opening day of the Russian fraud trial had unquestionably reached fever pitch. As a group of well-known news presenters jockeyed for prime positions in front of the entrance steps, the next eight weeks would be bedlam. It was headline breaking news, what sold newspapers, until everyone had grown tired of it all.

Further south, David Carlisle stepped out of his Rover P4 100 just as heavy spots of rain started. He wasn't looking forward to this one iota, and the tragic news of his colleague's ex-wife's death had shocked him to the core. They'd been good friends for as long as Carlisle could remember and had gone through thick and thin together over the years.

Carlisle entered the Chief Inspector's office with trepidation.

'What can I say, Jack? This has all come as such a terrible shock.'

Mason held his hands up as in surrender. 'It's strange,' the DCI reflected. 'After I got over the initial shock, my biggest concern was my daughter. At least I still have her and the granddaughter to cling to.'

Coffee arrived, and Carlisle took up a seat opposite.

'Is there anything I can do?'

Mason's facial expression never altered, but the look in his eyes showed sadness. 'I know this may sound dreadful, but after the divorce, the two of us had a nasty habit of speaking to each other with utter contempt. It's strange how some situations pan out, but once I sat down and really thought about it, I began to realise that it was time to put my own house in order. It was probably the wakeup call I needed. . . believe me. Life is never straight forward at the best of times, and you never know what lies around the corner.'

'That's one way at looking it, I suppose,' Carlisle said, relieved that his friend had some appetite for conversation at least. 'You haven't had much luck lately. Once this fraud case is behind you, you should seriously consider taking some time off.'

'As one door shuts another one opens.' Mason smiled.

'True.'

Mason looked at him oddly. 'Before this all happened, I'd intended to take a short weekend break to Florence with someone who is dear to me.'

'Who, your physiotherapist?'

Mason looked up at him warily. 'It's wasn't a crazy flash in the pan idea, this time it's serious. Barbara has helped me through an awful lot lately, and I'm beginning to look at life differently.'

Carlisle nodded, knowing that his colleague was fighting his own demons and didn't press the matter further. He knew what grief meant, having lost his own wife in a tragic holiday accident. No, he thought. Mason was mentally strong, so best let him cope with it as only he knew how.

'So, what happens to Operation Drawbridge now?' he asked.

'Now that Special Branch has brought in its own team of legal experts, they've taken the case to another level.'

'Hang on a minute, I thought the trial was moved away from the capital for the very opposite reason.'

'It seems that both the British and Russian governments are locked in diplomatic discussions over the list of names they uncovered on this USB memory stick we found in the back of Yavlinsky's stolen car. The problem is, once the Home Office are involved, we recede into insignificance, it seems.'

'Christ, not another cover up!'

'Who knows?' Mason shrugged.

'What then?'

'It would appear that people in higher office have a lot at stake and are using it as a bargaining chip.'

'What about the press?'

'That's no longer my responsibility either.' Mason shuffled a few papers around a cluttered desk. 'The Chief Constable and a team of so-called media experts will be dealing with that from now on. I'm still responsible for the day-to-day protection of those involved in the trial, but we don't anticipate any major problems now that the money laundering operation has been exposed.'

'And the boy, Martin?'

'What about him?'

'I thought he was in Scotland?'

'He is, but his father has finally got himself into a spot of bother again.' Mason levelled with him. 'It's not looking good for your friend Phillip Kennedy, and he could be facing another lengthy prison sentence I fear.'

'Bugger,' Carlisle swore, 'what's Phil been up to this time?'

'He's been charged with grievous bodily harm after he was involved in a nasty pub brawl over non-payment of rents.'

'But he was really doing well for himself.'

Mason shook his head. 'A leopard never changes its spots, that's for sure.'

'So, what will happen to young Martin now?'

'I've been in touch with Social Services and he seems quite settled in his new school and is doing remarkably well under the circumstances. Not so in his mother's case.' Mason gave him a smile that masked unease. 'She's still refusing to go into drug rehab so I doubt she will ever gain child custody again.'

'What a pity.'

'The strange thing is, this move has opened up a whole new world for Martin and I was wondering if you fancied a trip to Scotland to see him. I know he'd be pleased to see you.'

'Yes, of course.'

'Good. I've already arranged for Sue Carrington to visit him, as she's spent an awful lot of her free time with the boy these past few months. Like you, they seem to get on well together.' Mason sipped some coffee and laughed. 'Perhaps the pair of you should travel together. . . spend a few hours up in the Highlands and do a spot of bird twitching.'

'Is that why you invited me here today?'

'That amongst other things, yes.'

Carlisle listened as Mason brought him up to speed on all the latest developments, and he sat back and took it all in.

'What will happen to you once the trial is over?'

Mason allowed him a brief smug smile. 'I had an interesting conversation with the head of the Amsterdam Crime Squad yesterday evening. It appears the Dutch authorities are investigating an intriguing case involving a thirty-two-year-old male who was viciously murdered in the Binnenstad district of Amsterdam.'

'When was this?'

'Late on Tuesday night.'

'So, why contact you?'

'The suspect's name is Thomas Ballantine, and they thought he may be of particular interest to us.'

'Thomas Ballantine? That name doesn't ring a bell.' Carlisle shrugged.

'It will when I tell you what his real name is Patrick Stanley.'

Carlisle drew breath and could hardly believe what he was hearing. 'Is this some sort of hoax? Stanley drowned in the River Tyne, we both know that!'

'Unless the Dutch authorities are sadly mistaken, then we could be dealing with a known serial killer.'

Carlisle fell silent, thinking.

'I thought that would tickle your interest buds,' Mason continued, 'and to think that bastard nearly cost me my life.'

'It can't be him, surely not.'

Mason stood from his desk and walked over to his filing cabinet. 'They've asked me to assist them with their current enquiries, and I've faxed them a shit load of files on the Stanley case.'

'That sounds ominous.'

Mason was quick to signal his thoughts. 'Now that his partner in crime has been found guilty of three counts of murder, I'm questioning whether there is a connection here?'

'If it is Stanley, which I very much doubt, then sentencing Angelica Glebova to life imprisonment could have triggered all kinds of emotions inside his head.'

'Good.' Mason smiled. 'That answers an awful lot of questions.'

'So, where do you go from here?'

'I was wondering if you fancy joining me on a trip to Amsterdam?'

'I thought the Chief Constable was cutting back on external resources?'

'He is, but not on this particular case.' Mason clasped his hands together in thought. 'The only reason I never took you on until the very end of Operation Drawbridge, is because of Special Branch's involvement. That said, once the Russians uncovered the boy's whereabouts that put a whole new slant on the matter.'

'I thought as much. When were you thinking of going to Amsterdam?'

'Let's see what the Dutch Authorities come back with first.'

Carlisle gave a disconcerted shake of the head. '*The Suitcase Man*. Who would have thought it possible that his name would crop up again?'

Mason smiled cynically. 'And that's coming from a criminal profiler who previously worked on the case!'

CHAPTER

SIXTY-SIX

Kinfauns October 2016

The drive to Scotland took DC Carrington a little over three hours. After skirting Perth, they took the M90 towards Dundee for approximately two miles before taking the turn off for Kinfauns. There were smart, detached bungalows all around. Many with large plots of land overlooking the River Tay. It was a beautiful area, Carlisle thought, full of wildlife and rolling hills and an ideal place for young Martin Kennedy to grow up in.

It was shortly after eleven o'clock when they eventually pulled up outside the foster-parents' house, and Martin was waiting for them. The boy gave them a big wave and excitedly ran down the garden path and straight into Detective Carrington's open arms.

'Nice to see you again, Martin,' Carrington said, giving him a huge hug.

'Did you bring me any new bird books?' Martin asked eagerly.

'Yes, of course we did, and David has another surprise in store for you.'

Met at the front door by Martin's new foster mother, after short introductions they were ushered into a spacious lounge with beautiful scenic views overlooking the Carse of Gowrie. Martin looked at home in the place, relaxed, and his new foster mother was a breath of fresh air.

'So,' Carlisle began, handing Martin a small gift-wrapped package. 'What have you been up to lately?

The young boy's eyes narrowed as he studied the silver wrapping paper.

'I've started my new school, and it's really cool.'

'And what are your new teachers like?'

'They're really nice, and the school dinners are fantastic. And guess what?' Martin said enthusiastically.

Carlisle raised his eyebrows a fraction as he stared across at Carrington. 'No. What?'

'I've joined the after-school wildlife club, and we go for long walks in the countryside twice a week.

'Really?'

'Uh-huh. It's unbelievable. I've only been going three weeks, and I've spotted loads of Hen Harriers and Kestrels.'

'It sounds great.' The detective smiled. 'What else have you been doing with yourself?'

Martin stared at the box as the last of the wrapping paper fell from his shaking fingers. 'Crikey, Avalon 10x40 binoculars. How did you know I would like these?'

'They're perfect for your after-school wildlife adventures.'

'Thanks, a ton.' Martin smiled, as tears of joy filled his eyes.

'It's a pleasure.'

'Can I share them with my new friends?'

'Of course, you can. They're yours to do whatever you like.'

Carlisle remembered all those years ago when he too had been given surprise gifts. Those were amongst some of the most cherished moments of his childhood; where days seemed endless and the sun always shone.

It was a welcoming sight, and a credit to his new foster parents for opening their hearts and home to Martin. The young boy now had a bright future in front of him, and a safe and secure roof over his head where he felt valued, respected and cared for. Pleased he'd made the effort to visit him here today, things couldn't have worked out better, Carlisle thought. Apart from Martin's father falling by the wayside again, the boy seemed completely at ease with himself.

They talked about a lot of things that afternoon, and when the time finally came, the boy seemed genuinely sorry to see them go. The moment they reached the unmarked pool car Martin gave Carrington a huge parting hug. A new enduring friendship had been struck, and there seemed little doubt that this wasn't the detective's last visit to Kinfauns. It was strange, Carlisle reflected. What had been a long emotional rollercoaster ride had turned into nothing short of a fairy tale ending. Pleased with his findings, it felt as if someone had lifted a huge weight off his shoulders.

Carlisle held his hand out, and Martin took it.

'Take care of yourself, son, and be good.'

'I will.' Martin managed a weak smile as he turned to DC Carrington. 'Will you thank Jack Mason for me. Tell him he's welcome to come and visit me any time.'

'Yes, of course I will.' She nodded. 'I'm sure the Chief Inspector will visit you in the near future.'

★★★

It was shortly after four o'clock when they finally joined the M90 heading south, and Carlisle let his mind drift. Now thinking about his own workload, other than his brief involvement in Operation Drawbridge, these past few months had been relatively quiet as far as his business was concerned. Being a private investigator had its advantages, but it could be monotonous work at times. He loved his job and he'd worked with some fascinating people over the years. The only downside, if he could think of one, was too much meddling by politicians.

Carrington turned to face Carlisle. 'Hungry?' she asked.

'I'm famished. I could eat a horse if it was put in front of me.'

'I don't know about that, but on my way up here I spotted a nice B&B pub just before reaching Perth. What do you think?'

'Sounds good by me. Do you think they serve food?'

Carrington flashed her deep blue eyes at him. 'I was thinking more on the lines of the B&B actually?' she replied jokingly.

A log fire crackled in a cosy lounge as they entered the pub, and they soon found a corner table overlooking the River Tay. It was a beautiful spot, and they couldn't have chosen a better place to eat.

Carlisle picked up a pub menu, ordered a round of drinks, and turned to the landlady and said, 'Do you have many rooms available at the moment?'

'We do. Would that be two singles or a Queen-size bed?'

'I was just curious. . . that's all.'

'I'll fetch you the keys and you can take a look for yourselves.'

As the landlady returned to the bar, Carrington turned sharply to Carlisle and smiled. 'She must think we're a married couple, David.'

'I don't know about that.'

'If not, then she's determined we stop the night.'

Seconds later the landlady returned and dropped a small bunch of keys on the table in front of them. 'Room two. Turn right at the top of the stairs – it's the last door on your left.'

Carrington looked at Carlisle and giggled.

It had been a long day.

THE END

YOU HAVE TURNED THE LAST PAGE.

But it doesn't have to end there . . .

If you're looking for more action-packed reading in the Jack Mason crime thriller series, why not subscribe to my monthly newsletter at https://www.michaelkfoster.com

Here you will find behind the scene interviews, discount promotions, signed book giveaways, and more importantly new release dates.

If you enjoyed Chameleon, why not drop a review on Amazon and let other readers know what you thought of it. They are dying to hear from you!

THE WHARF BUTCHER

(Book 1) In the DCI Mason & Carlisle Crime Thriller Series

When Jack Mason is called to a brutal murder scene at an isolated farm in Northumberland, his worst nightmare has become a reality. Two people are dead, their bodies lie twisted and broken, but nobody knows why.

With the pressure to solve the case mounting, the clues don't add up. Far too many people are entangled in this crime – some with dark secrets to hide, others unwilling to cooperate. When things take an on unexpected twist, Jack fears a serial killer is at work and a criminal profiler is brought in to assist. But this killer makes his own rules and draws them ever closer into his twisted web.

A chilling psychological suspense thriller set in the rugged North of England, The Wharf Butcher is the first book in this gripping new series that will shake you to the core.

'Start to finish, the author hardly gives you time to catch your breath as horror piles on horror and the killer thumbs his nose at the pursuers.' *The Northern Echo.*

Satan's Beckoning

(Book 2) In the DCI Mason & Carlisle Crime Thriller Series

When a fatal road crash turns out to be murder, JACK MASON is sent to investigate. There are no clues, no motive, and the driver of the car is missing.

Within the seemingly dark vaults of the police missing persons files, lay untold dangers. Young women are easy pickings for a serial killer who is growing increasingly audacious. When criminal profiler DAVID CARLISLE is drafted in to assist, he is not able to protect anyone – least of all himself.

As the investigations intertwine, Jack is forced to face his own demons, but the closer to the truth he gets, the greater the danger he puts them in.

Satan's Beckoning is a fast-paced crime thriller with a cliffhanging conclusion.

'An outstanding writer of considerable talent and with this, his second novel he has proven yet again that he is a new force in British Crime Fiction.' *Booklover Catlady Reviews.*

THE SUITCASE MAN

(Book 3) In the DCI Mason & Carlisle Crime Thriller Series

When DCI Jack Mason is sent to investigate a gruesome double murder, his entire world is turned upside down. The ex-wife of a notorious gangster lies dead, a second victim's body is missing, and the evidence doesn't stack up. A few days later, when a young man's body turns up hidden inside a city storage locker, the head and hands are missing.

With Jack's powers of investigation tested to the limit, a criminal profiler is brought in. But, the inner workings of this killer's mind won't be easy to decipher. In a world of human trafficking, drugs, and gangland unrest, who can Jack trust?

'Once again the author has delivered a gripping tale of murders that leaves the reader wanting more. Very believable, gruesome, well written and engaging to the end.' *Dan Brown.*

MICHAEL K FOSTER

30327214R00213

Printed in Great
Britain
by Amazon